The Secret Lives of the Edmonts

OTHER BOOKS BY LUCY KAVALER

A Matter of Degree
Noise, the New Menace
Freezing Point
Mushrooms, Molds, and Miracles
The Astors
The Private World of High Society

FOR YOUNG READERS
Green Magic
The Dangers of Noise
Dangerous Air
Life Battles Cold
Cold Against Disease
The Astors: An American Legend
The Wonders of Fungi
The Artificial World Around Us
The Wonders of Algae

Lucy Kavaler

The Secret Lives of the Edmonts

E. P. DUTTON · NEW YORK

Published in the United States by E. P. Dutton,
a division of Penguin Books USA Inc.,
2 Park Avenue, New York, N.Y. 10016.

Published simultaneously in Canada by Fitzhenry and Whiteside,
Limited, Toronto.

Library of Congress Cataloging-in-Publication Data

Kavaler, Lucy.
The secret lives of the Edmonts / Lucy Kavaler.
p.   cm.
ISBN 0-525-24819-6
I. Title.
PS3561.A8684S44   1989
813'.54—dc20   89-32339
                                    CIP

Designed by Margo D. Barooshian

1 3 5 7 9 10 8 6 4 2

First Edition

To Andrea Kavaler,

my Fitzgerald,
with my love and thanks for your enthusiasm,
energy, encouragement, and expert help.

Acknowledgments

The social and financial history of New York City has been an abiding interest. Research, carried out over many years, was begun for previously published historical works and was continued and expanded more recently to provide the historical framework for *The Secret Lives of the Edmonts.*

When I began my investigations there were still a few very old people alive, members of New York's most prominent families, who remembered the 1890s and shared their recollections with me. It would not be feasible to list here individually the many people, living and dead, who contributed their knowledge. All have my thanks.

I should like to give mention to the New York Public Library where the special collections of books and nineteenth-century back files of newspapers and periodicals were invaluable, as was the New York Society Library with its histories and memoirs, many long out of print. These provided information on real-estate holdings, tenements, labor conditions, clothing, cosmetics, women's rights, menus, servants' salaries, home furnishings, prices, and other aspects of day-to-day living. The Newport (Rhode Island) Historical Society and the 1890s files of the *Newport Mercury* provided insights into the period. The Federal Reserve Bank gave me the 1895 exchange rate with the pound sterling.

In obtaining authentic detail I was also aided by the collections of costumes and memorabilia as well as the exhibitions of nineteenth-century photographs at the Metropolitan Museum of Art, the Museum of the City of New York, the New-York Historical Society, the Municipal Art Society of New York, and the Fashion Institute of Technology.

The Preservation Society of Newport County made it possible for me to visit and study the great mansions built during the "golden days" of Newport. In England I benefitted by the work of The National Trust, the Department of the Environment's Ancient Monuments and Public Buildings, and the owners, royals and peers of the realm, in maintaining and opening such castles and residences as Skipton, Hever, Blenheim, Syon, Windsor, and Hampton Court.

As I acknowledge the past I think of my governess, Tilla Sproge von Dippel, who told me from the time I was a child that I must write a book like this—and whose memory still gives me strength.

I should particularly like to thank Claire M. Smith, my agent, for her help and belief in the book from the start, and I greatly appreciate the interest shown and help offered by Margaret Blackstone, my editor. My husband has my thanks for giving assistance and being, as always, supportive.

Contents

The Secret Lives of the Edmonts

Logic versus Desire

When people look back on the summer of 1895, they will say, 'That was the summer Mrs. Wallace Montague Edmont V rode a camel into the great ballroom at Île de Joie.' "

Wallace found intolerable the way she spoke those words to him, the way she looked, giving him her bold and winning smile. The same smile she gave Harry Van Burgh, he was certain. Who could live with such a woman? Excessive, moody, tempestuous. Unfaithful, blatantly so, the subject of the lowest gossip, deservedly; her behavior was common knowledge in any home they visited. Melanie's "summer toy": that was how the local scandal sheet had described Van Burgh. Accurate, of course. Handsome Harry, as he was known, was in his twenties; it was the Van Burgh parents, not too much older than he, or than Melanie for that matter, who had been their friends. Crumpling the *Bourneham Bugle* in his hands, Wallace knew he should leave her.

Extravagant. Uncontrollably so. The cost in dollars of

maintaining her would be unimaginable to anyone else. The camel was only the latest of the fantastical ideas that had to be indulged. Everyone was talking about her, as she had known they would, and the already fabled ride was nearly a week away.

One of the most powerful men in New York, the largest property owner, a member of every club, of each city commission and committee of businessmen, the possessor of the most respected name in society, and people were whispering behind his back. The *Bugle*, a yellow rag, not fit to be in any gentleman's home, was in every gentleman's home. And this was just the current gossip, except for Van Burgh's youth, not much different from earlier scandals. It had gone on for years. He would come home from his office and she would be sitting in the little parlor off the great reception hall, her skin luminous. Oh, he knew what gave her skin that luminous look. And he would wonder who the man had been, why chosen, where embraced, and how. It was not to be endured.

And now for the first time he had met someone who had shown him how different a woman could be: comforting, respectable, frankly accepting middle age.

Divorce. How odious the idea was to him still. Yet three men among his acquaintance had been divorced and no one thought the less of them. Divorce had not reflected on them in business or society as it would have done a generation earlier in the more sober 1870s. He was a conventional man; marriage was for one's entire life. But who could have foretold what he would have to bear in a marriage with Melanie?

And yet . . . Every so often, and he never knew when it would be, he would be going to his room to bed and as he walked down the long corridor he would see the door of her bedroom wide open, and she would be standing there within doing nothing, just waiting for him, in her creamy satin robe with the maribou feathers. As soon as he came into view, she would smile and open her arms, welcoming him in. And

2

as she did so, the robe would fall open, revealing her naked body, the most beautiful he had ever seen. Still today, the most beautiful. He would enter and go to her as if mesmerized, put out his hand and lightly touch her skin, so soft, resilient, hot, heated by her excitement. She would throw off the robe, let it fall to the floor. And he would be "my sweet Wally," "my prince," and she would say that she would do "anything for you, anything you want, Wally, anything." Helping him out of his suit coat, his vest, his shirt, and then moving lower, she would not hesitate at the buttons, pulling his trousers down with her long slim fingers, trembling a little, his underdrawers. "My Wally, my prince."

At such moments it did not matter if other men had held that beautiful, passionate body in their arms. She was his, and it was not merely that he could demand his conjugal rights. (But when had he to demand? She had never refused him.) In bitter moods, he had wondered whether she were too clever to give him so overt a cause for putting her aside.

Yes. There was so much bitterness that he would try to see calculation in the timing of these episodes, to determine that they followed some particularly outrageous behavior on her part. Wallace was a logical man, but logic did not help.

Faithless . . . and yet . . . "I want you . . . my Wally . . . my prince." He would believe her as she spoke, believe for days afterwards that he came first.

At these moments the thought of divorcing her seemed the height of foolishness. Would any man give up such a woman? Such a wife?

CHAPTER 1

Ladies on
a Summer Morning

Any man will do."

"The way she turns her eyes on him . . . bending forward across the table as she does."

"What woman could not be beautiful devoting the time she does to her looks?"

"And having her husband's money to spend on herself."

"Poor Wallace. He's in terror of her temper. He'll put up with anything for peace. She calls Junior 'stupid.' The servants can hear her all over the house."

No need for her to ask whom they were talking about. Of course they were talking about her. In a moment Melanie Edmont would have to step out of the clubhouse onto the veranda overlooking Emerald Beach and say something outrageous. It was essential to maintaining her reputation. Her acerbic words would later be quoted behind fans at dinner tables with little smirks.

She was accustomed to being hated by women. When she stepped onto the veranda, she would see the golden sand

4

glittering in the sun and be surrounded by the hard glitter of malice. Taken by surprise, embarrassed, they would yet be pleased that she had overheard the hurtful words. Hardly a woman there who did not at least occasionally harbor the doubt that her husband (lately perhaps her son) had been with Melanie. Louise Van Burgh's voice was the most shrill; she had the most right to bitterness. Her son Harry, who could so easily rescue her and his sister, Evangeline, from their lives of bare gentility, was passing far too many of the summer hours at the Edmonts' Île de Joie when he should have been at the Woodruffs' Villa del Destino assuring his marriage to Iris by turning his considerable charm on her mother.

Melanie knew she must go out and face down the women; staying in concealment in the shadows was to concede defeat. Competitive by nature, she usually enjoyed deflecting the hostility with her wit. Tall, regal in bearing, slender yet voluptuous, her physical endowments assisted her in dominating any scene. A sense of excitement was felt in her presence. Her skin was always glowing. People made excuses to touch her.

Somehow she did not have the heart for clever badinage today. She had awakened with a heavy feeling pressing on her chest, filling her throat. Anxiety. It was not her style. She knew herself confident, able to deal with anything—until this unease had come upon her. The sense of misgiving had stayed with her while she was drinking coffee, having her massage, creaming her arms and breasts and face before being dressed to go out. All the while, the conversation of last night's dinner at the Woodruffs' ball kept running through her head. That conversation had seemed so casual at first that she had missed the portentousness, the threatening undertone hinting at disaster.

Returning home, agitated, she had walked into the tense, ugly scene with Wallace, another threat of another disaster. It had ended with their making love. Her doing really. She had been desperate to change the mood and excited by that

5

very desperation. The signs of their lovemaking had been evident on the sheets when she awakened this morning. But there was no joyous recollection. When he had been inside her, while she had her tongue in his mouth, she had forgotten the menace. In the clarity of morning she felt a sick fear that nothing had been changed between them, that they had merely succeeded in distracting themselves.

She took a step forward and glanced at the long row of bathing houses lining the beach alongside the clubhouse. Each had its little awninged porch, untenanted now, except for the maids and governesses waiting there. Another step and she could see the women strolling up and down the veranda of the clubhouse. Huge puffed sleeves belled out and the breeze from the ocean lifted the flounced sheer voile skirts. The yards and yards of light fabric swayed, making it appear as if the wearer were floating, though there was nothing sheer and light about the corset worn even for a lazy summer's morning at the beach.

The ocean glimmered in the sunshine, green-blue, cool, enticing, beckoning. But Melanie shuddered at the thought of the clamminess of the waterlogged navy alpaca swimming suit, sleeves extending to the elbow, the knee-length skirt with bloomers underneath. She hated the slimy feel of the long black stockings against her thighs and the heaviness of the low canvas shoes. The men swam nude at the cove; it was forbidden territory for women. Or so it had been until the day she went there with Harry. At first she had objected; nudity out-of-doors was different from nakedness in the bedroom. Harry made it seem so natural that without realizing she had agreed, and she had slipped off her swimming suit and run into the ocean, holding Harry's hand. And oh how wonderful the coolness of the water on her skin and how liberated her flesh from the constraints of her clothes. Their bodies came together in the water so easily, but what was not easy with Harry? Ease, pleasure was his forte. Kissing her, he pulled her under for a second, his mouth still on hers, delicious. Later he taught her to swim. Word of this had gotten about; there were few secrets in Bourneham.

The other women envied her daring. It fueled their hostility, which had more to do with her flair and appearance than with the fact that she had love affairs. After all, many of the women at the beach that morning had lovers too. The manner of their lives encouraged it. Most husbands were driven by the will to succeed, and were reluctant to make the trip to Bourneham, six hours by the best rail and steamboat connections, not much less by yacht. To take more than two weeks of vacation—and many took but one—was viewed as indolence, a proof of indifference to the most important thing in life, business. It had become the thing to remark at balls and dinner parties that a love affair could not be conducted in Bourneham, with hardly a man to be found, except on the weekends—and these had to be spent with his family. But, of course, ways were found.

"She likes the young ones best," the gossip continued.

"The older she gets, the younger she wants them."

The tone seemed particularly venomous today. It had to do with Harry, of course. All the Bourneham world loves a chaste lover, and Harry and Iris were the perfect pair—so young, so good-looking, she to join her family's great wealth to his family's great name. Woodruff to Van Burgh: this was a match made in the Bourneham heaven. And Iris was madly in love with Harry, and he was in love with her, or so it had seemed until he had fallen under Melanie's malign spell. Melanie was the stumbling block, it was believed, to this marital consummation.

The *Bourneham Bugle* had come out the previous day. They had all read it. Every week another scandal was unearthed, never with the principals named, only hinted at so cleverly that their identities were plain. The *Bugle* printed more falsehood than fact. Everyone knew that, but paradoxically persisted in believing every word written in it.

"What island beauty has taken a summer toy that another, younger heiress longs to play with?" This was the kind of coy writing that delighted Armand Wolfe, the editor of the *Bugle*. Everyone, of course, was able to guess that Melanie was the island beauty, a play on the name of her

Bourneham cottage, Île de Joie—after all, everyone who read the gossip paper had enjoyed the advantage of a French governess—and that Harry, alas, was all too obviously the summer toy that Iris so desperately wanted to play with. It was a perfect *Bugle* item: easy to understand, malicious, with just enough truth to be dangerous, just enough truth to display each person at his worst.

The "toy" accusation was not without a modicum of justification. Harry was filled with joy, displayed a carelessness quite lacking in the heaviness of Bourneham life. When he walked across the great lawn sloping up from the ocean to the terrace of Île de Joie, it seemed to Melanie that he shimmered in a golden haze.

She had always known Harry. Everyone in the small number of families making up society's inner circle knew everyone else. He had followed her about when he was a boy and she a young married woman. And in time she was ready for him.

It was not love she felt for Harry, she told herself; love was, always had been, Denis—flawed, bitter though it was for so much of the time. It was rather that Harry would come into a room, light of heart, light of spirit, and she should find herself smiling. Harry walked with a spring to his step. His hair curled. His teeth gleamed. Harry was made for joy.

In bed she would say to him, "You glow in the dark." His body hair was golden, his skin translucent, his eyes a yellow-brown.

She had married Wallace in good faith. If she had not loved him passionately, she had cared enough to think she could make him a good wife—and how many girls of her acquaintance passionately loved the men they agreed to marry? It seemed unthinkable that a married woman would be unfaithful. (Men were different; no matter how innocent, a girl would have to know that.) She had believed Wallace would obliterate the past for her, make her forget Denis. But it had not happened. She gave Wallace what he wanted out of marriage. He could never say that she did not. And some-

8

times she desired him, was happy with him, too. It changed nothing after all; she remained haunted by Denis. However seldom she saw him, however much she resisted, resented even, the attraction he held for her, she was painfully vulnerable not only to him, but to men who reminded her of him, dark men with a brilliance that had a hard edge, an undercurrent of egotism, in her worst moods she thought viciousness. Harry was different. She was never closer to forgetting Denis than when she was with Harry.

The most distasteful aspect of the affair with Harry, in fact, was his youth. Odd that all the other women missed the point that having a young lover made one more, rather than less, conscious of one's age. It was not that the comparison between their bodies was unfavorable to her. Her own well-exercised and massaged body was firm. But how carefully she had to guard her tongue so as to avoid references to events taking place too long before the present 1890s. Harry could share none of her early memories. She would have been embarrassed to admit to him how well she remembered the horror of Lincoln's assassination, the excitement of the Union victory celebrations. Melanie had been a child then, but Harry had not yet been born. He could not even remember the Tweed Ring scandals of the late sixties and early seventies.

Still, the women were right about one thing. She did fear growing old. Once during a quarrel with Wallace he had turned on her: "You will grow old, Melanie. You will grow old and lose your looks and I will be free of you." That brought her up short in the midst of an outburst of anger. Did he mean that the only thing holding him to her was her beauty? Wallace had succeeded in frightening her.

The words haunted her, though she tried to explain them away. It had been a harsh quarrel. She said unkind things herself, knew herself given to making the clever remark that cut. Yet she was unconvinced, and her doubt helped her justify her actions. What was their marriage after all if he could even in anger, even on an impulse suggest that he would so

9

easily put her aside? She wronged him far less by accepting the happiness Harry offered her.

Harry carried lightly the burdens of his mother and his unfortunate sister. All situations favored him. The bride his mother had found for him was fragile, lovely, virginal—and, of course (or Louise would not have singled her out), the heiress to a vast fortune. Harry courted her whenever Melanie was not free for him, a fact that was evident to Iris's mother, Nellie, who held the ultimate power of decision.

It was the same with business. Everything came easily to Harry. Immediately upon his graduation from Harvard, a position was made for him in a bank managed by a friend of his late father. Harry did not use this position as a springboard to success. He was bright and quick, and had many ideas and a surprisingly sound instinct for business trends, yet could not be induced to take the work as seriously as his colleagues did. Once the affair with Melanie began, he found every excuse to be absent.

This fecklessness, this lightness was his charm. Melanie knew their relationship was temporary. He was to marry Iris Woodruff and he was so young, she thought rather cynically, that he believed he would be faithful. She saw a kind of innocence in him, a lack of awareness as to how hard it would be for him to break with her and have only bloodless little Iris. The idea of having to face another stultifying New York season, then another stultifying Bourneham summer without Harry depressed her. So she sought by whatever means she could to postpone his marriage. Everyone in Bourneham blamed her for his dilatory behavior with the Woodruffs. But was it so unworthy for Melanie to hold him, noble for Louise to plot that he marry Iris for her money? Certainly that was the view held by the respectable women of Bourneham.

The conversation returned to Melanie's predilection for youth. It was a topic with an unending appeal.

"Have you noticed how she has that baby brought in at dinner parties to make her seem younger?"

Who could have imagined, thought Melanie, that having

children late could be turned to advantage? She had been thirty when Wallace Junior, the sixth of that name, was born, and she was just past forty when at last successfully delivered of Rosamunde. For years everyone said she had refused to have children, and then after Junior, to have more than one because she was afraid of ruining her perfect figure. She had encouraged the rumors, preferring to have people think she was vain rather than that she was barren.

How she had feared during all those years that she had damaged herself irreparably when at fifteen she had, all alone, in the rose marble bathtub with the golden eagles' feet, taken the knitting needle stolen from her governess, Miss Robertson, and pushed it in and up. Kneeling naked, trembling, the marble slippery and hard against her knees, her mother's heavy silver hand mirror (said to have belonged to Catherine the Great) placed beneath her to help her guide the hand that held the stolen knitting needle. She had not been certain of how far the needle point should go, why it should achieve the end that the whispered gossip indicated it would. But she must have moved it rightly, because a flood of blood poured from her body, and she was able to detect a slimy substance unlike the menstrual flow.

How cold the bathtub had been; she had never been in a cold bathtub before. Until she was mistress of a house, she did not know that servants warmed the marble before each bath by filling and refilling the tub with warm water half a dozen times. Nauseous, dizzy with cramping pain, so innocent had she been that the thought of Denis had sustained her. It did not occur to her then to blame him for anything. She loved him. (Later Denis introduced her to the pessary; she had the best ones imported for her from Vienna each year by the apothecary.)

Her bleeding periods did not resume for half a year and were never quite right thereafter. Still, in the end, it had all worked out better than she would have thought possible.

Did she have Rosamunde brought into the dining room at parties to show off a baby of her own when others her age were grandmothers already? That was only partly the reason: her spirits rose when she saw Rosamunde's fresh little face and the delicious flesh of her chubby little arms and neck in startling contrast to the world-weary faces around her.

"I hear that Wallace is thinking of getting a divorce."

She stopped where she stood and shuddered. A cold wind must be blowing up from the ocean; the hair on her arms was erect. Who had spoken? What did that matter? If one spoke, anyone else might have done so. Common knowledge. Divorce. Disaster. It had been in the air during that terrible quarrel the night before. Unspoken. She had not realized the rumors had gone so far. Yet it was true that Merwyn James, Wallace's lawyer, had been visiting the house quite a bit of late. Whereas in the past he had always sought out Melanie, flirted with her, implied the wish to see her alone, these days he was slow to meet her eyes.

Not since her wedding night had she been in such danger. She could not imagine what had changed Wallace. Quarrels had characterized their married life for many years. Still, to both of them marriage had always been immutable. A solid family background was essential for a man in business. Although several couples, even in the best society, had gotten divorced in recent years, Wallace had always spoken of them scornfully.

The few divorce cases she had heard about came to mind. Wallace's reputation for absolute probity in sexual matters would weigh heavily in the balance.

She could not actually be thinking about this as if it were to happen, but there was enough evidence to shake her confidence. Again she wondered what had made the difference. The "summer toy" accusation? Wallace said he never read the *Bugle*, yet that was the only explanation that made sense. With any other man, one would of course assume a woman was involved, but that was impossible with Wallace.

All the gossip about her would be repeated. Much of it was untrue or grossly exaggerated, but everyone would believe it.

There was a vast difference, she knew, between being a beautiful wife believed to have affairs of the heart and being a divorcée. Whatever the gossip, she was sustained by the solidity of the position and fortune of Wallace Montague Edmont V. It would not be at all the same thing if it were her money. And that—if Wallace adhered strictly to the prenuptial agreement—would be slightly less than one million dollars, a figure that looked considerably smaller now than it had when the lawyers had arranged it more than two decades ago. It would hardly be adequate for clothes, travel, maintaining a home with servants, and entertaining. But would she be entertaining and being entertained? A divorced woman was quickly déclassé, removed from visiting lists, unwelcome in the best homes, even in the not-so-good homes. She thought of Junior and Rosamunde and trembled at the possibility of losing them. Surely that would not happen. No court would separate a mother from her children. Still, the scandal would reflect on them, too. It struck her that the only way for a woman to rise above the disgrace of divorce was to remarry quickly and well. If she could do so. Whom could Melanie count on in the crisis? Denis? He was irrevocably bound to Adelaide. And Harry—what could one reasonably expect of a golden boy, even were he not promised to Iris?

Still, never had she faltered when confronted with obstacles. She walked forward, resolute, queenly. Everyone looked up and then exchanged glances. Wondering whether she had heard. Pretend she had not? Cowardice was not for her.

"I do believe the art of conversation would die if I did not exist," she remarked coolly. "Everyone would become mute and have to communicate by waving hands about, or like animals, with grunts and snarls."

While they stared at her, amused and admiring, she calmly stepped off the veranda onto the sand and started to stroll down the beach towards the children at play. Junior was tossing a ball with his friends. Rosamunde was sitting beside her nurse on a pale blue cashmere blanket, her soft face concealed by a big white sunbonnet. With every step Melanie's feet sank into the sand until, scorning convention, she bent down and took off her shoes and made her way to the water's edge. Her skirt, longer in the back, trailed over the sand, creating the appearance of a path behind her.

Everyone expected her to go to the pretty baby, she knew, but instead she called Junior and he came, too surprised to be reluctant, and she held him to her, letting the dampness and wet sand from his body and swimming suit stain the white linen skirt, the long tight white gloves. None of the other women would do that. But then none of the other women called their little boys "stupid." And of course she had. The child had come in to ask in an irritating piping voice: "Why does everyone but us get the *Bugle*? Buddy van der Cleeve said they read about you in the *Bugle* all the time. I asked Papa why we don't get it and he said to ask you."

What a dreadful man and what a foolish child. Surely Junior should have been able to perceive this was something one could not ask. Anyone else would have seen the malice in Buddy van der Cleeve's remark and in his father's reaction to it. How could a child of hers, and he was eleven years old, be so simple? Angry at Wallace, at Junior, at the van der Cleeves, the *Bugle*, and at herself for being in this position, she had lashed out: "Stupid." Of course the servants had heard; they heard everything. A moment later she was sorry for having frightened the child and pulled him to her and stroked his hair and said that they did not read the *Bugle* because it was so crudely written and ungrammatical. Junior was soon smiling again. As children do, he accepted his mother's quick temper as a part of her, did not take it too seriously. He knew she was as quick to be warm and loving. That did not help. Another legend about her had been born.

Returning to the veranda, she was alarmed to find her mother-in-law. Could Genevieve have been there all along to hear the gossip? Things were bad indeed if the women had dared to speak in front of so respectable and respected a person. "I did not see you, Genevieve," she said weakly. "Were you on the veranda?"

"No. I decided to sit inside the clubhouse today with Josephine van der Cleeve and her grandmother—she is a Langmuir, you will recall—who is ninety-three and has come to Bourneham for Josie's birthday party. The excitement and bustle of the veranda are too much for her. I came out just now to take a look at the children before going home."

Relieved, Melanie smiled at her mother-in-law warmly and observed how the women on the veranda were taking careful note of what Genevieve Edmont was wearing. Genevieve's short plump body was dressed in striped sky blue surah, black soutache circling the high neck and the cuffs of the enormous leg-of-mutton sleeves. She carried a blue surah parasol and a fan of ostrich plumes dyed apricot to match those on her hat. Her pearl-buttoned white kid gloves, changed four times a day to guarantee their whiteness, were exceedingly tight to display her surprisingly slender, beautifully shaped wrists and hands.

The mode of costume to be worn for a morning at Emerald Beach, as indeed for all occasions during the day, was determined by her. Whatever she did was accepted as unalterably correct and imitated. The surah dress had not been seen before. Genevieve brought ninety dresses to Bourneham for the eight-week season, each with matching parasol and hat, and two hundred pairs of white gloves.

In the years since her marriage and to her own astonishment, Melanie had come to appreciate her mother-in-law's kindness and to love her. It was her one true friendship with a woman. Alone among the women, Genevieve did not resent Melanie's beauty. Rather, she was proud of it, thinking it reflected well on Wallace. In this marriage as in all else, Wallace had triumphed. Genevieve could not have been more pleased if the glowing skin, the beautifully curved slender figure had been hers.

Looking at her mother-in-law more carefully, it seemed

to Melanie that she could trace the faintest of shadows. Could Genevieve have overheard the other women gossiping after all? Her composure proved nothing. That was the way she behaved. So had she been able to welcome back at regular intervals an openly errant husband, disregarding any and all gossip. That was the way women of her generation and social status had been trained to behave. Let it happen that a husband took a mistress or beggared his family by gambling, let a father die of the French disease, a sister run away with a footman, a son become addicted to laudanum, it would be ignored or falsified. Women known for their probity did not hesitate to prevaricate in such situations. Or let it be a story of embezzlement and corruption. To hear these women tell it, there had not been so much as a venal thought. Mrs. Carle had been the same. Melanie's brother Bunner's terrible death had been glossed over so skillfully that Melanie sometimes found herself believing that he truly had died, like so many other young men of good family, in a hunting accident.

Never in all the years had Genevieve indicated in any way an awareness of the gossip about Melanie.

"Where is your carriage, Melanie dear?"

"I didn't come by carriage, Genevieve. I came here on foot."

Hardly any adult woman besides Melanie walked. Even in the morning the other women wore shoes so tight as to make more than a brief stroll unendurable. Only Melanie refused to follow the custom. It was viewed as eccentricity in Bourneham. Her bootmaker practically wept at her insistence that her shoes be made to match the size of her feet.

"Let us drive back together then. And tell me what is wrong, Melanie." Genevieve ran her hand caressingly over the back of Melanie's neck; it was a way she had to be touching people she cared about. Melanie had never known another woman so tender.

"I still have a great deal to prepare for my ball," she equivocated.

Melanie's was the last great ball of the Bourneham sea-

son, as her mother-in-law's was the first. Only after Genevieve had held her ball could another hostess send out invitations. Similarly, no one would dare to preempt the last
Saturday in August, which was Melanie's.

Selecting a theme for the ball occupied her for weeks
each summer and the recognition of the fact sometimes depressed her. As a bride, she had imagined her life as a woman
would be so meaningful, filled with business activities. Her
determination had been to follow a course that bore no similarity to her mother's.

When she was a girl Melanie thought that never had
anyone been so idle as her mother. She did nothing, it
seemed, but was always too busy to stop to talk or accompany Melanie and Bunner anywhere. Everything she did was
so puffed up and out of proportion. A week was spent considering the theme for a ball. And the place cards, why the
place cards. She could stand there for hours pushing the
small cards beautifully lettered by Mrs. Bott, the housekeeper, from one little sterling silver swan card holder to
the next.

It was not until Melanie was married herself that she
discovered how time-consuming were the things her mother
did, how far from idleness was her life. The endless fittings
were obligatory if dresses were to hold their perfect line.
Each dinner had to be planned not only for taste, but also
for color, texture, originality, indeed uniqueness, rarity, and
obvious cost. Yes, it took time. Servants did not relieve one
of that. The mistress of a house was like the general of an
army, directing, planning every move. And there were so
many houses to run—the mansion in New York, the summer
cottage in Bourneham, the country estate to the north of the
city, the villa in the hills outside Florence.

As for the place cards. Why the place cards. Each required consideration. Days slipped by in planning, thinking, remembering, studying gossip columns, discreetly
questioning one's maid so as to be sure not to commit a gaffe.
Emmeline Gerard had never lived down the error of putting

Mrs. Carteret next to Mr. Bitner, across the table from her husband and his wife on the eve of the very day when a veiled account of their affair had appeared in the *Bugle*.

Except for spending more time with her children, Melanie's life was not too different from her mother's.

When she first came to Bourneham, Melanie had not intended to be swept up in social competition. She was a serious person who would spend her time more profitably. But profitable endeavors did not come her way and in time she came to realize that giving extravagant balls with startling themes fitted her personality: she liked to shock, to outdo; she liked to spend money.

"Does this make you happy?" Denis had asked her once.

A natural question for Harry, for any other lover, but not Denis who had so seldom cared, she thought, if anyone but he were happy, not his wife certainly, nor, it seemed, Melanie. (Though once long ago, he had put his hands over his face and wept for her—she had seen the tears trickling through his fingers.) Moments of softness came just often enough to keep her from extricating herself from the affair, even though she came to suspect him of using kindness in a calculating manner. Whether he loved her or not, and she was never quite sure, he did not want to lose her.

"I have been amused."

"And that is enough."

"It has had to be enough."

That was the best she could say. Surely he knew that balls, other men, amusements were not enough. Except that sometimes now, with Harry, it seemed enough. Misleading, of course. Harry would soon be gone to give all that brightness to Iris, and in time there would be someone else to amuse her while she waited for the moments with Denis. She knew what her life was.

As the footman helped them into the carriage, his hand lingered on Melanie's arm a fraction of a second longer than his support was needed. She hardly noticed, so used was she to such attention.

The shadow on Genevieve's face deepened; in anyone else, it would have been a frown. "Melanie, can it be true that you are planning to ride a camel at the ball? People are talking of nothing else and my maid tells me that palm trees and loads of sand are being delivered to Île de Joie, that a wooden ramp is being constructed from the back lawn into the ballroom, and crude pine boards are being laid over your beautiful ballroom floor. Now Mr. de Witte's footman claims to have seen the camel."

"Yes. It is quite true, Genevieve. I wanted it to be a surprise, but, of course, it is quite impossible to keep anything hidden in Bourneham, certainly anything as large as a camel. I had it brought in from the menagerie in New York on a specially built cart."

"What will people say?" Genevieve had been told it added to Wallace's reputation to have so flamboyant, orchidaceous a wife. (Everyone knew Melanie had spent four million dollars to remodel and furnish Île de Joie.) In fact, he had once remarked that such expenditures were good for business, though she was not quite certain why extravagance should be advantageous. But a camel was going too far.

CHAPTER 2

The Letter

When people look back on the summer of 1895 they will say, 'Why, that was the summer Mrs. Wallace Montague Edmont V rode a camel into the great ballroom at Île de Joie.' "

She should not have said that to Wallace, knowing how he felt about her extravagance, but she had not been able to resist. The image and the effect it would have were so clear. The vast ballroom had been modeled after the Hall of Mirrors at Versailles. Melanie on camelback would be reflected from all angles. The formality of the room contrasted with the crudeness of the beast would be a scene to remember.

Genevieve was still troubled. "Isn't a camel dangerous?"

"I spoke with the keeper, Abdelrahim, and asked if the creature could not be given a touch of laudanum to calm him down. But no one seems to know how much to give to quiet a camel. And you see, I simply will not ride in on a nodding, sluggish beast. Abdel says the camel will behave so long as nobody teases him, so we will have to control the guests rather than the animal."

Genevieve was not deflected by Melanie's humor. "It is not dignified to ride a wild creature from a menagerie in Bourneham."

"But are we so dignified in Bourneham? I can recall Petra Musgrove's ball where she brought a circus elephant and gave each of us a bag of peanuts to feed the animal as we danced by. The elephant also ate a couple of fans and a pair of gloves. And Johanna Harteland had monkeys in full-dress suits mingling with the guests. Then there was the party at the Olneys' where money was the theme and one-hundred-dollar bills were wrapped around the candied fruit and cigars given as favors." (Melanie had whispered to her dinner companion that French envelopes wrapped in the currency would have made better, or at least more useful, favors; the remark had gone around the table and was still quoted.)

"I did not approve of any of those balls, Melanie. I would not have gone to the Hartelands' had they not concealed the fact that monkeys would be there." The monkeys had misbehaved; several ball gowns had been damaged.

Melanie had gone too far with her plans to consider changing them. A Bedouin costume had been designed and fitted. Wearing trousers beneath the burnoose was daring, but she would be completely covered up to spare the sensibilities of her mother-in-law and Wallace. After the ride she would change and make her second appearance wearing the most spectacular of all the gowns Worth had ever designed for her.

Genevieve yielded with good grace; she had expressed her opinion and would not quarrel. Genevieve kept all relationships harmonious. The camel now, well it was ridiculous, but if anyone could carry it off, Melanie was that person.

"Where do you keep the camel?"

"I wanted to put it in the stables, but Wallace thought his horses would become nervous, so I have had the groundskeeper rent a barn from one of the farmers three miles to the north of Bourneham."

The carriage was taking them along the ocean drive that curved so as to afford a view of the shoreline. Genevieve's house, built for her grandfather in the 1840s, was the first of the row of mansions commanding the vista, and was the simplest. Designed by Richard Upjohn in early Victorian style, it was smaller and less opulent than the great castles that were to come. Wallace had offered to build his mother a new mansion when she relinquished Île de Joie (before Melanie it had borne the less enticing name of Seaside Rest). Genevieve had refused. For a few weeks each summer she relished the role of one who espoused the simple life and lived modestly in the old family home. She declared her jewels to be unsafe in a house that had but fourteen bedrooms and a staff of only fifteen and kept them in the vault at Île de Joie along with Melanie's. Every morning her butler and three footmen set off, all of them armed—for had not Elsie Morris's trunk containing $40,000 worth of jewels been stolen from the pier where the Morris yacht lay at anchor? The servants exchanged the jewels Genevieve had worn the previous evening for those she intended to wear for that night's ball.

Genevieve frowned as the Woodruffs' Villa del Destino came into sight, massive and imposing at the farthermost cliff overlooking the Atlantic. The sight reminded her of the worry she meant to discuss with Melanie.

"Junior came to breakfast with me this morning." To Genevieve, Wallace was still "Junior," her grandson, "little Wallace." Melanie started; the heavy feeling she had been holding at bay, distracting herself with chatter, was back.

"Junior is worried," said Genevieve.

Melanie wondered if Wallace had told his mother he thought to divorce. Were that so, the deed was as good as done.

"It's about that man at the Woodruffs' last night."

Melanie's immediate sense of relief was tempered by her recollection of what had passed between her and Elmer

Morgen. "Which man?" She did not wish to seem too know-ing, though she knew well enough.

"The journalist. The one who dared to seat himself next to you at dinner, Melanie. The utter gall of it. Such people have no idea of how to behave. I hope he was not rude to you. He runs that scurrilous newspaper, the *New York Journal*, that is always making trouble for someone. Now he is determined to make trouble for Junior."

"What kind of trouble could he make?"

"Junior did not go into details with me. Something to do with one of his properties. Innuendo, slurs. A man like that stops at nothing in his efforts to embarrass, to attract readers to his disreputable newspaper.

"No one could run a business more scrupulously, could be more concerned about the welfare of all the people in-volved, even the poorest of them, than Wallace. But a trou-blemaker can do a lot of mischief."

Genevieve sat up even straighter and declared firmly, "I will cease calling on the Woodruffs, Melanie. They do not know whom to invite to their home. One finds oneself associating with the most undesirable persons. No. I must draw the line. I told Junior and he agrees. I think it made him feel a great deal better to know that his mother would not sanction with her presence the appearance of so low-class and reprehensible a person."

It was clear that Genevieve was convinced she had made the appropriate and helpful response to Wallace's expressed worry. Melanie thought it a lack of sophistication, but maybe Genevieve was right. Melanie's efforts to involve herself in Wallace's business affairs had only angered him. "Nobody looks at my ledgers!" he had shouted. "Nobody!"

"I think I have upset you."

"I worry when Wallace worries," replied Melanie. She could not reveal the cause for the darkness of her thoughts, though she knew Genevieve loved her sincerely. If Wallace did mean divorce, she would lose Genevieve. The thought was surprisingly painful.

"I know that, Melanie. And so does he."

Melanie smiled wryly. She could think of no possible response, but fortunately there was no need to say more as they were approaching Île de Joie.

The coachman left Melanie just inside the gate, knowing that she liked to walk across the lawn to the house. The garden was entirely hers. Red. All the flowers were red, glowing, brilliant, pure tones with no hint of yellow, orange, blue, purple. Just a clear red, the color of blood, associated with life, with passion. Masses of rhododendrons, of cannas, of roses, of peonies, azaleas. The garden was planted in such a way as to look undisciplined—jungles of flowers and bushes one would think to hide in. The lack of discipline was only seeming: every flower and shrub had been placed according to her master plan.

The house, massive yet graceful, stood amidst the brilliance, its creamy exterior taking on a rosy glow. The glass in the windows had been angled so as to catch the rays of sun. At dawn and at sunset one might have thought Île de Joie aflame. All day long, reflecting the sunlight, the great house glittered, golden.

Leaving the garden she mounted the steps. The heavy door of bronze and steel topped with the Edmont initials and crest in gold opened at her approach. Never had Melanie lifted a hand to the knocker. A footman was always nearby listening for the carriage, waiting for her.

She stepped into the entrance hall out of a flood of sunlight outdoors into a flood of sunshine indoors. The floors, the columns, the walls were of the yellow Siena marble known as sunshine marble. From where she stood she could see all the way through the house. Archways and glass doors led the eye from one room to the next, to the one after that, and finally through a series of French doors to the terrace and velvety lawn sloping down to the ocean. So skillfully had the house been designed by Richard Morris Hunt that there was a feeling of lightness and airiness, despite the tapestried walls; the great curving staircase and stained-glass window on the landing, the mahogany furniture so heavy it took six men to move the dining table a few feet.

A footman brought her a letter on a silver tray. And there it was. The crest on the envelope, his handwriting, the stab in the groin, the heat. Denis. Not that his letters contained a word that of itself could excite. They were written with such care, such ambiguity that anyone could read them. Each contained a puzzle, a clue, and when they finally saw one another, he would explain this to her.

It had been so in the first letter he had sent her so many years earlier during that terrible time of fear and hope that without her doing anything to achieve this end, Denis would find out about the pregnancy and resolve her problem. The letter told that he had enjoyed her company, had found their meeting pleasurable, exceedingly so in fact; sent his compliments to her parents; expressed regret that her brother Bunner had been absent. Her mother had read the letter, expressed pleasure in its courtesy. Nowhere could Melanie find a suggestion that if she needed him, he would come to her.

Later he explained that the word *meeting* was the clue, intended to convey all that their meetings had contained. Yes, they had met. It was after getting the careful letter with the meeting and the compliments that Melanie knew she could wait no longer and would have to do whatever was necessary by herself. She had never lacked for courage, even at fifteen. But she had not the faintest idea what it was she could wait no longer to do. Fortuitously, Bunner, Bunny to her, had a bit of gossip too good to keep to himself: a girl in their set accused a friend of their parents of debauching her and admitted, the rumor went, having brought on a miscarriage by her own hand. Pleased by Melanie's rapt attention, Bunny had continued, ". . . with a knitting needle." There. She had her fact.

For years afterwards she could not bear to look at a woman knitting. She refused to allow any servant to knit in her presence. One of Melanie's many idiosyncracies, it was said, a way to make others bend to her will.

She opened the letter.

CHAPTER 3

Adelaide, 47, Bears a Son

Adelaide is dead."

For the first time Melanie had a letter from Denis with no ambiguities, no clues or hints, but a flat statement of fact.

With a sudden surge of guilt, Melanie realized that she had . . . not hoped . . . certainly she had not seriously gone that far . . . but felt some vague wish that Adelaide would be somehow removed from the scene. Melanie tried to feel sympathy for her. It was no more than decent. But she had suffered too much because of Adelaide—she knew it was not the woman's fault, but how did that lessen the pain?

Denis was free. She could hardly take it in. Standing in the large airy room at Île de Joie, she gasped for breath.

Those hours after giving birth must have been the happiest Adelaide had known since marrying Denis. What a gallant woman Adelaide had been, trying again and yet again, miscarriage after miscarriage, stillbirth after stillbirth. How had she stood the pain? Melanie's three postmarital miscarriages had been not much less painful than the other, the

26

concealed one carried out alone in the rose marble bathtub. Each time for months afterwards only the pessary ("womb veil" her apothecary called it) made it possible for her to tolerate marital relations. In contrast, Adelaide, well past the normal age for childbearing, had made this final effort that had killed her. Undergoing labor late in life was dangerous. There had been fears for Melanie's safety when pregnant with Rosamunde. And Adelaide had been so much older, forty-seven at least.

Looking at the letter again, it struck Melanie that something was wrong. The date. It was four months past. She had wondered why there had been no word from Denis since he had informed her of his father's death six months ago, or more. This letter must have been mislaid by a servant, found, and handed to her without comment out of fear. Four months and Denis had not written to her again. What should she do? What could she do in the face of that silence? If she had gotten the letter on time, she could have rushed to England and in the confusion done . . . something; surely there was something she could yet do.

The quarrel with Wallace. Perhaps it was fortuitous. What if she, like Denis, were free? Then she thought that were Wallace to follow through on his threats, the scandal would become known in England as well as the United States. She would be unacceptable in the social circles where Denis was prominent, in the world that meant so much to him. Her affairs with others, with him, would be made to appear ugly to everyone, perhaps even to him. She knew that Denis had always been conservative; he would be even more conventional now that the heir at last was born. Perhaps he was not freed at all but was more bound in having a son. Her fantasies had never gone so far as to explore the realities of divorce and scandal.

For years Melanie had believed that someday, somehow she would be mistress of Carnaugh Castle. This belief had persisted long after she was as bound by marriage, parenthood, and convention as Denis. She had continued to think

27

against all logic, against all odds, that it could still happen, that they could come together. Each time she visited, the vision was reinforced and she would think how it would be when she belonged there. The scene was so clear: entering the grounds through the huge marble arch with Denis beside her, she would share his pride as they drove down the avenue between rows of oaks, old when Henry VIII had visited, then crossed the bridge spanning the lake where white swans and black were gliding. Down other avenues they would go, past greenhouses, hedges, a maze, through other arches, to come at last to the huge courtyard, dominated by the bronze statue of that Marquess of Warburne who had been a formidable crusader. Before them across the moat would be the great castle, a massive stone building, flanked by two crenelated towers. Sometimes she saw the vision of Carnaugh more clearly than Île de Joie.

Whatever she wanted that money could buy, she possessed. At Carnaugh, however, paintings created by the greatest of artists—Holbein, Van Dyck, Romney—portrayed members of the family. There was Gainsborough's famed portrait of Denis's great grandmother. (He had once said she reminded him of Melanie.) The statue of a mounted knight in the armor worn by an earlier marquess was set on the landing between the two wings of the staircase. In a glass case, on a crimson velvet cushion, was the bullet that had felled Denis's great-grandfather at Waterloo, pried from his body to be returned to his widow.

Melanie had been so sure that she would someday be mistress of Carnaugh that she had gathered entire wardrobes of warm clothing to protect her from the chill of the great drafty rooms. The wind stole through cracks between the huge blocks of stone until the tapestries depicting the first Marquess of Warburne billowed out and formed incredible patterns. Threadbare, but so ancient, so valued that no replacement could be contemplated. Fires were laid in every room, the largest boasting half a dozen fireplaces, but so high were the vaulted ceilings, so vast in dimensions the rooms that they retained the chill nonetheless. The Oriental rugs taken from mosques during the Crusades had been worn down, had not for centuries been thick enough to protect against the cold of the stone floors.

Armoires were filled; trunks were filled with woolens from Ireland, cashmeres from Scotland, with camel's hair, and vicuña, alpaca, and llama. A dressmaker had become skilled in lining the fabrics too scratchy for Melanie's delicate skin. Into every dress soft silk, velvet, and chiffon had been inserted beneath the neckline, within the bodice, inside the sleeves and down the back. With the lining sewn into place with the tiniest of stitches, the silk and the wool appeared to be a single fabric. In Paris she ordered ball gowns of heavy velvet with ermine trimming the sleeves and mink-lined mantles to throw over her shoulders. Negligees were of quilted silk, boudoir slippers lined with fur, and lingerie a heavy weight of satin.

It had been ridiculous really. Melanie knew that, had known it almost from the beginning. Childish, like a game. And with the passing years perhaps a shade pathetic. Clear-eyed, she sometimes compared herself to the aging spinster still preparing her lace-trimmed chiffon underdrawers to entice the bridegroom who never appeared.

Eventually she came to understand why she had needed that dream, had been so obsessed all these years. The images—herself so foolish in her innocence, Denis vicious—were not to be endured. If she and Denis did not marry, those images would be all there was, would be true forever. Only were they to come together, could she tell herself that the relationship had been destined from the start, that theirs had been a great love, blighted only by the misfortune of his having been married when they met, married at a time when divorce was more unthinkable than now. Otherwise, all that suffering—the loss of virginity, the pregnancy, the self-induced miscarriage, the terrors of discovery, of annulment and disgrace, the loneliness of separation—would have counted for so little. For years she had refused to believe that with all her passion and energy and enthusiasm and cleverness, she would not succeed and walk the halls of Carnaugh.

Wallace had no idea of all this. Consumed by business as he was, her activities were not of particular concern to him so long as she maintained their social position.

During this time, between their infrequent meetings, were Denis's letters, careful, cryptic, enigmatic, sending compliments, glad they had met or hoping they would do so soon.

Long after she had given up adding to the contents, she retained the trunks, the armoires, the boxes until the garments became hopelessly out of date, out of vogue, as was her dream. It had always been possessed of unreality. Reality was Adelaide whom she had disliked from their very first meeting, irritated by the superior manner of speech. "I will go now to make my ablutions," Adelaide would remark. Or, "Why, Denis, the pater might serve as a paradigm of the aristocracy." Mrs. Carle insisted this was the way the upper-class British women spoke, but the dislike remained. By then it was because Adelaide was with Denis, always with Denis.

It was inevitable that they should meet. They were in a manner related. A cousin of Melanie's mother had married Denis's uncle; that made a connection. The Carles had stayed in Carnaugh Castle on several of their annual trips to England, but though Melanie had been fourteen, old enough to accompany them the last time, Denis had been visiting the sheep farms in Scotland; their paths had not crossed. Mrs. Carle frequently found occasion to mention her cousin, Lord Warburne, the fifteenth marquess, and his son, the Earl of Lowndes, thirteenth earl, she believed it was. When Denis and Adelaide made their first trip to New York in 1869, of course, they stayed with the Carles.

Before their arrival, Melanie had asked what they were like. "She is attractive on the large scale, Junoesque, I would say," replied her mother, "but he's ugly."

Was he ugly? She supposed he was. Oh who, upon seeing him without prior knowledge, could have guessed that Denis was an aristocrat? Heavy dark hair grew so low on his forehead as to practically meet his thick eyebrows. With shaggy beard and mustache, his face was almost simian. And out of this mass of hair shone his eyes, a gray so pale as to have been washed with white. In a dimly lit room, the pupils of his eyes shone black; the rest was white, gleaming. His teeth were very white and gleaming, too, his mouth soft and full.

He was slightly below average height and stockily built; his legs were short to carry the powerful torso and shoulders. And he perspired. Streams of perspiration ran down his face, his neck, into his collar, onto his tie. When he took off his suit coat, his shirt clung to him, wet all the way down the back.

But with Denis none of that mattered. He carried with him an air of promise, a feeling that at any moment, maybe the next moment, he would make something happen. Ugly perhaps. But women were attracted by him.

And his voice—there was the aristocrat after all—low, deep, with flawless diction.

Seeing him that first time in the drawing room, and looking into his pale gray eyes, Melanie forgot to curtsy, offer her hand, say a word of greeting, barely aware of Miss Robertson's disapproval of her poor manners. Denis half smiled: Oh, I know what you are thinking. But she did not know what she was thinking. Not then.

Another day he led her through room after room. And she was certain that in this room or the next, they would find someone, her mother, her aunt, Adelaide, Mrs. Van Burgh, sitting and reading, drinking coffee, gossiping, talking about dressmakers. And at any moment a voice would call, "Why there you are, Melanie."

"Where can we go to be alone? What a terrible house," he said laughing. "Every room opens in all directions." Of course there were at least two doors and three or four in most rooms. How else could the servants come in to bring coffee and shawls unobtrusively? Were there but one door, they would have to pass in front of the people in the room.

He was holding her hand; to her surprise, his was trembling, too. She knew how much older he was than she, that he was married to Adelaide, that paradigm of English womanhood. It could not stop her. For all her innocence, she sensed what it was he planned, though not how it would be brought about. Sexual feelings were not fully identified as such, as being that sharp sensation discovered by accident on horseback and reproduced by one means or another, pressing against a chair, letting the stream of water from the faucet strike her, putting the hand just so. It was best, she had found, to do this thinking about a boy, and he did not need to be someone she knew well; the gardener's son, the youngest footman would do. Sometimes just looking at him, she thought she could not wait to be alone to relieve the feeling of pressure, the heat gathering at the groin.

Yes, she was dimly aware, but could not imagine anyone else doing for her what she did for herself. She was not sure how it was between a man and a woman. No one would tell a girl until the night before her wedding. Even Bunny had turned prudish.

Finally they arrived at the music room where Melanie dutifully spent an hour a day practicing the piano. It was the last room in the east wing of the house, and so had only one door. Denis made a sound in his throat, she did not know if it was a laugh, and closed the door. He bent to lock it, and shook his head to see there was no lock. After all, why would anyone ever lock a music room door? He took a position against the door, his back flat against it. She stood facing him, nervous, eager, already gasping a little; they had moved so quickly, and her unaccustomed corset was so tightly laced.

Reaching out, he put his hand on her face, very gently. "My Melody." She was so nervous, not about doing the act, but about the possibility that he might yet decide *not* to do it, think her too young, a child. She did not know what he was to do, only that he must do it.

He pressed against her and she thought that perhaps this was what making love must be. She knew in general the part of the body that was used, but not how it was to be used, to be touched. That pressure again, of his hips against hers. His hand perhaps instead of her own probing her body?

Close against the door in his embrace, so excited and her rib cage so compressed by the corset, she could not catch her breath. "Don't be afraid." Yes, she felt fear, but only that he would remember Adelaide and stop. She believed he could only make love to her by forgetting Adelaide. No married man would behave so if he allowed himself time to think.

She was terrified, too, that at any moment Miss Robertson would call or her mother send a servant to fetch her. "Quick, quick someone will come."

He took off his suit coat and threw it on the floor and she felt the wetness of his shirt. His hands went under her skirt, lifting it and her lace-edged petticoat, and then he was unfastening the waistband of her drawers. Suddenly she remembered and felt sick with shame that his hands would touch the bloody cloths. Even Dena, a woman herself, made a little grimace of distaste when she picked up Melanie's bloodied underdrawers and cloths to give to the laundress. Should she push away his hands and take off the cloths herself? But he might misunderstand the gesture, go away, and now she had to have it, the pressure that would bring her relief. But he would be repelled, disgusted. Oh, how hard it was to be a woman.

And as she worried, his hands reached down and touched the cloths. She expected to see repugnance on his face, to feel him draw away from her. But he only took a breath and murmured, "Thank heaven for small favors." It was years before she knew what he had meant.

He was opening his trousers then, taking something out. How could it be so big, so hard and not have shown against the tight trousers? She had suspected that men looked different there, but had not thought in this way. This was what he would press against her, she thought—the act, the mystery—as murmuring her name, he lifted her, his hands beneath her buttocks. Her legs went around his waist, her arms

33

around his neck, and she clung to him. Gasping against the corset, she struggled for air. If she could only fill her lungs, get one full deep breath. But the tightness of the stays allowed her breath to come only shallowly. She felt as if she were being cut in two. Quick, quick someone will come. In the midst of her excitement was the fear that she would be sick. She was terrified that she would vomit and repel him utterly. The blood was bad enough. The room was spinning.

But Denis, she later learned, had thought she was so girlish, fainting at the unfamiliar male touch, never considering the imprisoning corset laced too tightly.

"Don't be afraid, Melody, Melody," he said and what was he doing? It became evident to her at last that he did not mean to press, but was forcing his way inside her body, creating by his thrusts a space large enough to hold him. She could not stand it. Her muscles tightened in an instinctive effort to keep him out, reduce the pain. But he only pushed again, harder, tearing. This then was how it was done, with such suffering. She pulled, strained away from him, arching her back. He was intent, holding her in a tight grip, moving, thrusting, oblivious to her pain. If only it would be over quickly. Yet even while thinking this, she knew that she would not have him stop now, no matter how great the hurt. Wet, slippery, the excitement was overcoming the pain. Denis, Denis. Melanie. Melody.

Panting, moaning, she had to scream. "Shh. Someone will hear. Put my ascot in your mouth." She tasted dye, acrid and unpleasing. Now she could not breathe at all. "I can't." She spat it out. "Better like this?" he asked and a second later she realized all astonished that it was his tongue that he had placed in her mouth. His lips were around hers, slippery, sticky with saliva, repelling and enticing at once.

Years afterwards she would accuse him of viciousness, knowing as he had to know the value placed on virginity. "I was young, too." But he had been twenty-four. "You wanted it as much as I did." Justifying himself. "You were practically panting." It was true. She had been fifteen and burning with it.

34

And was she ever closer to ecstasy in her life than in those frantic moments, behind the door, with her skirts and petticoats up, her drawers and the bloodied cloths on the floor at their feet, and Denis, Denis, hot, wet, pushing inside her, in and out, back and forth, his trousers unbuttoned and his shirttails out, holding her buttocks, holding her, fainting with pain, excitement, and fear, gasping for breath in the little space left between his lips over hers, his breathing heavy, his perspiration pouring onto her hair, into her ears, down the bodice of her dress between her breasts? The smell of his perspiration, the scent of blood, the light floral perfume, the only one her mother allowed her to wear, combined to make a jarring aroma, sensual and virginal at once.

His muscles tightened, expanded, and he took his mouth away from hers to groan aloud. As he leaned back, withdrew, she felt another wetness mixed with the wetness of her blood. Another odor, fishy, rank, mixed with the odors of perspiration and perfume and blood.

Relaxing his grip, he put her down. Denis pushed his shirt into his trousers. There was blood on the shirttails.

Looking at the viscous pool on the floor, he smiled, stroked her hair, damp with perspiration, and her face, murmuring Melody, my Melody, mine, mine, you are so lovely, so beautiful, and my own darling, my own, and we must meet again, I will arrange it, watch for my signal. And at his words, she remembered Adelaide, but did not care.

She picked up the cloths, mopping the blood off her legs. But a pool remained on the floor and if she used the cloths to wipe it up, the blood would come through on her clothes. "Leave it," said Denis. "Ring for a maid to clean it up."

"What will I say?"

"One never explains to servants."

She had not the nerve then, knowing it would not be Dena who would answer a ring from this room, but a downstairs maid. Melanie could only say, stammering and blushing, her voice high, "I had a nosebleed."

She trailed Denis back through the rooms they had traversed earlier, dreading the passage through the drawing room; it was the only way to reach the staircase leading to her bedroom, to the bath. The servants' staircase would have offered an escape, but it never occurred to Melanie that it was a way she might go. No member of the family ever used it. She was hoping to meet no one. Instead who would be sitting there but her mother and Adelaide, the tea service in front of them?

"Whatever have you been doing to get so overheated?" said her mother, concealing her irritation with poor grace. Melanie could not answer, but stood there blushing, trying to smooth down her hair, and feeling so wet. Surely the blood, the other liquid would drip down her legs and onto the floor and everyone would see. She glanced at Denis, but his habitual dishevelment made it impossible to tell that only moments before he had stood panting and groaning behind a door.

He came over to Adelaide pleasant as ever and seated himself beside her. And she without hesitation said, "Do not ask of him if he desires hot tea, Mrs. Carle. He likes only frigid beverages. My Denis is always so hot." My Denis. And she put out her hand in the most natural way, feeling his damp forehead. It was her right. Seeing Adelaide's hand on him, Melanie's stomach lurched. She swallowed hard, tasting vomit. The perspiration had poured down his face onto her hair, into her ears. That Adelaide should know how he perspired was unbearable. And Denis just took it as a matter of course. He was so cool, despite the perspiration.

"Denis," said Adelaide, "I was just telling Mrs. Carle that my maid could hardly fasten this frock." She leaned forward. "See how the fabric strains at the seams."

Denis smiled, touching Adelaide's hand to his lips.

At first the conversation meant nothing to Melanie. Then she noticed that her mother was frowning, indicating Melanie's presence with a slight movement of her head, and Adelaide was putting her hand over her mouth in mock repentance. Despite the frown, her mother, too, had a benign expression quite uncharacteristic of her.

36

Denis had been casual when, close to tears, Melanie had asked him later how he could have . . . when Adelaide was expecting.

"Adelaide is frequently with child. She is proud when in that state, so proud that she shows herself everywhere, despite all convention. My father encourages her in this. He thinks of nothing but continuing the line. For fifteen generations, he declares, the marquisate has been in our family, the title passed from eldest son to eldest son without a break. He has taken Adelaide's misfortunes as a personal blow."

"What misfortunes?"

"In our four years of marriage, Adelaide has had four miscarriages, but she will not give up. Adelaide and my father are as one in this endeavor. As if it is of such overriding importance whether in the end, when both my father and I are dead, drafty old Carnaugh goes to my heirs or a cousin's."

Adelaide would suffer, thought Melanie, and for the first time knew the terrible feeling of joy at the misfortunes of a rival that jealousy produces. Shivering with guilt, she nonetheless thought that if Adelaide died, she might walk through the drafty halls of Carnaugh Castle, tense with cold and excitement.

Long afterwards, when she was herself pregnant, she remembered her malign wishes for Adelaide and a superstitious terror came over her. As she miscarried, she felt it was justice being performed. And when at last Junior was born, she was so sure she had given birth to a two-headed monster or twisted dwarf that she was terrified to look when the doctor and midwife held the baby up for her to see and at first waved them away. Everyone was appalled, thought her an unnatural mother. Another legend was created.

In later years, as Melanie came to know Denis better, she was to recognize the insincerity of his claim that he, in contrast to his father, was indifferent to the succession. Rather it was Denis who was obsessed. Adelaide no doubt shared the obsession; she was continually expecting, and one had

37

to assume that there was no need for an upper-class woman to become pregnant if she did not choose to. Melanie could not ask, made dumb by the realization that Denis was in Adelaide's bed so often, in hers so seldom. It was unbearable to see them together; Adelaide was always touching him, putting her hand on his arm, on his brow. Melanie knew no other married woman who was so demonstrative in public.

Melanie had not seen Denis for four years after that first visit, refusing steadfastly to go to England in the fear that they would meet. "There is no point in traveling to Europe," she would remark lightly. "We have seen it already."

If the stained glass from the rose window of a French cathedral decorated the medieval dining room at the Devereux', what could one possibly see at the cathedral itself? Perhaps a scene of the Resurrection lacking the figure of Christ who had been replaced with a pane of ordinary window glass? If the great stone blocks that made up the floors of a castle in Yorkshire had been lifted one by one for use in the Arnolds' entryway, who would care to enter the castle itself and stand on bare ground? Melanie was already gaining a reputation for the wittily outrageous. Her remarks were quoted at dinner tables and received with amusement and some chagrin.

Melanie's mother, setting off on her annual visit, would exclaim at the rudeness of declining all invitations. She was nurturing the British relationship, was delighted at being asked to Carnaugh.

Each time Melanie had waited desperately for her parents' return from England. Had Denis asked after her? He had hoped she was in good health. Even the news of her engagement did not prompt a personal response. The gift of a large silver bowl had arrived, the wedding message written by Adelaide. "What did he say?" "He said to give you his felicitations."

It was a relief to her when only his father came in response to her parents' return invitations. Adelaide's physician was now forbidding her to travel while pregnant.

Once married, it became impossible to avoid the trips abroad. Wallace expected them to follow the pattern set for society by his mother—New York, Bourneham, Paris, London, little vacations elsewhere. Each had its turn. Although at that time Melanie did not look for pleasure, sexual release from Wallace—she induced that herself with her hand after he had gone to sleep—there were compensations in having joined her life to his. A wife, she enjoyed her position and wanted to please him. A daughter-in-law, she had found a friend and was moved when Genevieve declared Melanie's absence would detract from her own pleasure in any trip. Melanie agreed to include England on the itinerary, insisting only that they stay in drab comfortable Brown's Hotel in London, instead of journeying out to be houseguests at Carnaugh.

Having yielded, she convinced herself that as Carnaugh was at some distance from London, she would not come into contact with Denis. In England, however, she soon learned, as in America, a social pattern was followed and the set of those belonging to the great families and the very rich was so small that everyone within that circle visited everyone else. In London for the season, Denis and Adelaide were likely to be on any invitations list that included the Edmonts. The family connection increased the probability.

Melanie steeled herself for the meeting whenever, with Wallace beside her, she entered a London town house for dinner. As the footmen passed the sherry, she was watching for Denis. Yet when he finally appeared, she was unprepared. On that evening they had arrived late, delayed by a cable from Wallace's grandfather, and had entered the Heathcotes' house in Belgravia only in time to go in to dinner. Melanie was seated on her host's right.

The footman set a cup of turtle soup at her place and withdrew a few paces behind her chair. Before picking up her spoon, she looked down the table. Ten people away from her—Denis. Trembling, she began to breathe quickly, shallowly as she had learned to do against the now familiar constriction of the corset. He had seen her, was smiling in complicity. From the time she had received his felicitations on her engagement, she knew that it would never again be possible for her to smile at him with her private smile, to speak with him beyond the briefest courtesies, to be alone, certainly not alone, not in his arms, not with her skirts up and his trousers open and quick, quick someone will come.

She glanced at Denis more closely, trying not to make her observation obvious. He was not handsome. The hair grew down too low, almost covering his forehead. Why was he still so attractive to her? His teeth were so white, his mouth barely visible between the mustache and beard was so soft, so red. Licking his lips, he made her remember his tongue inside her mouth. His smile. With such a smile four years ago he had brought her to the rose marble bathtub. A cramp so sharp she could not believe it was memory induced seized her. Denis was looking at her, waiting for her attention.

George Heathcote asked if she were ill. No, no; she flushed at his knowing look, but there was nothing he could have guessed, was there? She looked again and saw that Adelaide was not present. With child, of course, Heathcote remarked.

When she turned back towards Denis, he was no longer looking at her, but at a young girl seated some distance from him on the opposite side of the table. Well, why should any man not look at a girl like that? She was lovely, no more than fifteen, surely no more than fifteen, a little doll, delicious, all pink skin and yellow hair dressed in the palest blue faille with a white chiffon modesty filling in the neckline, a small string of pearls circling her neck.

Denis had a look she thought she remembered, a look of conspiracy, a look of possession. So had he looked at her in the drawing room at home . . . afterwards. The girl was his.

"Valerie Latherington," her host informed her, smiling unpleasantly.

The girl was staring without any attempt at concealment at Denis. She could not take her eyes off him. The smell of soup rising from the cup in front of Melanie was nauseating; she indicated to the footman that he should take it away.

Later, among the women in the drawing room, the gossip began. With meaningful glances first towards Valerie and then towards a haggard, beautifully dressed woman who kept herself apart, the hostess, Marjorie Heathcote, revealed the gossip of the moment, which concerned, she might have guessed it, Valerie and Denis. Everyone hung on the speaker's carefully enunciated whispered words. While at the dressmaker's for a fitting, Valerie had given her governess the slip and not returned home for hours, and . . . She is just a child, everyone kept saying. Just a child. Innocent. Melanie knew what it was to be a child and innocent. Mrs. Heathcote was delighted at the scandal and the opportunity to pass it along. Adelaide, she went on, was in bed seeking to prevent yet another miscarried pregnancy.

Escaped from her governess, been lifted up—this little girl—her legs around his waist, his hands on her bare skin. But of course it need not have been done that way. He was on home ground in England. Probably he had a thickly carpeted room, draperies, a soft bed with hangings, a comforter. No need to put his tongue in her mouth to muffle her cries of passion.

As the men entered the room and Denis walked past, Valerie's mother turned her face away so as not to greet him. He came up to Melanie then and they exchanged pleasantries; her responses were clumsy. Every statement of his, however simple, seemed to her to have a double meaning. He had not known she was visiting England or he would have been in touch, he so often thought of his visit to her parents' home and their hospitality, wished her to come to Carnaugh. There was a portrait by Gainsborough of his great-grandmother, a beauty of the age; he thought Melanie had the same look around the eyes and mouth. And all the while, Valerie's large round eyes were on them, expecting her turn.

41

Observing that, Melanie could not wait for Denis to be gone. It was a relief to her when Wallace came over to introduce the gentlemen with whom he had been speaking. He towered over the others in the room, large, solid, her husband. A feeling of unaccustomed warmth, tenderness towards him came over her. What had passed between her and Denis was over. She was nineteen now, married, safe. Denis had been a part of growing up. Like Valerie—she had been no different, had meant no more to him. Adelaide was pregnant again. Melanie thought herself pregnant now, too. Their lives might touch; there was the relationship after all, but never again any intimacy. She felt quite sure of it.

In this conviction, she did not object when her mother accepted an invitation to Carnaugh for all of them the next year. The day they arrived, she told Denis what had happened in the cold rose marble bathtub, the silver-backed mirror of Catherine the Great helping her guide the insertion of the knitting needle. He had put his hands over his face and wept; she had seen the tears trickling through his fingers.

CHAPTER 4

To Be
a Virgin Again

Could a marriage be annulled if the bride were not a virgin? Reading Denis's letter, it all came back to her, the fears, the feeling that she was in a trap, caught, thrashing around, trying to find the way out.

One afternoon she had discovered a brief section on "nullity of marriage" in a legal reference book in her father's library. Hope died as she read the dread words that a marriage was void if there were fraud, such as concealment of sterility or sexual impotence. Could a lack of virginity constitute fraud? An annulment, she read on, rendered the marriage void, as if it had never been, and relieved both parties of all their obligations to one another, all vows, all promises to cherish until death. She could not even be sure that the reference book with its unsatisfactory account was up-to-date. The year on the flyleaf was 1852 and perhaps the law had become more stringent since then.

Such dire legal consequences had helped to explain the fanaticism with which she and all the young girls she knew were chaperoned.

The danger she was in had been clear to her the day she had agreed to marry Wallace, but what alternative to marriage did she have? Once she was engaged, on all sides she heard nothing but approbation. The brilliant match she was making. She was admired and praised by her parents, admired and praised by his.

Plans moved inexorably forward and all she could think was that a wedding day was followed by a wedding night and how would she get through it? A simple solution then occurred to her: schedule the wedding date to coincide with her monthly bleeding. Her cycle was somewhat irregular since the miscarriage; still, with luck, the bleeding would come on time.

But she had not been able to conceal the significance of the date from her mother. The laundress kept the time for all the women in the household.

"Melanie, dear," her mother had said, smiling faintly. "I think we had better have a little talk. You see, my child, we must arrange a wedding for the right time of the month and that means the time when you are most certain not to be having . . . um . . . your monthly flow of blood. Men, husbands, do not like . . . bleeding."

Thank heaven for small favors, Denis had said. The bloody cloths on the floor, the blood on his shirttails. He had smiled.

Melanie was frantic. What if she were to steal a knife and cut herself at the critical moment? However, she had hardly ever been in the kitchen and when she did go, the cook was all over her. Then, what if she were to cut Wallace by accident, not herself? Sometimes when his name was mentioned she would imagine the horror on his face when he discovered her fatal lack and excused herself hurriedly.

Her mother held the obligatory preparatory talk with her, describing what the act entailed ambiguously, but being perfectly clear in stating that this was a wifely duty, part of the bargain one might say, given in return for receiving care and support. Of pleasure, the remembered rapture, there was

44

not a hint. The blood was important, though her mother again spoke in terms so vague that lacking prior knowledge Melanie would never have been able to guess where the blood came from. Her mother meant kindness, kept reassuring Melanie that the blood in this case was good, that it was not the kind of blood husbands did not like, but rather did like, did prize as a proof of virginity. If her mother knew that, surely Wallace could know no less.

Good blood versus bad. As if the color would be more brilliant, more crimson. Good blood mixed with bad running down her legs when she had stood with Denis behind the door, good blood mixed with bad forming a pool on the floor at their feet.

Her wedding gown and trousseau dresses were taken in a second time, a third. And everyone thought it was simply charming for so headstrong a girl as Melanie—why there was talk about her even then—to be so shy, so nervous about getting married.

Every so often, however, when she was with Wallace, she could briefly forget her dread, believe that the marriage would bring her happiness. He was so clearly infatuated with her. Everyone was sure it was the correct step to take; perhaps they were right. Wallace was a good responsible man; he would never hurt her as Denis had done. She could not imagine that she would ever feel the passion for Wallace she had known with Denis. Though she had gained sufficient experience by then to recognize how thoughtless, no, call it vicious, had been Denis's treatment of her, his was still the face, the body, seen in her erotic fantasies when caressing herself. That would change once it was Wallace making love to her. She felt enough for Wallace to make him a good wife, if only she could get past the wedding night and be a wife at all. Her husband; she would have someone to embrace and be embraced by for the rest of her life, to satisfy her hunger, her longing. She imagined how it would be to lie clasped in his arms all night, free of clothing, free from the fear of discovery.

Moreover she found Wallace attractive. While his face was not handsome, his brown hair straight, his beard and mustache sparse, he had a good figure, strong and well built; his hands were large with long fingers that she imagined touching her. Best of all, he was tall, taller than she, and as she stood five feet, nine inches, this was true of few men. (Why, Denis was barely her height.)

Panic soon returned. She felt desperate with the need to talk openly with someone, but there was no confidante. Girls had always shied away from intimacy with her, envious of her looks, of the attention she received.

Denis knew of her engagement and for a time she had hoped he would arrange to come to see her before the marriage took place and she could ask him what to do. He was older than she, a man of the world; probably, she thought bitterly, she was not the first girl he had taken and left. But after the silver bowl and the felicitations offered in Adelaide's hand, she knew he did not care.

And then, beyond all imaginings, she made a discovery that led her to consider her father as a possible source of help. She had gone back to her father's library to study his books with greater care and she discovered that in books purporting to be about law, biology, economics, military history, or shipping, there were etchings and woodcuts of nude or seminude figures in unnatural postures, riding one another as if on horseback, sitting on one another's laps, lying contorted like acrobats.

On a high shelf that she could barely reach, she had noticed a book with a French title. She pulled it out, not because she had heard of either author or title—De Sade, *Justine, ou, Les Malheurs de la vertu*—but because of surprise at finding a book in that language in her father's bookcase. His inability to learn French had been a family joke. Glancing at the book at first only casually, Melanie soon was transfixed. A naked woman was tied to a tree with three huge dogs biting at the most private parts of her body while a man stood by smiling, his trousers misshapen by the stiffened

46

phallus pushing at the buttons. Turning the page, she come upon another scene of violence, a woman pinned down by a rapist in the midst of a circle of men holding rods.

Sickened, fascinated, she went on. Here was the unfortunate woman chained to a wheel to be beaten with a spike-studded hammer. The next scene did not at first seem so terrible until she realized what it was the man was doing: squatting over the face of the woman helpless on the ground, he was defecating. Her flesh crawled. Some pages on, the victim was standing on a stool with a noose around her neck, the end of the rope held by a man with trousers open to reveal his large erect phallus curving upward.

Her repulsion was accompanied by a curiously heightened sexuality. Aching with desire, she put her hand inside her dress, against her fine cambric drawers to press harder.

She tried to read the text, but though, unlike her father, she was praised for her ability at languages, her vocabulary was inadequate for this. About to return the book to the shelf, she observed a small notebook next to the empty space on the shelf where the book had stood. The writing inside was so minuscule that she could not puzzle it out. A magnifying glass lay on the shelf beside the book, and with its aid, she began to read a translation into English of the pornographic French. The translation was clumsy, stilted, but the meaning was clear. As she read on, it struck her that there was something familiar about the precise tiny handwriting; it was the writing of Monsieur Toulouse, her French tutor.

Looking through the magnifying glass, she discovered a world different from any she had known or imagined, a world in which men tormented, degraded, abased women, a world of pain inflicted and pain accepted. Surely, she thought, if a man could write of such terrible happenings, someone had experienced them. Sitting there, her hand pressing hard, she would stop every so often to think that her father had read this, her father.

Over the next few days she waited only for the moment when she could steal away from the wedding planning.

Sometimes just holding the book on her lap was enough to give her an orgasmic shudder. In at least one way she could identify with the heroine of the book. Like Justine, she had been innocent. Pain. Denis in the music room. Pain and ecstasy to follow. Then pain again. The rose marble bathtub.

The only person who could understand and so come to her aid, she now saw was her father. With gray waving hair, lined face, and deeply shadowed eyes, it was often said of him that he would be handsome if only he would smile. The heir, Bunner Renvereau Carle, Melanie's Bunny, had lived in fear of angering or disappointing him. Melanie was his pet, or so in the old days he had led her to believe, but she, too, found him forbidding. She would never have dared to ask the father she had known for help in her quandary, but this man, the man she now knew him to be was different. This was his book. Because of his use, it fell open to the most vile and salacious illustrations. Unable to comprehend the language, he had engaged his children's tutor to do the translation.

It proved impossible, however, for her to engage his attention. Instead he followed his own train of thought about her forthcoming marriage. "Your mother is smiling . . . for the first time since your brother died. The Edmonts are a fine family, Melanie. Today Genevieve Edmont stands for the best in our society. The fact is, Melanie, there is a correct way to behave. And in these increasingly lax times when propriety is being abandoned and loose living becomes commonplace, it is good to have people like the Edmonts who set a high standard and live by it. Wallace Edmont is an excellent man. I can tell you, Melanie, that I have never heard a word, not a hint of gossip about him at any of the clubs. He is absolutely honorable and upright."

Absolutely honorable and upright. Good in these lax times. How far removed she was from Edmont standards. Denis. Adelaide in the drawing room, her expanding waistline pushing against the seams of her dress. The knitting needle. The mirror, once owned by Catherine the Great, the heavily embossed mirror that her mother had generously pressed on her for a wedding gift, priceless really.

The wedding, the wedding night would have to be gone through. The possibility existed that Wallace would not wish to admit the mistake he had made. It was a slim hope, but she clung to it.

The morning of her wedding day Melanie went in to thank Miss Robertson for the beautifully embroidered table-cloths, the traditional gift of the governess. Unlike other governesses, Miss Robertson had never hinted of a glamorous past, a fiancé dead in war or of consumption or accident. She told only of a widowed mother, poverty, nothing for it but to become a governess.

"Thank you for the tablecloths. I'll think of you every time I use your gift."

"Sometimes information is the best gift of all," remarked Miss Robertson coolly, and began to speak of the night ahead.

Surely, thought Melanie, Miss Robertson must be aware that Mrs. Carle would have given the needed information. At first she hardly listened, and then all at once she realized that this was no account of duty done, a husband satisfied, but was instead a graphic account of how to simulate virginity. Miss Robertson left no detail unsaid, making a fist at one point to clarify her meaning. "If you are clever, there should be a bit of blood."

"Clever?"

"What might be reasonable for you to keep close at hand? A nail file perhaps. A little prick anywhere with the sharp point. All that is wanted is a few spots of blood on the sheets."

Melanie had been thinking of kitchen knives and stabbing, nothing so simple as this. "But will he believe it?"

"If you have made entry hard enough, he will believe it." So there had been the lover dead in war or accident after all.

That night, lying in bed waiting for Wallace, the nail file carefully placed beneath her pillow, she rehearsed how it was she was to act, what there was for her to do. When he got into bed beside her and pulled the covers over them both, her heart began to pound violently and she could not catch her breath. She hoped he would not hear her panting, guess the source of her nervousness. He put his hand on her breast. "How your heart is beating," he said. Yes, he knew. "Like mine." He did not know. Not yet. Could she bring off the deception?

Trembling with apprehension, she was aware of his pulling up his nightshirt, then her frilly nightgown and moving to begin the conjugal act. In the moment, to her surprise, it had been quite easy to follow Miss Robertson's instructions, to remember the clenched fist, the nail file. She pricked as hard as she could and felt the blood start and run onto the sheets. Wallace, intent, did not seem to notice. Pleasure she did not expect or look for. This was a serious matter. Only he was hurting her. She had not thought there would be pain. After the first time Denis had slipped in so easily, wet and smooth and slippery. When Wallace at last forced his way through her tightened muscles, she felt hot blood at the tissues' parting, but inside she was dry, so dry it felt as if she were being rubbed back and forth by an object covered with heavy fabric. At last he withdrew. Now she would know, for surely he must express his disappointment and anger. The suspense was intolerable. Had she responded as a virgin would? Was there enough blood?

In silence he pulled back the blankets, the sheet, and in the moonlight she saw the relief on his face at the tiny spots of blood, at the knowledge that she was truly his own, his valuable possession. He had not been sure of her virginity, she thought; there had been gossip because so many men clustered about her. Miss Robertson had helped her, discharging the last responsibility to bring her girl safely into marriage. She had gotten away with it and should have felt relief greater than that written on Wallace's face. But she felt only a dull ache of misery that it had not been Denis.

She could not help it and began to weep. Wallace bent

over her and kissed her face gently. As he did so, desire absent during the performance of the crucial act arose and she felt tense, unsatisfied, hot. Timidly she took Wallace's hand, thinking to guide it, but he did not appear to know what she wanted and pulled away. Melanie reminded herself then of how much was to be offered her as his wife. With a lifting of her spirits, she realized that she was married to a man who recognized her intelligence, her interest in business, often told her what a pleasure it was to talk with a girl who grasped the essence of economic life. She recalled going over the balance sheets of their father's bank with her brother, Bunny, longing to be given a place in the financial world, too. What she had longed for then was to happen now—with Wallace.

"When we are married, I think we should hire a tutor to teach me business law and accounting," she had told him a few days before the wedding, her eyes shining. Wallace had smiled and kissed her hand.

Lying in bed beside Wallace, her frustration forgotten, she remembered the hours she had spent studying statements of earnings, assets, losses, loans, debits with Bunny. How Bunny would have laughed to know that on her wedding night, in the bridal bed, she was consoling herself with thoughts of business.

CHAPTER 5

I Asked You First, Wallace

How relieved he had been, almost crazy with relief when on their wedding night he had pulled back the sheet and seen, in the moonlight streaming in through the open window, beneath the lace and ruffles of the nightdress bunched at her hips, the spots of red on the pure white linen sheets.

"Melanie, my own," he had said and kissed her.

The kiss tasted of salt and he saw the tears streaming down her face. Why, she was just a girl, innocent, and he had hurt her. He had tried to be gentle. But what did a man like him who had never been with any but paid companions know of the delicate ways of a virgin? He marveled at this. So beautiful. Just the thought of the body beneath the modest nightdress was enough to make him stiff. These were, he often thought afterwards, the proudest and happiest moments of his life as a husband. He had not yet discovered her temper, her demands, her extravagance, and her infidelities.

Later, though, the things she had wished him to do. A

bride of only a week, she had lit the lamp one night and asked him to take off his nightshirt. She wanted to look at him, she had declared. Just like that, baldly, look at him, in the lamplight. Then a few months later, he had approached her, not realizing that it was her bleeding time. With barely an instant's hesitation, she had rolled over, indicated her buttocks. "Try it this way," she had urged. He had been repelled. What knowledgeable lewdness did this show? How had she learned about this? He feared to ask. Even he had only heard it discussed among men returning from visits to French brothels. Like dogs. But no well-bred young woman would ever have been allowed to see animals coupling. Innate lasciviousness was all he could attribute it to.

And then, during the first summer they spent with his parents at Bourneham, he had awakened one night startled to find that Melanie was not in bed. (They shared a bedroom then.) He got up and started looking for her, and drawing the curtains back from the windows, saw someone on the lawn. He leaned forward, alarmed. Could a burglar have climbed over the fence, eluded the watchman and entered the grounds? A sound must have awakened Melanie and, fearless, she had gone down to investigate. And then suddenly with stunning surprise he recognized the person on the lawn to be Melanie, completely naked. She must be sleepwalking. He had to go to her. How lovely she was, slender, almost thin, but her breasts were full. She had insisted that he touch them, hold them—really she had no modest bridal hesitation.

Filled with apprehension at the thought that his parents might awaken and see her, he hastily put on the brocaded dressing gown and matching slippers left by his bed and softly made his way out of the room, down the hall, which had never before seemed quite so long, past the doors of his parents' rooms, of his sisters'. It seemed to him he heard someone moving or sighing behind every door.

The French doors from the ballroom onto the lawn were open. Melanie's nightclothes lay just inside in a heap. He

53

stepped outside. She looked up, saw him, and held out her arms. She was not sleepwalking, thought Wallace stupefied. "Come to me, Wallace." Her hips pushed forward; her intention was perfectly clear.

"Let's go inside, Melanie."

"No. This is the place for love with all this beauty and the sound of the sea." Her arms outstretched, so white, gleaming in the moonlight. It was cold with the wind blowing in from the ocean, and he was shivering a little in his heavy brocaded dressing gown. Her breasts stood out, the nipples erect, but she seemed not to notice the cold.

"Not here. My mother's windows look out on this lawn." He was desperate to induce her to come in, and she kept shaking her head and holding out her arms. "Come in, come in, my mother will see."

At last she nodded, seeming to yield. But instead of coming towards the house, she turned and ran across the lawn and lay down on the ground beneath a weeping beech-wood tree. He turned his head, annoyed and nervous, certain that at any moment his parents would come to their windows, the servants appear, the guard dogs start barking. What could she be doing? he thought, as she lay facedown on the grass, her arms beneath her. Her hips were moving up and down, then around and around. The thought that flashed across his mind was too improbable, too repellent, impossible to accept. But even while he was seeking to dismiss the idea, he knew it to be true. His body knew it, too; he felt himself harden, knew the sudden rush, ache of desire. Yet he did not move. Then she stood up and came towards the house at last, breathless and perspiring, with bits of wet grass and damp earth sticking to her body, caught in her pubic hair. He averted his eyes hastily, but could not keep himself from putting out his hand and brushing off a blade of grass, caressing. Too late.

Her large round dark brown eyes were shining in the moonlight. "I asked you first, Wallace. I asked you first."

But what if he had overlooked the unsuitable nature of the act, given way to her and, yes, his, desire? He would have been aware, even while taking her, that someone, his mother, might see, might come. Perhaps it was this combination of fears that had held him immobile. He believed her action disreputable, disgusting, indecent. At the same time he could not bear what he was feeling.

The next morning it was not possible for him to meet her gaze, but she was perfectly natural. They never referred to the episode again, but it marked a certain change in their relationship, so slight at first that one could not be sure it had occurred. She was just a trifle sharper with him, less conciliatory, more likely to raise her voice when she did not get her way. Just occasionally, a portent of what lay ahead. Years afterwards when Wallace first suspected her infidelity, it seemed to him that he could hear her voice, throaty, breathy, "I asked you first, Wallace." Through the years, "I asked you first, Wallace. I asked you first."

Would it have changed anything at all between them had he done as she wanted, had it not taken so many years for him to recognize how far she would go to satisfy her sexual urges? At that time, onanism had seemed excess enough. But as a bridegroom, Wallace had been possessed of a certain innocence, too. Before his marriage, he had visited the actresses and dancers who made themselves available to the rich men in his set. Although these women expected gifts of money, there were those who appeared genuinely swayed by sexual passion. It did not occur to him that a woman of good family might have these feelings, too. He had been brought up to consider that in the upper class, sexuality was a male attribute.

There was no question that among married couples, the man alone could be expected to be unfaithful. That belief, too, belonged to a time of innocence. Not that Wallace behaved in this manner. His own behavior towards the woman who might become Melanie's successor was respectful. Even his gifts to her were discreet. He smiled, thinking of the brooch he had ordered for her at Dreicer's, a small fleur-de-lis of diamonds. Imagine giving so small, so delicate a gift to Melanie. His last gift to her had been a fifteen-carat blue-white diamond, surrounded by a sunburst of thirty perfectly matched star sapphires.

Wallace had leaned over backwards in his determination not to emulate his father. Why, his father had died in the bed of a young actress in New Orleans. In those days it had been possible for a rich and powerful family to keep the newspapers from publishing that titillating bit of gossip.

His father had been sixty the year of his death and stout, having trouble bending over to put on his shoes and fasten his spats. Still whenever he saw a pretty woman, he would straighten up, throw out his chest, draw in his stomach, and offer his charming smile. Wallace's father committed adultery as it if were natural, required, his right.

Working at his desk all these years later, on the eve of the Woodruffs' ball, he wondered what Melanie was up to now? Her summer toy, the *Bugle* had called that young Van Burgh. Did Melanie plan to meet Van Burgh at the ball? That could be why she was so determined to attend despite Wallace's refusal to join her.

There was also the fact that Melanie simply refused to curb her extravagance, and this at a time when the press was whipping up antagonism towards the rich. Since the panics of 1890 and 1893, conspicuous expenditures were being described as morally indefensible. As if there were anything immoral about spending money that had been earned honestly. But that was not the way it was characterized. Surely Melanie was the most orchidaceous of women. This was an asset during times when he was seeking expansion capital, but was becoming a detriment today. Muckrakers were raising an outcry at conditions among the poor, drawing a totally illogical comparison between the slum dwellers and the well-to-do in their mansions. The fact that the former refused to work and the latter worked day and night was simply ignored. Wait until the yellow press got onto the story of Melanie's camel. It was bad for business, and when you came right down to basics, that was the most important factor in all their lives.

Wallace opened his desk drawer and took out one of the

huge black ledgers listing his properties below Fourteenth Street. There were more than a dozen ledgers in his study at Île de Joie, four times that number in New York, hidden in a cabinet specially constructed to hold them. Not one of his business managers, not even Jessop, the chief, had ever seen all of them. Wallace kept them up to date himself, correcting, altering, expanding each entry by hand. His grandfather whose business genius he recognized had advised him to do so.

Wallace looked at his ledger without really seeing it. Melanie's presence seemed to be everywhere. Even in his study, with the door closed, he was aware of her so close by in her dressing room preparing for the evening. It was odd for so large a ball to be held on a Monday. There must be some reason for it; Woodruff never did anything without a reason. Everyone would be looking at Melanie. They always did, of course, but not as they would tonight with the *Bugle* in every house in Bourneham. Thinking about Melanie, he had forgotten for a little while why he had remained in Bourneham instead of returning to the office as he usually did on Monday. Trouble was brewing and whenever anything went wrong in the slums where he owned property, he was immediately under siege. It did not matter what had precipitated the immediate crisis—whether it was, as in this case, a tenement fire, or buildings collapsing, roofs giving way, cholera epidemics, let alone banks failing and clothing prices falling and precipitating wage cuts—troublemakers were at his office door demanding to see him. Jessop had urged him to spend the week in Bourneham, wait until the bad feeling blew over. But he could not stand it. A day or two more and he would go to New York and determine what needed to be done.

Wallace oversaw every detail himself. Each agent reported to him monthly on the state of the property. Like his grandfather, he insisted that basic repairs be made, a thoroughly unusual practice for the time. Wallace knew it did not take long for the smallest leak to reduce the value of a $50,000 tenement building to $45,000 or even $30,000.

The other lesson he had learned from his grandfather was that success lies in being the first to see potential, and expand. His grandfather had bought beyond the northernmost boundaries of the city. Some of this land had originally been part of what was then known as the Annexed District where a vast estate had been granted Lewis Morris in 1697. The property had been virtually worthless when his grandfather bought it, but all that had changed with the growth of the city. Wallace had since bought farmland even farther to the north. Now there was talk that this area, too, would be incorporated into the city.

Oddly, he recalled Melanie's telling him that her father had inherited property in this northern agricultural region. A family connection could be traced to that Jonas Bronck who had settled the area above the Harlem River in the name of the Dutch West Indies Company two centuries earlier. Mr. Carle had sold that land twenty-five years ago; he had no instinct for making money.

Not only did Wallace buy new properties, he found ways of enhancing the value of those he held. Certainly the idea of locating small manufacturing plants in tenement rooms was not his, but he had seen the possibilities. Much higher rents could be charged an entrepreneur running a factory than an individual renting rooms for himself and his family. To this end, Wallace had hired agents to seek out factory owners and suggest that they contract out their simpler tasks to home workers; shirts, suits, hats, cigars could be partially produced by piecework.

In time, would-be manufacturers came to Wallace with the request for funds to create workrooms, to purchase long tables, sewing machines, and other simple equipment. He became known for his generosity in this regard, but he recognized the value. A few hundred dollars would set up a man in business. Over the objections of his sublandlords and agents, Wallace sometimes allowed a tenant a few months of grace to get on his feet, or would carry him a month or two rent-free when business was slack. Once the factory owner had a steady supply of orders, he could pay a higher rent—twenty-five or thirty dollars a month—and employ more workers.

Accommodating manufacturing plants and ordinary tenants, housing became ever more crowded. One newspaper reporter, disguised in rags, sneaked into a tenement building and counted the number of people living there—101 adults and 91 children. In some places, he wrote, the homeless paid five cents for a night's sleep on the floor of a hallway, three cents to squat there.

Reading this, Wallace was struck more by what the writer omitted than what he expressed. According to Wallace's research, and he kept a staff of clerks busy amassing facts that might be useful to him, more than five million immigrants from Europe had entered the United States in the previous decade, most crowding into the New York slums, and though the numbers had declined slightly in the 1890s, they were still high. If the slums did not house these immigrants, they would lie in the streets; if the "sweaters" did not employ them, they would surely starve.

Wallace contributed more than any other man in the city to his church's fund drives for the homeless. Epidemics raged through the slums each summer. City health officials made regular visits, demanded improvements in sanitation, and went so far as to call the police to issue summonses. Most property owners ignored them, preferring to pay the fines and forget about making changes. Not Wallace. In front of Jessop, he took a jocular tone, pointing out that sick men, not to mention dead men, did not pay rent. Jessop would dutifully laugh at this point. Humor aside, Wallace read the reports of the Department of Health with the most careful attention.

But it was neither feasible nor sensible to follow the recommendations to the letter. Amory van der Cleeve, for example, wishing to further a career in politics by well-publicized good works, had ordered his building managers to remove the foul-smelling outdoor privies and install water closets on each floor of his buildings and fit them out with the most modern plumbing equipment (ignoring the fact that

59

most of the immigrants had never had a water closet at all, thought Wallace, that they did not know what they were supposed to do in it). Soon the water closets were made unusable. Sinks with running water were put in, but the faucets were left open and the water spilled over until the floorboards rotted. What was necessary was to strike a balance between what people needed and what they knew how to use properly. No one understood the tenants better than Wallace. For someone else, a city official for example, to tell him what to do was absurd and invariably turned out to be wasteful.

In order to impress the unknowing reader, the newspapers had taken to blaming the property owners for matters that were not in their province—that tenements were dark and dirty, that men, women, and children in the sweatshops worked from daybreak until nine or ten at night, earning but a few cents for each pitiful thing they made. But was a tenant to be the slave of the property owner, to perform at his bidding? Wallace could hardly demand character references of each tenant, each sweatshop owner, refuse rooms to a person found to be greedy and exploitative. Were that to become a policy, there would be many respectable citizens with no place but the open fields in which to rest their heads at night.

This sensible view did not prevail. Instead, he would pick up the *New York Journal* and read a heartrending story of a garment worker dying bent over her sewing machine, and on the same page a flood of excessive adjectives decorating the vivid account of Mrs. Wallace Montague Edmont V at Worth, Paquin, Pingat, purchasing forty thousand dollars' worth (conservatively estimated, inserted the journalist) of velvets, brocades, satins, feathers, and handmade laces for the coming season of balls, dinners, and entertainments. Private entertainments, too, he thought, his business forgotten. No conservative or other estimate need be given for what was purchased to delight young Van Burgh's eyes. Yes, it was time to leave her.

60

CHAPTER 6

Unsuitable Ambitions

When she could forget how he died, the happiest memories of her girlhood were of Bunny.

Despite the age difference of five years, Melanie and Bunny might have been twins, so similar were their features. They were dark haired, with large, very round, brown eyes, fair complexions, Roman noses, and beautifully carved lips. Nearly the same height, both of them were well built and strong. However, the resemblance was only physical. Bunny was easygoing, lacking in drive and ambition, whereas Melanie had too much vigor. There seemed no way to contain her. But Bunny was the heir.

By his senior year at Columbia College, Bunny had already been made a junior officer in their father's bank, spent vacations and holidays there. He enjoyed the workday, talking to the other men, having a pleasant lunch, stepping out to stretch his legs. In the evenings Bunny would take home the reports he had not finished in the office. There would be his father: "Give me your opinion on this, Bunner. Is the company sound?"

All this came so hard to Bunny. It was not that he was stupid, but he had no tolerance for routine tasks. His attention span was short, his patience limited. He wanted to be off drinking with his friends, hunting, swimming, making love. That was Bunny.

He would take the balance sheets to his room to escape being under his father's eyes. By unspoken agreement, Melanie would follow him. This was the part of the day she waited for, the opportunity to see the listings of assets and liabilities, borrowings and lendings, to calculate percentages and rates, figure on probable growth and possible losses. She read the financial pages of the newspaper and the business journals Bunny brought home every day. Her parents did not approve; knowledge about financial matters made a woman unappealing to men, if not downright masculine.

While she read over the reports, Bunny would come and sit next to her, close, warm, friendly. He, too, thought it humorous that she was so adept at calculations, but in his easygoing way, he was pleased to take advantage of it. "This company wants to borrow more money than it is likely to be able to repay," she would declare to Bunny firmly. "Just see the earnings for the last five years, and consider that the demand for their product is going down, not up. The *Financial and Commercial Chronicle* had an article about it."

All the figures seemed alive to her. The plots for a thousand novels lay in those balance sheets if one knew how to read them. There was a heady sense of power, too, that what she would say might influence their father's bank to make or withhold a loan. To be sure, her words had to be passed through Bunny. Mr. Carle would never have taken seriously an opinion on the male world of finance given by his daughter. But when they sat in Bunny's room companionably after dinner, she was happy.

Melanie believed that at some suitable time, they would disclose to their parents that she had learned the business and she would be given a position in the bank, subordinate to Bunny's of course; he was, after all, the male, the heir.

"Look, Bunny, this coal mining company wants a loan of a quarter of a million dollars to buy control of coke ovens in Pennsylvania. That will put them in direct competition with this Joseph Woodruff who is buying out competitors and by now owns hundreds, maybe a couple of thousand coke ovens. Papa says he's coming up fast and he's hard and ruthless and unscrupulous. Do you think he will let any other company get in without a fight? Should Papa's bank give the loan and take a chance on who wins out in that cutthroat competition? Will the owners of the company dare to stand up to Mr. Woodruff?"

Sometimes she became carried away by the excitement and Bunny would laugh at her kindly. They were so close, cared so much for one another. That happiness ended so quickly, so horribly. She had awakened at night to hear Bunny being sick, noisily, agonizingly sick in the bathroom down the hall. Running out, she summoned servants to help him, gasped and gagged as the door opened and the footmen, still in their nightshirts, carried him to his room. The rest of the night was all confusion as her parents were aroused, the doctor called, followed by nurses. And always the sound of illness and the smell pervading the air, filling the house with foulness. There had been an argument. The doctor wanted to take Bunny to the hospital. Her mother became hysterical and her father was firm in his insistence that Bunny remain at home with a doctor and nurses they could trust. He would receive better care there. Even then Melanie had grasped the fact that they did not wish word to get out. Servants would be silent—they were loyal to the family after all—and the doctor and nurses were trained to secrecy. Once in the hospital, the situation would be out of their control. They were terrified that people should know. The shame of it. Afterwards, Melanie sometimes wondered if Bunny might have been saved had he been taken to a hospital.

Her parents wanted to send her away to the country, to Grandfather Bunner's. She would not go. What if Bunny were to ask for her? She still believed he was suffering some terrible form of food poisoning and that by her presence she could make him feel better. No one had the time or energy to argue with her. They let her stay, provided she would remain in a room prepared for her in another part of the house.

But she had to see him. In the afternoon of the third day of his illness, she crept out and waited in the corridor, watching the door of his room. There was much coming and going, with pans, with linens. Finally, two nurses came out and she went in and stood just inside the doorway.

There were the sounds of his retching, hiccuping, gasping. She had been braced for the foul smell that had permeated the house on the first night, but the smell, while persistent, was rather weak and not really like that of typical body wastes.

She would not have recognized him. His skin was flaccid, as if it would be cold and clammy to the touch, but wrinkled at the same time. His eyes were deeply shadowed and sunken, his cheeks hollow. He was lying limp, apathetic, at a rather odd angle and then it occurred to her that he was lying on a pan.

When he saw Melanie he tried to rouse himself and the worried expression on his face lifted. He smiled, his teeth so white against his bluish-colored lips. "That's my Melly," he said in a strange husky voice. "Melly. Afraid of nothing."

"Not of you."

His face became contorted with pain as cramps seized him. The nurses returned then, horrified to see her, and sent her away. She could hear Bunny retching again as she went down the corridor.

He died that same week. A monstrous dying, cholera, "the death of a dog" (the French call it *le mort de chien*). How did he catch it? A disease of the poor, of people living crowded together in the tenements? What could have brought him there?

Her parents insisted on the lie. The manner of his dying reflected on them. A hunting accident; the son of a prominent family could easily have died in a hunting accident. That sort of thing happened with some frequency. Not this. Oddly the true story never leaked out. And after a while, it almost came to seem as if Bunny had really died in that way, as if no one but she remembered his retching in misery. *Le mort de chien.*

She never recovered from Bunny's loss. If some incident or sight brought back the memory of those evenings in his room or the memory of the horror of the days of his dying, she would stop whatever she was doing and weep. She seldom spoke of Bunny. After they were through with all the lying about the manner of his death, what was there to be said?

Once, soon after she was married, she had thought to tell Wallace. Perhaps she selected the wrong time; he had barely listened, glancing over his papers while she spoke. She left the story unfinished. This indifference, remembered over the years, had made it easier to deceive him.

Bunny died in the summer. The winter weather came early that year, damp so that the chill ate into one's bones. The house, always before so warm and pleasant, held the chill, the dankness. It fitted the gloom that hung over them all. Her parents sat in the drawing room hardly speaking.

This was to have been her debut year, but to everyone's relief, society's arbiter, Genevieve Edmont, advised a year's postponement. By then, as it turned out, Melanie was married to Wallace despite the impropriety of not having come out.

There seemed so little for her to do that year. And when the first shock had passed, it occurred to her that with Bunny gone, her father might bring her into the business. It made her feel guilty to wish she could take his place. But Bunny was gone and devoting herself to practicing the piano and doing needlepoint would not bring him back.

Occasionally she would even allow herself to daydream of going downtown to the bank and learning all the secrets about business that men knew—the pulsing life behind the

65

assets and liabilities, credit lines, new stock issues, and bankruptcies.

"A man without an heir is at a great disadvantage, Melanie," her father would sigh. "Everyone knows that the business will die with him."

Melanie was encouraged by the tenor of his words. "Papa," she said, "you know Bunner told me a great deal about the business. Don't you think I could be trained to come into the bank?"

Mr. Carle was almost smiling; he smiled so seldom that it made his face look unnatural to Melanie. "My dear, marriage is something for you to daydream about, not business. You probably have no idea what marriage opportunities you have. Your mother and I are continually approached with suitors for your hand. Young men from the best and most eminent families. We did not think it proper to discuss weddings so soon after Bunner's death." Her father paused. "Why Bunner had a real talent. My colleagues could not believe what excellent recommendations he used to make. Just a young fellow like that. One time George Smilers asked for a loan for his company. Seemed straightforward enough on the surface, but Bunner quickly realized that this could lead to a struggle to the death for control of the coke ovens with that upstart Woodruff and warned me of the risks of my participation. I had, of course, made this calculation myself and was testing Bunner. But he passed every test." Seeing her face fall, Mr. Carle had added: "Do not think me unappreciative of your desire to help me."

Later, in the music room, lifting her hands from the piano she could hear him chatting with her mother in the drawing room. "Why I would be the laughingstock of the banking community if I brought my daughter into the bank."

There was a long pause. He sighed and muttered in a voice broken with grief. "What a pity it was the boy."

"Ah, yes," said her mother.

The words hung in the air, threatening her, as if palpable, closing her throat. Sometimes in later years, she had been able to block out those words temporarily, but they were always close by somewhere in her mind, lying in wait as it were, to be recalled with all their pain.

Pity it was the boy. Pity, pity. What a pity it was the boy. Ah, yes.

From then on, always, she drew away from her father's touch. Not knowing that she had overheard, he thought her foolish, brooding about her mad idea to go into business. It had become a good story to tell his friends downtown. When dinner parties began again, Melanie noticed his business associates looking at her and smiling. She hated those smiles, suspected her father had told them and that they were laughing at her. Why then, after so great a rejection had she thought to ask her father for help before her marriage? But of course, it was all too obvious: the one thing her father did value her for was her marriageability. The bank was doing poorly; she was not too naïve to realize the need for a wealthy son-in-law.

Wallace's proposal came as a relief. The main reason he was chosen over her other suitors was that he spoke to her of business, offered her, or so she then believed, an opportunity to satisfy the ambitions her father and his friends found laughable. It never occurred to her he was not serious. Later, looking back, she marveled that she should not have seen that this was his way of courting her, no more sincere than the elaborate compliments of his rivals.

During the early months of her marriage, Melanie enjoyed a brief popularity with women that she was never to know again. For a time—and she was not then to know how evanescent her good reputation would be—she was the pet of society's matrons. It was as if having taken her beauty to the marital bed, she was no longer a competitor. Women confided in her, shared the names of their dressmakers, traded footmen with her for dinner parties. (The intimacy could not last, of course. Husbands, fiancés, fathers were too openly admiring. They flirted, pursued; soon it seemed no one believed the prize had not been captured.)

67

Melanie was surprisingly happy; Wallace, filled with pride, looked at her possessively. Remembering how he had kissed her tears on their wedding night, belatedly it comforted her. She still had hopes of finding sexual fulfillment in bed with him, and beyond that she still believed a place would be found for her in Wallace's business. The problem was that she was no better able to engage his full attention than her father's when she talked business.

When they dined at home it was Wallace's custom to spend a few hours afterwards working on his ledgers; if they attended a ball or the opera, he would repair to the study upon their return. Melanie recalled his telling her that most women were so ignorant of business that were they to see his ledgers, they would not understand them. It seemed to her that he had been scornful of such ignorance, had contrasted her interest and intelligence favorably. But when he came home from his office one evening and found her in his study going over his ledgers, he had flown into a rage. "No one looks at my ledgers! No one!"

It was the first time he had raised his voice to her; the menace was unmistakable. The expression on his face terrified her.

Later that evening he came into the drawing room and sat down with the newspaper. After a while he looked up at her: "Everyone in this world has a role, Melanie. I have mine in business. And you have yours as my wife, a role you fit exceptionally well. I do not ask how you carry out your duties; I do not expect you to investigate how I carry out mine."

Pity to be a girl.

She felt that she had been cheated of what she had been led to expect. He was disingenuous, not quite worthy of respect. His methodical ways that had seemed to her a part of the business personality now became irritants.

A woman's life seemed to her a succession of stultifying events, of balls, intimate suppers at which thirty other people were present and always, always meaningless conversation.

Wallace, working at his desk, barely noticed as she left the room. When he sat over his ledgers until midnight, he would occasionally go to bed in one of the guest rooms. Not to disturb her. But soon so many of his belongings were in the other room that without either of them making the decision, it became his bedroom. Of course he came to hers, but she felt a rejection. When she objected, they quarreled and quarrels became an integral part of their relationship. Only then was she able to engage his attention fully, only in the aftermath would his lovemaking come to life.

And all the while other men were waiting, seeking a response. Still, long after the romance with Denis had resumed—an inevitability she later thought; certainly she had fought against his attraction for her—she had refused even to consider anyone else. (Denis was her past, her dream of her future.) She felt her duty to Wallace, accepted his view of her role. It was not without a struggle that she took another step into the secret world that was to be rumored in the gossip columns. The years passed, bringing her a greater sense of isolation in her marriage and all the time there were the other men waiting, wanting, as she was waiting, wanting. Denis gave too little, made her more rather than less aware of what she lacked.

Once she had taken that step, she was astonished to discover how much was offered. She had anticipated the warmth, the intimacy and sexual pleasure, but had been unaware of another benefit, a benefit few other women would have appreciated. Only with a lover, she was to learn, could she engage in meaningful conversation about the world of finance. The very man who spoke nothing but the most innocuous of small talk to a woman at the dinner table would in bed after sex reveal not only marital but also business worries, plans, plots, chicaneries, competitions, mergers, stock issues, loans, and expansion possibilities.

Only with a lover could she respond with her full intelligence, have her words weighed seriously, her advice sought and taken. Only with a lover could she achieve a modicum of her unsuitable ambitions. When guilt, remorse, regret, responsibility, and yes, there was affection after all, sent her back to Wallace—she was not so easily unfaithful as was generally believed—she missed the business talk quite as much as the sexual activity.

Pity it was the boy.

CHAPTER 7

So Do They Pass
Their Golden Hours

Just thinking Harry's name made her recall the feel of his body in her arms. So vivid was the recollection that she shivered. Thinking of Harry always had a physical quality. If anyone had told Melanie a month before, a week before, even an hour before it happened that she and Harry were to become lovers, she would have scoffed at the idea. Harry was not the sort of man she became involved with. He belonged to the younger set that went partying after the formal parties ended, wagered on winning swimming and tennis contests, and was the focus of attention for the debutantes and their mothers. Certainly she saw Harry at some social event every week. She liked to look at him. What woman did not like to look at Harry? He was the handsomest of the young men. The debutantes vied for his interest and each season his name was linked with one and then another. Now the name was Iris Woodruff and common wisdom held that he was to marry her. It was time; Harry was nearly twenty-eight and he could not postpone the capture of a rich bride—for the sake of his mother and sister if not his own—much longer.

Melanie found it pleasant to be with Harry, who knew how to make the most trivial small talk seem amusing, and she quite looked forward to dancing with him, to be that close to his appealing person. Her thoughts of him went no further. Her family had joked about his obvious admiration for her when he was a boy. It did not seem too different now.

He had appeared without advance warning at her house one evening in early spring to see Wallace, he said, a business his bank was interested in that involved Edmont properties. However, Wallace was inspecting real estate possibilities in Philadelphia that day and was not to return before midnight. Was the visit contrived? She had not thought so at that time, believed Harry to be ingenuous. Later she was not so sure.

She had taken him into the garden, as it was unusually warm for March, and they sat beneath the trees, chatting in a desultory way. All at once, making the movement in so natural a manner that, sensitive as she usually was to male advances, she was barely aware something was to happen, he bent forward and kissed her. "How can I resist you?" he said. "You were my daydream when I was a boy. I've been half in love with you all my life."

She had drawn back. "Half is quite enough." But her voice did not carry the tone of finality she had intended.

"I think it's time to try for the other half."

He stood up, took her hand, and without hesitation led her to the gazebo. It was her house, her garden, but he knew where to go to be alone and unobserved. She had not meant to accompany him, to be with him, *but how can I resist you?* Even while she was saying to herself that it could not be happening, he was unbuttoning the long rows of tiny buttons with skillful fingers, unlacing the tight corset—and she was curiously unwilling to stop him.

She had never held a body like his in her arms. There

was about it a cleanness, a smoothness, a strength. In the dimness of the gazebo, his body shone golden. And his touch. It was as if the joyousness that was so integral a part of his personality flowed through his fingertips onto the surface of her body and within. How easy it was to be caught in his mood, to think of nothing but what was happening between them.

"Tell me what you like. What do you want me to do for you?"

His body lay on hers lightly, but with a heavy pressure against the groin, hard, ready. What do you want me to do for you? She could guide his hand, his body to her pleasure and he would not draw back. Their tongues touched; his breath, the taste of his mouth was so sweet. "My Melanie, my Melody." She was not even stopped by the remembered pet name.

Afterwards she thought about Iris. She knew men so well that she was certain Harry made no connection between the marriage he was intending with chaste Iris and the love affair that was beginning with Melanie now. Neither situation had anything to do with the other. This was not serious; how could it be serious? There was only one serious affair in her life and no room for more. But a lighthearted romance with so charming a young man: that would suit her quite as well as it suited him. She wondered idly if she were to be Harry's last fling. At the moment she rather liked the idea. It was only later that she found how irksome this could be.

Tonight, for instance, she would have to watch Harry dance at the Woodruffs' ball. With Iris. A lovely couple. But how disagreeable to see them dancing together. It would be a pleasing sight, he so tall and well built, and she so small and fragile—a pleasant sight if it did not turn the stomach. The affair of a married woman with a younger man was transitory, but she did not like to see him embrace his younger fiancée.

Melanie wished she had not agreed to go to the Woodruffs' ball. To make matters worse, Joseph Woodruff would be watching for signs of discomfiture. She could hardly bear to be in the same house with him. Unfortunately, staying away from this particular ball—and with Wallace in Bourneham but refusing to attend—would revive the gossip that had taken so long to die down as a result of Joseph's efforts. It satisfied his pride to have people know of her, so long as his wife did not, of course.

Joseph had been her greatest mistake; she could not imagine now how she could have been so stupid. Well, it had not been stupidity. She had succumbed to a surprising desire for coarse, vulgar Joseph Woodruff. It would be an unparalleled experience, she had believed, to be with, in the sense of having intercourse, a man possessed of such drive, such achievement. He was the prime example of the self-made man, scorned by members of the old families, but admired at the same time. Joseph had been nobody, a butcher's son, helping to hang and carve the carcasses, cutting chops for the customers, cleaning the blood and intestines off the counters, spreading sawdust on the floor. He had no education to speak of, no money. Marriage had not been to someone who could help him advance, but to Nellie Green, the daughter of the butcher who had the shop next door. Somehow, and with no one to point the way, he had the prescience to see the extent to which the expanding economy would need fuel, had succeeded in finding and convincing a financier to back him with the funds needed to gain control of one small coal mine in Pennsylvania. With that as a base, he paid off his backers and was on his way. Soon he was able to form a company to operate coke ovens. The Panic of 1873 gave him the opportunity to buy up businesses in trouble. Woodruff gained control of coal mines, of coke ovens, bought rights to iron ore in Canada, made deals with steel manufacturers. He had the nerve to try anything, to take any business risk. His interests went so far as a line of freighters and small railroad lines—enough to keep his coal, coke, and ore moving, not so many as to go into competition with Vanderbilt. All his companies were profitable;

in times of economic depression he would pay the lowest wages, demand the most work in regions where unemployment was highest. By the time of Villa del Destino in Bourneham and the mansion just a few blocks down from the Edmonts on Fifth Avenue in New York, he controlled most of the nation's coke ovens, had a major share of the steel industry in the East and was occupied with a plan to take over the western market as well. At his instigation, the state legislature passed regulations favoring heavy industry. It was said that Woodruff owned more politicians than any man in New York, excepting perhaps Edmont.

At the time Melanie met them, the Woodruffs had not yet gained acceptance to the narrow circle of society in which the Edmonts moved, but occasionally would be present at one of the larger balls given to honor actresses or opera stars, balls that Genevieve would not dream of attending but Melanie would go to out of ennui.

Melanie had been so bored then, moving almost always with a group carefully culled from society's greatest families, following the inexorable pattern of the social seasons. There had been a time when it seemed that Joseph Woodruff might save her from this boredom.

She found him strangely attractive; his very ugliness added to the fascination he held for her as a man of exceptional potency. His skin was pitted, his nose large, and his jowls heavy. The powerful body excited her, aware as she was that the muscles had been developed lifting sides of beef and hog. His wrists were thick. The very crudeness of his table manners appeared virile to her, the way he pushed up peas with his knife, gulped his overly sweetened coffee. His manner of speech was vulgar, with errors in pronunciation and grammar. She had never known a man who had not been born to wealth, to social position. A cruder man, a man of the people would bring her something new, exciting. What a lover he would be, Melanie had thought.

Well, it had not worked out that way. The drive that characterized his business dealings, which she had been convinced would add vigor to his sexual behavior, was not in evidence in the bedroom. In fact, he was barely able to maintain his erection long enough to enter and climax himself. He apparently had no idea that a woman should be satisfied, too, and when the hint was dropped, had no idea of how to provide for her. Melanie found him slower to pick up her cues than Wallace had been as a bridegroom, as easily shocked by her suggestions, appalled by her taking the lead in any way.

She had imagined a naturalism in lovemaking, animalistic, but no man could have been more conventional. The draperies had to be drawn and the lamp extinguished, as many undergarments as possible retained, the blankets pulled over them. The only interesting part of the affair was becoming privy to some of his business stratagems, to information about the rivalries between the industrial tycoons. This soon sickened her, too. As he became more open, she learned how unscrupulous were his business methods. He spoke, and with pride, of cheating, lying, all but stealing to achieve his ends; he took actual pleasure in bringing about the ruin of any who stood in his way, boasted that he had arranged to have a railroad train burned to prevent a rival's shipment from reaching its destination. To deceive Wallace, and with such a man.

It had proved extremely difficult for Melanie to extricate herself from the affair. Joseph was used to acquisition, not loss. Proud of possessing so legendary a mistress, he viewed himself as a notable lover as well as a notable businessman. When Melanie made it evident that she wished to break with him, he turned vicious. The final scene between them had been so terrible that she tried to forget it had ever happened; he had terrified her with his threats of revenge.

It turned out that there was something he wanted enough to let her go. Admission to the inner circle of society had become his own as well as his wife's greatest ambition. Melanie could give them entrée. The thought of inflicting the crude Woodruffs on her mother-in-law, her friends, was repugnant to her, but she was at her wit's end. So she agreed to invite Nellie Woodruff to tea, to introduce her to Genevieve Edmont, to sponsor them for a good box at the Metropolitan Opera on Monday, society's night. It was the first time she realized how great a motivating force was social ambition, that there were people who would do anything to gain entry to the world she had been born into and took without question as her due. For all his millions, for all the businessmen he could, as he liked to say, buy and sell, for all the politicians he controlled, Woodruff was helpless in the face of rebuffs when he sought membership in the clubs and learned that he and his wife were passed over when invitations to the inner circle homes were sent out.

So it was that on a Monday evening years later, Melanie was preparing to attend the Woodruffs' ball. The evening began badly. Melanie had ordered the mauve lace gown with cream appliqués to be laid out for her. Harry had admired it and there was no need to wear something new for the Woodruffs. Her personal maid, Dena, held out the gown for Melanie to slip on. The dress was too large; material hung slack at the waist. "Why Dena," she said sharply, "surely you know which dress to bring me."

It was then that she observed the wrong response. Dena was smiling faintly. Maliciously? The maid said nothing, although the error meant that she had to climb the stairs to the closet rooms on the third floor again. She returned some minutes later with a dress that appeared to be identical, but was more sharply tapered through the bodice and inches narrower at the waist. This was the gown created in Worth's workrooms in Paris. The other was a copy made by Melanie's dressmaker to be worn without corseting. To obtain such replicas, she ordered yards and yards of additional chiffon, satin, velvet, lace, on the pretext they were needed for scarfs, fans, parasols. The reason given was irrelevant. Even the greatest designer in the world as Worth was known to be would not wish to challenge Melanie.

The servants knew, of course, and a lover could tell if

she intended to engage in sexual activity simply by glancing at her waist.

Dena then explained that Nellie Woodruff had offered her a position for seventy dollars a month, nearly as much as a butler earned.

Melanie was stunned. It was taken as an assumption, rather as a fact no more alterable than a geometric theorem, that a woman would steal another's husband sooner than her personal maid. Nellie might even believe that the maid would give her Melanie's beauty as well as her other secrets.

"My mother may need an operation," said Dena in a placating manner. "I wouldn't think of it otherwise, madam. Working for you has been my whole life."

My life, too, thought Melanie, remembering with pain how it had been Dena who came to her aid when she had miscarried by her own hand. Dena had not been summoned, but she was there. Smaller than Melanie, she had, nonetheless, lifted the fainting girl from the deep marble tub and carried her to bed. That whole day Melanie had lain there inert, waiting only for Dena to come and change the bloody cloths, put a cold towel on her head, bring her drinks of aromatic ginger ale and Hazard's Nerve Tonic from the apothecary. Later Dena washed the towels and bed linens herself so that the laundress would not gossip, scrubbed the Persian rug in the bathroom, the Aubusson in Melanie's bedroom. Perhaps she had even washed and returned the knitting needle. Miss Robertson had never commented on its loss, and until the wedding night there was no reason to suspect that she knew what had happened.

Dena. The only reason Melanie had even taken notice of her before that day was her name, Dena. Denis. It had seemed prophetic. She was the least of the upstairs maids, the one assigned the tedious task of caring for the dust ruffles that lined the trains and wide sweeping skirts. She cut them off for cleaning and then when that had been done, sewed them back on, row upon row upon row, with stitches that had to be tiny, perfect, though no one but the wearer would ever see them. To become a personal maid was an unhoped-for step up. They never again referred to that day, but Melanie had taken Dena with her when she married. After years of discretion, would Dena tell all this to Nellie?

When Melanie did not speak, Dena said softly, "I would hate to leave you."

Melanie picked up the emphasis on "would." The foolish girl thought Melanie was going to make a counteroffer. A disloyal maid was finished. No other woman in their circle would dare to employ her. Nellie surely planned to send Dena away as soon as she had gleaned from her the information she sought. The way down was quick, so quick. Melanie needed to say only that she wished to terminate Dena's employment, the maid was clumsy, perhaps mislaid small pieces of jewelry, bathed too seldom. Even if she sought employment lower in the social scale, she would find that women who paid their maids twelve dollars a month were no less concerned about honesty, loyalty, and cleanliness than those paying four and five times as much.

Dena became nervous; she knew Melanie so well that she could tell her news had not been taken quite as she had planned.

"Do you have my cosmetics ready?" asked Melanie coldly. "Let us begin."

Dena's hands shook as she started the elaborate makeup procedures. Putting on a white kid glove, she dipped the forefinger in blue salve and faintly traced the veins of the breasts as far down as would be revealed by the round low neck of the gown. Most of the women she knew would hesitate to have this done, but Melanie was ready to try almost any makeup practice she heard about—using it subtly, of course. Removing the makeup glove, Dena creamed Melanie's neck and face and lightly dusted them with a fine tinted rice powder, scented with dried rose petals from the garden. A hint of carthamous rouge, sent specially from Spain, the only one of the rouges that Melanie would allow; the cheaper carmine roughened the skin. Then a touch of powder again.

And it was time to pass a piece of the softest flannel over the face so as to leave the glow, remove the appearance of being made up. When Melanie's makeup was completed, it would look as if she had used none at all. A bit of almond oil highlighted her dark eyebrows and sparkled on her lashes and just the faintest blush of rose colored her lips; anything more was the sign of the painted woman. Her hair, brushed until it shone with blue lights, was combed high and allowed to fall into its natural waves before being pinned up, and held with a diamond-studded tortoiseshell comb.

Only then did the dressing begin. Dena kept fastening the sixty-four tiny hooks and eyes down the back of the dress improperly and having to start over. Her hands were perspiring and Melanie reminded her rather sharply to wipe them on a cloth before touching the gown.

Even when all was completed, Melanie did not feel that she looked quite right. One could always tell when a woman had not been properly dressed by her maid. Everyone had known that Alfred Van Burgh's business was failing when Louise appeared at a dinner party with the sleeve on her right arm pushed higher than that of the left and a tiny smudge on the tip of her gray satin shoe. While Melanie did not care about the Woodruffs, Harry would be there. He would be seated beside Iris, but his eyes, Melanie knew, would turn regularly to her.

She stopped in the nursery to kiss Rosamunde goodnight and then went in to Junior's room to talk with him as was her habit before going out to dinner. His tutor complained that she interrupted the boy's summer assignments, but they both looked forward to these moments together. Tonight he hid something under the blotter on his desk when he heard her come in. A picture probably; he preferred drawing to doing his arithmetic. He was such a serious little boy that only in this way did he remind her of Bunny, putting work aside for pleasure. The memory was painful.

After a few minutes she left him and went on to Wallace's study. She did not really mind his refusal to accompany her, but wondered why he had stayed in Bourneham after the weekend. As was his way, he had ignored her questions. For once he was not studying his ledgers.

"Is something wrong? Would you rather I didn't go but stayed here with you?"

"Nothing is wrong, nothing you would understand. Just business. Business. You cannot imagine what worries, what problems a businessman must deal with." Words like those still had the power to irritate her. "Of course, you must go. My mother is waiting for you."

Genevieve had agreed to consider the Woodruffs socially only because Melanie had asked her to do so. Her acceptance had not been absolute, to be sure; she came to Nellie's balls, but only the most elaborate, and invited Nellie and Joseph to her own balls, but only the least important.

Neither woman had been looking forward to the evening and they took little pleasure in the beauty of the ocean views on the ride to Villa del Destino. Nellie Woodruff gave no sign of suspecting their lack of enthusiasm, greeting them warmly, her six-strand ruby necklace bobbing up and down on her ample bosom. Iris stood beside her on her father's arm. It was odd that Harry, the acknowledged suitor, was not standing with them, but was with his mother and sister. Melanie observed Joseph glancing at Harry, looking him up and down, and then smiling at her, licking his lips. Joseph was making it evident that he knew about Harry.

Seeing Iris without the distraction of Harry beside her, Melanie was able to study her and to realize sadly how lovely she was and how slight. Imagining that frail body so unlike hers in Harry's arms was painful. Of course, Harry had surely never seen that body naked. Not yet.

Iris's waist was so small, the smallest in Bourneham, it was said. The rumor was that her mother had started lacing her tightly when she was a child. Some other mothers put little canvas belts around the waists of their small daughters, but Nellie was accused of having used a rigorous lacing.

Entering the ballroom side by side, Melanie and Genevieve were dazzled by the brilliance. Nellie had combined all light sources, illuminating the vast room with candles, gas lamps, and the new incandescent electric lights. The gowns appeared splendid, the diamonds and rubies sparkled, but many faces, certainly Nellie's own, looked older, more lined, hollow or jowly, haggard, ravaged, rapacious. As was true of many Bourneham ballrooms, all four walls were mirrored. From odd angles one would catch sight of a tête-à-tête thought to be unobserved, hands held too long at the conclusion of a waltz. Tonight, however, the mirrors were covered over with painted screens.

Once her eyes had accommodated to the brilliant light, Melanie observed that the screens depicted the interior of a great English castle, with baronial dining hall, picture galleries, stone staircases. Feeling an unexpected pang, Melanie realized the scenes reminded her of Carnaugh. She supposed that there were similarities among the English castles.

Looking about more carefully Melanie observed that the English motif was continued in a profusion of pale pink tea roses contained in vases of Wedgwood blue. Nellie apparently saw no contradiction between the English scenes and the livery of her footmen who were dressed as for the court of Louis XIV in blue velvet with an allover pattern of tiny fleur-de-lis and poufs of cream-colored lace at neck and wrists. Their hair was powdered and drawn back with thin blue velvet ribbon.

The ballroom was crowded; representatives of the great families of Bourneham mingled with members of the less important European royalty.

Harry came up then to exchange small talk. There was a little buzz of conversation; everyone had read the *Bugle*. Everyone had noticed he was not with the Woodruffs. Harry was too polished to give any indication of embarrassment. He did not mention having seen the damning article. And if being conspicuously separated from Iris troubled him, he gave no sign. After a suitable period of small talk, he returned to his sister's side, perfectly at ease. Aware that nothing else was possible, Melanie nonetheless felt let down.

Conscious then of someone looking at her, Melanie became aware of a man she had never seen before. He was standing a little apart from the other guests, surveying the vast, brilliantly lit room, the magnificently dressed guests with a faint look of distaste on his ugly, strong, deeply lined face. He had dark red hair cut short and standing up straight on his head like bristles on a brush and long sideburns. His chest and arms looked too heavy for his tightly fitted evening coat.

"Who is he?" she asked Josephine van der Cleeve, who knew everybody in society. But Josie had no idea. Melanie found the mystery surrounding him intriguing.

At that moment dinner was announced. Melanie scrutinized the crowd. No matter where she was, Melanie always had to be aware of what Harry was doing. Surely he would join the Woodruffs now. Instead Iris, her face heavy with despair, was being taken in to dinner by her father.

Harry's gift for not appearing at a loss was never more in evidence as he was shepherded by Nellie Woodruff to the side of Eleanor de Witte. At one time everyone thought Harry would marry her. Harry was looking down at Eleanor, talking, smiling. Melanie knew just how charming he must be. She remembered his face above hers after they made love. That look, was it not almost the same? And then he caught sight of Melanie and smiled at her and she saw how casual, how meaningless had been the smile he gave Eleanor de Witte. But how did he smile at Iris? Deliberately she turned away.

"Well, I suppose we are now in for one of those famous Woodruff anything-goes free-for-alls," said Josephine scornfully. She was referring to Nellie Woodruff's custom of informal seating for dinner; everyone knew this was the only way she could handle a dinner party. When she had first started entertaining members of society, she had made gaffes in seating people next to those they most sought to avoid, because no one would confide in Nellie. So she declared place cards spoiled the "fun" for a party. People should sit as they would (except for Iris and Harry, whose position she ordered). It made for confusion and discomfort; guests at a ball were accustomed to having everything arranged so as to go smoothly.

Melanie noticed the stranger again. He had an interesting face. She wondered if she could contrive to go in to dinner with him. There was no problem as it turned out. Having brought Harry and Eleanor together, Nellie rushed over to Melanie to arrange an introduction. "Elmer Morgan." The name sounded familiar to Melanie, but she could not quite place it. No doubt a relative of J. P. Morgan, she decided, refusing his arm but accepting his company to enter the dining room beside him.

As they went to the dining table, she was surprised that he made a move as if to pull out her chair for her, a clear sign of gaucherie, of a man unaccustomed to having footmen do all the work. Pushing the heavy mahogany dinner chairs was work indeed. The footmen perspired in their velvet coats.

He quickly corrected any impression of a connection with the House of Morgan, saying boldly, "It is spelled differently. *E - n*, not *a - n*."

Now that she thought of it, he spoke properly, but his accent was unrefined.

"I like your spelling of the name," she replied pleasantly. "Morning in German. That is my favorite time of day." She sometimes met a lover in the morning when Wallace was in his office. "Early in the day, anything still can happen. Later on it often becomes muddied, dull, drab, ugly." She was flirting with him; it was early in their acquaintance and she did not think how quickly the situation between them might be muddied.

"Ah yes, you society ladies know every language you might possibly need, don't you? A governess for German, another for French, and whatever else is proper. Am I right?" But he spoke with seeming kindness. "Did your German governess know how you felt about the morning?"

"Yes. It worried her."

"And what do you do in Bourneham in the evenings?" he asked, a hint of suggestiveness in his voice.

"We either gossip or eat. Some prefer the former, some the latter," she remarked. She was smiling, but she spoke the bitter truth.

"It is clear which you prefer," he returned, glancing without subtlety at her slender arms and narrow waist and from her waist to her barely touched plate.

"Melanie counts the bites of everything she eats," said Jenny Olney, seated diagonally across the table. "She allows herself just so many for each course."

The statement was spoken with clear malice, but was quite accurate. How else was one to get through the series of courses at a Bourneham or New York dinner without becoming porcine? The pâtés and the bisques and the lobsters and the Muscovy duck, the sorbet, and the filet of beef, the duchesse potatoes, wild rice, the broccoli, brussels sprouts, mushrooms drenched in butter, the artichokes, asparagus with rich Hollandaise, the rolls and muffins, then the puddings and little cakes and candied cherries and pineapple and chocolate-covered mints, all accompanied by glass upon glass of champagne and sauterne and bordeaux and sweet claret. She looked around the room at the faces bent over their plates. There was hardly a woman—or man—over thirty without a double chin, the features blurred. Sometimes a portrait hanging on a side wall in plain view presented a cruel contrast, revealing the face long since hidden in fat.

Melanie had devised a meal plan—five spoonfuls of soup, six bites for the fish, ten for the roast, one of pudding. It kept her amused. She seldom lost count.

The footmen were offering the food, holding heavy gold bowls and platters. Twelve pieces of cutlery were at each place, each embossed with a crest that every scion of an old family knew to be bogus. After twice passing a course, the footmen would set the serving dishes in the center of the table so that the truly greedy could take something more to nibble on. The weight of the dishes and cutlery was so great that if the tables had not been reinforced with wooden bars, they would have buckled.

The next week everyone knew the *Bugle* would describe such a ball. Although not invited himself, Armand Wolfe had his informants, young men in society not beyond providing tidbits, hints of scandals, real and imagined, in return for small sums of money or sometimes just to make mischief.

Melanie was usually amused by the way other women kept repeating the story about the bites, thinking to harm her, not realizing that it added to her luster, made every man who heard it take another look at the slenderness of her body, with only the beautiful breasts half revealed by her low-cut gown giving any hint of fullness. But there was something about Morgen's scrutiny that disturbed her. She noticed for the first time how dark his eyes were, a brown so close to black, there seemed no difference between iris and pupil. It was impossible to imagine them softening, moistening with emotion.

"How are the plans for your ball coming, Melanie? I hear the most fascinating rumors." It was Jenny again. "Melanie's balls are the high point of the season, Mr. Morgen. Last year she appeared as the snow maiden all in white with feathers and pearls. And the ballroom was decorated to mimic the North Pole with mountains of snow and ice. It was such a hot night, but they just kept on bringing the ice from the ice boxes in the basement. I can't wait to see what the theme will be this year."

"So do they pass their golden hours," said Morgen.

"You are an observer of our ways."

"I am a journalist. My father's name was Morgenstern, but I found it too long for the byline."

The editor of the scurrilous *New York Journal*. Wallace often cursed him for making a career out of "exposing," that was the word Morgen used, the activities of the wealthy. He had already written thousands of words about the tenements and the sweaters and there was talk that he planned to have these published in book form.

Being seated next to such a man, thought Melanie, could happen only at the Woodruffs'. It would make a good story to tell Harry. Wallace would not be amused. She felt put on her mettle.

"You are thinking that tomorrow you will in your columns describe a woman so wealthy she throws away her food while millions starve, and plans to exceed last year's Snow-in-Summer ball while millions swelter in the tenements," she said allowing the footman to take away another barely touched plate. Morgen colored slightly. Clearly that had been the story he planned to write. *So do they pass their golden hours.* She was more amused than annoyed; there was a slight bite to his words; she both liked and disliked it. From a nearby table, Joseph Woodruff was staring at her. She recognized the meaning of the hint of a smile he allowed himself. Just so did a man look at a woman who had once been his lover, that look, oh, what a gay dog I am. But there was something more to his expression she could not quite read.

With the extra sensitivity she had where Harry was concerned, Melanie was aware that his eyes were on her. He was apparently conversing with Miss de Witte, but he was really observing Melanie's interchange with Morgen. He did not like it.

Talking in animated fashion to Eleanor de Witte, Harry was at the same time thinking he had never been so uncomfortable at a social event. Nellie Woodruff was showing him, in front of everyone, that he could not expect to continue to receive treatment as a favored suitor without going through the negotiations for the marriage settlement and showing himself eager for a specific wedding date. Certain that all was understood, he had let the formalities lapse. This was just a warning, he knew; Iris's miserable face revealed that she was not responsible for his banishment to another table. His attention was drifting away from Eleanor. It was not fair to her; she really was a good sort. Why, only a year ago he had been close to asking her to marry him, but somehow, the romance, if such it were, had faded away. They had remained friends; no one was ever angry with Harry. Nellie Woodruff would be won around again, too.

He looked over at the table where Melanie was seated with that journalist, Elmer Morgen. What an unlikely combination they were, he thought, disquieted to observe how interested they appeared in one another. Melanie had a way, he knew, of making the man she was with feel he was the only one in the room. It was easier when Wallace accompanied her. A husband was somehow well safer than another man, thought Harry, but of course when Wallace was not with her, she was paired with someone else. He was, after all, almost always with Iris. But he wished her eyes were not shining so brightly, that she was not leaning towards Morgen, though he knew it absurd to think Melanie's manner to her dinner companion had any importance.

Morgen had been so charming, so flattering, commenting with a smile on Mr. Edmont's absence from the ball that she was quite startled when as the strawberries with chantilly were being offered, he said without any hesitation or transition from his flatteries, still in that charming way, "There's some ugly talk about your husband's tenements."

She saw the animosity then, remembered that Morgen was a muckraking editor and was furious with herself for having fallen into his trap. Vanity makes one intellectually lazy, she thought. Admired for her appearance, fawned over for so long, she had forgotten that beauty was not of itself a reason for every person to be eager to be with her.

Joseph was looking at her. This time she could see the malice. He would like to see her brought down.

Wallace had been in a strange mood since arriving in Bourneham. Though tempted to ignore Morgen, she realized that she needed to find out what was being said. Perhaps she could influence Morgen not to write about it. Oh, vanity dies hard, she thought. "There is what you call ugly talk about all men of property." She was trying for a light touch.

When he did not respond, she could not help but ask: "What ugly talk?"

He smiled. "Don't you know? I would think a man with a wife as clever as you would discuss his business with you. I admire the intelligence of women. The *Journal* stands firmly for women's suffrage, you know."

The journalist, trying one ploy, then another. But his statement was accurate. The *Journal* did support suffrage. Under any other circumstances, she would have warmed to him. *No one looks at my ledgers.* Morgen had struck home. "Mr. Edmont could not be engaged in any business activity that might validly arouse the kind of gossip you are hinting at."

Morgen's eyes were shining in his eagerness to tell his story, see her reaction. "Whether he has told you or not, you have surely learned about the Heron garment factory fire. Vests for men's suits were made there. I would call it a sweatshop, but I daresay that is not a term you would use. *Sweat*, I mean." He managed to give the word a suggestive nuance.

The release from tension was so great that she was able to smile at Morgen, at Joseph watching, always watching. Yes, she knew about that fire. The newspapers had been full of it and yes, she had felt a flicker of unease when she began to read the first news report and looked for the name of the holder of the property. It was not given, but the address was enough. Wallace did not own buildings on that block. It was in uncomfortable proximity to the Edmont Hotel and he had mentioned it to her, had named the owner.

"I saw the fire myself you know, got to the scene when the flames were at their height. The workers were mostly women, and some not even that, little girls really. I saw them jumping out of the windows. I saw them fall, their hair, their blouses ablaze, their eyes staring with horror. And they were the lucky ones; many of them survived, though with serious injuries. Most of the others could not get to any window, but died at their sewing machines. Men were rushing up, fighting the police and firemen, trying to get into the building, screaming and crying that their wives and daughters were there. It was a heartrending scene."

Morgen did not look as if anyone or anything could rend his heart; he selected his words as if he were writing for a newspaper audience, not speaking to one person. "And they work for a pittance, you know. What would you think a woman takes home after working six twelve-hour days in a week? Six dollars maybe, some of them less.

"And for that, forty died and as many more were injured. And do you know why they had to die?"

Melanie waited for his argument to lead to Wallace. Then she would speak and deflate him.

"They had to die for want of proper fireproofing, for lack of sufficient sinks with water in the building, and most important, for lack of windows and usable fire escapes.

"Perhaps you have guessed by now that Wallace Montague Edmont V is being blamed for these deaths."

"I understand your eagerness to obtain a sensational newspaper story, Mr. Morgen. But in this case I think you are laboring mightily to force a mouse to bring forth a full-grown tiger."

"I like your witticism even if it is at my expense." He was still in good humor.

"You should obtain new sources of information, Mr. Morgen. With regard to the Heron factory, the fact is that Mr. Edmont is not the owner—not of the land the building stood on nor of the building itself. If he were, I can assure you, Mr. Morgen, there would have been sufficient fire escapes."

She did not hesitate to say this, though what did she know of the specifics of Wallace's business? But he was so responsible a man, it was reasonable to assume he would never risk valuable property, and, of course, human life.

Morgen was still smiling. "No, Mrs. Edmont; I don't think I need better informants. I know as well as you that Mr. Edmont does not own the tenement that housed the Heron factory. In fact, that is the point. He wants it. You asked me what the ugly talk was about. I'll tell you. People are saying Mr. Edmont had the fire set so that the owner of the property would be forced to sell."

Melanie knew that wealthy men were viewed as fair game by the scandalmongering press. Journalists of Morgen's stripe were capable of writing anything to attract readers, not caring what the results of their slander might be.

"Such an accusation could only be made out of malice, in a vile attempt to blacken Mr. Edmont's reputation."

"Oh, I agree." His expression was still pleasant, but his dark eyes studying her face seemed particularly intent for their lack of a defined pupil. "However, people are every bit as vile as that, Mrs. Edmont. On the other hand, Mr. Edmont's detractors offer a good basis for their suspicions." He paused, building up the suspense and when she did not speak went on. "The Heron sweatshop was in a building in the middle of a row of tenements that Mr. Edmont has been trying to buy for the past year. His agents have made offer after offer. Until now, the owner didn't need money badly enough to accept any of these. He preferred to remain a thorn in Mr. Edmont's flesh. He has flatly refused to sell."

"What if he has? No single piece of property could be so desirable as to make any man do something so dastardly as to arrange for arson."

"Men just as decent as your husband have done such dastardly deeds," Morgen returned coolly. "Most businessmen nowadays have contacts with criminals. These are hard times, with riots and strikes becoming commonplace, Mrs. Edmont. The masses of poor are no longer quiescent. The volcano is smoldering. At the very least, wealthy men now need protection. Ask your husband about that some time."

She prepared to deny it, but all at once remembered the men she caught sight of from time to time in the back room behind Wallace's office or following him when he went about the city. Ill-dressed, crude, powerfully built, they seemed out of place in their surroundings.

"It is said that Mr. Edmont wants that property desperately. He is losing money on the elegant Edmont Hotel because of the propinquity of the slums."

For the first time it occurred to Melanie that the story might not be so easy to refute. She did not doubt Wallace. He could not have sanctioned arson; he was too good a man. But she thought again about the property, the row of run-down tenements, the worst housing the Heron garment factory. Wallace wanted to build a new mansion for himself and Melanie, another for his mother farther up on Fifth Avenue nearer the Edmont Hotel. The commission to design the house had already been given to White, McKim, and Mead. The presence of the Edmont family as neighbors would enhance the reputation of the hotel. Others of their social set would be eager to follow the Edmonts and the area would become a symbol for luxury, for all that was best in New York City—if only he could obtain the title to the offending tenement. Rat-infested, filthy. Every month he spoke more intemperately of the intransigence of the owner, who, delighting in Wallace's discomfiture, was refusing to sell. He had to have that property. Melanie had heard him say so a dozen times. As had others.

"After a fire like that, a property owner may be ready, even eager to sell."

"Mr. Edmont had nothing to do with the fire and those who hint that he did," she was careful not to name Morgen, "are despicable."

He went on as if she had not spoken. "Every day the tenement stands, the Edmont Hotel loses money."

The man was insufferable, but how many people thought as he did? How many people might he influence through his newspaper to think that way?

"Losing money is of no importance to Mr. Edmont. He does not *need* money. He *has* money."

"Ah, but can any man have enough money? The more one has, the more one needs. They say you could invite all of us here to dinner any night on the spur of the moment—

how many would you say there are—six hundred guests?"
He looked around the room, filled with dining tables. "And
have the food to serve us and the servants to prepare and
bring it to the table without sending out for so much as a
pullet egg or borrowing a footman from your mother-in-law.
You are a costly sort of wife for a man, however rich, I should
think."

For the first time she fully understood and sympathized
with Wallace's complaints about modern muckraking journalists. "In my grandfather's time," he would say, "if a
newspaper just once printed something he didn't like, he
would say the word, and it would be shut down." She had
argued with Wallace about freedom of the press, a concept
that appealed to her. "These newspapers arouse the common people by distorting the truth, and making them unhappy about things they can't do anything about. What we
need is responsible journalism," he had said.

It would be a relief to have these stories choked off, the
sneering smile wiped from Morgen's lips. Perhaps reformers
had a vicious streak for all they claimed such charity.

Melanie felt exhausted by the strain and the long dinner
had not yet approached its conclusions. The plates that had
held strawberries were to be taken away, the sweet wines,
the petit fours still to be gone through. Looking up, she was
aware of the covert but unmistakable attention of all the
diners. They had talked too long, too intensely. It was fortuitous for once that due to her reputation anyone who saw
her talking with a man thought immediately of a new affair.
Certainly, Harry's reaction, which for all his social smoothness he could not quite conceal, supported this impression.
Eyebrows were raised. Morgen was not of their set, of unknown origin. Melanie's penchant for the unusual was in
evidence, they believed.

Indeed as if to prove them right, Morgen was looking at
her figure then, crudely, letting her see him observing the
cleavage between her breasts. The mood was changing, the
dangerous topic being abandoned.

Luckily no one had been close enough to hear what they were really talking about. The tables were so large that guests had to raise their voices in order to be audible to those seated opposite them. The only person in a position to have heard everything was Harry's sister and with her hearing handicap, she could not do so. Melanie observed that Evangeline was seated beside Hiram Genever, a recent widower. He was twice her age, but then, as everyone said, a totally deaf young woman could not afford to be fussy.

Morgen was leaning forward, observing the attention with avid interest. Melanie, aware of the many eyes upon her, tried to appear unconcerned, flirtatious.

"I wonder," Morgen said softly, as if there were collusion between them, "whether you will tell your husband of our conversation."

"Perhaps I will tell him that I had a dream in which a specter appeared and the false was presented to me as true. A nightmare." She was trying to choose her words carefully but could not restrain herself.

He was unaffected by her scorn. "Don't forget that my name means morning. And it is in the morning when one awakens and discovers . . . perhaps . . . that the specter was real after all." His voice was barely polite. The threat was clear.

"Perhaps I have not given the proper name after all, Mrs. Edmont." He took a deep breath, hesitated, and then plunged forward. "Anathema. Possibly that's the name I should have given, anathema to Mr. Edmont and his kind."

She gasped; no one of her acquaintance would ever trade insults with a lady. Perhaps he hoped to goad her into saying something he could report. Forcing herself to smile, she returned: "Oh, I did not realize you were joking with me, Mr. Morgen. One never credits a journalist with humor somehow. Anathema. That is really quite good. I daresay you have as clever a descriptive word for Mr. Edmont and his, how did you put it, kind? But I think I will not ask you what that is."

94

Still, she began to feel afraid of him. To appear calm, she picked up her glass of wine, not realizing that her hand was shaking, and a few drops spilled onto the white-and-gold lace tablecloth.

"I like you better for spilling the wine," said Morgen so very, very softly, with again a hint of intimacy. "I thought you had no feelings."

He looked into her eyes; she could not help but look up at him. Something was there after all. She was too experienced to miss it. Someday if that should prove necessary, she might be able to make use of it.

CHAPTER 8

Clara Awakens Memories

It was a tradition Melanie hated, analogous to being sent to bed as a child when the grown-ups were still up and doing interesting things. Even now when there was a sense of relief at being able to escape from Morgen, she felt at the same time resentful that as soon as Nellie rose, she, along with the other women, was literally being ordered from the table.

She hesitated in the doorway of the music room, reluctant to enter and join the conversation. There was nothing about her own childbirth experiences that she wished to share with anyone, nor her bleeding irregularities, nor the inadequacies of servants. Except for Dena who had yielded to Nellie's tempting, she had few problems. Difficult employer though she was, servants knew what she wanted, came to expect the scenes and demands she made as part of her grandeur.

Seeing Melanie standing on the threshold of the music room, Nellie rushed over, overcome with joy at having an

Edmont in her home, proof that she, the daughter of a butcher, was the equal of any in society. In a moment, she was stroking Melanie's arm, breathing in her perfume, begging her recipe for facial cream, telling her how young she looked, how sinuous. Nellie was always effusive, but this time Melanie could sense an awkwardness of manner. In that instant Melanie realized that the seating with Morgen had been planned in advance. She had maneuvered to be Morgen's dinner partner, not analyzing why it had been all too easy to arrange. He and Nellie Woodruff had done the maneuvering.

Why would a muckraking journalist be made welcome in this home? Morgen had viciously attacked Joseph Woodruff's recent strikebreaking tactics: Pinkerton men had been brought in with orders to shoot the workers on strike against the Woodruffs' steel mills if they did not give way. Several men had been killed. The *Journal* had given this event damning attention.

The scheme—whether conceived by Nellie or Joseph himself—was as clear to Melanie as if she had been told of it by the plotters. The Edmonts were to be used to draw Morgen's fire. Morgen was willing; aware that the public was tiring of the steel mill strike, he needed a new objective to attack. His placement at dinner had been arranged in the belief that Morgen had the skill to obtain from Melanie a remark, a thought, an idea, a plan that could be distorted so as to sound reprehensible. Her words would be twisted to implicate Wallace in the arson at the Heron factory.

Extricating herself gracefully from Nellie's encircling arm, Melanie entered the music room alone, and as she did so there was a . . . no, not a pause, the break in the conversation was too brief for that, but a *something* in the air. Melanie was used to producing an effect, but this was different in kind. She felt the downy hairs on her arms rise. Nothing exceptional was apparent. That they had been talking about her was probable in view of the *Bugle* article and the supposed flirtation with Morgen, but she was used to that, and

Genevieve's presence in the room kept the gossip within bounds. The air felt different; yet the scene was so ordinary, a group of women in glowing satins, stiff brocades with millefleurs designs, velvets, laces, feathers, braids, arranging themselves just far enough apart so as not to crush one another's skirts, talking in the soft after-dinner voices cultivated for the exchange of intimacies.

Harry's sister, Evangeline, had placed herself outside the circle of women. Melanie usually paid attention to the young woman, tried to converse with her, and Evangeline did appear to have some understanding of what was being said. Tonight Melanie was too disturbed, distracted to make the effort.

She looked around nervously. A few strangers were present, guests at one or another of the great houses. Perhaps it was their presence that changed the ambience, but there was nothing remarkable about any of them; this woman was too thin, another too stout.

One of the voices, though, had an odd timbre. It was low and deep and had a cooing sound, tremolo, like doves about to mate, a caressing voice, sensual, awakening dreams. Surely she had heard that voice before. Where had it been? Melanie looked more closely at the woman speaking. There was nothing familiar about her. She was the stout one, not fashionably curvaceous, but merely stout, a solid front, no separation between the breasts. Her face, lightly dusted with golden-tinted rice powder to take off the shine, had beads of perspiration on the upper lip. The woman appeared to be in her late forties, possibly fifty, though this may have been because she made no effort to look younger. Her gown was clearly costly; Melanie could think of only two French couturiers who used that particular satin, so soft it hugged the body, so heavy that the folds of the skirt fell like velvet. On this woman, the effect was lost. The dress merely covered her body decently. And yet that voice.

Nellie, suddenly recalling her duty as hostess, brought the newcomers to meet Genevieve first, then Melanie. Again, that feeling in the room as the introductions were made, that hesitation, almost a pause. The name of the woman with the voice, Clara Ribley, was not familiar to Melanie, but clearly the reverse was not the case. Upon hearing Melanie's name Clara blushed and looked down. Her "It is a pleasure to meet you" was delivered in the softest tone, the coo subdued, barely a quiver.

There was the lightest of touches on Melanie's arm. She looked up and saw, to her surprise, Evangeline, frowning slightly. Melanie smiled and turned away; she could not manage the difficulty of speaking with the deaf girl at this moment.

And suddenly Melanie remembered where she had heard the voice before. So many years ago. She had been unhappy then, with Denis gone forever as she had believed. Wishing only to be alone, she had spent hours reading and day-dreaming in the airy cool gazebo behind the English garden. The bottom half of the structure was solid, white painted wood with a design of green leaves going all around, but the top was partially open to the air, the sides made of bamboo elaborately twisted into patterns of monkeys, vines, and flowers. Melanie still had a tactile response to the memory of wicker furniture, which for all the overstuffed cushions, was uncomfortable. The backs of the armchairs tilted so far that the feet could not touch the floor and the settee was too short to lie on, too high to sit on easily.

On the afternoon that came to mind, Melanie was about to enter the gazebo when she heard a laugh. "No, Bunner, no, no." That was it, of course, the cooing tremolo of the voice that day turning the negative into an affirmative. "Clara. Damn. I wish Mamma would get a decent-sized sofa in here. But I haven't been able to figure out a way of suggesting it without suggesting why," he laughed.

There was a silence, then murmurs, breathing. Melanie had known she should go away, not stand outside listening. But she could not move. Desire came over her, a rush of heat to the groin. Only a year before—not even that—Denis had been embracing her. It did not bear thinking of. Never again. She sank down on the grass outside the gazebo, lifting her dress, putting her hand inside. "Right there, right there, oh, Bunner that's it, that's it, that's the way. It feels so good." Outside on the grass Melanie trembled, put a finger to the tiny protuberance of flesh where pleasure lay, pressing hard right there, right there, where Denis had touched her, where Bunny was touching the girl with the cooing voice. Denis. Bunny. She was not even sure whom she had desired at that moment. To be inside the gazebo, touching, seeing. She had never seen Bunny naked. Sin. Sin. To think of a brother so. But she could not force herself to leave. This other girl could see, could touch him. "Let me put it between your breasts. They're so lovely, Clara." The thought of Bunny's male organ between Clara's breasts filled her with excitement as if it were lying between her own. Her finger pressed harder, moving faster and faster bringing her climax.

A few minutes later she saw Bunny and then the girl slip stealthily out of the gazebo, straightening their clothes, smoothing their hair. They did not turn or they would have seen her. And it was then that she recognized Clara and was astounded to discover her as belonging to a family in their own social set. Clara's parents attended dinner parties at the Carles'. Melanie had automatically assumed that the girl with Bunny was a seamstress, governess, even a maid. Those were the women whom men had their fun with. The girls of families like theirs, the girls they met in dancing class and at the debutante balls were sacrosanct, not to be touched until marriage.

This was the first time Melanie had realized that other girls of good family wanted what she did, wanted to rise to that ecstatic spasm to fall again.

A few days later, she heard Bunny mention Clara to his friend Gaynor. "She's so high-spirited and she'll do anything for me. She really likes me."

Gaynor had replied laughing. "Likes to be fucked, you

mean." Melanie had not heard the word before, but the sense of it was plain. "Don't make a fool of yourself, Bunner. Any man will do."

At the recollection of that phrase familiar to her now for other reasons, Melanie shuddered. A ghost walked over her grave was the saying. But it was Bunny in the grave.

"I think you're a fool, Bunner, to take a girl from one of the families we know. Oh, she wants it so much and you're so wonderful. You think you are in luck, and then she gets scared and runs to Papa and next thing you know, the lawyers are meeting in the library and the agreements are being gone over clause by clause. That's why I never touch the girls our family sees socially. I get what I need somewhere else, somewhere safe."

"Not safe from the French disease, my friend."

"You can get rid of the French disease faster than a wife, my friend."

"Maybe it's time for me to change my style," Bunny said laughing. Maybe he had.

Get rid of a wife, get rid of the French disease; Bunny had not needed to do either.

It was years before she would admit to herself that the onanistic pleasure of that day outside the gazebo—one sin augmenting the other—would rarely be matched in intercourse.

Now, looking at the solid front of bosom that had once held Bunny's erect, swollen phallus, Melanie could imagine a faint imprint still, a stain, a whiff of his semen, his perspiration, his body odor. Bunny seemed closer than in years. She could have embraced Clara, torn away the gown, the corset, chemise, and laid her hand where Bunny had lain. So might she feel close again to her dead brother.

She was so overwrought with the emotion that she rose to her feet, seized Clara's hands in hers. Clara blushed a deeper brilliant unlovely crimson. Perhaps she too was remembering Bunny. Clara was wearing a wedding ring. Melanie wondered whether she had "proved" her virginity on her wedding night. The women were exchanging glances. Melanie, always so sensitive, was indifferent, so great was her need to make contact. "I think you were a friend of my brother's, Bunny, Bunner, that is."

Clara looked bewildered. "Bunner?"

"It is a long time ago," said Melanie. Could Clara have forgotten?

Clara's eyes darted about; how shifty the woman looked. Melanie wished she had not spoken. But she was curious now. It seemed important that Clara not have forgotten. Because if she had, Bunny would be that much more dead.

"I remember," said Clara, speaking so quickly that the cooing was gone from the voice and it was just a low, flat tone that you would hardly hear from outside a gazebo. "He was so nice; my mother liked him. She used to say he was a gentlemanly boy, so polite and respectful."

Where in that description was Bunny to be found? Bunny with his easygoing ways and readiness to seduce girls of good family.

Melanie at last became conscious of the attention of the women in the room. There was an awkward silence. She tried to remove herself from the situation, but now Clara would not let her go, became suddenly effusive.

"What do you hear from your sister-in-law, Jocelyn? Or must we now call her the Contessa di Valli?" said a sweet husky voice.

Nellie Woodruff, who had been watching the scene between Melanie and Clara with a faint but unmistakable look of pleasure, turned to stare at Evangeline, who spoke so seldom. Melanie gave a start. How could Evangeline, isolated, cut off from conversation by her handicap have known this would be the one topic certain to turn the conversation?

Jocelyn was Genevieve's eldest daughter, now the triumphant (the triumph being Genevieve's) countess. "The Duke Paolo has just had Jocelyn and the count for the weekend," Genevieve put in happily, "and they will be going to the Italian Riviera next month for the bathing."

Genevieve had the rare ability of recognizing ahead of anyone else where society was heading and had been the first woman in New York's inner circle to arrange a marriage between her daughter and a member of the European nobility in need of the funds the Edmonts were able so amply to provide.

Nellie responded to this account of Genevieve's aristocratic connection with a whisper so loud it was audible throughout the room. "I think the Italian nobility does not hold a candle to the English."

Taking Melanie's arm, Genevieve walked away from the group. "As you know, Melanie, I do not like to make harsh judgments, but I fear that Nellie Woodruff's envy causes her to behave in a crude and boorish way."

Envy. It did not appear so to Melanie. The entire evening had been as carefully plotted as a play. A role had been assigned to her. She wondered what it was.

CHAPTER 9

Luxury, Poverty, and Violence

Huge rats jumped out of overflowing trash barrels. Starved cats fought belly to belly striking one another with emaciated arms and extended claws. The carriage lurched over broken pavements and mud-filled holes.

It had seemed like fun when Harry suggested that Melanie meet him downtown, that he would slip away from his office for an hour or two. This was the week before the Woodruffs' ball and there was a brief hiatus in the schedule of social events in Bourneham. Melanie was in New York at Wallace's urging; it was his wish, virtually his command that she come to take coffee at the Edmont Hotel from time to time. Hardly an exciting way to spend an afternoon. Hardly worth making the long journey by yacht back and forth to Bourneham. Until Harry's suggestion. She would arrive later than expected at the hotel, but who was to know the reason?

They could go to the Van Burghs' town house, Harry told her, his mother and sister being in Bourneham. With

104

foresight when it came to planning this type of endeavor, he had hired a carriage; the Edmont coach could pick her up later. Dena would accompany them, wait downstairs until Melanie called for her help in restoring the formal appearance required for a visit to the Edmont Hotel. With all eyes upon her, she did not dare to go uncorseted.

Upstairs at the Van Burghs' for the first time in many years, she was startled to observe the mahogany furniture had been replaced with pine, the velvety Aubusson rugs with early American. Louise's plight was so grim that she was selling off her possessions. For an instant it seemed as if Louise had stepped into the room right then and was looking at Melanie with reproachful eyes. Melanie shuddered. What was she doing here with this boy? But really, Louise had nothing to reproach her for. This was the way young men were expected to behave, even young men about to be married. The wedding would take place, and once Harry was married, their relationship would be over. That had been understood from the start.

Still, she was conscious of a slight sense of discomfort as she watched Harry undress. With her new awareness, she noticed for the first time that though his suit and shirt were elegant, his underwear was neatly darned. Naked, Harry came towards her smiling and helped her off with her many layers of clothing. How nice it was to look at him, feel him. She had never minded imperfections in a man, but surely it was a pleasure to see a body so perfect, without a hint of future change, to run her hands over that smoothness, that firmness of muscle and skin.

As he drew her down onto the bed, the sheets so soft from many washings, an image flashed through her mind of Iris, who would one day not too far away be lying just so, her legs entwined with his. When Harry bent forward and kissed her throat, Melanie forgot Iris and everything else in her life. It happened each time they were together. She could not understand why when he was not her type at all. *What do you want me to do for you?* Lying in his arms on a sum-

105

mer's afternoon gave her a sense of such ease. She never thought of Harry with the mixture of pain, bitterness, and regret that was locked into her passion for Denis.

The hired carriage returned them to the spot where the Edmont coach had been stationed. The plan was for Harry to leave and Melanie with Dena to proceed uptown to the Edmont Hotel, but no sooner had Harry handed Melanie into the coach than he climbed in after her. He could not bear to leave Melanie a moment earlier than was necessary. They could have another half hour together if he drove with her to the hotel. His work had been at a particularly interesting point when he left, a loan application that looked valid on the face of it, yet he sensed something odd. Perhaps the loan applicant was controlled by Woodruff. Harry liked delving into such matters, calling people he knew to obtain information, but the importance of this project receded in Melanie's presence. His work could wait; anything could wait so long as he was with her. He had wanted her since boyhood, could still scarcely believe that he possessed her.

"Harry," Melanie began to remonstrate. It was charming for him to put his work second, but really the time had come for him to return to his office. Then she broke off; she had no wish to play the sensible older woman, was not his wife to remind him of his duties. And as Woodruff's son-in-law, he really would not need to work hard, if indeed he needed to work at all.

The carriage left the downtown area and starting going north and then east towards Fifth Avenue. Buildings were going up on what had been farmland and the disruption of the construction caused the carriage to pass through streets of incredible squalor. For all his efforts at whipping the horses, it was not possible for Cough, the coachman, to get the carriage through quickly.

From inside the buildings came the clattering, banging, whirring of machines. Shouts, cries, a cacophony of languages. And at every window and on every doorstoop were amassed the indigent idle. Drunken men stumbled out of

106

first-floor grogshops. A murmur, hostile, followed the carriage. A stone, feces covered, and an apple core were thrown and the malefactors quickly lost in the crowd. Who would have thought they would dare? The whole fabric of society was loosening, as her mother-in-law often said.

When they approached Fifth Avenue where the Edmont Hotel stood, only a few blocks from that horror, the carriage stopped short, throwing Melanie sharply against Harry and Dena onto the floor. Looking out, she saw Cough whipping the horses, seeking to shake off a tramp who had seized the reins and was shouting in a harsh gutteral voice. The coach lurched forward as the man released the reins, leaped to the step, wrenched open the door, and stepped within. With fear and horror Melanie saw that he had a knife and for the first time understood that the words he was shouting were "Death to Edmont."

The attacker stood there, the arm with the knife upraised. He was stopped for a moment by the sight of Harry, clearly uncertain whether this young man could really be the dread Edmont, but he had come too far to retreat, and so he lunged. At that same moment Harry rose from his seat and threw himself upon the man. Clutching at the assailant's body in an effort to disarm him, Harry fell with him through the open door of the coach, bumped over the step and onto the ground. The two men struggled there. Harry was much the stronger, but the other had the knife and a madness in him. Immobilized for no more than a few seconds by the shock, Melanie leaped from the carriage to come to Harry's aid. A frilly tangerine-colored silk parasol was her only weapon. As the man rolled over on top of Harry, she struck at his back as hard as she could and was horrified to have the parasol break off in her hands, doing no damage, not even startling him. She looked around for help. Cough was struggling with the horses; Dena was cowering in the corner of the carriage.

The fight went on until Melanie saw the grubby hand with the knife strike at Harry's throat. Aroused by the pain and the closeness of death, with one more violent effort, Harry pulled himself up to a half-sitting position and twisted the hand holding the knife. The weapon fell and rolled into the gutter. Melanie bent down and picked it up out of the dirt. As if the loss of the knife made him lose all heart and spirit, the man went limp. After a moment Harry rose a little shakily to his feet. His clothes were stained with mud and filth. The man had injured him; a cut on his neck was bleeding.

"He might have killed you, Harry."

"It would have been quite a disappointment to him then to learn that I was not Edmont," remarked Harry, smiling at her, the lightness of his tone contradicted by his still gasping breath.

Melanie was too shaken to smile back. And yet lying cowering on the ground, the assailant appeared little more than a bag of rags. Now that the immediate threat was passed, she recognized that but for the lucky chance that Harry had decided to come with her, it would have been she who would have received the attack and most probably been killed. Of course, it was not either luck or chance. Harry was always ready to give up his work for her.

Harry pulled the man to his feet. How thin the arm was, like a matchstick. If he twisted it just a little further, it would snap. Desperation out of a sense of being wronged had given the strength to stop the carriage, wield the knife, if possible to kill. What was to be done with the man whose frail underfed body was trembling in Harry's grip? Disarmed, he no longer seemed dangerous, but merely pathetic, as if that one gesture had worn him out.

The man's eyes were dull, shadowed, until becoming aware that Melanie was staring at him, he raised his head and looked her full in the face. And as he did, it struck her that something about him was familiar. Where had she seen that reddish scraggly beard and sparse red grizzled hair, the inflamed nose and small bloodshot eyes? His hands were very small, with short stubby fingers ending in long broken blackened nails, and his feet, the toes misshapen, were exposed by his torn shoes. She remembered the feet.

108

Melanie recoiled, sickened by the memory this man aroused. Years earlier she had arranged to have Joseph Woodruff meet her in one of the guest rooms of the Fifth Avenue house. He was to slip in through a side door where Dena would be waiting to direct him. Melanie stood outside the guest room listening to the sound of his steps coming down the hall towards her. Without a word she opened the door to the room and had then been driven back by a repellent odor. She would have thought it impossible for such a smell ever to be in her house. Any one of the twenty guest rooms could be put to use at a moment's notice.

She gasped, putting up her perfumed hand to cover her nose. The smell seemed to be one of putrefaction. Could a rodent or a pigeon have gotten into the house and died there? "What is that odor?"

"Don't you know what it is?" asked Joseph; he seemed amused.

"It smells like death."

"Not like death, but like life. Of course you don't know the smell, Melanie. That is the stink of an outhouse, of a water closet that is not cleaned. It is a long time since I lived like that, but it is something you don't forget."

Fascinated, half sick at the smell, she took a step into the room. The sky blue curtains were drawn, but as her eyes became accustomed to the dimness of the room, Melanie saw the man sprawled over the large double bed. No question but that the smell emanated from him. He had wet himself. There were dark patches around the crotch and down the legs of his trousers. Melanie stared at his feet. The toes, crooked, and with a corn on each joint, stuck out through his torn shoes. He had been sleeping, but suddenly awoke, rubbed his eyes with a filthy hand, scratched his reddish, grizzled hair.

It seemed impossible, but he had gotten past the police patrolling the avenue, had somehow scaled the wall, avoided the gatekeeper, the gardeners, the butler, the footmen, the maids, to sneak up the servants' staircase to the room where

Melanie and Joseph made love, to lie with his soiled trousers and muddy boots on the millefleurs brocade bedspread.

He jumped to his feet. How small he was, half a head shorter than Melanie. "I meant no harm," he started babbling. "Thrown out of my room. I'm new in this country. I got no place to go."

"Then you must go to jail," said Joseph firmly, smiling. Melanie could tell he was enjoying the scene.

"I'll hold the man while you ring for a footman," said Joseph. "Then I'll get out of here. I guess the footman knows better than to talk. Once I'm gone, the butler can call the police."

The man was bent over, and Melanie realized he was crying. "It's not right. Not right." He straightened his back then, stealing looks at Joseph, then at Melanie. His eyes focused on her breasts, the cleavage between them, and he drew in his breath sharply, almost whistling. Horrible as the man was, at that moment something passed between them.

The poor had seemed so different to her that they might have belonged to another species. She now realized, and it was for the first time in her life, that though poor, a tramp, he was yet a man, not so different from other men, looking down the bosom of her dress. The dampness made his trousers cling to his crotch. The bulge was clearly outlined. She looked again at the deformed, filthy feet. How far had he walked in his broken shoes? Her hand on the bell's rope, she hesitated. This shattered bit of humanity. What would be done with him?

Later she had suggested to Wallace that they look into alternatives rather than proceeding to prosecution. After all, the man had stolen nothing, had hurt no one.

Wallace had been first shocked, then obdurate. "It is degrading that this . . . this scum has been in my house. He deserves a prison sentence to teach him respect for property."

The episode with the tramp was never again mentioned. And now, suddenly, years later, here was the derelict brandishing a knife in his dirty hands.

Just then the man turned and looked at her and she realized it was not the same tramp after all. This knife wielder appeared familiar to her because he was poor, filthy, and ragged, and the tramp had been the only other poor, filthy man she had ever seen at close range.

"What's to be done with him, Harry?"

"We'll have to let him go. Otherwise the newspapermen at the police station will pick it up and Edmont will learn you were here with me. I don't even want to think how he might react, what that might mean to you. I can't let any harm come to you, Melanie."

It had not even occurred to him to wonder how his employer might react were he to learn the true reason for Harry's absence, Melanie thought. Careers had been destroyed by no more than that.

"And you know, I have a grudging pity for him," Harry continued. "Imagine what his life must be. And I don't think he's a danger anymore. This was his one chance and he missed it."

Relaxing his grip, Harry let the tramp get away and in an instant he was lost in the crowd. Harry clasped Melanie's hand hurriedly and disappeared down the street as well.

Cough and Dena were staring at her, numb with astonishment. "Never speak of this to anyone."

When Cough handed Melanie down at the hotel a few minutes later, she was aware that he was eyeing her askance. One never explains to servants, Denis had said as the blood and semen ran down her legs to form a pool on the parquet floor.

That evening Wallace was horrified to learn of the detour through the slum blocks. (Melanie did not mention the man with the knife.) Melanie's experience was one more proof that the proximity of the slum blocks was at the root of his problems with the Edmont Hotel.

Profits were disappointing, yet the plan, he was still convinced, was sound: he had created a hotel more elegant than any other in the entire United States. The time was propitious, as steamships were crossing the Atlantic with in-

111

creasing frequency, bringing wealthy Europeans to New York in numbers too great for all to be accommodated in the homes of their friends. They perforce stayed in hotels adequate for ordinary businessmen perhaps, but not for those accustomed to the very best of furnishings and services.

In contrast, paintings of the French Barbizon school and the Italian Renaissance hung in the public rooms of the Edmont Hotel. Rugs had been imported from Persia, tapestries from Belgium. Furniture was inlaid with rare woods, mother-of-pearl, and onyx. There were five hundred huge bedrooms, their walls covered with silk, and private bathrooms having marble floors and gilded fixtures. It was a hotel with more servants than guests. Room service, hitherto unknown in American hotels, was available at any hour.

But the hotel could not live up to its promise so long as the stench of garbage and human wastes assaulted the senses of those approaching from the wrong direction. Something had to be done. He must make use of every possibility that offered itself. This fire at the Heron garment factory yesterday had been in one of Quigley's ill-kept tenements, lacking all safety precautions. He knew how men like Quigley thought: they rejected fireproofing as too costly. If the careless tenants did not smoke in their beds, fires would not break out. Maybe so. But he would not care to be Quigley today. Women had died. Children.

Jessop would have to be instructed to make an immediate offer to Quigley for his entire row of dilapidated tenements. After the losses incurred by the fire, Quigley would need the money too badly to hold out any longer. There was no room for sentiment in business. And, of course, his refraining from buying Quigley out would not bring one person back to life. If he did not buy the tenements, someone less responsible, more greedy, would do so and replace the burned-out shell with the shoddiest of tenements, setting the stage for another fire.

In the wake of the fire would come a host of new legislative hearings and regulations. Worse yet, once legislators saw how advantageous such rulings were to them politically, they would go on intruding into areas they knew nothing about. Only four or five years ago a regulation had actually been passed prohibiting the manufacture of tobacco products in the tenements. Cigar making was one of the most profitable of home manufacturing ventures, profitable for workers as well as owners. Of course it had proved possible to have the law declared unconstitutional, but achieving that exceedingly reasonable judgment had taken a great deal of time and a great sum of money.

At the back of one of the ledgers listing properties he no longer held was a list known only to Jessop. Year by year were listed Wallace's contributions to political campaigns, his gifts to politicians, to judges, to commissioners.

Wallace kept his list of influential politicians up-to-date, crossing off a man who had lost an election or been charged with fraud, adding another who was rising to power through inheritance of wealth or by marriage or ability. Every aspect of urban life affected real estate. It was necessary to purchase information as well as votes. If a thoroughfare were to be cut through farmland, a new trolley car line or elevated constructed, a new bus route opened, the person who knew that first was the person to prosper.

Repugnant as he found such dealings, they were a necessary part of doing business in the 1890s. How else could he have been appointed a member of the most recent commission to investigate conditions in the tenements, a commission formed in response to public outcry (aroused by such newspapers as the *Journal*, no doubt)?

CHAPTER 10
Marital Strife

Every so often, and she never knew when it would be, she would feel a sudden desire for his heavy body under his heavy clothes. Prepared for the night, she would open the door of her room, and wait for the sound of his step going down the corridor from his study to his bedroom. Her heart would pound and her breathing quicken as she would beckon him into the softly lit, warm, perfumed room. And for a little while it would all be true, the excitement, passion. "My own Wally." "My prince." All true.

He would be slow in his movements; he was always slow-moving. But when she wanted him, his very slowness aroused her. Clasping him to her, feeling the heat in the groin, the wetness between her legs, she could not believe how often she had needed to pretend desire without feeling. Afterwards lying beside him, holding his hand, she would feel for him a strange emotion compounded of love, regret, compassion, and peace. They had been together so long, had, for all their differences, so many memories in common. He was the constant in her life; she was in his.

It was said that she dominated him with her temper. An exaggeration. Wallace gave as good as he got, was a stubborn, dogged adversary in argument, refusing to yield on the most minor matters.

Wallace was not so quick as she to take a point, make a clever remark. She was always surprised that he was so brilliant a businessman, an impressive figure in the world of commerce, bold and foresighted, yet how careful of details. Seeing him in his study was to see another man. When they were engaged (he had spoken to her of business then), he had boasted in a quiet way that he could tell her at any moment the exact state of any one of his myriad pieces of property.

Returning home after the Woodruffs' ball, Melanie felt exhausted by the nervous strain of the conversation with Elmer Morgen. It had been instinctive for her to defend Wallace, but she was unable to put Morgen's words out of her mind. Could Wallace have been involved in the fire after all? Not directly, of course; at the most he might have suggested some minor harassment and it had gotten out of hand.

As she mounted the stairs, her gown's long train lined with dozens of rows of protective dust ruffles weighed her down, pulled her body backwards.

She could hardly wait to reach her bedroom. The atmosphere of this room never failed to calm her. Designed and built in Paris in the workshop of Allard and Sons, it had been dismantled, crated, and sent to Bourneham along with the French craftsmen who would put it together again. The room was shaped to form an oval; even the glass in the windows overlooking the lawn and the ocean had been blown to maintain the curve.

When she was lying on her chaise longue, Melanie could see the lighthearted paintings by Fragonard reflected in the mirror. On one wall hung a botanical drawing that Junior had made for her last birthday. The fresco on the ceiling depicted the sky at sunrise. I like the mornings, she had told Morgen. That is when the day is young and full of hope.

As she walked down the hall, she observed that the lamps in Wallace's study were still lit. On an impulse she went in. Tonight at the Woodruffs' ball she had been required to make a show of loyalty, and having done the right thing, she felt a degree of warmth for Wallace that had become rare to her. She approached the desk; his ledgers were, as she knew they would be, open.

Becoming aware of her presence, he slammed the ledgers shut. She felt her face getting hot and drew back, her good feelings about him vanishing abruptly. Strange that after so many years his harsh rejection of her interest in his work should still rankle.

Long after she was married, she had remained an avid reader of the *Wall Street Journal* and the *Commercial and Financial Chronicle*, missing no detail of the financing of Andrew Carnegie's steel mills, John D. Rockefeller's Standard Oil Company, Astor's real estate empire, and Woodruff's intricate maneuvers to expand and consolidate his iron ore and coke oven holdings. Observing the role of the great banking houses, she was dismayed that Carle & Company was inactive in financing industrial expansion or serving as intermediary in business deals.

As a bridegroom Wallace had put up three million dollars to save Carle & Company during the panic that followed the collapse of Jay Cooke's bank in 1873, and had been called upon many times thereafter. Her father had no daring, no foresight. After much hesitation, when he was already suffering from the pulmonary congestion that was to kill him, her father finally called a distant cousin, Desmond Carle, to help run the bank and in time take it over. The man had nothing to recommend him except the Carle name and relationship. He had never run a large business nor shown any particular aptitude.

After her father's death, Melanie had arranged to meet Desmond, ostensibly to discuss the provisions of the will,

116

but actually to broach a suggestion so daring, so unusual, that she had been unable to sleep since it first came to her.

Melanie's plan was for her to become the operating head of the company, leaving Desmond as titular head. She knew how essential was gender. Approval by the board of directors would still be a problem, but with a strong recommendation from Desmond, she thought they could be brought around. Melanie had expected Desmond to be receptive to such a plan. Each time he paid one of his duty calls to Melanie and her mother he complained how heavy the burden, how much he needed relief, yet whom could one trust with a family business? From the way he kept glancing at her figure, surreptitiously but suggestively, it occurred to Melanie that he saw a love affair rather than a business relationship between them. There was no man so seemingly bloodless or dull that he did not view himself as a lover. It might be an advantage in putting forward her plan. But the cousin simply had not grasped what she was talking about for a time and when he did he saw it as a rich woman's whim. She looked at his face, unlined for a man of his years, thought of his unimaginative, cautious approach to finance. But there it was. Any man would do. Any man. Harry. Anybody. Not she.

She never told Wallace about this attempt, thinking that had he known, he would have laughed at her. As it was, he continued to provide infusions of capital to keep the bank afloat under Desmond as he had in her father's lifetime. Major shares of stock in the bank had been left to Melanie and her mother and she would, upon her mother's death, be the largest stockholder. Wallace viewed it his duty as husband and son-in-law to protect this source of income, but the banking business did not excite him as did property and he never gave it his personal stamp.

The knowledge of what she could have done angered her as she watched Carle & Company miss the opportunities being seized by Morgan, Brown Brothers, and Kidder, Peabody to make financial deals and control vast industrial interests through credit lines.

Then one day she saw the situation clearly. There was nothing she could have done, nothing that business acumen on her part could have achieved that would have compared in any way with what she had done for her father, for the bank, in marrying Wallace and bringing a never-ending source of capital. It was one of the bitterest moments of her life.

Wallace heard the click of her heels as she climbed the marble stairs, then the rustle of her gown as the train trailed across the floor, and was unaccountably annoyed by the sounds. Here he sat, consumed with worry, while she was enjoying herself, sweeping the floor heedlessly at a ball given by that scoundrel Woodruff. Oh, he could just imagine how she had been, with what interest she had turned to her dinner partner, leaning forward, her eyes melting, toying with her food, her manner indicating that it was of no interest compared to what he was saying. Clara was to be at the ball, too. That was one of the reasons he had not gone. There was no gossip (he was sure of that), but still it was best to be careful, even excessively so. He must first complete his plan, work out with Merwyn James, his lawyer, what settlement to offer. He would not be foolish enough to take the blame. George Carrington, a fellow member of the Union League Club, had done the so-called gentlemanly thing, and what was the result? Elena Carrington had gotten the houses, the land, and heaven knows what else in the settlement.

What sort of a settlement should he agree to? Melanie spent money as if it fell from the heavens on command, but he would not have her scrounge for it like Louise Van Burgh. There would also be separate funds for the children. The children. He could not quite reconcile himself to that aspect of a divorce. They would go with their mother; there was no other way. And he had to concede that she cared for them.

He forced his thoughts back to Clara. Here was his chance to be with a woman, easy and gentle, interested in him, not herself, not obsessed with her appearance, not extravagant or willful. Clara was large, a bit stout, somewhat older than Melanie, but satisfied to be middle-aged. Her clothes were well made yet unexceptional, her blond hair mixed with gray, her face lined, free of cosmetics. She had a strange voice, though; he did not like it. Seated beside her, he would think how soft her body was. He could sink into it, rest in it. She would seek no lovers, behave in no way the scandal sheets could pick up, never drive him mad with jealousy—all the times he had come home to find Melanie glowing. There was no getting used to the forced knowledge of her affairs, the glances when they would enter a room together. He knew what people were thinking, were saying when his back was turned.

But even while Wallace was telling himself that divorce was wise and overdue and the only thing to do, he had almost physically the sensation of holding Melanie's body in his arms. Wally, my prince, the loving things she would say when the mood took her. Never again. Better not to think about that. Think instead of her irritability, the way she snapped at him over nothing, it seemed. Clara was never irritable.

The door opened and Melanie was standing there, graceful in mauve lace. She had insisted on his buying her amethysts in a shade to match the dress. He had demurred, reminding her that she already had amethysts. But these were too purple or not purple enough, and considering the way she carried on when crossed, it was easier to let her have her way. Money. How Melanie could spend it.

And now there was that camel. Could anyone have devised a more ridiculous extravagance? It had been all he could do to prevent her from stabling a wild beast that could barely be contained in a menagerie with his valuable horses. He wondered what it had cost to transport the camel here. Probably as much as the improvements on a nice bit of property on Avenue A or Essex Street.

"Well, how much is it? What is it costing?"

She stared at him, bewildered.

"The camel. The blasted camel for your ball."

Melanie's intention had been to give him an account of

her confrontation with Elmer Morgen, but with Wallace glaring at her, she had no choice but to answer: "Not so much, really. It's quite a bargain when you consider that the camel had to be brought from the menagerie in New York in a cart specially built for the trip and its trainer and an assistant had to come along." She thought it too insignificant to mention the extra workmen, each being paid three dollars a day, or the cost of the sand, the ramp, the little shed being constructed on the back lawn to shelter the camel on the day of the ball. "I think the whole thing will come to five thousand dollars. Perhaps a little more, perhaps a little less."

"Consider this. Consider that. Consider that you will in time succeed in ruining me with your extravagance." The topic was raised each time they quarreled, regardless of what they were quarreling about. Well, of course, they did not really quarrel about anything but their mutual discontent.

"Not at all, Wallace. You attract even more money than you otherwise might because I spend it where it shows— not in private printings of my family history." Despite the provocation, it was a mean remark, and as soon as it was spoken, she would have recalled it. A weakness to be unable to resist the outrageous when it was merely rude or cutting rather than witty.

Wallace's interest in his family was his one great enthusiasm outside of business. He spent hours in research and tens of thousands of dollars sending scholars to Europe to trace his forebears. An expanded volume was published every five years, privately. The latest scholar had managed to find a link with royalty many generations back, an ancestor killed in the French Revolution during a peasant uprising, impossible to verify or prove false.

Intolerable for Melanie to talk in this manner. She appeared to delight in opposing him. His search for familial origins was a worthy activity for a man with children; he was doing it for them, whereas Melanie's spending was beyond all reason. And though no one recognized better than he the commercial value derived from appearing to have limitless liquid assets, he sensed a change coming. Other successful businessmen sneered at journalists seeking the sensational by attacking the rich; Wallace did, too, but he learned from them. Others saw only that workers' strikes were broken, that pay scales could be dropped when times were bad. They were secretly proud of the infinite detail with which the furnishings of their mansions, the elaborate nature of their balls were described. Sometimes it seemed to Wallace that he alone was troubled by the juxtaposition of society news and reports of strikes (the Homestead mill workers' strike against Carnegie had lasted five months, after all) and the increasing unemployment following the business collapses during the panics of 1890 and 1893 (when he had once again been forced to rescue Carle & Company). His fellow businessmen despised public opinion, but it was bad business to allow the public to become disaffected. And here was Melanie, unregenerate.

"You change the subject when it does not suit you," he said coldly. "The fact remains that there are more important things for you to do than bring camels into a civilized society. I would be ashamed to have no better idea of how to use my energies and money." Sanctimonious, she thought. "Is it possible you do not recognize all I have done to keep Carle & Company from going bankrupt? It would certainly be less costly for me to give your mother an allowance. Instead I have sought to protect your family's good name."

A bankruptcy in the family would have reflected on him, Melanie thought bitterly, bad for his business, too.

"Now there is more for me to worry about. As you will be the majority stockholder, the directors naturally have called me in. Desmond Carle is getting older and unfortunately he has no heir. As usual, overburdened with work as I am, it is left to me to resolve the problem, to find someone else to succeed him as bank president." There was a pause, and seeing the way she was looking at him, he gave a supercilious smile. "I suppose you think it should be you. Is not being a wife and mother enough for you? It is a sacred vocation for most women."

She was close to hating him, his condescension, his refusal to see her as anything but his possession. She tried and failed to recapture the feeling she had had when defending Wallace to Elmer Morgen. "You know I love my children and perform my . . ." For a moment she could not think how to put it. ". . . social duties as your wife. But I am a person who can do all that—and more. You have never taken me seriously; you have insisted that I spend my life in the drawing room, the ballroom, never where things are happening." Unable to help herself, she was raising her voice, even knowing that he would respond in a quiet manner and that the servants would describe this as a typical Edmont quarrel dominated by her temper.

"I think you have done the insisting. You live for all the things my money makes possible. A woman who must spend forty thousand dollars for clothes in a single year, squander five thousand dollars to transport a camel from New York, and import gallons of French perfume at a hundred and fifty dollars an ounce to spray in the air must have an indulgent and wealthy husband like me."

Pity it was the boy.

"You should take up charitable work, Melanie. Other women do." Clara, he thought, newly returned from the Midwest, was already heading a committee at Trinity Church—preparing tracts for missionaries, he believed.

"I have been thinking about a charity. Perhaps I should start a Bourneham branch of the Malthusian League. Or if that does not suit your principles, what would you say to my joining the Society for the Suppression of Vice?" This was, as always, the point in a quarrel when she turned to sarcasm. "I could participate in their next raid on pharmacists covertly selling contraceptives."

Wallace was annoyed, though he assumed she was joking. Melanie often complained that he lacked a sense of humor. Well, if charity were a topic for humor, then she was right. In another moment, he thought, she would be talking about woman suffrage, another topic on which she was misguided. She announced at regular intervals that she wished

122

to stand with Lucy Stone, Elizabeth Cady Stanton, and Susan B. Anthony in fighting for the vote when everyone knew the movement was carried on by ugly women with no better opportunities in life. She would make herself and him a laughingstock.

"I suppose you will next be saying you would like to join the National American Suffrage Association. Even the name is ridiculous."

Melanie knew that other women dared to join the movement despite the opposition of their husbands while she could not withstand Wallace's pressure. He was a ruthless man in business; she knew him capable of finding a way to stop her. For all her display of independence, she dared not take this stand without winning his approval. *You may not look at my ledgers.* And for more than twenty years she had obeyed. It was said that she ruled Wallace, but she was helpless. For all her high spirits and demands he ruled her life.

"The name may be redundant, but the aim is clear and true."

"Even most women don't think that. Why I remember hearing the last time I was in England that one of your heroines, what's her name, Lydia Becker, and her suffrage society are backing the idea of excluding wives from the vote— just giving it to widows and spinsters who don't have the good fortune of having a man to look after and care for them."

"Lydia Becker is not one of my heroines. I think she is endangering the cause of suffrage." She was surprised Wallace knew so much about women active in politics, tending to think him indifferent to everything that did not affect his business.

"And would you prefer the backing of a worthless adulterer like Henry Ward Beecher?" asked Wallace. "There's a supporter of women's rights for you—the right to be debauched by him, a preacher having to stand in the dock at a public trial of his morals."

Beecher's trial for the seduction of Libby Tilton had taken place some two decades earlier and had ended in disagreement by the jury, but Wallace brushed aside Melanie's efforts to point that out. He was in full stride. "You get your ideas from those ridiculous books you read. What was that Mill thing I saw on your table the other day? *Subjection of Women,* I think it was called. I would like to see what women are being subjected to, except having too much money. That's all you know how to do, spend money."

What a mean man Wallace could be, she thought, and to the world outside, he presented so calm an exterior that she alone was blamed for the quarrels the servants duly described.

"Maybe we would know how to do other things if we had the vote and opportunities that men do. Men have not made such a success of the world."

"Can you really think that giving the vote to a silly woman like Nellie Woodruff is going to improve the world? Nellie would pick among political candidates on the basis of who was the handsomer, came from an older family, or had not snubbed her at the opera Monday night."

"Joseph Woodruff is no better. And he does have the vote."

"Woodruff is a scoundrel, but I would not call him silly. He has built up a business worth millions of dollars; he is one of the most powerful men in the Northeast."

"No one ever wanted a useful life more than I, Wallace. That was how I saw our marriage. I wanted to work with you side by side, to help you."

Not that again, he thought, in exasperation. "Now I suppose we're going to hear again how your father never gave you a chance to run his business." He recalled how charming he had thought her interest in his work before they were married. But what had seemed delightful in an engaged girl appeared singularly unsuitable for a married woman. There was more than enough for a woman in her position to do, activities suitable for a wife, for his wife, to be exact.

"Times are changing," said Melanie. "I would like to think that Rosamunde will have the vote."

"The best thing you can do for Rosamunde is to prepare her for marriage and then find her a good husband."

Melanie began to reply: perhaps they would find her the ruler of a small kingdom in the Balkans—and then suddenly in the midst of the quarrel she lost her momentum. It was always like this. She would all at once remember that she was the one who was wronging him, that she was unfaithful to him. Then she would tell herself that she did her part in the marriage, had given him the son he needed as heir, the daughter he loved, made their home magnificent, did him credit with her beauty, her entertaining. None of these would appear to balance the wrong she did him. And there was no changing it. Life would be unbearable without Harry, without the hope for Denis. She could not give this up. Her voice trailed off and she left the victory to him.

It was then that she remembered Morgen. Knowing the danger he was in, she suddenly saw Wallace as vulnerable. "There was a man at the Woodruffs'," she began tentatively. "The editor of the *Journal*."

Wallace stared at her, startled by the change of subject. "The *Journal*?" he repeated; then as it sank in: "My God, Nellie will invite anyone to her disreputable affairs. And with my mother and wife present! I know the fellow—Elmer Morgen. He will say and write anything for effect. He doesn't know the first thing about how a gentleman should behave. I had him investigated: his father was an unschooled immigrant, worked as a porter. This is very odd. Woodruff has been threatening to send thugs to beat the man up for the articles he wrote about Woodruff's calling in the Pinkertons to shoot down the strikers." Wallace smiled thinly. "He made Woodruff out to be callous, monstrous. And Morgen was at the Woodruff ball after this. I wonder what it means. I don't like it." He frowned at Melanie. "What do you know about all this?"

"He talked to me about you."

"Do you mean to tell me that scoundrel dared to address you?"

"Nellie seated him next to me at dinner." It was only a slight exaggeration; certainly Nellie had planned for that to happen.

Wallace struck the surface of his desk. "So you—I indirectly—were their motive in inviting Morgen. That explains it. They had the intention of getting at me through you. But how? I still don't see that. Tell me. What did Morgen say? Did he try to get information about me from you?" Without waiting for her to reply, he went on. "The Woodruffs are immoral as well as shameless. I knew you should not have gone; I should have stopped you. The thought crossed my mind that they were quite capable of using your presence for some purpose of their own. But my mother had decided to attend and I have never questioned her judgment. This time, though, I fear she was in error. My mother is so good a woman she could not conceive how creatures like the Woodruffs behave."

Melanie had to concede the accuracy of this remark. Genevieve's only criticism of the Woodruffs had been their lack of breeding.

"Well, what did he find to say about me?"

"It was the fire at the Heron factory. He was there, saw them leaping from the windows. Many were killed. A heart-rending scene, he said it was."

"Yes, yes. I hear it was a tragedy on the grand scale. One of Quigley's buildings, you know, and he always looks for the cheapest way to do anything. It doesn't pay in the long run. Now all of us who own property, those who take good care of it as well as those who like Quigley use it heedlessly for quick profit, will suffer. There will be another of these endless, useless, costly investigations by incompetent city employees, demands for regulations. Wasting my time, interfering."

At last he paused. Uncertain of the best way of rephrasing Morgen's taunts, she began hesitantly. "He made an insinuation."

Wallace's face was grim. "I am not surprised. I knew he

would make everyone believe the fire was in one of my buildings. Quigley is small-fry, too small a fish. Not worth attacking. An Edmont, now there is a name to conjure with. This kind of suggestion is the hardest to counter. To deny it is to give it life."

"It is worse than that. He says you wanted that property, Wallace, because of the Edmont Hotel, and that the owner refused to sell."

Wallace turned white. "He could not! Not even he could dare to suggest that I ordered arson! But, of course, he did. That is what you are telling me, is it not, Melanie?"

She nodded.

"The scum. Excuse me for using so crude a word. Did he say it outright?"

"He put it that people are saying so."

"Who besides you heard him?"

"I don't think anyone else could have; he was speaking very softly, for my ears alone." Wallace frowned and looked down and she realized she had spoken carelessly, made him aware of the implications of that intimacy. She went on hurriedly. "We were fortunate that the person nearest to us was Evangeline Van Burgh."

They had been sitting together, dinner partners, and close by, Harry Van Burgh's sister. Totally deaf it was said. But who could be certain of that? And even if true the girl might have guessed something from the intensity of the conversation, ask her brother about it, and the less that family knew about the Edmonts the better.

"I wonder how Morgen plans to handle this situation. He is a skillful journalist, I must give him that. He names names seldom, only when it is possible to obtain absolute proof, as with Woodruff's handling of the strike. Lacking that, he depends on innuendo. Much like the editor of our own *Bugle*, wouldn't you say, Melanie?"

Despite her long schooling at self-control, she gasped: he had read the *Bugle*. That was the reason why this quarrel, for all its similarity to hundreds of past quarrels, had yet seemed different, nastier, more venomous. One small item, snidely worded.

"My wife," he said. "And you allow fools to laugh at you and through you at me. You allow a dangerous man to maneuver you into a tête-à-tête for everyone to see. Do you think I will put up with this sort of thing forever? My patience is not limitless."

This was the moment, he thought. Now he had gone far enough to continue to the end, to make the break. But he hesitated again; as many times as he had determined to proceed, so many times had he drawn back.

Melanie, appalled by his words and what she sensed in his voice, saw in his face, rushed into the silence with a flood of words, placating, gentle, Rosamunde and her sweetness, anything. She stood on the brink of the abyss; somehow she had to find her way back to safety. Wallace could not mean what he was implying; it was a part of the quarrel. But she was afraid, shivered—a ghost walked over her grave, as Miss Robertson used to say. A breach was unthinkable. Couples were incompatible, said nasty, bitter things to one another, but they did not . . . give one another up. Her position would be untenable. Talk of suffrage. Talk of opportunities to play a part in business life. When it came right down to it, a woman was as nothing in their society without a man. A protector. Harry was to be Iris's protector. Denis? He had not come to her rescue before; he would not now. It was months since she had heard from him. She had been a fool to quarrel with Wallace now, with the *Bugle* item fresh. She returned to Morgen: "I informed him firmly and without question that such a suggestion could only be brought out of malice, in a vile attempt to damage your reputation." She caught his eye, held it. "I think I was convincing; I should have been. Because that is what I believe, Wallace. I am, after all, your . . . helpmeet . . . your wife."

Those words stopped him from speaking further. The harshness with which he had addressed her earlier embarrassed him. He could not doubt that in the crisis she had spoken as she claimed. Her disloyalty took a different form. And yet surely Melanie was his greatest liability; he wanted to think that. It made easier his flight to Clara. "Even so," he said finally, speaking so quietly she had to strain to hear him, "no matter what Nellie had planned, I know you too well to believe you would have accepted a dinner partner you did not care to sit beside." He stood up, preparing to leave the room.

She was so tired but afraid to let him go. He had read the *Bugle*, had turned the conversation with Morgen against her. Somehow she had to gain control over the evening. My patience is not limitless, he had said. Tired, but she dared not be too tired for the one course of action that had turned away trouble in the past.

"It's late, Wallace." Her voice, soft, throbbing, emphasized his name ever so slightly. Your helpmeet . . . your wife.

"Should I ring for Dena? Or would you help me unfasten my gown and open the laces?"

His tensions drained away and the atmosphere in the room lightened.

She bent towards him. Oh, he knew her ways, that almost imperceptible bending movement from the waist, just enough to draw the attention to the cleavage between the full beautiful breasts. A practiced movement. He knew that, had seen her practicing in front of a mirror. How she could disarm him. He remembered one time returning home after overhearing gossip about her, he had turned on her, accusing her of everything but what he knew she was. It was impossible for him to admit his knowledge. For once she did not pick up the quarrel and only bent forward in that way and said, "But what would you have me do?" She had spoken so simply and with such sweetness, that what was there for him to do but take her in his arms, caress, stroke, hold? How she could disarm him.

The invitation still had the power to excite. How many men, he thought, with his old sense of pride, had wives of

129

such seductiveness? She was his. He forced the thought away. He was determined to break away. This was no life—quarreling like cat and dog, mendacity upon mendacity, betrayal on betrayal. He had his fill. But he had not realized until recently, until Clara, how Melanie had changed him, what she had brought him to do, to need the seductions that had once so shocked him. Without his noticing. How had it happened? Clara would be the one to be shocked, he thought, smiling at the irony, were she to know that sometimes he came to Melanie's bed without his nightshirt, the lamp still lit. Once he had lain with Melanie on the floor of his study, on the rug, his head whirling as he looked down at the swirls of designs created, he had been told, by starving hallucinating weavers in Persia hundreds of years earlier. Melanie would take on a husband like this, like a lover.

Clara, Clara: her body was ample, stout really, not like the voluptuous figure bending towards him. But he could rest on Clara's bosom, secure, pillowed. Think of the repose, the restorative quality of the calm, tranquil, smooth, easy. At the same time, he was imagining, no remembering, how it was to unfasten that long row of hooks and eyes, so tiny they resisted his clumsy, eager fingers. And the way at last the gown would fall forward and she would turn to stand before him, her shoulders and then her breasts revealed with the faint blue tracery of veins contrasting with the whiteness of her skin. He knew she at least sometimes created that tracery, had come into her dressing room once unexpectedly to see Dena touch Melanie's breasts with a blue-stained finger. Like a courtesan, he had thought. But what did it matter when, as now, it was for him? Her breath came quickly, almost panting already. For him. And when he would unlace the brocaded corset slowly, oh, so slowly and take it off and the sheer chiffon chemise beneath, he would gently touch the red marks outlining her slender waist, the harsh bruises left on her soft skin by the whalebone ribs. She would reach out and take a jar from her dressing table, open and hold it out to him to take the pink, fluffy scented cream on his fingers, to rub on the marks, over and over, his fingers, then his lips. He did not want to think of it, to allow his desire to take control of him.

Clara, Clara: she was his future, his hope for peace. Not Melanie with the shrill tone that would come into her voice when angry, the barely concealed impatience, the discontent, the extravagance, the vanity, the infidelities. He said her faults over and over, a litany. He tried to summon the memory of the pleasing, fresh lemony scent that Clara wore. But it was overpowered by Melanie's perfume, musky, woody, green, the fragrance one might come upon within a grove of flowering trees, a perfume like no other, specially blended in Paris for Melanie alone, he knew at what excessive cost. To press his lips and tongue up and down and inside that hot perfumed body.

Wallace stood immobile, wishing not to yield to the desire he felt. He threw out his hand as if to push her away, but the gesture was weak. Melanie reached out, undid the buttons on his trousers and placed her hand inside. Tumescent, hard. She fastened the top button again, led him by the hand down the hall to the dressing room, the scented cream, the bedroom, the satin sheets.

CHAPTER 11

Iris
"Needs" Harry

As soon as Harry started down the walk to the house, his spirits sank. The pavement was broken and the weeds had taken root in the cracks, the lawn was brown in spots and shaggy, the rose garden for which the cottage had been named was a mass of tangled stems with drooping heads. A single gardener, and he close to eighty and coming but twice a summer, could not restore the damage. Nonetheless at first glance, Rose Cottage still had dignity; well designed, it represented the best of late eighteenth-century architecture. A closer look revealed that the blue paint on the wooden exterior had peeled off in great strips and the mansard roof needed repair. Upon entering the house, the initial impression was also one of grandeur, for the first object to meet the eye was an enormous mirror, twenty feet in width, twelve in height, with a heavy gilded frame boasting a design of entwined leaves and clusters of grapes with drops of dew. The mirror had been imported from France a hundred years earlier by Harry's great-great-grandfather and was his mother's proudest possession, though to seek one's reflection was to see a wavering distortion in the worn-off silvering.

A familiar depression that he felt nowhere else seized Harry as he stood on the doorstep waiting for Agatha to respond to his knock. He knew how slowly and painfully, head down and shoulders stooped, she would make her way from the kitchen or dining room to the front door.

Inside, even at the height of summer with brilliance all around, the house was dim. The curtains in the parlor were drawn all afternoon to protect the color of the Oriental rugs, the few paintings left, the damask, velvet, and needlepoint upholstery worked in a flower pattern, the sole indication that this was a summer cottage after all. As in the New York town house, the upstairs furnishings had been secretly sold off room by room.

His father's former business manager, Donald Kirby, regularly came to call on Louise and advise her on managing her small sums of money. Harry determined to enlist Kirby's support to induce his mother to sell Rose Cottage. She could still come to Bourneham for the season by taking rooms in the best hotel, the Ocean House. He had suggested it before, but Louise refused to discuss it.

No sooner was Harry home than he longed to be elsewhere. At Île de Joie the flowers were brighter than anywhere else; the sun streamed in through every window, reflected in crystal chandeliers, in mirrored walls that also reflected Melanie's image, her brown eyes shining, her dark hair lustrous. When alone with him, she would draw the curtains and little bands of gold crept through, making a magical world.

Hearing his step, his mother came in. She had taken on the soft faded look of her house. Even now she was attractive, with her slender waist, long curving neck, and swaying walk. Were wealth restored, she would quickly be able to assume the proper look and manner, showing no signs of the years of deprivation.

Out of the corner of his eye Harry caught sight of the *Bourneham Bugle*, lying on the bois de rose end table with the chipped legs, so neatly folded that it might seem to the casual observer not to have been read at all. But of course it had been read down to the belittling paragraph. It was not the insinuation about the affair with Melanie that rankled, but that catchphrase "summer toy" reduced him. No one could say he did not work. Still, it was true that the other day the manager of the bank had remarked on the amount of time he was taking off this summer. It had not seemed like so much to Harry, considering how enticing were afternoons with Melanie. Nonetheless from now on he would try harder to prove himself.

As was the custom, Harry had been apprised of the forthcoming item (though not its snide wording) by editor Armand Wolfe and been given every opportunity, indeed almost been begged, to buy the man off. Bribery, blackmail really, was paid all the time, as Harry was well aware. But he did not have the money. If only this had come up a week later, he would have been able to pay. George de Witte, ever the gambler, had put up five thousand dollars as a prize for a swimming race across the narrows, a distance of eight and a half miles. Harry and Andrew Arnold had accepted the challenge and the date had been set. Contests of this nature were held every summer and Harry had come to count on them to augment his inadequate earnings, to give his mother a sum that would briefly make her smile. Harry was sure he would win the race; Andrew Arnold was not in as good condition, had the beginnings of a paunch. Arnold had declared and been quoted to that effect in the more reputable local newspaper, the *Bourneham Gazette*, that if he won he would donate the prize to the Men's Club to pay for paneling the bar room. Anyone else would see through this gesture as done out of malice, a malice all the nastier for posing as generosity, a slap at Harry's penurious state. But Harry could think ill of no one. Old Andrew and he had always been friends. Harry saw this action as inspired by Andrew's competitiveness, a trait that had been in evidence since boyhood.

To his surprise his mother did not mention the *Bugle*, but gave him a letter with trembling hand. "One of the Woodruffs' footmen brought it." The Woodruffs had a telephone; the Van Burghs, of course, had none.

Iris needed—the word was underlined—to see him at once. But if he went to Villa del Destino now, he might miss being with Melanie that afternoon. She had said to come early if he came at all, for she was to go and practice riding that accursed camel. At the thought of Melanie, Iris faded slightly, like his mother, like his sister, like the furniture in his home.

Harry had not seen Melanie since the Woodruffs' ball, having left for New York on the Olneys' yacht immediately afterwards. But Tuesday he had been too uneasy to settle to his work at the bank and had rushed back to Bourneham by train and boat. He could not stand it, had to reassure himself today that nothing of importance had passed between Melanie and that journalist at the Woodruffs' ball. If he could just see her, he would know without asking.

"What does Iris say?" At last Louise could not resist the question.

"She says she needs to see me."

"Needs?" Louise appeared quite cheered by the choice of word. "Go. Make the most of it."

Harry found his mother's insistence particularly troublesome today, because Mrs. Woodruff's coldness to him at her ball had been marked. He meant to repair the damage as quickly as possible and would speak with Iris's father, who for once was staying in Bourneham through the week. He found it hard to explain to himself, let alone his mother, why he had been so dilatory. He loved Iris. It was not just that he was flattered by her obvious adoration. That was the odd part. He was as fully convinced as his mother that Iris was the right bride for him. When they stood together her whole body seemed to bend towards him. His feelings about

Iris were quite separate from his passion for Melanie. He never thought what the future without Melanie would really be like, intended to be a good husband.

In his mother's presence, he felt the *Bugle* would have been more accurate describing him as the Woodruffs' rather than Melanie's toy. He paid his own way with her, and not with his family name and lineage. He had heard the jokes; they had increased in number since the *Bugle* item. "Does she give the orders in bed, Harry?" "Move this. Put that there." Expressed more crudely, of course. It did not bother him; he alone knew her to be so different as a lover from what others believed. No one could be more responsive to a touch, turning to him, yielding to him, whispering, caressing, all his own.

Observing his withdrawal, Louise could not keep herself from saying the words that when calm she knew were best unsaid: "You must break with Melanie Edmont. How can you, Harry? She's practically as old as I am."

It was quite true, thought Harry. He remembered meeting Melanie, a married woman, at his parents' dinner parties when he was on vacation from Phillips Exeter. Yes, she was older than he. Yet her experience was a part of her fascination for him. Lying beside her after making love and thinking of all the other men—prominent, rich, successful—who had desired her made him feel that in taking Melanie he had taken to himself all that prominence, wealth, and success. The sense of power acted on him like an aphrodisiac. His mother had no idea of how he felt holding all that vitality in his arms.

It seemed incredible to Louise that something so simple should have become so difficult. The last thing she wanted was for Harry to sacrifice himself for her and Evangeline. But how could marrying sweet, beautiful, loving Iris be viewed a sacrifice by anyone? This marriage, this perfect marriage that would make Harry happy, would change their lives, pay their debts, provide a marriage settlement for Evangeline.

"Don't worry, Mother," said Harry. "Iris and I will marry."

He always said that. But she knew too well that all he meant was that *he* would not worry.

Louise had done all she could, smiled, touched his hand, and left the room. It was only then that Harry saw Evangeline sitting in the corner darning a damask tablecloth in the dim light. "Well, Harry, is it all settled that you are to sell yourself to the Woodruffs and restore Mamma to a house full of servants and induce some desperate man to marry me?"

"Any man would be lucky to get you, Evie." Harry faced her as he spoke to let her read his lips. She was so expert that as long as he did not turn his face or cover his mouth he could ignore her handicap. "Marriage settlements are taken as a matter of course." But how many other people in Bourneham saw his suit of Iris in that light?

"You don't need to marry Iris to get a marriage settlement for me, Harry. I don't want a husband that much. Were it not for Mamma's tears, I don't think I would want one at all."

Harry could not believe her sincere. Of course she wanted to marry; every girl did. A husband had to be found. Even Harry who saw the world as a happy place knew how hard was the life of a spinster. Yet he could not help but admire her pride and independence. Another woman would have been bitter: pretty, slim, intelligent, well-read—without money her deafness made her virtually unmarriageable.

The loss of hearing had come as a result of scarlet fever at thirteen. Louise had wept more over what deafness would do to her daughter's chances of finding a husband than over any other aspect of the loss. After this initial weeping, Louise shifted to denial. The girl could hear if only she would try. Alfred was still alive then and reacted quite differently. He obtained the services of a woman who had studied with Harriet Birbank Rodgers at the Clarke Institute for Deaf-Mutes to teach Evangeline the lip language. Alfred also purchased an ear trumpet; Louise would not allow Evangeline to use it. There were plans to take her to Vienna, where an ear specialist was said to be working miracles, and of buying a new instrument able to magnify voices. All that ended with Alfred's financial reverses and death.

"Don't you want love, tenderness, companionship?"

"I am not aware that any of these would exist in a marriage arranged for me, Harry, if indeed they exist in any marriage. But for me, I can see the face of my selected dinner companion fall at having drawn me as his partner. It is no use for me to tell him I can read his lips perfectly if he will just look at me. He never does. And the person on the other side and the one across the table also act as if I do not exist."

Cheerful Harry was appalled by this glimpse of her life. Why hadn't he rescued her? Made people pay attention? How could he have been pleased with himself for getting someone—anyone—to take her in to dinner?

"Yes, Harry, that is why a deaf person gets to be an observer. And oh, what she observes. No love or tenderness or warmth between the couples, except just at the beginning of a marriage, and not always even then." Looking around a table, Evangeline could see each member of a couple desperate to attract the attention of someone else, anyone else but the marital partner.

"They are not all like that. Not if they have the right partner."

Evangeline would not yield. "They look so unhappy—all of them. Even your beautiful Melanie," she added, and observed how he brightened. That was one marriage he did not wish to think happy. Melanie's face had a certain look when Harry was present; one could not call it swollen, but somehow filled with a suffusion of blood, heavy yet at the same time bright. The look of love, of lust perhaps. How could Evangeline tell? That Melanie cared for Harry pleased Evangeline. Melanie was nicer to her than were any of the other women, made a point of seeking her out. There was no question how Harry felt. In Melanie's presence he positively glowed; his hair looked more golden, his eyes brighter.

"Some couples are happy," Harry persisted. "Our parents, for instance."

He would not see things as they were, thought Evangeline. Their parents—she had been able to hear then—the acerbic tone in which the simplest remark was made, the quarrels; later she had read on their lips the recriminations after her father's business began to fail.

She wondered what Harry would think if he were to learn what had taken place between Melanie and Elmer Morgen at the Woodruff ball. Hidden by her deafness, Evangeline had sat directly across from Melanie, following the conversation. The fire at the Heron factory. With what pleasure Morgen threw the blame at Edmont. A look of uncertainty had crossed Melanie's face so rapidly it was barely there. Evangeline did not even consider telling Harry what had been discussed. She had once read on Melanie's lips, "Harry, you are made for joy." These devious plots had no place in Harry's life.

"But how about love, Evangeline . . . I mean . . . the physical manifestation of love? Desire?" Since becoming Melanie's lover, he had gained a new insight into how young girls felt. Before then he had thought they had no interest in that sort of thing. Melanie had opened to him another world of young girls panting for fulfillment, desperately longing for a man, trying to catch sight of their brothers' nakedness, watching the gardener's boys, the footmen, their parents' dinner guests in tight evening clothes, waiting, pressing their bodies against the backs of chairs, letting the water from the tap flow over their genitalia, pressing their hands to just that place. Almost the way boys did, if no one caught them. It would have been called self-abuse in a boy, he thought, recalling the warnings against onanism and its dread results. He supposed no one ever gave girls similar warnings, for no one thought that sweet young innocents sought such pleasure. He had not admitted to Melanie how shocked he had been. From then on, he had looked at young girls differently. (Except for Iris; somehow, he still thought of her as being without physical desires.)

Desire. Harry glittering. Melanie's face suffused with blood. That heavy look. Andrew Arnold used to have that look when he was dancing with her. Desire? Was it the look of desire or had she only longed to think so? Andrew had sat with her, danced with her. One summer afternoon at Emerald Beach, he had taken a stick and written in the sand, "My pretty." My. My. Had he meant "my"? Leaning forward to let the sand run through his fingers, his arm had accidentally brushed across her breasts. Accidentally. Or had he meant it? The movement was so natural, the touch so light. Her mouth had opened in surprise and pleasure. He had kissed her then, improperly, but she had not stopped him and fresh from swimming his mouth had tasted of salt. It was then that she made her mistake. "Andrew," she had said softly. "You can speak to me as to any other woman, so long as you face me. I have learned the lip language." It made him uneasy, she realized then. He had found her deafness soothing; her isolation meant he had nothing to contend with. Later, it had even occurred to her that he had dared to kiss her, improperly, because he knew she would not cry out, speak of it to others. Who would listen to her? The idea of her as helpless had been part of her attraction for him; he did not wish her otherwise.

Evangeline had never really dared to hope. It was just as well. After he became engaged to Martita Langrave, he hardly spoke with her again, acted as if he were angry with her. Perhaps he was only angry at himself for having wanted her when she was so unsuitable a match. But she was not even certain this was not taking too much credit to herself. "My pretty." That was not like saying "I love you" though for a little while it had seemed that way. Now, this business with Harry about the race. She wondered whether she figured in it in some way. Andrew was developing a little paunch; it pleased her to see that. Her waist was laced to barely seventeen inches around; she hoped he noticed.

Desire? She would not allow herself to feel it, the way it had been when Andrew kissed her and she opened her mouth to him. There was no point. The physical manifestation of love. For her it would be experienced with an old man, endured with eyes closed and teeth clenched.

"It's not as if I were likely to get an attractive man, Harry. And better no husband than one who is dull and old and ugly."

Their mother was now encouraging the suit of Mr. Genever, who could certainly be described with those words, as could the previous candidate, a widower with three children who had in the end settled on someone else. Harry had grown weary with Louise's insistence that he marry Iris, but without that kind of money, could a better husband for Evangeline be found? His mother clearly thought not. Evangeline had never made such a demand on him. What other sister would have been so generous?

Andrew Arnold had once confided to Harry that he was "fascinated," that was how he had put it, with Evangeline. Nothing had come of it. How could it? Louise had said from the start that he would never marry Evie. At that time the Arnolds had been as much in need of a wealthy bride as the Van Burghs were now. But Harry could remember the expression on Andrew's face when he danced with Evangeline at Genevieve Edmont's ball, and once coming out of the water after a swim he had seen Andrew sitting beside Evangeline on the beach. There was something about the languid yet tense way they were leaning towards one another than made him think they had been kissing. Andrew had wanted Evangeline. No doubt as to that. But money talks, as his mother often said, money talks.

Though she was keeping out of sight, Harry knew his mother was hovering nearby, willing him on his way to Villa del Destino to meet Iris's need. It was his need, too, and he could not imagine why he felt so strangely reluctant to be on his way.

As soon as she heard the front door close behind Harry, Louise returned to the living room. Observing the worried look, Evangeline wished her mother would recognize the need for resolving their problems without depending on Harry. She loved Harry, but with the hard clarity of vision encouraged by her handicap did not believe he would see this marriage through. They must change their way of life. As for her, she did not even wish to be married. These efforts to find her a husband should stop. She repeated the gist of what she had said to Harry in an effort to convince her mother.

For once Louise held her tongue; she had reached the end of her resources. Were Harry not to marry, by winter she would have to go and live with Mildred, her sister-in-law, in Boston. Evangeline, too.

Rose Cottage was sold already. The price had been ridiculously low, but who would pay more for such disrepair? They remained here on sufferance of the new owners, the Langraves, who intended to make the house over as a wedding gift to their youngest daughter. Only the fact that the marriage had been postponed to the New Year's had enabled the Van Burghs to remain for one last season. The Langraves had been insufferable, condescending in allowing her this privilege. Louise would have refused, but swallowed her pride out of necessity. Appearances must be kept up while Harry pursued his courtship of Iris. Everything hinged on that marriage; small wonder she irritated him with her hysterical appeals.

No one had a warmer heart than Harry. But she could not count on him in this particular. What was he doing now? She wished she could be certain he was at Villa del Destino giving his golden smile to Nellie Woodruff, but it was just as likely that he was at this moment reflected in the triple mirror set on the rosewood dressing table in the boudoir with windows overlooking the ocean, the boudoir at Île de Joie. Disaster had threatened from the moment when Melanie Edmont bent over the table to reveal the cleavage between her breasts to Harry seated opposite and Louise had realized that the marriage to Iris was no longer assured.

Evangeline broke in on these thoughts with another plea for a device. "I know you keep thinking that a device has to

142

be big, like an ear trumpet. But these are modern times. New ones have been developed that are small."

Suddenly it seemed to Louise that if she were to agree to the hearing aid, it might bring them all luck, almost as if it were a way to propitiate the gods, halt the Erinyes who had pursued them for so long. She could laugh at herself for superstition, as if this yielding could possibly affect anything going on at Villa del Destino this afternoon. But still. "I think you might start to investigate the kinds of devices available and their cost, Evie. Discreetly."

Seeing her mother so reasonable about the device, Evangeline thought this the moment again to repeat her most practical advice. "Harry and I think Rose Cottage should be put up for sale," she declared. "We could live quite comfortably on the proceeds for a long time to come."

"Evangeline!" Despite the lines on her mother's face, the beauty of the delicate features was notable. Louise's eyes were so bright, so bright, and in a moment the tears coursed down her face, making tracks in the powder.

At this evidence of her mother's distress, Evangeline became silent.

Louise went over to the bay window and looked out at the once cherished garden, seeing brown clumps of earth, crabgrass, patches of dandelion, clover, a statue of Cupid with his wings broken. The Langraves would restore it, she thought. Their gardener had come to ask the names of the varieties of roses—huge floppy blossoms and small tightly rolled ones, in colors ranging from the palest pink to flaming red, from the softest cream to a brilliant orange. If she were to close her eyes, she would see the garden as it had looked when she first came to Rose Cottage with Alfred. Harry had been a baby then, the most beautiful child anyone had ever seen, and so lovable. Her friends had marveled at him, envied her. And for all the years afterwards. Was he really going to throw it all away? His charm? Brightness? His handsome person? His great name? Throw it all away? For one summer with Melanie Edmont?

CHAPTER 12

The Woodruff Choice

If he did not linger at the Woodruffs' too long, he could still be with Melanie before the camel ride. Looking towards the drive leading to the ocean, he imagined that he caught sight of the sun's reflection flaming on the skylights of Île de Joie. Harry walked rapidly to Villa del Destino, standing massive and imposing on the farthermost cliff overlooking the ocean.

Admitted by the gatekeeper guarding the entrance to the walls, Harry passed through gardens resembling those of the Roman Villa d'Este with rows of fountains lining the walk leading to the house. Two onyx sphinxes with golden peacocks riding on their backs flanked the entrance. Cupids perched atop the roof, their small fat legs hanging over the gutters.

Harry stepped into the great hall that was ringed by Corinthian columns, the sworls of the capitals outlined in gold. Beside the archway to the drawing room stood two marble statues, a Greek kouros with an archaic smile and the goddess Diana. The beauty of their nudity was concealed by small drapes of velvet fastened to the fingers of their outstretched hands and falling to cover their genitalia. Joseph, not Nellie, it was said, was the prude.

False doors on one wall balanced the real doors on the opposite side of the room. Such perfect symmetry was to be found in all Bourneham mansions, following the style of Louis XIV's Grand Trianon at Versailles. A fleur-de-lis was carved into each panel of the doors and an enormous golden W on top.

Nellie Woodruff rushed into the drawing room. She could never resist coming to see who had arrived instead of waiting as dignity required for the footman to bring her the calling card. Her face fell at the sight of Harry. He was still being punished for his dilatory ways with Iris. Perhaps he should suggest the fateful meeting with Joseph Woodruff this very afternoon. He would not be able to see Melanie. Harry turned his golden smile on Nellie, but her eyes focused on a point to the left of his head; she might have been studying the bronze bust of Augustus Caesar atop a black marble pedestal.

Iris came running in just then, a trifle breathless as she always was. It was said she had trouble breathing, a result of her mother's having insisted on her being so tightly laced from childhood on. Iris was usually laced to barely seventeen inches, and for formal evenings to a perfect sixteen.

"I must speak to Harry."

Nellie shrugged her shoulders very slightly, just enough to reveal her feelings. "You may do so in the conservatory."

Her intent was clear. From her vantage point in the drawing room, she could keep watch on Harry and Iris through the glass-windowed walls of the conservatory. What did she think he meant to do, make Iris his, seduce her then and there? Iris seemed to him so frail, so delicate that his hand pressing too firmly would bruise her. His love for her was barely sexual; at most he imagined holding in his arms her lovely light body in a frilly white nightdress with pink

145

satin ribbons tied at the neck. He avoided thinking how hard the separation from Melanie would be in his very proper marriage. Yet all summer any day he did not see Melanie seemed dull. Even now while reacting with pleasure to Iris's perfect oval face, graceful figure, and her way of leaning towards him, he was at the same time already bored, eager to be away, to be with Melanie.

She was expecting him, but he knew that if he did not come, Melanie would never refer to the broken engagement afterwards. If he asked about the afternoon he had missed, she would say she had found something else to do.

They walked into the conservatory. The air inside was hot and humid, heavy. In a second Harry was sweating. Iris looked cool; she never seemed to perspire. Nellie Woodruff had created a jungle in her conservatory. Running the width of the villa, it rivaled any hothouse at Kew in England. Heavy vines, their stems as thick as ropes, their leaves huge, green, speckled, hung from the palm trees. Orchids were everywhere, ranging in size and hue from large white-and-purple blooms to tiny freckled ones of cream and tan, brown, russet, black. Planted in profusion were cannas of a brilliant red, surrounded by luxuriant tree ferns and slender fiddleheads. Purple berries covered the magenta branches of the pokeweed and yellow flowers bloomed in the small reddish purslane. Balls of fluffy cotton fell from the flowering tops of the tall cattails, contrasting with the coarseness of the shiny leathery reddish green leaves of the ti plant. Bunches of bananas clung to the trunks formed of huge leaves overlapping one another. Nellie's heart had been set on having a breadfruit tree, but its height was excessive so she had agreed to settle for a small sweetsop tree with slender leaves, tiny flowers and heart-shaped fruit. In the midst of this luxuriant plant life, fountains cascaded into rippling pools, the surface covered with water lettuce and white, pink, and yellow blooming water lilies. The odor in the conservatory was very slightly rank, the heavy wet leaves and damp earth overlaid with the scent of the flowers. It was a smell that caught one

146

by surprise coming from the drawing room, a smell that aroused the senses.

It would have been easy to go deep inside to be concealed behind the heavy foliage and Iris clearly would have preferred that. If only he were not so proper and would show his affection for her then and there in front of her mother, Iris thought. "Mamma says I can't marry you, Harry," she stated without any preamble. Her voice was low. Another man might have seen a sexual promise in it, but Harry considered her as the bride, Melanie as the sexual being.

"She's just angry that I haven't formally asked for your hand, Iris. I should have done so, of course. But everything has been understood among us all for months. I'll ask to speak to your father today, right now." They would set a wedding date. January would be good, a New Year's wedding.

Iris touched his arm; her hand was trembling. "It's too late, Harry. Mamma is planning to have me marry an English lord, Harry. And Father agrees."

She was holding a small piece of newspaper and now handed it to Harry. It came from the same issue of the *Bugle* as the damning item and he had not read anything else: "An important event of the Bourneham season will be the visit of one of England's titled gentlemen. It is important, because this member of the nobility is recently widowed and hence marriageable and can trade a British title for an American fortune."

"He is here, Harry. In this house. Upstairs. With his cousin. And, Harry, he's awful. He's old and he's fat and he's all hairy. And . . . he's not you, Harry." Her voice rose hysterically. "Mamma says it's all settled, that the reason the cousin came is that he is to handle the arrangements for the marriage contract. It is beneath a nobleman's position to negotiate on his own behalf. Father is staying in Bourneham this week so as to see more of him."

In the hot conservatory Harry's skin felt clammy. "But how did all this happen so quickly?" Suddenly it seemed that an English nobleman had just appeared as if born

147

from Nellie Woodruff's head like a latter-day male version of Athena.

"She's been planning this for months, Harry, but I didn't pay much attention to her talk about English nobility. I didn't see what it had to do with me. I was thinking about you, Harry."

Nellie had been fanatic in her insistence that everything be just so for the visit, with the intended suitor given the suite of rooms with windows facing the ocean, and his cousin the walnut-paneled rooms across the hall. Nellie's personal maid was to be put out of her room so that it could be given to the lord's valet.

"I barely listened to all these plans," said Iris, "about how English wildflowers were to be put in every room and tea served on Wedgwood china instead of our silver tea set. The wildflowers were grown from seedlings, Harry, the Wedgwood china ordered to come by sea from England. Once the dates of the visit were fixed, an English artist who has done portraits of the British nobility was brought to the United States to paint scenes of the interior of the lord's castle to be mounted on screens in the ballroom to fulfill the theme of the ball."

Listening to Iris, Harry realized that at the same time she had been encouraging him, Nellie Woodruff had covertly been making plans to ensnare the Englishman. What kind of a lord could someone like that capture? A baronet at best. Harry castigated himself for having been so careless, so confident of his position.

The ball, Iris continued, had been scheduled to welcome the Englishmen. They had been due to dock in New York on Sunday and so the ball had been set for Monday, the day before yesterday. Bad weather delayed the ship's landing and her mother had learned of this catastrophe too late to postpone the ball. Only then did her mother reveal the whole story to Iris with obvious pride. Iris was appalled. "But it's Harry I'm to marry." She could not quite take in what she was being told. Her parents had smiled on her romance; her mother always described Harry as charming, dwelt frequently on the two Dutch patroons (both sides of his family).

Iris was weeping now and Harry would have liked to put his arms around her, but that was impossible in full view of Mrs. Woodruff. Their marriage would not take place. He could hardly bear the thought of telling his mother, seeing her tears. And Evangeline. Who would marry her now? "Am I to take it that your mother ordered you to marry this English lord, like it or not?"

"That is not how she put it, Harry, but we both know that is what she means. She talked right over my words about how wonderful life is in England and how happy I will be to join a family with a history that can be traced to the time of King Edward the Third. I will not merely be presented to Queen Victoria, Mamma tells me. I will dine with her."

Harry took this account of possessions and prominence with a grain of salt. This was what Nellie wanted people to believe.

"I do not wish to dine with Queen Victoria, Harry. I have heard it said that she is an implacable enemy of women's right to the vote."

Harry was startled. He had never heard such a view from anyone besides Melanie. If two women so different as Iris and Melanie were in agreement on suffrage, perhaps women would get it some day after all.

Harry listened, murmuring words of agreement whenever she paused. Now that the first shock was passed, despite the desperate seriousness of the situation, oddly, as with his mother, he found his mind wandering while Iris continued her recital. Even as he spoke and felt he really cared for Iris, he was aware of time passing. Melanie. She was waiting for him, lush and lovely, with her long slow kisses, his tongue in her mouth, in and out, around and around.

Iris looked up at him, troubled. He was listening, hearing, reacting, but at the same time he kept slipping away from her somehow; she could not seem to hold his attention.

149

"Mamma said that since his wife died he's been looking for a new wife and he doesn't seem to mind my being so much younger. I find that odd. You would think a mature man would pick someone his own age." Harry thought her innocence charming. "He had no children and Mamma says mine will inherit all, Harry."

In every exchange she spoke his name over and over as if just the act of saying it gave her possession of a sort. "What are we going to do?" The "we" touched him. He told her that he loved her, she was lovely, and he felt guilty that his mind had begun wandering.

Iris, waiting for him to answer, was not quite trusting. She was innocent, but not foolish, and her love for Harry did not blind her to his failings. Why hadn't he asked her father formally for her hand? Her mother had asked that question and she could only look away. Why hadn't he insisted on marrying her sooner?

The worst, the very worst thing that had happened the day before—and she would not tell Harry this—was the moment when Nellie, seeing her daughter recalcitrant, had brought out the *Bourneham Bugle* and handed it over. Iris read the scurrilous paragraph without changing expression, so well had she been trained by her governess. "It is completely untrue," she declared, and her voice did not tremble. "Armand Wolfe makes up such stories to attract attention. He is a dreadful man, vulpine like his name."

Toy. She was the toy, not Harry. Everyone thought she had such an easy life. She was always hearing that. Pretty, rich. Rich, pretty. The order changed, but not the words. Her father called her his little bird. People picked that up. Little bird, little bird. What an unhappy comparison. In what way did she resemble a bird? Birds were plump, like women with big bosoms. And everyone said she had such an easy life. It was common knowledge that she was ruled by her mother and Nellie was admired for this success. When she reached marriageable age, she and her mother at last found a mutually agreeable goal. Marriage offered her an acceptable escape from her mother's loving, she could not deny there was love, but implacable supervision. Soon people were adding a few words to the refrain. Rich, pretty, and loved by Harry. It had seemed that everyone was smiling at this love. Until now.

Shocked by the disclosure of the gossip column, she tried not to believe it, to remind herself that any man seen talking to Melanie was her putative lover. Harry loved her, Iris. He had said so. And he could not possibly be having an affair with Melanie Edmont. It was an absurdity, a perfectly sickening idea. Little as she liked to, Iris had to concede that Melanie was good-looking for someone of her age. But that was quite different from being desirable to a young man, to Harry. Why, Melanie was too old, nearly as old as Iris's mother, and she was married besides. It was impossible.

Then all at once Iris remembered having stopped on the threshold of her mother's bedroom one day just as the masseuse was leaving. Nellie was lying on the chaise longue all pink from the kneading of her flesh, breathing heavily. "I would give anything," she said to the masseuse, "to have Melanie Edmont's figure for just one month."

"And what would you do in that month, madam?"

"Why, I guess I'd do just what Melanie does." Nellie's laugh had a coarseness to it Iris had never heard before.

"Oh, madam, your daughter wouldn't like that!"

At the time, Iris staying carefully out of sight had not understood. But reading the *Bugle* she realized what the masseuse had meant. Her Harry would not do that with Melanie. Not something so dirty and disgusting.

Right now he was smiling at her in the way that made it hard for her to catch her breath. The story was made up out of whole cloth, she knew that. Except that here, in the conservatory, this afternoon, while she was telling him her story, her really terrible story, every so often it seemed to her that he acted, well, almost as if he wished to be elsewhere. With Melanie? Impossible. Harry did not like trouble; it was no more than that. This time he simply had to

151

face trouble, to find a solution for them. If only the very intensity of her thought would convey the solution to him without her speaking. Because how could she, a woman, possibly speak of such a thing? The fact that they were (had been?) virtually engaged made no difference.

Watching from the drawing room, Nellie could see that Harry was barely responding to Iris's story, was, it would seem, quite ready to concede her to the Woodruffs' choice. She had expected nothing more of him. But Iris, innocent, kept touching Harry's sleeve, looking up at him adoringly, weeping; Nellie could have wept, too. She was offering—no, more than that, arranging for—her daughter a life so much better than any Harry Van Burgh could offer, a life out of a fairy tale: a butcher's granddaughter to become a member of the British nobility. In another era, troubadours would have sung such a story.

How far they had come. Iris had no idea. Last winter in New York, feeling restless one morning, Nellie had ordered the coachman to drive down Second Avenue past the butcher shops with their huge carcasses hanging in front of the windows. What memories were aroused by the smell of freshly killed flesh, the ranker smell of aged flesh, the sawdust on the floor—did she really smell them from her carriage, or did she only imagine that she did? She drove past William Kuehn's shop, caught a glimpse of the butchers inside with their bowler hats, their bloodstained white aprons. For a moment she was tempted to order the carriage to stop so she could enter. Willie was probably running the shop now. She might have married him. He was always in and out of her father's shop. They used to kiss in the cold room or behind the counter, hidden between the huge sides of beef and mutton. He had a strange way of kissing, would suck her lips inside his mouth. She had been violently excited, had let him take her hand and put it against the hardness at his crotch, her heart beating as if to jump out of her chest. She never forgot it. And how had she ever had the luck to pick Joseph, who had seemed no better a catch? She liked to say that she had recognized Joseph's brilliance and where it would take him from the start but that was not true. It could have gone either way. She had quarreled with Willie, who charged that her father added water to the hams he sold to increase their weight. Of course he did, as did Willie's father, but each defended his own, and there was Joseph. He had been earnest, no kisses in the cold room, asking her father first.

Yet it had been so hard, moving up with Joseph. He did not care what people thought of him, so long as he was on top, had the power. But it was different for a woman. She became aware of all she lacked, hired a tutor to teach her to speak properly. People heard of it and laughed, but she went ahead with it anyway; eventually they forgot.

Growing wealth had brought a new series of snubs. She did not falter. Nothing but the top circle of society ruled by Genevieve Edmont was good enough for Iris. Nellie's four other children, born in the early impoverished days of her marriage, had died of the fevers that swept through the slums with grim regularity. Nellie would look at her own heavy, powerful arms and hands, her waist so thickened by years of helping out with heavy work in the butcher shop that no amount of massage, no stricture of whalebone construction and lacing could bring below thirty-two inches, and marvel that this aristocratic child had come from her body.

Joseph said she caused the girl to become a nonentity, making all decisions for her, but that was how young girls in society were brought up. Iris would grow. A few years in England as a lady of noble rank would develop her character.

The idea of finding a European aristocrat husband for Iris had been at the back of Nellie's mind ever since Jocelyn Edmont had, through her mother's intervention, been made an Italian contessa. Of course, it had been easy for an Edmont who possessed not only money but also an old and respected family name. Nellie never expected anything to be easy. She decided to concentrate on the British; it had been hard enough for her to learn to speak proper English. Traveling to England with Joseph every year from the time Iris was fourteen, she sought to meet noble families who might put her in the way of finding a titled gentleman more impoverished than the Edmonts' count and willing to consider wealth alone sufficient to compensate for any lack in lineage.

The previous year, in fact, they had been put in touch with the family of a baronet, aged twenty, whose father had been so charming that Nellie had become suspicious. It had been too good. The detective Joseph hired was embarrassed to reveal to them that the young man was said to have the French disease, a result of a life of licentiousness begun at the age of fifteen. Nellie for once had been shocked. She had thought that upon leaving the slums she had left behind the pox, the French disease, the disfiguring exuding lesions.

The English aristocrat whom she finally settled on had as impeccable a reputation as Nellie required. It was chance that he had become available to her. In one of her many efforts to advance to the highest levels of British society, Nellie had, through a person indebted to Joseph, contrived an invitation to meet the nobleman and his wife. They had been cool, barely courteous, but the contact was made and the next time she came to England, he was widowed. It was then that she learned his estates were inherited from a father so profligate as to have run through the family fortunes. He was said to be close to financial ruin. This time he was more courteous, less cool.

Dazzled by his prominence and the magnificence of his castle, not really daring to hope, Nellie continued to search for other likely candidates in England and the United States. Among the young men in the innermost circle of New York society, she settled on Harry Van Burgh. Joseph actually preferred him; while he had not opposed Nellie's search for a nobleman (finding a good husband for the daughter was, after all, a mother's duty), he really believed that foreigners were inferior to Americans.

She was so taken with Harry, with the idea of being intimate with the Van Burghs, that she was genuinely delighted when Iris fell in love with him and he (before becoming entangled with Melanie) appeared to return that love. For all her leanings towards the aristocracy, if Harry had moved quickly, shown himself determined to win Iris, Nellie would have accepted him. Yes, earlier in the year Harry might have had Iris for the asking. But that was precisely what he had not done.

Harry's affair with Melanie had not detracted from his eligibility. A relationship with an older woman, a member of the best society, glamorous, experienced, did a young man good, enhanced his reputation, made him a better husband when the time came. She would have wished that Joseph had come to her so tutored. There was a rumor that Joseph had been Melanie's lover once, too, but it was absurd to assume that a woman of such sexual allure and so wide a choice of men would have accepted Joseph with his crude in-and-out lovemaking. He had probably started the rumor himself.

Once the scandalous account appeared in the *Bugle*, her attitude to Harry changed. Melanie Edmont's summer toy; Harry was finished for her.

Now it appeared that the Englishman was there for the taking. And Iris could only weep and murmur Harry, Harry. Nellie sympathized, could understand Iris's reaction. But what was Harry after all? A pretty boy with a handsome face and a lean, well-exercised body. There would be pretty boys enough later. A wealthy woman had no dearth of suitors. Even she, with her weathered skin and heavy body, had her choice of lovers. If they made it clear that costly gifts were expected, well, Nellie was prepared to pay for what she wanted. And Iris was so beautiful. Like Melanie, she would be the recipient of gifts as well as of sexual pleasure. One did not have to marry the pretty boys in order to enjoy them. Iris looked unhappy now; she would get over it.

Seeing Nellie's eyes upon them, it seemed to Harry that he read a trace of scorn on her face. In that moment he knew what he had to do. He did not need to allow Nellie to push him aside for this aging Englishman, cause him to let down his mother and sister; he did not need to lose Iris. Elopement. That was the answer. He would take Iris away from here, secretly, and travel with her to another city where a minister would be found to marry them. Then they would spend the night in a little inn in some beautiful secluded spot in the countryside. The romantic possibilities were entrancing. Iris would be so happy. When they returned to Bourneham as man and wife, Woodruff would have to accept them. Nellie would probably insist on another wedding ceremony, formal, with members of society in attendance and Iris dressed in virgin white despite the impropriety of the clandestine wedding night.

He turned to Iris, smiling, but she was looking away, disconsolate, mistrusting.

If Harry's change in mood did not reach the drooping Iris, Nellie, watching, grasped it at once. The recognition of Harry as a possible risk brought her to her feet and into the conservatory so precipitously that Harry was cut off before he had a chance to speak the words that were to tell Iris of his plan. She would not let him see Iris alone again, thought Nellie, calling the footman to bring Harry's hat and show him to the door, rushing him out without ceremony or courtesy.

Harry tried to give Iris a signal that he would be back, but was not sure she saw him. She was standing with her head bent, perhaps thinking him a poor suitor. It would add to his pleasure on his return to make her smile again, look at him lovingly, admiringly as she always had. For the moment Harry had no choice but to go.

His spirits were high as the great doors to the villa closed behind him. Nellie could put him out now; she would find it impossible to do so when Iris was his wife. How delighted his mother would be. He was half tempted to go home and confide his plans, but it would be better not to tell her in advance, let it come as a surprise. And if he went home, he certainly would not be able to reach Melanie this afternoon.

Taking out his pocket watch, he observed that due to Nellie's intrusion there was still time to visit Melanie before her camel ride. Actually, it was sensible to see her, tell her his intention and obtain her advice on how to proceed. Careful planning was needed to bring off the elopement and Melanie's practical turn of mind would be helpful. With a spring to his step, Iris's passionate suitor made his way to Île de Joie.

CHAPTER 13

How to Hold Harry

Will I marry again? Oh, no, madam. I am past all that. I am nearly forty-two."

Melanie recoiled, wondering what Harry would think if he knew this woman applying to be her maid was of an age with her, tried to imagine him putting his arm around that thickened waist, kissing that pale, lined skin.

Past all that. Melanie surreptitiously looked at her own glowing face reflected in the mirror opposite for reassurance. Past that. She could not imagine it, past the desperate hunger for Denis, past the desire for Harry's sweet, hard body. She could not accept that. So much still ahead. In time Melanie and Beryl would come to play the roles of younger mistress, older servant. It suited them both.

Learning of Dena's imperfections on the way to the Woodruffs' ball, Genevieve had immediately thought of Beryl as replacement, and an interview was arranged for Wednesday. Beryl had left domestic service to marry Genevieve's butler; now he was dead and she sought to return to work, knew how an Edmont home was run.

Once the matter with Beryl was settled, Melanie found she could not concentrate on anything else. Harry was late. Of course he was at Villa del Destino mending his fences so to speak. She could imagine how charming he was being. Perhaps right now while she was at her desk, the seating plan for the dinner at her ball laid out on the mother-of-pearl-inlaid surface, he was closeted with Nellie fixing the date of the wedding.

The realization of what he must be doing gave Melanie a pang and a feeling of unaccustomed irritation at Harry came over her. She had known of Iris at the time she accepted Harry's—well, invitation—but not how galling his relationship with Iris would come to be. Not much better than having had Adelaide as a companion, present whether she were there or not.

Mrs. Karling, the housekeeper, knocked and came in then with the food bill. Melanie was glad of the interruption to her thoughts. Checking the household bills was mandatory; otherwise, her mother had explained, one gave the servants a license to steal. The bills for the past month were typical, $550 to the butcher, $175 to the grocer. All bills were padded, that was understood, to allow an outstanding chef like Monsieur Alphonse a larger profit than the ten percent of food bills openly added to his salary of $100 a month.

For all his talent, Monsieur Alphonse was not in Melanie's class when it came to devising a menu that was dramatic, shocking, talked about. Melanie let her imagination run to such food fantasies as black caviar packed into mushroom caps and mounds of crabmeat mixed with mayonnaise, whipped with red caviar and topped with the yolk of a quail's egg. She conceived of melon rinds filled with sweetbreads finely ground, greened with imported pistachio nuts, and capped with a perfect red cherry the exact size of the ruby Melanie was to wear at her throat the night of the ball. A footman was to bring the ruby to the kitchen two days earlier for the measurement to be taken. The remainder of the meal would be noteworthy for the superb quality of preparation by Monsieur Alphonse—gray sole lightly grilled and topped with watercress cut to size with scissors; lobster meat removed, cut, dipped in lemon butter, and returned to the shell before baking; filet de boeuf roasted to be charred outside and rosy within, covered with a mahogany dark truffled gravy and served with tiny potatoes identical in size, crisp on the outside, firm within. The asparagus, topped with a subtly flavored hollandaise, would be so tender a spoon could cut them.

She decided to wait no longer for Harry, but to go down to the pantries and kitchen to encourage the preparations for the ball. It was customary for the servants to work themselves into a frenzy for a week before a major ball. Nothing could let down as to meals and laundry for the family in the interim, including the separate servings for the nursery and for the staff. A common saying in Bourneham was that it was not a proper ball until all the servants were exhausted and reduced to tears.

Melanie's appearance guaranteed a redoubled effort, kept each staff member at fever pitch. Groves, the butler, she thought with amusement, was irritated each time she arrived unannounced. He sought to run the house in the English fashion, with the mistress making an appointment through him to visit the kitchens and servants' domains. Today, to capture attention more fully, Melanie sent Dena, who was hovering nervously, to the top floor room where hats, gloves, purses, and shoes were kept, to bring her the hat trimmed with an aigrette and mauve-colored ostrich plumes made for her on the Rue de la Paix in Paris by Mme. Virot. This sort of effect was expected of her. And the servants knew that just before the ball, she would come down to the kitchen, gloriously gowned and blazing with jewels, to praise them. A footman would accompany her, so that she could hand each kitchen maid a rose; the chef's assistants, cigars; the chef, a bottle of French brandy. Money tips would be given the next day. Most other women never set foot in their kitchen, thought it sufficient to send the butler to proffer thanks and tips.

About to enter the kitchen, going past the laundry room,

she observed the laundress and her helpers pressing the dozens of damask tablecloths and thousands of napkins. Fresh napkins were given four times during the dinner, each set being a different shade of rose.

In the pantry the parlor maids were helping the kitchen maids to shine the vermeil cutlery popular this year as a change from silver.

The kitchen was orderly, like an army camp on the evening of battle. Dinner preparations for the Saturday ball were already underway; foods were stored in the huge walk-in ice boxes in the basement. Chef Alphonse considered himself a general with troops to deploy. There was no relaxation in dress; it was said that he did not allow anyone above the level of scullery maid to perspire. Certainly he never did himself.

The kitchen maids were sitting at the long counters, piles of melons in front of each place. They scooped the insides out of melon after melon and painted the rinds with broad brushes dipped in a solution of sugar and flecks of gold to make the fruit hold its size and shape. Younger maids ran back and forth, taking away the discarded fruit, bringing clean knives and brushes. Grinding, chopping, hacking, whipping; everyone was busy; bits of food flew off boards and out of bowls. The maids and assistant cooks had been working since five o'clock that morning and had been drooping before Melanie's appearance caused them to straighten up.

Monsieur Alphonse stood at a counter modeling with softened wax. Coming closer, Melanie observed it was a camel, a model for the sculpture that would be carved out of ice just before the ball began. She walked back and forth, her skirts brushing over melon seeds and pistachio shells, admiring this, criticizing that, encouraging, urging. A few minutes in the kitchen could make the difference, she had learned, between an excellent meal and one that was inspired.

She returned to her dressing room to find Junior waiting for her, demanding to ride the camel. He was stubborn like his father and kept insisting that it was not fair to deprive him. "All my friends are asking me if I get to ride it. Everyone thinks I'll have a chance."

The story of the camel was ubiquitous in Bourneham, discussed by children as well as parents, thought Melanie with pleasure. As she had intended, her ball with the camel ride would be the major event of the summer. It might be fun to take Junior along this afternoon, but then she thought that she would be embarrassed to have him observe her efforts to ride the beast. She needed more practice.

"You can't ride the camel," she said firmly, relieved that one did not have to give children reasons for one's decisions.

Junior had no sooner given up and gone off to play than Harry appeared unannounced. The servants knew he was to be passed through without the customary formalities.

Although Harry had been thinking over the problem with Iris and wondering what Melanie would have to say about his elopement plans, as soon as he saw her, from long habit his eyes went to her waist. Sometimes even with the corset on, he could sway her, but quite as often she would smilingly refuse. Just a few inches to make such a difference. Noting that her waist was not at its narrowest, despite himself he began to feel excited. They had spoken of making love when they arranged for his visit.

Following his glance, Melanie remarked lightly, "I do not wear a corset for four activities: playing tennis, swimming, making love, and riding camels. There is of course no way for you to guess which one I have in mind. The camel has been waiting for me all day and I don't want it to become nervous."

Harry knew he was expected to respond with some half-joking remark whether she thought it better for him to become nervous. She would answer in kind and they would advance to caresses. Tempted to postpone his announcement until after the afternoon had proceeded along its accustomed lines, he gave the anticipated suggestive response. Seating himself opposite her on a rose velvet arm-chair, Harry felt himself relaxing. The chairs in Melanie's rooms were more comfortable than those anywhere else. He wondered how she managed it. They looked no larger, deeper, softer than any others until one sat down.

In Harry's presence, Melanie's irritation left her. She thought how attractive he was, glowing in the sunlight streaming in through the windows. He was hot; the heat of his body warmed her. There was the familiar dampness be-tween her legs; she was in the mood now. The camel could wait. So do we pass our golden hours.

And then Harry broke into a cold sweat of shame as it struck him that from the instant he had seen Melanie, Iris and her troubles—his troubles, too, he rapidly amended the thought—had become less significant. He must speak of what had happened and tell her of the elopement plan immedi-ately. Only it was hard to think clearly when Melanie was so close. There was something about the texture of her skin that made him long to touch it, so soft and yet so firm, press it and release your finger and the flesh would spring back. Her skin was always hot, as if the blood were coursing too near the surface. Other people also were aware; he had no-ticed how they brushed up against her, put their hands on her unnecessarily.

"Don't you want to know why I was late, Melanie?" She raised her shoulders; it was not quite a shrug, but suggested that she was not really interested in reasons. He had not been here; she had done other things.

"I received so frantic a message from Iris Woodruff that I had to go to the villa."

At his words, her high spirits left her and she felt let down. For him to recall Iris before they made love—she had seen the direction of his eyes—made evident to her that something definitive had happened this afternoon. Never before had he spoken of Iris until afterwards. And in that moment she saw the inevitable future without Harry draw-ing nearer, an inevitability that was unpalatable. Somehow until now she had seen his marriage as taking place at some distant future date, a time when the love affair would have run its course. Not now when she was not ready.

"I was impatient, wanting to come to you. But then I learned that there really is a crisis. Iris's mother says we are not to marry."

Melanie's first reaction was pleasure. She would not lose Harry yet; they could go on being lovers.

"Mrs. Woodruff has decided that Iris is to marry an English nobleman, who is fat, old, and hairy. Awful."

"Have you seen him?"

"No. Iris has described him in those terms. I just missed seeing him, as did you. Mrs. Woodruff scheduled her ball to coincide with the night of his arrival, but the ship was delayed."

The Monday date. The English motif for the ball. She had wondered about these things. An English nobleman for a son-in-law. Despite herself, Melanie had to admire Nellie Woodruff. In her own way, she was as formidable as Joseph. In the course of a generation, the butchers in the background would be forgotten. The Woodruffs would be well within the inner circle, with others vying for their approval. Nothing was ever due to chance; one simply had to know the reason.

"By now the Englishman has arrived, accompanied by a cousin who is to conduct the marriage negotiations."

He could hear Iris's breathy voice. The china had been ordered in time to come by sea from England; a long well-thought-out campaign. He had been the backup if the plan failed.

"I think I have been a dupe."

Feeling remarkably cheered by his news—and guilty at the same time to feel so—Melanie hastened to offer comfort, though Harry merely appeared troubled, not really cast down. It seemed to her that he was more disturbed at having been credulous than at having lost Iris. But perhaps that was how he wished to appear in front of her, thought Melanie out of her long experience.

"When Iris first started telling me about this, I thought her mother was threatening us with the nobleman because she was angry with me for not having asked Mr. Woodruff formally for Iris's hand."

Melanie with difficulty concealed her surprise. Feckless she knew Harry to be, but it had never occurred to her that he had failed to take this so necessary step. Oversight? She wondered. Well, it was pleasing to her. A compliment really. She wished Harry the best of everything, of course, and had always said that included Iris, but she could not help feeling some triumph that he had been so distracted by her as to let the formal proposal wait for so long, too long.

"The saddest part of this, Melanie, is that it is not as if the English lord wants Iris in particular. He had not met her before this prenuptial visit. Clearly he would have taken any American heiress to provide him with money and an heir."

He found this the saddest part, thought Melanie. An odd way for a lover to talk, for surely the saddest part should be his loss.

"Iris must be so upset. And you, too, Harry." She found that she was quite able to make appropriate remarks. It was easy now that his engagement was in trouble.

A fat old Englishman. In the long run it would be of little moment. The fact of his being old meant Iris would find herself a widow when still young and lovely. Entrenched among the British nobility, she could then find a husband more to her liking. Melanie realized of course that these were the thoughts that came to a woman who had experience of the world, hardly a girl of eighteen, and one who was in love with Harry at that.

"When Iris was telling me about the English suitor, I was thinking that perhaps we should . . . well, we should elope."

The word was out and with it came the thought that if they eloped, she would not be alone with Harry again ever, that this afternoon would be their last private meeting. Certainly married men conducted affairs and Harry in time would, too. When they had been approaching intimacy, but still just friends, Harry had been firm in his quite conventional views of marriage and fidelity. There had been women in his life, but he intended to be a faithful husband. Harry had not talked about marital fidelity lately, but that did not mean much either.

The years were her enemies. By the time Harry was ready to return to her she would be too old, perhaps not too old to want it, to want him, but too old for him to want her. *You will grow old and lose your looks and I will be free of you.* Wallace had said that to her once; she had never been so frightened. That attitude must be held by all men.

Harry was talking on, the elopement taking shape in his mind. It appealed to his sense of the romantic. There was a carriage to hire, a minister to be found, a country inn located, no, he knew just the place. It was true that he had spent his salary and payday was still some time away. But any one of his friends, good fellows all, would be happy to stake him. And next week the swimming race would come off and he would be able to pay back the loan.

Elope. Melanie wondered if Harry had thought anything through. It was at moments like these that she realized how young he was. Elope, he said. With what? She had seen the denuded upstairs rooms in the Van Burgh town house. Why, Iris had never dressed or undressed herself in her life, viewed a thousand dollars as the kind of small change carried to buy something that caught her eye.

"Have you any idea, Harry, what these things cost? Quite aside from the immediate expenses of the elopement, what it will take to set up housekeeping with Iris?" Melanie feared she was presenting herself as the sensible older woman, an image particularly hateful to her in Harry's presence, but the desire to make him postpone the elopement was upon her.

Women were so practical, thought Harry sighing, quite forgetting that obtaining practical advice from Melanie had been the ostensible reason for coming to see her this afternoon. In his experience, women, girls even, who appeared

166

to think of nothing but balls and gowns knew to the penny what everything cost. He supposed little Iris would in time be telling him the same things.

And it was then when be began to speak and defend his position that it dawned on him and for the first time that the elopement was not a romantic dream, but was reality, was immediate. The break with Melanie was upon him. It was not something to happen in January when he would be ready for it. But right now. At the image of Melanie, naked against him, slippery with his sweat, he found himself hoping—well, almost hoping—that another solution could be found. No. He must not think this way. Everything required him to elope with Iris—his mother, Evangeline—and he did love her, of course he did. He must not let himself be distracted by the desire Melanie could always arouse in him. His future, his real life, was with Iris, and he had to work out the problems attendant on the elopement. They were not as serious as Melanie made out. It was not as if his lack of money would be that important anyway. Once he and Iris were married, Woodruff would come around and accept them.

He began to explain that to Melanie when suddenly it struck him that there was no certainty at all that Joseph Woodruff would accept him warmly as son-in-law as soon as the deed were done. He could not assume that Woodruff would behave in the same manner as his mother. No matter how unsuitable a marriage he made, were he to marry Melanie, for example, he knew his mother would put a good face on it, welcome the bride. But Woodruff was ruthless; he might cut off an adored daughter who displeased him. If that were to happen, there was no way Harry could support Iris as well as his mother and sister. For the first time in his life, Harry recognized that in his work, he was behaving more like a dilettante than a serious young banker on the way up. He would apply himself from this day on. Even if he did, how in his circle, where an Edmont or a van der Cleeve controlled tens of millions of dollars, could he earn any sum that counted? The situation would be hopeless without

Woodruff's blessing. If only he could predict how Woodruff was likely to act. Iris would not know. She would not believe her father capable of any harshness; she most certainly had not seen the vicious side he was known for. How would such a man behave?

It was then that Harry remembered the rumor. There were so many rumors about Melanie that it was impossible to separate the true from the false and she never mentioned a previous lover to him. But of course there had been lovers, and the worst of the rumors linked Melanie with Joseph Woodruff. Adept at shutting out the unpleasant and hurtful, Harry had never allowed himself to think that the men who had preceded him had actually performed the act of love. Even his unease about Morgen had focused on the attention she was paying, had hardly touched on sexual congress. But somehow now, in the heightened emotion of the day, he felt a certainty that Joseph had been here in this room, had sat where he was sitting, had looked to Melanie's waist, to Melanie's mood, had followed her into this or another bedroom where she drew the drapes tightly shut and created a secret world. Melanie was by no means incapable of taking such a man, coarse though he was, as lover. Seeking variety, escape from boredom, excitement, she might indeed have thought Joseph Woodruff different from the society men she knew, more interesting than they (more interesting than he?). The two of them, naked, embracing. Harry shuddered in jealousy and distaste.

Watching the expression on his face, Melanie was aware of the exact moment when he thought of the link between her and Woodruff. What other man so entangled in the Woodruffs' lives would have failed to find out more about that? But Harry ignored the disagreeable. Her golden boy, out of his depth. Another man would never have left the Woodruff house without Iris.

At the same time Harry was realizing that he had been inexcusably dense. As Iris's suitor, this was one rumor he should have investigated. Perhaps Woodruff harbored an

168

animus against Harry for having superseded him with Melanie. It was even possible that Woodruff had never intended to allow Harry to marry Iris, had been playing with him.

How could he find out? There was nothing for it but to ask Melanie, who would be aware, as women always were, how Woodruff felt about her romances with other men.

Harry took a deep breath. "Melanie, how do you think Joseph Woodruff will react to my eloping with Iris? Do you know . . . think . . . he has any particular reason to . . . dislike me?" Now that he was thinking about it, Harry was becoming increasingly uneasy about flouting the wishes of a man known to be crude and violent, not above using the lowest intimidation tactics to get his way. Cutting off funds for a disobedient daughter and unwanted son-in-law might not satisfy his desire for revenge. "I wonder what Woodruff would do if he were really angry, Melanie. At the club I have heard stories of the most terrible sort. Woodruff is said to have nearly killed a plant manager who told him a new kind of coke oven he had designed himself was inferior. I suppose it's absurd to imagine his resorting to violence against me. The man isn't a brute, after all."

Not absurd at all, she thought; the man was a brute. There was nothing Joseph would stick at, as she knew too well. The rules that governed the behavior of members of society did not apply to him.

Melanie remembered the last time she had been alone with Joseph, the blood, the pain, the fear. "You want to get rid of me so you can fuck someone else." And he had twisted her arm, thrown her down, hurt her; the blood had poured down her face, her body. "I had a nosebleed." She could almost hear her own girlish voice explaining to the maid at the beginning of the lies and lying.

Joseph's heavy weight had held her down as he entered her roughly and began to thrust, in and out, in and out. His erection was stronger than she had ever felt it to be. In the past she had been disappointed in his too rapid ejaculations;

169

now it seemed that he could continue the act endlessly. And as she had struggled, knowing herself helpless against him, the images, forgotten for years, flashed through her mind. As if the book were in front of her, the pages turning to one illustration after the other, she could see the naked girl, the dogs, the spike-studded hammer, the circle of men erect, the stool, the noose. *Les Malheurs de la vertu.*

Joseph had been indifferent to the bruises and lacerations that would prove impossible to conceal with cosmetics. She could tell what he was thinking: he had been a little rough, she had deserved it for playing with him as if he were no different from any other lover to be discarded when she grew weary of him. The affair would end when he chose, not sooner. Well, she had found her way out of the affair after all.

But he would not turn to violence with Harry. Dislike Harry? Why Harry was a feather in Joseph's cap. She had often observed him looking at Harry, appraising him—the cultivated manner and well-modulated voice, the handsome face, the figure narrow of waist and hips. Joseph took pleasure in each of Harry's assets. They reflected credit on him, for had he not preceded Harry with Melanie, proved himself the sexual equal of this young man with a great name and illustrious family history, the superior really? That was why he had favored Harry's suit. Melanie had known this all along. If it came to an elopement, nothing would please Woodruff more. That was the kind of action he understood, respected. Aggressiveness, determination, ruthlessness were the qualities he admired. Iris was his pet and he had been angry about Harry's vagueness. But Melanie did not know that she wanted to say any of this to Harry.

It was certainly sensible for Harry to have left his sweetheart and come to her for information about Woodruff, but it was hurtful all the same. She felt angry, used.

Always perceptive, Harry could tell she was annoyed with him and all this talk of elopement. As the affair between them intensified, he had been careful not to speak too much of Iris. But all summer Melanie had repeatedly told him he must keep his relationship with Iris alive, had warned him that theirs was sweet, fleeting, a summer romance. Now when the moment had come when he must act on all she had said, she was offended. "When I was with Iris, the elopement seemed so logical and I felt that I must come here and ask your advice. But I realize now that I was seeking an excuse to see you again, be with you."

Seeking an excuse to postpone his marriage, she wondered? Or just an excuse to make love one last time? Still, he was charming, her Harry. She could not bear to give him up so soon. New Year's was a time for weddings, not an elopement right away.

Well, Harry had put the means to hold that off into her hands. He would postpone action on the basis of her words. She could always change her advice if circumstances demanded. An elopement was a last-ditch effort. With Harry's bent for procrastination, she knew he would prefer to wait. And it might not be a mistake. Negotiations broke down as often as they succeeded.

Melanie had been silent for so long that Harry was looking at her, puzzled. "I have known Woodruff well enough to be able to tell you that I would not care to put myself in a position where I was at his mercy." That much was true and would not need to be repudiated later. "There is no certainty the Englishman will come to terms with Woodruff, who can be a most obnoxious person. Many things may yet happen, Harry. The Woodruffs adore Iris and she may be able to persuade them to give her what she wants." What she wanted was Harry.

"But what if the marriage settlement is made and a wedding date set?"

"You can elope with Iris then, next week, next month. They will hardly marry her off in an hour. You can elope at any time short of the actual moment when she enters the church on Joseph's arm and starts walking down the aisle."

That was true, and he needed to postpone the elopement. The swimming race would take place and give him the necessary funds to cover the immediate costs. But what would happen afterwards? Melanie had not fully answered his questions about Woodruff. It did not matter. The decision was his. If the marriage to the Englishman appeared inevitable, he would have to take the chance, elope with Iris, and hope for the best.

It would be hard to tell Iris that he was going to let negotiations for her marriage to another man go forward. Her look had been a bit distrustful. He would have to make her see that all he was doing was waiting to determine whether they could yet be married in proper style in a church with their families and friends standing by. Melanie was looking up at him from under her eyelashes. Many women did that, none so effectively. He wondered then at her advice that he postpone the elopement. It was logical, of course, but was unlike her, nonetheless. She invariably urged action; if she had criticized him for anything, it had been for procrastination. He recalled that she had once said to him that she lived on the assumption that nothing was as it seemed, that there was always a reason behind the reasons given and sometimes another reason behind that. The thought came to him— and it was undeniably pleasing—that she was not so eager to have him elope, that her desire for him might be the reason behind the reason given. Then he realized that there could be yet another reason, one not so pleasing, and that reason was Edmont and his new romance. Certainly it could not be serious; though there were rumors of divorce, Harry put these down to the general astonishment at Edmont's lapse. When you came right down to it, there was no one more conventional than Edmont, and as for his mother, she would never allow it. But knowing of this affair, Melanie might very well feel the need of a man by her side. She had always been the great beauty admired by all men. The role of the deceived wife was not one she would accept. In this new situation it would be natural for her to seek to avoid what might be taken as another abandonment, Harry's marriage to Iris. Harry felt uncomfortable with all these plots and counterplots going through his head when he liked things to be simple.

"Does any of this," he was unwilling to pin down just what "this" referred to, but thought she would guess, "have something to do with Mr. Edmont's . . . well, you know?"

"What do you mean, Harry?"

"The woman, the stout one from Chicago."

She stared at him. Clara Ribley. Bunny's Clara. Mr. Edmont's well-you-know.

So she had not known about Edmont's affair. Harry felt better, until he saw that she appeared stunned. Was it possible that Edmont was the one she cared about after all? Well, no. Of course, she cared about her husband but in a way that had nothing to do with the passion a woman felt for her lover, for him. Still, he could see it was a blow.

Once again he recalled the rumors about divorce and for an instant the thought flashed across his mind that Melanie might be free, as free as any nubile girl, and he felt a thrill of pleasure. Ridiculous of course. Even if convention did not make divorce impossible, to imagine Edmont replacing Melanie with Clara Ribley quite staggered the mind.

Why had it not been in the *Bugle*, which she read assiduously, wondered Melanie? But of course Wolfe would be afraid to tangle with Wallace Edmont; he knew he could be put out of business, forced to leave town. He knew just how far he could go.

Everything was clear to her now. The rumors about divorce. Wallace's threatening manner during their quarrel. She had been so convinced his personal life was irreproachable that she had not even troubled to tip his valet for information. An upright man, her father had said years before, never a hint of scandal about him at the clubs. Until now.

She understood why the women had acted so strangely Monday night at the Woodruffs' ball, the expectation in the room. The love affair she had believed Wallace would never have could change her life. Until now, for all her anxiety, she had not fully accepted that Wallace could leave her.

Clara Ribley. Bunny's Clara returned, but so changed

from the afternoon Melanie had sat concealed behind the gazebo, listening to her cooing voice, her moans of pleasure. Stout, middle-aged, dowdy. Nonetheless her rival.

Harry was waiting for her response, but she was beyond speaking. Shocked? Was there hurt as well? Yes, oddly, for all the times she had been unfaithful to Wallace, she found it, illogically, hurtful that he should turn to someone else. And fear. The specter of divorce, of ruin, drew closer.

A conservative man. Wallace weighed every decision. He must have considered whether divorce would be bad for business, whether financiers might draw back from giving capital and credit to a man who had been involved in a scandal. And there would be a separation from the children. His mother would be appalled. There were many arguments against divorce. And in its favor? An end to their quarrels. Revenge for her having known other men. But both of those factors had existed for years. What then was new? Clara Ribley. And the report in the *Bugle*, which Wallace insisted he never read. Odd that this little item with its catchphrase proved more ruinous than all the previous gossip. The timing had been disastrous. Melanie's summer toy. And Wallace's Clara.

The memory of standing with the women in the music room at the Woodruffs' came over her again and she flushed with shame. "So that was why Evangeline broke into the conversation. She quite took us all by surprise. And she did it for me, turned the conversation skillfully. I think she had been trying to warn me before that, but I didn't pay enough attention. It didn't occur to me that Evangeline might know something I did not." She turned to Harry. "I had understood that she could not hear at all."

"Evangeline has been taught a rare skill; merely from the way the lips move she can tell exactly what is being spoken. And because she is known to be deaf, no one troubles to guard his words. She could tear Bourneham and New York society apart if she had the interest and taste for it."

He was impatient at this talk of Evangeline, a digression enabling Melanie to conceal from him the way she felt about Wallace's affair. "I'm afraid I have been the bearer of unwelcome news." He took her upset personally. His jealousy was soothing to her. "I had thought you knew about Mrs. Ribley."

Clara had been at the Woodruffs' ball. Nellie had really outdone herself in terms of malice.

The sunlight streaming in through the window picked up the gold in Harry's hair and eyebrows. In spite of, perhaps because of the strain she was under, she was even more conscious of his desirability. Her whole life was falling apart. Harry, too, would be leaving her. One time, maybe this afternoon, would be the last time. Well, why not?

Sensing her change of mood, Harry began to relax and felt guilty at doing so. He really must leave Melanie, and return to Villa del Destino and reassure Iris.

Melanie stood up. "I should change into my riding habit. Will you wait for me here, Harry, until I return from my practice ride on camelback, or does one say 'on camel hump'?"

When Melanie smiled at him in that intimate way, Harry's resolve to see Iris immediately weakened. It was impossible to refuse Melanie. There was no knowing how long the visit to Villa del Destino might last. The best plan would be to go in the early evening and bribe one of the footmen to let Iris know he was there. Mrs. Woodruff would be out of the way getting dressed for dinner. There might not be many more opportunities to make love to Melanie. And he would spend the rest of his life with Iris.

He found himself smiling back at Melanie in the old way. "I will consider whether *hump* or *back* is more correct until you return."

Harry settled onto the chaise longue; it was scented with her perfume, heady with musk, fern, and sandalwood, the magic of a hidden grove. When he went home, his mother would smell it on him and sigh, but he could tell her quite honestly that he would not allow his suit with Iris to fail.

Harry was cheerful sitting there by the window looking out at the sun's reflection on the water, thinking about Melanie.

Leaving the house by way of the terrace, Melanie glanced up at his blond head by the window. If she were Iris, she would have made Harry elope with her that very day. But Iris waited for Harry, and Harry . . . well, he was still hers.

CHAPTER 14

A Camel Ride
and Other Events

An expanse of sand rising to
dunes in the background, desolation, the unrelenting brilliance of the sun—that should have been the scene. Instead
the camel trainer Abdelrahim, his boy Ali, and the camel
formed an incongruous group amidst the lush green farmland. They stood there patiently, men and beast, surveying
the scene with unblinking eyes. Perhaps they had been
waiting all day for Melanie (she never gave the hour of her
arrival), and would have waited another day or more, hardly
moving.

Melanie approached the camel, feeling as she did each
time a faint apprehension. It was a beast, freed from its com-
pound in the menagerie, a beast, unpredictable, for all its
motionless stance. The camel pulled back its soft lips, un-
covering large protruding teeth, some of them pointed. The
noises it was making seemed threatening to her, though they
resembled nothing so much as a stomach rumbling. Years
before at a reception she had met a zoologist, who had de-

scribed to her his experiences with desert animals. The camel, he declared, would seize its prey by the leg, and using the power of those frightful jaws, hurl it to the ground and beat on it with heavy, callused knee joints.

But as she came up to it, the camel looked at her so sadly with large limpid eyes beneath long fringes of eyelashes that she had a sudden feeling of fellowship. It had a sorrowful beauty. Grand and majestic, bizarre, like no other creature on earth, captive, it had no choice but to get down on its callused knees on command.

The beast was huge; the hump she was to sit on was so high off the ground and the sidesaddle with its hanging red tassels was precariously perched atop. Ali hissed loudly and in response the camel folded its hairy legs and settled onto the ground. The men lifted her into the saddle. Abdel rested his hand on her leg just a trifle too long, as did any man who touched her. She was used to it, barely noticed. Before she was ready, the camel, trained to rise at the weight of a body, lurched up in great swaying motions. A surge of pure fear came over her. This was the third time she had ridden the camel, but the initial moments were always bad. She would have to conquer the fear before the night of the ball.

Once up, she felt exhilarated at being so high, higher than on horseback, in command, not only of the camel but of the entire surroundings. The camel put its head down to sniff at the grass, but turned away. This herbage was too juicy, too green; dry shrubs, cactus, and thornbush were its proper diet. Looking down the long expanse of neck gave Melanie a jolt, her stomach tightened, but pleasurably, as before some great excitement. Led by the trainer and his boy, the camel walked down the dirt road onto the farmland, careless of the rows of corn trampled beneath the heavy flat hooves, then back again to the road. Melanie rocked back and forth, yielding herself to the animal's movement. That was the summer Mrs. Wallace Montague Edmont V rode a camel into the great ballroom of Île de Joie. Imagining eyes upon her, she straightened her back and lifted her head. Now she was beginning to enjoy herself.

Seated on the camel, she was conscious of the rank animal smell. Like the odors of sex, it was not unpleasant to her. The air of the ballroom would be unscented so that the smell of the camel would come through, adding to the sense of the unusual, unknown, wild, juxtaposing the desert with the overcivilized decor, the mirrors, the crystal chandeliers, the gilded sconces, the family crest. The rankness would not be allowed to remain for so long as to disgust the fastidious. After she had dismounted and the camel was tethered by the palm trees, the room would be sprayed with a perfume that had been specially formulated for the occasion by her perfumer in Paris.

What of her own body? Each day when she returned from riding the camel she bathed in scented water and stepped out into a cloud of perfume sprayed by her maid from a huge atomizer, cut from a single piece of onyx.

Abdel touched her leg again as if by accident. She noticed it now, but was indifferent. She knew that many women, as they grew older, found men like this exciting. How often did not the *Bugle* hint at respectable matrons taking footmen, gardeners, chauffeurs as lovers? She would not say it could never happen to her. All the things one thought would never happen did. One thought one would never paint one's face, but, of course, in time, the shadows under the eyes, the pallor of the cheeks demanded it, or tint one's hair, but, of course, at the first sign of gray, color was added to the rinse water.

"Let us run," she told Abdel and he, shaking his head and reluctant, struck the camel on the rump and it began to race, pitching her back and forth, and just visible in the distance was the long road leading to Bourneham, the mansions with windows golden in the afternoon sun. Oh, this was freedom.

From afar she noticed a horseman approaching, but he seemed so remote from her atop the camel that she did not expect him to ride up so quickly. As the camel ran—one could not call it a gallop or a canter or trot, but rather a rocking run—the trainer and his boy were left behind. Suddenly the horse was directly ahead of her, the rider reining in sharply. The camel stopped short and shuddered so violently that if she had not grasped the pommel of the ill-conceived side-saddle with both hands, she would have fallen. She was so angry she could not help but raise her voice. It was the tone she used when quarreling with Wallace: "Surely you will not tell me you were unable to see the camel!"

"I will tell you just that," the horseman replied very softly and distinctly. "I observed nothing but its rider."

She looked up, saw the ruddy face, the dark hair growing down to thick eyebrows.

"I have often imagined you riding, Melanie. Although until today it never entered my mind that a camel would be the creature involved."

Denis. There it was again. The heat in the groin. The cramp in the stomach. The difficulty breathing. Nothing had changed. Despite the birth of the heir, he had come back to her.

Abdel came running up, Ali close behind him. "Take me down," she ordered, so dizzy with emotion she could hardly tolerate the great seesawing movements as the camel knelt, down with the front legs, down with the back. Abdel steadied her; she clutched at his arm, glad of it this time.

Denis had dismounted, too, and stood waiting for her, smiling. He handed the reins of his horse to Ali, barely glancing at him, certain there would always be a servant to come to his assistance. Followed by Ali leading the horse and Abdel the camel, they formed a procession walking down the road. Melanie thought of the infant boy and felt a sharp pain in her side. "Why are you here?"

"This is why I am here." Denis enjoyed such elliptical talk. "To tell you why I am here before you learn it from someone else."

"As I recall you always said late August in the United States was unbearable. Too hot."

"We change. We must change with the times. I have come to make my fortune . . . remake it I suppose I should say."

180

"I thought you had a fortune, Denis."

"Fortunes too change with the times."

And then she knew. He had changed so little really to become Iris's awful Englishman. A bit thicker around the middle, his waistcoat strained over a small paunch and under the whiskers of his beard she could see jowls. His hair was still black, but the beard was flecked with gray. What was it Harry had said? A fat old Englishman. Hairy. Awful. To Iris. But still her Denis. Heart-stopping. He had not come for her after all. Iris was to walk the drafty halls of Carnaugh, swathed in ermine, kept warm with silk-lined woolens. This had been arranged during these past four months. No wonder he had not written again.

"The communications system in Bourneham is faster than you think it," she said. "You have waited too long to tell me; the word is out already that you wish to call Joseph Woodruff 'father-in-law.' "

If her choice of words disturbed him, he was far too well schooled to give any indication. "Why didn't you write, Melanie? I had expected to hear from you after sending you letters with such terrible news." He appeared angry, hurt.

"Letters?"

"Yes, I wrote again of the child's death a week after Adelaide's."

"But I never received the second letter and the one informing me of Adelaide's death arrived only yesterday." She knew then what had happened. The letters had not been lost by accident, but by design. Nellie Woodruff, the careful campaigner, had been in England, Melanie realized, right after Adelaide's death. Once she had fixed on Denis as a husband for Iris, she had planned for every contingency. Poor foolish misguided Dena had surely been paid to hold back any letters from England. Nellie missed nothing; she alone must have guessed at the carefully concealed affair with Denis, never gossiped about, never mentioned in the scandal columns. She had feared what Melanie might do upon learning such news. Take ship to England? Divorce Wallace? Anything had been possible. What was still possible?

He had come for Iris, but that did not mean he would leave with Iris. It was not for this that she had waited a quarter of a century.

A marquess since his father's death. Who would have imagined Nellie could capture such a prize? Harry had never mentioned the title. She had known Carnaugh was in disrepair, but such a union spoke of absolute disaster. Unless Harry had been wrong and Denis really had seen Iris before, wanted her, and found the Woodruff fortune a mere added inducement. Denis liked young girls.

But if it were money, and that was the likelier story, the death of the heir meant she might yet live her dream and become mistress of Carnaugh. For the first time since Harry had told her of Wallace's unaccountable desire for Clara, she saw that her husband's affair might work to her benefit. Wallace's fall from grace reversed their positions in the event of divorce. No longer would he have the upper hand. No longer would she be in a poor bargaining position when it came to a settlement. The guilt would be his, the bargaining advantage hers.

She could not think how to proceed, how to make happen what she wished. Melanie had been taught from childhood on that plans were made by men, direct actions taken by them. For all her determination and high spirits, she saw no way to achieve her ends other than through indirection and feminine wiles. She had come to believe in the power of her seductiveness. But seductiveness took time and that was lacking.

Over the years she had found that Denis was never more loving than when she refused to meet with him alone, spoke of another lover (he knew of her lovers; she saw to it that he knew). She could make him suffer, would observe him turn white when in the course of a dinner party she would let him see how she gave her attention to another man. No one could be more charming than Denis when in pursuit. Once she gave way, his manner would change. After having told her about pessaries in the first place, he would appear contemptuous to learn that she had carried one concealed in her corset cover from the moment she arrived in England. Yes, they had learned to torture each other—he to make her unsure of his love, she to make him doubt hers. She did not trust him; how could she trust him after so bad a beginning? After the cold careful letters that followed the most rapturous meetings? After the dinners at Carnaugh where she would look down the table and there would be the inevitable young girl staring avidly at Denis? These girls with their soft rosy flesh seemed interchangeable to Melanie, sweet as puff pastry in their fluffy gowns. Adelaide would be sitting beside him, touching him, unless recovering from miscarriage or stillbirth.

Often she had wished herself free of Denis. She would glance at him, pleased to see how stocky he looked, how short even when seated, how hairy his face. What was there in this man to have led her to such excess?

But if one moment afterwards Denis sent a maid to her with a note arranging to meet her, she was unable to feign indifference. Nothing could stop her, not an affair with another man, not knowing as she always did that Wallace was the person deserving her loyalty, not the child growing beneath Adelaide's loosened gown, not the pretty little girl in flowered blue voile. She was driven. Trust or mistrust had nothing to do with desire. For all their cruel games with one another, the passion between them remained, the resistance to it token and short-lived.

And when they would embrace, standing as in the past, she would remember only that he had wept for her and love would be there again, only with no hope for them of more than this. Until now, with Adelaide and the child dead and Wallace for the first time unfaithful. A divorce would free her—for Denis. Except that he had not come here for her. He had come for Iris. At the ugly thought the pain in her side became more acute, but she straightened her back, held her head high.

They walked side by side, Abdel and Ali following at a

distance with the animals, the coachman and Beryl waiting in the carriage. There was no one else within miles to see, yet so ingrained was the habit of caution that they did not touch.

"Now I understand why you never wrote. You know, Melanie, for a moment I thought, hoped, you would leave for England when you received my letter. You have always had a touch of the impetuous in you, Melanie. And the fact is that actions just so impetuous are taken, by people like us. I have personal knowledge of that." She could not imagine what he was talking about. Could Adelaide . . . ?

The pain in her side had disappeared at his words. He had hoped she would come to him. She stepped lightly on the balls of her feet, feeling young again, younger than Harry, than Iris. Walking down the road with Denis, she walked back into her past. It was always like that. Afterwards she would go home and in the mirrored walls of her dressing room expect to see the dewy skin, the bold look in the big round eyes showing a spirit uncaged, untamed, the lips wet and smooth and trembling, the softness, not fat—she had lost her baby fat before she met Denis—but there was a delicious roundness of arms, of breasts. The elegance and perfection of her present appearance, the veiled look in her eyes, startled, saddened her. It was not that she was less beautiful now; perhaps she was more so, queenly, people called her, striking. But not young.

Walking down the road with Denis, she could see him as he had been that afternoon when she walked into the drawing room at her mother's call and saw him, desirable before she knew the true meaning of that word. He had stood there in front of her in the music room, his sex outlined in his tight trousers, perspiring, the heavy look she had since come to know so well, the heavy look of lust on his face. She looked again and saw the older man, Iris's fat old Englishman superimposed on the young man she remembered.

"You neither wrote nor came—I did not know you had not received my letters—and of course, I quickly realized that it could never happen. The Woodruffs and I are the logical combination, incongruous as we may appear together. As for you and me, nothing has really changed except for one member of the cast of characters. We will go on together as people in our positions do."

Melanie was about to tell him it did not need to be that way, but he went on talking, deflecting her. They walked down the road together and he told her that she was beautiful, never more so, and desirable, never more so. They must arrange to meet again, more privately, if she took his meaning. He was looking about for place and opportunity. And he did not speak of Iris and she did not know if he were being kind or cruel. He caressed her with his voice. He had come to marry Iris but how caressingly he talked. What was lacking in the man? And yet she found herself slipping back into the dream with him, the dream in which the rest of her life dimmed. They walked and around the bend of the road it seemed that she would meet her young self walking towards her.

The road was shimmering in the sunlight. Waves of heat rose from the surface. Melanie imagined for a second that the trunks filled with cashmeres, with furs, brocades, velvets, the collections of years were blocking the path, as in a mirage. She shook her head. This was a time for thinking clearly. What was said today, decided today, could change her whole life. How beautiful his voice was; sometimes the sound distracted her so that she listened to that, not the meaning of his words. They stood by the side of the road. The camel trainer and his boy holding the reins of the animals stopped a distance away. The horse appeared restless, pawing the ground, lifting its head, tossing its mane. The men and the camel waited with infinite patience. Time that mattered so greatly to her did not matter to them.

Denis became silent then. An advantageous marriage was mandatory now, he was thinking, in view of the disaster following his father's death the previous year. He had known that things were bad. The winter before last he had discovered his father's sale of the best of their Rembrandts. An agent had been sent to Holland secretly. The sale had been revealed by chance when one of the maids reported to Adelaide that a painting was missing from the north gallery. Denis seldom went there himself. He had little interest in any art that was not English and preferred the Constables, Gainsboroughs, and Turners hanging in the central hall. But sure enough, there was a rectangle of pale cream where the painting used to hang, startling against the time-darkened wall all around. At first he had thought of burglary; that would have been preferable. And the Rembrandt had been just a beginning.

Afterwards he could not have said he had not been warned. Adelaide of all people had seen what was happening more clearly than he, had urged him—stammering a little because it was so unlike her to proffer advice—to insist on his father's opening the books to him, to take a strong stand and protect his heritage. But he could not oppose his father. Waiting to inherit a title, being an heir, kept one a boy in some ways for too long, he thought bitterly. He had thought Adelaide exaggerating; she had no sense of proportion where dynasty was concerned. Now his regret was that his father had died, the catastrophe fallen before her death. The knowledge that she had been right had been cold comfort to her. Swollen with child, worrying. Poor girl.

As she lay dying, Adelaide had called Denis to her. "At least save Carnaugh," she had whispered, "whatever you have to do, whatever it is."

At the time he had not grasped the import of her words; it was only later when Nellie Woodruff had him to tea and spoke of Iris that it dawned upon him that she had been urging even such a second marriage upon him. If Adelaide had lived, there would have been no way to save Carnaugh, no way at all.

Well, Melanie and he would go on. He could not imagine his life without her. Her skin still had the quality he had never found in anyone else, roseate, as if heated by an inner fire. To touch her was to sense that heat, that fire. Perhaps they would see one another more often now. Shipping was so much improved; the *Kaiser Wilhelm* made its way from Southampton in England to New York in but eleven days.

"I did not come only to give you news, but to see you ride the camel, Melanie. All Bourneham is talking of it; anticipation is high."

"You would see me on Saturday anyway, Denis. I had already urged Nellie Woodruff to bring her guests with her. She was very arch about my invitation, would not tell the names, insisted her guests would surprise me."

"I could not be satisfied by watching a ride across a ballroom, Melanie, in the company of others. I cannot describe how I felt riding up the road and seeing you erect, regal, high above the countryside on that great mysterious beast of the desert. Oh, that will be something to tell my grandchildren."

Iris, the seams of her velvet gown straining at the waist. Melanie stumbled though there was no unevenness in the road. She caught at his arm. He could feel her trembling. Grandchildren. The heir. That was the one thing she had forgotten in making her calculations. His obsession. Adelaide's too, she supposed, or perhaps adopted as a way to hold him. Poor Adelaide had died for it. Rosamunde was still a baby. Could she become pregnant again? Adelaide had been older than she would be even given a year or more for the divorce to go through. Her mother had not undergone the change until she was past fifty and the tendency ran in families. "Rosamunde is not yet two, Denis."

Could Melanie possibly be implying that a marriage between them was feasible? And that were it to take place, she could yet bear him a child? It was hard to attribute the remark about Rosamunde to any other purpose. The thought appalled him: one wife lost in late childbirth to reproach himself with and she suggested another. It was not like Melanie to be so fanciful. Surely she recognized that Adelaide's dying freed only him; she was still bound in marriage to

Edmont. She was usually so clear-eyed. Then Denis remembered that even he, with all there was against it, had guiltily allowed himself that fantasy for a moment after Adelaide's death.

Adelaide's death. It had been unexpected. Strange to say, despite her advanced age for motherhood, the pregnancy had gone well, better than any of the previous ones. They had hoped . . . the doctors had given them reason to hope . . . for a living child at last. Adelaide's funeral. It had not rained. Denis could hardly remember a day for a gathering in his part of the country, were it wedding or garden party, let alone funeral, when it had not been lowering and gray, pouring down rain, or at least an intermittent drizzle. But on that day the weather had been perfection, balmy and clear, the clouds white and puffy, the lawn emerald green, the golden daffodils pushing up between the graves. Somehow it made everything seem worse. The boy, too, was dead, dying in those few days while the preparations for the mother's funeral were being made. A small grave by the larger one.

Melanie wondered at his look of desolation. "I was remembering Adelaide's death and the funeral." By speaking of Rosamunde, Melanie had hoped to make Denis think of her as wife, mother, to use this as a way to lead into telling him what had happened with Wallace; instead she had turned his thoughts back to his own infant, his loss, back to Adelaide.

"We were standing by the grave. And my wife's governess . . . I know her name as well as my own, but somehow it eludes me . . . she came up to me, crippled with arthritis, limped up on two canes, stumbling on the uneven ground. She is ninety or more, shriveled and bent, beyond observing the proprieties. From her expression I feared for a moment she meant to spit in my face, but then she drew back. 'How could you get my girl with child so late? It was criminal, unconscionable.' Her speech was so indistinct that it took me a moment to grasp what she had said. I could not be angry at her presumption, knowing she spoke out of love."

188

Perhaps more love than he had felt. "I knew it my responsibility to answer and I did so, with difficulty. I told her than Adelaide—I spoke of Lady Warburne familiarly to her governess—had wanted it so." But he was not quite sure. Had she recoiled, flinched those last times he had taken her? Standing there in the brilliant sunshine, under the accusing reddened eyes of the ancient governess, he had felt sick with guilt and regret. He would have liked to cry out that he had not meant it to work out this way, that he had done his duty as he had seen it with the utmost probity. He had allowed himself so little, had relegated his love for Melanie to the background, to the most occasional visit, so as to fulfill his obligations to Adelaide, to his family.

Looking down at the grave, he felt guilty that even then he was wanting Melanie. He had returned to Carnaugh sunk in melancholy to struggle with his burdens. Walking about the estate, marquess at last, he had recalled his family's great history: the lands on which the village stood had been given by Edward III to his ancestor as a reward for courage and loyalty, the only charge a battle standard to be sent to the ruling monarch each year. His father had carried on this tradition. Now it was for him. As things turned out, its successful maintenance depended on his marrying little Miss Woodruff. "I do not know what I would have done . . ." His voice trailed off, as he realized that he was saying too much. If the Woodruffs had not turned up. Providential, he was thinking. Melanie knew it.

"I have heard it said that Iris Woodruff is in love with someone else," she said, and thought all at once of Harry. Not much more than an hour had passed since she watched the sun pick up glints of gold in his hair. How light he seemed, how bright. Even in the sunshine, she was aware of the darkness in her relationship with Denis who was unperturbed by her words.

"I will win Iris around. I know how to please young girls."

She gasped, never knowing when in conversation he

would hurt her, put in the knife. How could it matter so much? Years went by and she did not see him. How to please young girls. Did he want her to remember her own past, to think now of the child he meant to take in the huge four-poster bed in his icy bedroom? Despite her control, she looked stricken.

Denis was taken aback. He had not wished to hurt her, only to make her see the marriage would happen. He wondered that, with all her experience of the world, she could not understand that his marrying Miss Woodruff would not alter his feeling for her. What did an obligatory marriage have to do with love?

"Forgive me. I did not mean that as it sounded."

She forced herself to be calm: the conclusion to their history was not yet written. "You could have meant it," she said coolly. "I have reason to know how very well you please young girls. Your words are true."

"True for us both perhaps." He was annoyed. When it came down to it, there was no excuse for her taking offense. "I had hardly arrived in Bourneham when I learned that you are 'playing'—I think that is the word being bandied about—with the very young yourself."

They were both annoyed now. She felt he had no right to throw the *Bugle* and her age in her face. His bringing up Harry upset her. She had always been able to keep all other relationships separate from her feeling for Denis. His power stemmed from the past, unalterable. Anyway it was not as if her romance with Harry, perforce temporary, bore a resemblance to Denis's planning a lifetime with Iris. Their interplay so often had an edge.

It was on her mind to speak nastily, to remind him that by his standards little Miss Woodruff was not among the very young, was a full three years past the age he favored. Fifteen, gasping for breath against the unaccustomed corset. All these years and at last the opportunity to make it come right. She must not quarrel with him now.

Denis also was thinking better of his words, seeking to

end the hostile interchange. "I must return to Villa del Destino," he said pleasantly, changing the subject. "My hostess has instituted a policy of serving English tea in my honor each afternoon. I have never cared for hot tea." (*He likes only frigid beverages. My Denis is always so hot.* How his perspiration had dripped onto her face, down her neck.) "But her courtesy demands my pretense."

The meeting was ending and she had yet to suggest to him the way they could go. At tea in the villa, he would remember her words, contrast her vitality, sexuality, with the etiolated charm of little Iris. In the conservatory with Iris, Harry had been unable to put Melanie out of his mind. At Adelaide's grave Denis had longed for her. Denis would yet be hers. She must make a start. "Perhaps you have moved into an engagement too rapidly, Denis. We have so often talked of what might happen were we to be free. Can you bear to give that up for Iris Woodruff? What if I too could free myself?"

Bed talk, he was recalling, pillow talk with Melanie. It had nothing to do with reality. She could not bear the thought of his making love to Iris; he understood that. But free herself? Divorce? She could not be serious. People like them did not divorce. Not even his father, and certainly no man had a greater provocation. Her jealousy was blinding her, an insight infinitely pleasing to him. "You speak as if I had a choice when I have none. Without the Woodruffs, I lose what I have no right to lose."

"I would not come empty-handed," she told him. "My nuptial agreement was favorable and there would be a divorce settlement."

Denis found it hard to believe she was discussing this as a possibility. What could she hope to get from Edmont if she left him (which he would never let her do no matter how many men's names were linked with hers)?

Seeing his disbelief, she went on. "Denis, there is talk of divorce, serious talk. Wallace's lawyer is too frequently at the house now."

That did startle him, but he appeared unmoved by her words. Perhaps he was thinking of the scandal and how it would affect him with his hereditary title, his position as a member of the House of Lords. He did not know that far from being the guilty party, she was now the wronged wife, a distinction that could make all the difference where propriety was involved. It was not as if, in these advanced times, there were no divorces in England.

The advantages of her new position were so clear to her now. Junior would see his father for the first time in an unfavorable light as profligate, deceitful. And her friendship with Genevieve, the only deep friendship with another woman she had ever known, need not be forfeit. For all her doting on Wallace, Genevieve would sympathize with Melanie. Losing her mother-in-law had been one of the most distressing thoughts aroused by the specter of divorce. Now all that was changed. If only she could make Denis understand. "Something strange and unexpected has happened. There is a . . . a woman."

Denis had not thought Edmont had it in him, but then what did it change after all? Husbands took mistresses as wives took lovers and marriages went on. Melanie should certainly know that; she was snatching at straws. In any event, Edmont could not be serious. With a wife like Melanie, another woman could at best be a diversion. In the end they would make it up. Melanie would not be able to manage without the Edmont name and money any more than he without the Woodruff fortune. A divorce settlement! The way she lived, he could imagine how rapidly she would run through it. The marquisate required money on the grand scale.

"He will appear as the guilty party," she went on. "The settlement will have to be generous, very generous."

It was not for him to convince her that her best course was to resolve her difficulties with Edmont. She was temporarily deluded. Nothing good could come to her out of a divorce. He had known a few divorced women; any one of them would have given all she possessed to have gone back to her marriage, however miserable it had been. But he knew she would take this ill coming from him. At least he could pretend to take her seriously, make her see that divorce would not make it possible for him to give up the Woodruffs and marry her. He wondered how much could be told her without his losing face altogether. It was bad enough to come here hat in hand, as it were, having everyone gossip that he was trading his title for money—as indeed he was.

He spoke of the Carnaugh payroll. "It fills me with consternation, just seeing the list for the house—the butler, four footmen and six oddmen for the heavy work, the housekeeper and half a dozen housemaids, a chief cook and an assistant and five kitchen workers, my valet, Adelaide's personal maid who can hardly be put out after a quarter century of service and her governess. It takes six women to do the laundry and the ironing. Then there are the grounds and the gardens and the greenhouses, requiring a staff of twenty."

Melanie was not impressed. Everyone she knew had a plethora of servants.

Well, the plumbing, then, thought Denis. Americans seemed to react most strongly to that shortcoming. "We live at Carnaugh as if we were not in the nineteenth century." Trips to the water closet had to be timed when the house was filled with visitors. For the lack of bathrooms, guests took baths in tubs set up in their bedrooms. Melanie used to comment on the incongruity of it, the towels and sponges, the soaps and the jugs of hot water and cold water amidst the decaying splendor of the furniture. And then of course the cold, which did not bother him. He thought cold healthy, but Americans could not get over the chill. It was as if the stones held in the cold of seven hundred years.

Now he did take her hand; it felt hot and dry, burning. "There is nothing I would like more, Melanie, than to take you back to Carnaugh. You would fill those rooms, fill my life. Quite differently from pale little, frail little Miss Woodruff. But she is my fate."

193

Denis did not gloss over his decision. Not a word here of love, barely of regret. Nothing he would like more. But not enough to act on. No, not that much liking. She was exaggerating. It was that he did not see marriage in those terms, but as a business arrangement, and she did not offer good enough terms.

Not for the first time she thought of the stock she owned in Carle & Company; if only she could become active in the company, she was sure she could make it profitable. If she ran the bank, there might be money to rebuild Carnaugh.

Would that make the difference? She was filled with doubt as to his love, wondering if he were using his financial plight as an excuse. No, she could not believe that. Of course, he wanted her. She could not think he did not care. He had put his head in his hands and wept. She had seen the tears slipping through his fingers. But then she thought that grief, those tears were shed twenty years or more ago. Decades had passed since that rapture behind the door. Oh quick, quick someone will come. What since? Why, Harry spoke of love more feelingly.

Denis was looking at her, his eyes, underneath the heavy eyebrows, were very shiny. "Melanie. Nothing changes between us. We will go on together."

"Everything will change if you marry Iris." Melanie was vehement. "Everything. This is our last opportunity. Don't throw it away."

"I have found a way, Melanie, or rather the way has found me. You must believe that it has nothing to do with my feeling for you."

"Marrying Iris has nothing to do with the way you feel about me." She said it contemptuously, seeing it as an absurdity.

He wished she would not make it so hard for him. She did not see that he was suffering, too. As usual it was left to him to shoulder his responsibilities and do what must be done. His parents, careless, selfish, had left it all for him; and his resentment at being in this position made him speak

194

more impatiently than he meant. "It is all settled really. Before dawn tomorrow my cousin and I are to leave for New York with Woodruff on his yacht. There we will meet with Woodruff's lawyers and draw up the marriage contract."

All settled. The end of her hopes. She would never be able to make it come right. The pregnancy. The self-induced miscarriage. She would never be able to say that their relationship had started badly, blighted by obstacles, but look how well it had ended. Forever, she would be the foolish virgin, he the seducer.

And then she saw the solution. It was simple, so very simple. The power was hers now, not Denis's, nor Wallace's, nor scheming Nellie Woodruff's. She had but to return home where Harry was expecting her and proffer a different piece of advice. Reverse herself. Everyone knew that women changed their minds. A few words and Harry would remove Iris from the scene out of Denis's reach.

Unexpectedly she felt a pang. Earlier this day she had been so sure she did not wish Harry to marry Iris too quickly. An odd thought crossed her mind: what if Nellie's plan were the one to succeed and Harry were left free? Well, what difference would that make to her? His mother would find him another rich young girl and it would all have to be gone through again. The difficulty of the scene with Denis was making her think foolishly. She knew whom she wanted, whom she had wanted all her life as a woman.

With the Woodruff fortune lost to Denis, the divorce settlement would no longer appear negligible. Another wealthy bride? It was not likely that Denis would accept a second American heiress after so great a loss of face.

The fact was that he still wanted her, Melanie. That was the source of her greatest power. Whether her doubts were grounded in reality and in truth his love for her was shallow, his desire was still strong. She could sense his longing to touch her skin. Brushing against him, she felt his excitement. She could make it all happen; there was no need to wait as she had been taught, to allow the man to make the

195

decision. A woman sometimes had to take the action that would save them both.

Strangely, she still felt disquieted, a qualm perhaps though she could not see why. Certainly, this plan was good for each of them. Not only for her. It would provide what they wanted. Harry would marry Iris, as he wished to do, as of course she wished him to do, as his mother desperately wished him to do. It would be better for Denis, too. He had been dazzled by the Woodruff money. But she would make him happy, happier than he had ever been with Adelaide, happier than he could ever be with pale unwilling shrinking virgin Iris. And yet there was this unease, almost as if she were betraying she could not imagine whom.

Denis was going to New York tomorrow. She would contrive to go, too. Her ball . . . she felt distress at absenting herself for a day during the preparations. How could she explain it to Wallace? What would she say to Harry? It was to visit her mother, she rehearsed excuses; the house was so unsettled and filled with cleaning people as to be quite unlivable this week.

"I plan to go to New York tomorrow myself, Denis."

"How so?"

"It's time to visit my mother. You remember her, I am sure."

"Ah, yes," he said, not thinking of her mother, but rather of what use, what sweet, familiar, always exciting use might be made of that visit. She could tell by the way a little vein in his forehead began to throb.

"Perhaps I will stop in to offer my compliments. Your mother was a most generous hostess to Adelaide and me. Woodruff must yield me up for a few hours to make my courtesy call."

As they talked they had been walking back down the road to the spot where Melanie's carriage was waiting for her. Ali came up with Denis's horse and by the time he was mounted she felt almost confident. The meeting in the city had been settled between them. They would be together, really together. Nothing would change, he had said, but what had been was never enough. She would send him back to the Woodruffs, back to Bourneham filled with her, her touch, her body heat, her perfume. There he would learn of Iris's defection. Watching Denis ride away, her heartbeat quickened to see him rein in his horse just before the curve in the road, stop to look back at her one last time. The situation would favor her yet.

Melanie stepped into the waiting carriage, rehearsing what she would say to Harry. Iris was not to be Denis's fate, but Harry's. Again that pang of . . . she did not know what to call it. She must keep in mind the fact that she was acting in Harry's best interest. But still she was uneasy.

CHAPTER 15

How to
Hold Melanie

$\mathbf{A}$s Denis rode back to Bourne-
ham and the Woodruffs', he was thinking he had handled
the situation with Melanie rather well. It was necessary to
keep a certain distance, to leave her slightly unsure of his
feeling, his intentions. In this manner, he was convinced, he
had held her interest over all these years against the romantic promises and eternal vows of other men. Captives, they
lost value for their servitude, their ready availability. Alone
among the men of her experience, he had shown himself
elusive, remained free, able to disappear at any moment. She
had to try to capture him.

He had not come to this mode of behavior by design. It
had been forced upon him by the mistrust Melanie never
lost; everything had reinforced it. The seduction (though he
had been as much seduced as seducer), the cool letters he
had written, proud of himself for having worded them so
that her mother and later Edmont could read them without
suspicion, the gossip about him beginning with that little
Valerie.

Melanie? He had been young then himself and at the time they met had not suspected her to be merely fifteen. She had seemed older, tall, and already something regal in her posture. Then her manner, the way she brushed her hips against him, catching her breath, her breasts pushing against the tight bodice of her dress so that the nipples showed—he had not thought her a virgin. She had been so lovely, her large round eyes gleaming, her Roman nose making a flawless profile when she turned her head. There was an incredible sensuality in her figure, slender, curving, voluptuous. The dress she wore had sleeves only to the elbow and her arms and hands were so beautifully shaped, the wrists slender, the fingers long and tapering. But it was the quality of her skin, her flesh, that had undone him. One ached to touch it, caress it with fingers, lips, tongue. Even in the Carles' drawing room with Adelaide beside him, it had taken an effort of will to keep his hands quiet.

If she had resisted in the slightest, demurred, played the virgin, ignorant of his intentions, he would not have gone forward. But she had been as driven as he. And by the time he realized the innocence, the purity of her passion, no man, he believed, could have turned back. Melanie, his Melody. He had thought himself careful; that first occasion had been her monthly time of safety. Later he had withdrawn. But perhaps not quickly enough.

When it happened, Melanie told him later, she had not known to blame him. "That is how innocent I was." She spoke with bitterness. Ironically, she pointed out, it was only when the experience was safely behind her, the knitting needle returned to its place, that she saw him as seducer, debaucher, vicious. Yet she had felt she still must love him, had to love him, she said, with an undercurrent of anger. How could she bear to recall that rapture, that agony, if not dignified by love?

It was not to be borne the way she was looking at him. He wanted to cry out that this was not how he behaved, was not the kind of person he was. It was out of character, against his nature. There was no man more responsible, more concerned about doing his duty than he.

But he had not known. There was the mitigating circumstance: he had not known; she had not informed him. Had she done so, he would have helped, located a physician, paid; that sort of thing was done all the time. American connections could be found.

"Why didn't you let me know? Write to me?"

She looked away from him then. "You sent me your compliments."

And it was at the memory of his carefully phrased, cold letter that he had broken down. He could hardly believe it of himself. There could not have been another time in his adult life that he had so given way. Even as a boy when his mother had caused such grief, he had retained control almost to the same extent as his father.

But how was he to endure the knowledge of what he had done, of his guilt, the knowledge of having behaved in the most feckless manner?

His mother's son, one might have said. Not to be endured. And he had felt guilt, though Melanie could not believe it; he would awaken in a cold sweat of shame in those dark hours before the dawn. Once back in England he had been consumed by it, had determined not to put Melanie at risk again, had not known how he could face her. He had used Adelaide's pregnancies as excuses not to visit America, been relieved when Melanie did not accompany her parents to England. With what genuine pleasure he had heard she was engaged. He had sent her his felicitations and they had been sincere. If he had harbored the thought that afterwards they could begin again . . . well, an affair with a married woman was quite a different matter, almost safe.

Later she would recall his tears and accuse him of having used them cynically to win her once again. Had he appeared always indifferent, callous to her pain, she would have been free of him, she said bitterly. It was this unexpected rare softness, suspect though it was, that sustained her passion for him.

He would have liked to justify himself to her, recognizing that she expressed her bitterness so that he would deny that she had cause. But it would have been a mistake, he came to realize, a way to lose her—and that he could not bear. Uncertainty, unpredictability, these were the qualities that held her, made him perversely more desirable. These, and the fact that he had been her first lover. And what lasting damage had been done, after all? Her life should have been ruined; she should have been dishonored, her chances destroyed. Yet far from being ruined, dishonored, destroyed, she had made the most brilliant match of any girl in New York society, captured the wealthiest, the most respectable and respected of men as husband.

He had possessed Melanie to a greater degree than Edmont, he was convinced, yet at the same time knew himself inextricably bound to Adelaide in his compulsion to guarantee that the marquisate and Castle Carnaugh remain in the direct line of descent.

Adelaide had been overwhelmed by Denis's charm. She made no demands on him; being accepted everywhere as his choice, as his wife, touching him, finding ways to reveal her intimate knowledge of him, these were her satisfactions. They had little in common. How could it have been otherwise? She lacked the intellectual curiosity that had enabled Melanie to go beyond the limited education commonly given then to women, even the wellborn. What could an Oxford graduate, well-traveled and well-read, discuss with her?

It was a marriage no different from countless others among the aristocracy, were it not for the tragic misadventures of her obstetrical history. So obsessed was she with her childless state that there seemed room in her life for nothing else. Each pregnancy was greeted with joy at the outset. What a good sport was Adelaide going on a regular cycle of hope, illness, loss, illness, despair, and then to hope again. Her skin coarsened, her hair became thin and limp, her figure thickened.

And the saddest part of it, he realized, was Adelaide's discovery that this was the way she could please him, command his attention. Only when she was pregnant did his eyes light up at the sight of her, did he kiss her hand and her face.

Yet there had been a time, Adelaide's physician had seen fit to tell Denis, when she had asked whether there were not a way to space out one's pregnancies. The physician had been embarrassed and told her nothing. But she had not given up; this was the part that haunted Denis after her death. Later she had admitted to having consulted her governess, whom one would have thought the most unlikely of sources. The governess had revealed to a shocked Adelaide the practice of coitus interruptus, rubber condoms, a pessary. Adelaide had blushed when she hesitantly mentioned these stratagems to Denis. Of course he had agreed at once; he was after all a gentleman. But these techniques and devices had not seemed worth the trouble. It was not as if he were consumed by a raging desire for Adelaide; it was her pregnancy not her body he wanted. And so he suggested periods of abstinence, which, it turned out, was the one method she refused. He knew what she was thinking: if he did not come regularly to her bed, what was their relationship then?

And so she accepted that it was her destiny to bear the long-desired son. She embraced it as she embraced him. The illness, the cramping and bleeding: they lasted too short a time to be important, she told him. There were occasional moments when he would come upon her all alone weeping. Had it been out of fear? Had she been forcing herself to try again, rise above her weakness?

Of course, Denis thought after her death, he had cared about her. One could not spend a quarter of a century with such a woman and feel nothing at all. He sometimes missed her, the sweetness of her smile with which she had always greeted him, the way she had of putting her cool hand on his forehead, always so damp, so hot. It had been time to stop. This trying for a child had gone on too long. She was too old. He had been the first to say so, more tactfully, of course, but the meaning had been clear, that they put an end to their efforts at childbearing. Adelaide had refused to consider giving up. She would still have a son. Why, a great-aunt by marriage was reputed to have borne a first child when older than Adelaide. They would stand together at the baptismal font; the christening robe that Denis, his father, and grandfather had worn was clean and ironed. But now when he recalled how that last year when he had come to her bedroom and bent over her, touching her shoulder lightly in his meaningful way, it seemed to him that she had flinched. Oh, surely not. He was never the man to demand his conjugal rights of an unwilling spouse. But that almost a memory of what might have been a recoil, a spasm perhaps of fear passing over her face. Surely not. "How could you get my girl with child so late?" the old governess had asked. Because he had not loved her enough to protect her? Unconscionable. And the act had been for nothing—another failure of conception and birth.

Now he rode towards Bourneham, towards the Woodruff heiress who was to make good that failure. Away from Melanie's distracting presence, he reviewed what she had said about divorce. The thought crossed his mind that she had been using this as a device to induce him to call off the marriage to Iris. He doubted that another woman was central in this business. An Edmont so swept away by passion as to agree to any terms did not fit his understanding of the man. It was likelier that Edmont had finally decided Melanie had gone too far: this Van Burgh business everyone was talking about. That was probably quite a minor matter to Melanie, but Denis knew that sometimes it is the unimportant affair that leads to disclosure, divorce.

Nothing irrevocable had taken place between him and the Woodruffs. It was still within his power to call off the negotiations. Melanie at Carnaugh. How she would fill the great halls, the emptiness. She would lie with him, naked, gleaming in the huge canopied bed where he had doggedly performed his conjugal duties with Adelaide. His heart was pounding. The carriage had not yet passed him. Melanie must still be with the camel. He reined in his horse, thinking to ride back to her.

Then he realized the hopelessness of his desire and continued on his way. Even were it true that Edmont was intent on divorce and regardless of who was guilty, responsible enough to provide for her, what kind of a settlement might he make? Denis had a pretty clear idea of this type of economic management. One million dollars? What would that be worth in pounds? Malcolm had checked the exchange rate before they left England; it stood at $4.86 to the pound. Why that was practically nothing. Such a settlement would be far too small to restore his estate. And surely there was something repugnant about taking Edmont money; he would not have considered it for a second were not Melanie the prize. As for her, the million dollars would not last her five years.

And there was Joseph Woodruff, whose first offer for the marriage settlement had been five million dollars, seven figures in pounds. Joseph would go higher, much higher for a marquess and marquisate. It was common knowledge that he had spent a cool five million dollars to build and furnish Villa del Destino; he knew the cost of getting what he wanted. The man was a boor and gloried in it, would make an error, say "ain't," mispronounce a word, misuse a Greek or Latin expression, and then declare with a kind of relish, "Of course I never had the classical education you fellows did. I've had to work hard all my life." Denis's cousin Malcolm was handling the negotiations. Eyes fixed firmly on the goal, he would ignore the boorishness, not allow the slightest sign of a sneer to cross his face until the settlement was made, the marriage to Miss Woodruff profitably arranged.

How could a man not be moved by the thought of holding that slight body in his arms, introducing her to physical love? He would charm her. He knew how to make young girls want him, even little Miss Woodruff who now looked so miserable; her eyes were quite pink and the lacy handkerchief she clutched was moist. It was said that she was in love with handsome Harry Van Burgh. But one got over these early loves; they were not serious. Certainly Harry was not serious. Poor Iris. And everyone knew. This was the man who had been pilloried in the gossip columns as Melanie's summer toy. Truth to tell, the thought of that toy, those games were enough to sicken him. A young man. Melanie often told him that men became better lovers as they grew older. But it was never wise to take a woman at her word; Melanie was adept at the uses of flattery.

No matter what woman he started thinking about, Adelaide, now Iris, within moments he was thinking of Melanie. Once past the initial days—and nights—this second marriage would be no different from the first, an arrangement made for economic and childbearing purposes, having no relevance to his love for Melanie, which would remain the dominant emotion of his life. Melanie did not take readily to being crossed, but Denis did not believe she really meant to break with him. Once he was married, to Iris, Melanie would make it up with Edmont and life would resume much as it had been in the past. But what if she could not do so? There was, after all, the possibility that Edmont was too angry to back down. He considered Melanie's position then— a divorced woman with a married lover. It would never do. A successor to Edmont would have to be found in short order, and he had no doubt it would be done. He felt a pang, brushed it aside, unwilling to believe any husband, any other lover, could keep her from him.

Tomorrow in New York they would be lovers again. She would be panting in his arms wet with desire. There had been other men over the years, surely some handsomer, wealthier, and wittier, now younger, and still when he appeared she wanted him. He took precedence. She had never been able to give him up. Oh, he could still hold Melanie.

CHAPTER 16

Oh, Where
Is Lady Aurora?

To this day Denis had not succeeded in unscrambling his father's affairs. Bills, letters of credit, purchase orders, loan applications were all jumbled together. Negotiations involving thousands upon thousands of pounds were inscribed in a minute hand on tiny scraps of paper thrown willy-nilly into cubbyholes in Lord Warburne's desk, into his bureau drawers. One was found in the seamstress's sewing table. He had borrowed money, offering as security the most prized possessions. Denis had made a list of the mortgaged treasures—the Gothic ivory caskets, the German carved wood altars, the tapestries, the suit of armor made in France in 1545 for Henry II, the Gainsborough and Romney portraits—was there anything to which he still held full title?

There were notes with no security at all, monies given his father just on the strength of his title. Now Denis's title. Every day new creditors appeared. On they came, bearing more papers, more documents; some, as word of the debacle

206

got out, ingeniously forged. He had to hire detectives, hand-writing experts.

Every pound Lord Warburne could raise went to support his folly, the *London Global News*. For this newspaper, Denis was in time to realize, his father threw away his inheritance, let Carnaugh fall into disrepair, left the tenants' homes without improvements, caused farmers to abandon acres tilled for generations, and was seen in the Lords only when an issue affecting the press was raised.

The newspaper could not prosper under his control. Viewing himself as a journalist, Lord Warburne traveled extensively, talked with presidents, diplomats, royalty, military commanders. Correspondents were stationed at great expense in Siam and India, in Casablanca, Cairo, and Rio de Janeiro as well as all European capitals and major American cities to make good his claim that the *News* was truly *Global*.

A dozen Rembrandts could not have saved the *Global News*. After his father's death, Denis sold the newspaper for a pittance and counted himself lucky to find a taker, considering the debts.

Later Denis was to view it as the height of irony that during all these years he had prided himself on his diligence and sense of responsibility. It was tradition for the eldest son to inherit the sheep farms in Scotland and the coal mines in Wales outright at birth, and Denis depended on the income from these to meet his own payroll and personal expenses. He oversaw the farmers in Scotland personally and due to his intervention his had been the only farms where the herds were not decimated by disease time and again. His coal mines in Wales, the most productive in the region, were visited on a regular basis.

Even though he did not suspect the full range of his father's extravagance, Denis had occasionally been moved to remonstrate, but his father's arrogance was such as to reject any opposition. "Your turn will come," Lord Warburne returned coldly. "Do not be in such a hurry."

It was strange, Denis sometimes thought, that he was so

conscientious when no one could have been more self-indulgent than his parents.

His mother—throughout his boyhood, servants were dispatched to seek Lady Aurora. Oh, where is Lady Aurora? The state banquet was about to begin. The guests who included both major and minor members of European royalty were standing impatiently, wanting to go in to dinner. But where was Lady Aurora? And she would be standing in the upstairs gallery looking at the Rembrandts and Frans Hals, on the terrace enjoying the night air, or in the nursery laughing with Denis, one, finger to her lips. Aurora was not even her proper name; she had been christened Augusta Christine Evelyn, but liked the airy sound and connotations of Aurora better. She would not allow anyone to address her as Your Ladyship or Lady Warburne. At all times she was Lady Aurora. It suited her.

Self-indulgent. Yes. That was his mother. She, it seemed, did nothing but what suited her. His father was often angry with her. She did not care. The duties of a marchioness. She did not see them. Occasional attendance at state dinners was as much as she would offer. The housekeeper, butler, and cook could manage the household, the gardeners the grounds, her sister-in-law (the one who had been born a Carle and so ultimately brought about the fateful meeting with Melanie) could substitute for her at the village fairs and church socials, at flower shows and ship launchings, could give out prizes at horse races and livestock contests.

Aurora did not have a classic beauty, but her face was unforgettable—the sharp, clean-cut features, the pointed nose, the almond-shaped green eyes, the hollows below the prominent cheekbones, the forehead high and square with her straight red-gold hair pulled back. Her face was always in motion, laughing, smiling. The way she dressed shocked the tenantry, enraged his father, and delighted Denis as a boy. She would go into the village wearing gray-striped trousers with a darker gray vest, a rose-colored shirt frilled all down the front, and a velvet cap like a schoolboy's. Her hips were slim, her abdomen flat; she was built like a twelve-year-old boy. At the castle she preferred a pair of black velvet knickerbockers. On days when Denis was home on holiday she would come looking for him and off they would go to run on the vast lawns of Carnaugh. She ran with incredible speed, kicking up her heels, scampering over the velvety lawns. When he was a small boy, Denis could not keep up with her for speed or endurance. Collapsing on the ground, he would watch her running and running far ahead, around through the copse of trees, across the bridge over the pond and back across the lawn. All his life, he could close his eyes and see her small thin boyish figure in the little knickerbockers running and running with what looked to be joyous abandon. No one could be more merry and bright.

In later years he was stunned to discover that Carnaugh to her had been "a vast emptiness." At night she could not sleep and walked up and down the long halls, the heels of her slippers slapping the stone floor with each step. Denis would come out of his room, but she acknowledged his presence only once, saying, "The night is too long without love." Then she laughed, not merrily this time, and sent him to his room.

There were other nights when he would awaken, alert to some unpleasantness of atmosphere. He would leave his room, walk down the long hall, and turn down another longer hall leading to his parents' bedrooms, one on each side. The door of his mother's room would be ajar and she would be insisting in her low husky voice that his father leave her alone. And his father would be shouting: why would she not do her duty, behave as it was reasonable for her to do? Why her parents had promised him. She had been willful as a girl; everyone had said marriage would settle her down. And she would just go on saying no and no again, again.

Occasionally, though, perhaps out of weariness, she would give way to his father's wishes. He did not know, of course, if she yielded anything else inside the room as well, but she would politely agree that she did have her duties as marchioness and she would perform them. At the next ball she would appear promptly to greet the guests, resplendent in ermine-trimmed satin with diamonds in her ears and around her throat. The red-gold hair would be loosened and elaborately dressed around the tiara.

Seeing her like this, Denis would be struck both by her beauty and by the fact that she behaved as if in fancy dress for a masked ball. The tight trousers, the velvet knicker-bockers, the vest, the school cap: those were the clothes that looked natural on her. Like a twelve-year-old boy. Slim of hips, flat of abdomen, light of foot. When she put her hair inside the velvet cap, she looked more a brother to Denis than his mother. Aurora. Lightness. Dawn.

One afternoon when passing by the drawing room, he heard his mother's voice: "Sometimes when I see him play-ing with his toy soldiers . . ." Denis stopped, realizing she was speaking of him. The soldiers had been passed down in the family; they had been specially made for his great-grandfather, each representing a member of the great-great-grandfather's regiment, the features exact. "I think that it is lonely for him here. He should have a brother or sister. Ste-phen keeps after me, too. But I found it too disgusting. I could not go through all that again."

Child though he was, the words sank in, hurtful. Dis-gusting. She was speaking of him. The manner of his birth.

The year he was thirteen he returned home from school on holiday to discover his mother absent, his father frown-ing, gray and silent. That night, unable to sleep, he went to his father's study hoping to get some word of what had hap-pened. The room was empty and cold. Papers were neatly piled on his father's massive leather-topped oak desk, ex-cept for one thrown to the side. A single sheet of heavy cream-colored paper with the family crest was lying faceup. His mother's handwriting was unmistakable, a scrawl despite years of painstakingly taught penmanship. He knew he should not pick it up; no gentleman read what was intended for another, but he could not bear the suspense. In gingerly

210

fashion, almost as if he were not doing so, he picked up the paper and barely was able to make out his father's name— the scrawl was worse than ever. Then one line: "Any kind of love is better than no love at all." That was the message. It hinted rather than defined.

Oh, where is Lady Aurora? At school Denis had heard of mothers who decamped, disappeared. From what other boys had told him, from the note, the secrecy, the long faces, he assumed she must have run off with a man.

Finally an uncle decided Denis had to be told and spoke in so vague and confusing a manner that it took an entire day to find the bit of truth almost lost in the flood of words. His mother had gone away with the wife of one of the lesser German princes. Denis recalled having seen the princess at Carnaugh on a number of occasions, a large plump woman with blond hair tightly drawn back into braids that she kept patting with hands disproportionately small for her heavy arms. His mother had seemed to be even merrier when the princess was there. He could remember her laughing so that all her teeth showed and calling this woman "meine Trude." He had been relieved at first. Two women together were respectable. It was only later that the words were spoken. Pervert. Deviant. As he grew older he would defend her from the charges. It seemed to him to be his duty as a son, Baron Beaufort, Earl of Lowndes, someday to be Marquess of Warburne, regardless of how poorly she had performed her duty as marchioness, as mother.

The letter. At first he had denied any applicability to him. The words were directed to his father. But he could not let it go at that. Any kind of love is better than no love at all. Not better than no love from a husband. Better than no love *at all*. Those words encompassed him, too, rejected him as well as his father. Too disgusting to go through all that again. Any kind of love. A fat German princess. Anyone.

She wrote him letters; he opened them, threw them away unread. To see the scrawl was to remember the note. Sometimes he found a train ticket enclosed. He sent it back without comment. She moved from Cannes to Monte Carlo to Bath. Ten years passed before he could bring himself to visit.

Once Aurora was gone, his father became completely absorbed with the newspaper, and all but ignored his son. In time Denis came to feel a kinship, unwilling though it was, with his mother. Walking up and down the long corridors in his heavy velvet dressing gown, he would think how long, too long, was the night without love.

Once his father returning late from a diplomatic reception had come upon him. "Like your mother."

"You of course always sleep well." His voice was cold.

Lord Warburne had put a hand on Denis's shoulder. It was the only time he could remember his father touching him. "My boy," he said softly, "do you think I haven't suffered?"

If that meant his father had buried himself in his newspaper so as to forget, why then there was hope that the man was capable of caring. But the brief warmth of that encounter never returned.

Denis insisted that his mother's portrait be hung in the upstairs gallery after his father had it removed from the drawing room. Yes, he defended Aurora and her life-style with such fervor that when at last he had gone to visit her, he was actually disappointed to find no trace of the princess and instead an unquestionably male companion, a viscount.

Aurora had laughed; she missed nothing. "But surely it does not matter if the lips kissing mine are beneath a mustache or not."

He had never been so shocked. Was any son ever so spoken to by his mother? Except, it was hard to think of her as a mother. Whenever he thought of her, it was in her velvet knickerbockers running, running across the lawn. Thinner than before, she had abandoned boyish clothing and was wearing an emerald green skirt cut so tightly in disregard of the fashion as to reveal the pelvic bones, the concave abdomen.

"What happened to the princess?" he asked with the intent to be unkind.

But his mother did not care. "Meine Trude?" she asked lightly. "Once we were living together I found her boring. I sent her back to her husband. Being boring, docile, agreeable are admirable traits in a wife—your father was always seeking them—but not in a lover. Be sure to select a wife who is docile and boring."

"I am married already." He said this stiffly, aware that she had not been invited to the wedding and that he had not brought Adelaide to meet her.

Then he realized that she was looking straight at him, her almond-shaped green eyes shining with a touch of malice that told him she knew all about his marriage, all about Adelaide, about the evenings sitting at opposite ends of the table with nothing to talk about, about the nights spent without passion seeking to beget an heir.

The viscount had joined them. And despite the suitability of his gender, Denis disliked his mother's lover at once. On the head of the golden stickpin fastening his tie Denis noted a small circle of precious stones, a ruby surrounded by sapphires. The sight of it was strangely unpleasant, causing a shudder to run down his spine. He remembered then where he had seen that circle of jewels before. It came from his mother's ring.

Later, when the viscount had left the room, Aurora turned to him and without preamble remarked lightly, "I always disliked that ring, Denis." She paused and added without a change of tone, "It was an engagement present from your father." She waited for a comment and when he could not bring himself to speak added, "And anyway I can afford it." The Bath town house was luxurious.

She was not living in penury as might have befitted one who had thrown away a marquisate. Not at all. So skillfully had the marriage settlement been drawn up by her father's lawyers—far more skillful than those of Denis's father—that she had succeeded in retaining most of it after her flight. None reverted to the abandoned husband or went to Denis. Although lawyers, bookkeepers, and in time detectives were dispatched to go over her affairs after her death, they failed to determine where the property had gone. It was perhaps her intention up to the very end to stand by her rejection of the role of marchioness, her refusal to do her duty as wife. For wife she remained. The marquess had never divorced her, too fearful of the scandal to bring the case to court.

CHAPTER 17

Plots and Counterplots

The bride on his arm, in his bed. What Denis had not reckoned with was that she could not bear to go through it all again . . . another quarter century of lovemaking to be revealed in pregnancies and miscarriages (Melanie would not imagine Iris more fertile than Adelaide, bearing his child).

Denis thought he had arranged it so skillfully, that he would have the millions of dollars, the virgin bride, the heir, and go on with Melanie as in the past. Year following year. The carefully phrased letters that could be left lying about for anyone to read. Year following year. *You will grow old and lose your looks and I will be free of you.* Nothing else Wallace had ever said to her in the most bitter of their quarrels had such devastating impact. He would be free of her. Denis, too, would be free of her. She had to make the most of this chance, and Harry would have to play his part.

Odd, though, that standing on the threshold of her sitting room, seeing Harry before he saw her, full of Denis, of plans, coming to the culmination of a lifetime of waiting, she felt a pang. He glittered in the sunlight. So dazzling, so light, so joyous, his very failings were a source of pleasure. Being with Harry was a vacation in a sense from the real life she had been planning for all the years of gathering the cashmeres and the furs and the velvets. The moment to open the trunks was almost at hand.

Harry had leaped to his feet at her entrance and approached, putting out his arms, eager to begin making love. But something about her manner stopped him. A sense of foreboding came over him, Harry, who always assumed things would go well for him. What was there about Melanie to give him such a feeling? He recognized a quality of suppressed excitement; her eyes glinted, and her face was slightly flushed. As if she had been making love or planning to make love. That air of barely suppressed excitement—it was not for him. That was plain as she sat down at a little distance from him and began to talk without preamble.

Aware of how inconsistent she must appear, Melanie spoke too quickly, reversing the position taken earlier that afternoon, insisting that an elopement with Iris would impress Woodruff, please him, that another delay now would be counter to Harry's interests.

She found Harry resistant, as close to irritability as he ever came, not wanting to listen to her. For once Harry who suspected no one of devious methods appeared suspicious, reminding her of the advice she had given barely two hours earlier. What was so galling about this was that her statements now were far more accurate than those spoken earlier. What she was telling him about Joseph now was perfectly true. Nothing was more likely to win his support and admiration than for Harry to show himself importunate, determined to have Iris whatever the cost.

Let down and disappointed, Harry did not know what to make of this reversal. "Woodruff was Woodruff before you went on the camel ride," he declared stubbornly. "Am I to believe that you had a sudden flash of insight while on camelback, or did we decide to call it camelhump?" Sarcasm was so unlike Harry that Melanie was shaken.

"I gave you bad advice then, Harry . . . knowingly. I wanted to keep you with me a little longer. I didn't think postponing the elopement for a few weeks would matter. Now I know that it would."

Harry did not understand why he felt so stricken, so lost at her obvious desire for him to rush into the elopement. Nothing was really changed by his marrying Iris sooner rather than later. What hurt was Melanie's as good as saying she did not want him anymore. Maybe he was reading too much into her words. Perhaps she merely meant that she had discovered something to indicate that an elopement had to take place now or never. Indeed that was what she immediately said.

"I have learned that the marriage settlement is to be made tomorrow. Joseph Woodruff and the Englishmen will leave before dawn to meet with the lawyers in New York."

"Still, they may not come to terms. Woodruff is so coarse." He was repeating the gist of what she had said earlier.

"They will come to terms. The Englishman will accept. To his way of thinking, he has no choice; he is desperate for money."

Harry knew how it was when someone was desperate for money. "How did you find all this out?" He would have thought she had not been on the camel ride if the rank animal smell were not still on her, arousing as her perfume. "The marquess came riding out to meet me, Harry."

"A marquess? Are you sure? Iris never mentioned his title to me." Harry found it hard to believe that the Woodruffs had ensnared a marquess.

"The Marquess of Warburne and I are old acquaintances."

Had the Englishman known Melanie would be on that particular bit of farmland? And riding a camel? Harry did not like the idea. What did it mean?

Seeing his grim look and guessing its cause, Melanie

thought how unreasonable were lovers. He had always made it clear that they would separate when he married Iris, but here he was offended, jealous at her meeting with another man.

"You would not want Iris to marry the marquess, Harry. And once the marriage arrangements are made, I doubt you will be able to stop them. Harry, you can't really know people like the Woodruffs, like the marquess. They are of a kind."

"I should think the Woodruffs and a marquess could hardly be more dissimilar."

"They are different from one another in all particulars, except one, that no one crosses them. You have no idea how ruthless and cynical they are. The marquess quite as much as Joseph Woodruff."

"And you know that?"

"Yes. No one better than I."

He did not trust her, was looking for a motive for her change of heart. Perhaps she had made a mistake in thinking Harry could be so easily manipulated. Her summer toy. The trouble with the gossip sheets was that one knew the lies and yet came to believe them, to act on them.

And all at once she knew how to convince him. Perhaps this was what she had saved her story for all these years, never telling anyone. The moment had come when that tragedy could serve a purpose.

Everything has its use, Miss Robertson used to say, and she never gave her clothing away. "You see!" she would declare triumphantly, pulling out a fifteen-year-old visiting dress. "I was right. Puffed sleeves are back in style." And so with this, as if it had been lying in a trunk for all these years, like Miss Robertson's dresses, awaiting the right moment to be brought out and put to use, was her story.

The passion, the rapture standing up behind the door. The blood. She had been little more than a child, unable to understand what he had known too well, the danger that lay in yielding to that passion, the ecstasy standing up behind the door. The blood. And then the fear. The knitting needle.

218

The blood. The pain. Everything has its use, she thought, as she spoke. What she said was the truth, but not the entire truth. Denis had wept; she had seen the tears slipping through his fingers.

Harry had never imagined a tragic past for Melanie, thinking she went through life doing as she would, with whom she would, in control. He found it hard to put together the young, vulnerable, yes helpless Melanie who had been so badly treated, with the woman he knew. It had not occurred to him that such strength was achieved by facing and dealing with so much that was painful, that was hard. Alone. Melanie who was never alone except by choice. He put his arms around her as if he could give her the comfort now she had lacked then. This was the first time since they became lovers that he saw himself as her comforter.

At the time Denis had first taken her, Harry was a baby, thought Melanie. But how sweet was his compassion today. She could lose herself in it. Oh, she was too experienced to allow herself to be deflected by a moment's tenderness in a summer romance. It would be too easy to give way, make love, let this last opportunity slip away carelessly. But she knew better. Not for this fleeting pleasure would she throw away the quarter of a century of waiting.

She stepped back, told Harry it would be best if he would act before the Woodruff party returned to Bourneham with the marriage contract signed. Once Nellie Woodruff were sure of the marquess, she would make quick work of getting rid of Harry. In all probability she would take Iris off to England, out of his reach. Well aware of Harry's proclivity for delay, she did not tell him there would be a few days' grace, because Nellie would never leave Bourneham before attending Melanie's ball. The invitation had been proffered before the contretemps at the Woodruffs' ball. Although the Woodruffs had not before been included in the guest list for so major an Edmont social event, Wallace had gone so far as to suggest it, saying that this was not a good time for two of New York's leading citizens to be at odds: they needed to present a united front when these so-called reformers in the legislature passed ill-considered laws that interfered with sensible ways of operating a business.

Melanie observed that Harry was looking at her speculatively, almost with hostility. Perhaps the story saved for so long was like Miss Robertson's puffed sleeves—not really in style after all, not really quite right for the time. Again, the expression was so unnatural to him that she was taken aback.

Harry was forcing himself to admit that the suspicion haunting him since Melanie first mentioned meeting the marquess that afternoon was true. She had confessed he had been her lover once. That would not have mattered could Harry believe the man was relegated to the past. But were that the case, why had Melanie told him? Oblivious as a rule to plots and counterplots, Harry was a lover, and jealousy confirmed the suspicion he would otherwise not have held. He was being replaced by another lover. Melanie was no longer interested in postponing the marriage to Iris; it was the marquess she was thinking about.

Though he did not doubt what she had said, he sensed that she had come to love the man who had seduced her. A common enough story. Even Harry knew that. Older, more experienced, British, an aristocrat: there were reasons enough why she might prefer the other man. She was looking at the floor, unwilling to meet his glance, plotting, he was sure of it. This must have to do with the rumors of divorce fueled by Edmont's love affair with that stout woman from Chicago. Possibly Melanie meant to have Lord Warburne not as a lover, but as a husband. And what a triumph it would be for her to capture a marquess.

Perhaps he had set the whole thing in motion, thought Harry gloomily. She had learned about Mrs. Ribley from him, recognized the gossip that Wallace would divorce her had a sound base. And this realization had come just before she went out and saw the marquess and learned that he was Iris's suitor. She had to make fast work of it, get Iris out of the picture to leave the marquess free for her. Harry's part in this was evident to him. Melanie was assigning a role to him as if he were indeed her summer toy. No, this was the role he had assigned to himself. He alone had decided to elope with Iris now, a decision made when Iris revealed how much she needed him. It was good to be needed; that would be his role, his life from now on as Iris's husband. The only deviation from his plan had been going to Melanie for her help. Of course that had just been an excuse to see her. And once in her presence, he had become distracted by her desirability.

The marquess in Melanie's arms . . . the image flashed through his mind and he felt a sickening jolt; it was more repugnant to imagine Melanie in the marquess's bed than fresh young Iris. He had to accept that inevitability. Harry liked to live in the present, never to look ahead. Now he had to look ahead and know that if not the marquess, it would be someone else. Melanie would never be without a man at her side. How could she? Still the most beautiful, seductive of all women.

A summer romance. That was what she had invariably called it and what he had to accept. The moment of parting from Melanie that he had always known would have to come was upon him. Melanie. And they had not made love for one last time.

CHAPTER 18

Before Dawn
on the Falcon

Could that be Harry walking down the drive leading to Emerald Beach? Driving to the pier in the eerie hour before dawn on Thursday, Melanie thought she caught a glimpse of him. No doubt he was refreshing himself with ocean air after a late night of partying. The dense fog rolled in then and she thought that it probably had not been Harry at all. What would he be doing there on the dawn of what was to be his wedding day?

Melanie had not expected to be going to New York on the *Falcon* and would have preferred to travel by herself on one of the luxurious ships of the Beecham Steamship Line. With staterooms the size of drawing rooms, lounges with Oriental carpets and wall frescoes painted by artists in Whistler's circle, these ships had become acceptable to members of New York society. They could not, of course, compare with the *Falcon* where she had supervised the decoration herself, installing a mosaic floor taken from a villa in Sicily, obtaining upholstery that exactly matched the greens and browns of the Corot country scene hanging in Wallace's stateroom. But when she spoke to Wallace of her intended visit to her mother, she learned that he had arranged to go back to his office that day.

As a concession, Wallace agreed to postpone his departure until nearly dawn. Most weekends he arrived at Bourneham at one or two in the morning on Saturday to leave again at one or two on Monday morning.

Figures of crew members rushing back and forth with boxes came into visibility and disappeared again. At some moments the fog would drift away, revealing row upon row of yachts and naval vessels, sailboats and launches, commercial liners, and ferries. The mast of the *Falcon* topped by a burgundy-and-cream pennant stood out. As she boarded the yacht, Melanie observed that the next berth belonging to the Woodruffs was vacant. The *Jonella*, a union of the names Joseph and Nellie, had set off even earlier carrying Joseph, Denis, and his cousin Malcolm to New York where the terms of the marriage settlement were to be arranged, where Denis was to come to her.

Denis had assured Melanie that it would be best for Malcolm to go alone to the offices of Woodruff's lawyers. Malcolm was a hard bargainer; indeed he had enriched himself for life by a marriage settlement so cleverly planned that on his wife's death her entire fortune came to him; nothing reverted to her family. Leaving the negotiations to Malcolm, Denis would break away and go to pay a call on his aged cousin, Mrs. Carle.

In her stateroom, watching Beryl put away clothing in the armoire, Melanie thought of the visit to her mother that lay ahead. No matter how she prepared herself for the decline, for the wandering look, the vague talk, the anhedonia, when she entered the drawing room where her mother was waiting, it was always a shock.

Senile, Mrs. Carle should have been pitiable, but whenever Melanie was present, she would suddenly rouse herself from inanition to reveal a streak of nastiness. A hard visit to be gone through for the sake of being with Denis. But what would she not do? It sometimes seemed that she would sell her soul for an hour alone with him, an hour in bed with him. What would she not do? She had given up Harry. The action common sense had not enabled her to take, she had done on hope of Denis.

Melanie thought of the *Jonella* on its way to New York. There was no way for Denis or Joseph Woodruff to know that she had rendered the trip, the agreeing to this and standing firm on that, to be for nothing. They might as well have had a good night's sleep in their comfortable beds at Villa del Destino.

While the *Jonella* was traveling at top speed through the waters, Harry was eloping with Iris. It could not have been he she had seen in the dawn. He had proved surprisingly refractory, but he knew she was right and he would act on it. She would return to Bourneham and he would be gone.

Following the information given her by Harry, Melanie had studied Wallace's face with particular care as they boarded the yacht, and later as they breakfasted together. The news she had brought from Morgen had upset him and it occurred to her that this might be a good time to make mention of Clara. Perhaps now, preoccupied, he would be more revealing. It would be well to know where she stood before seeing Denis.

"I met an old friend of my brother Bunner's at the Woodruffs' ball," she remarked. Wallace looked up. "Clara Ribley." She completed the statement and had the satisfaction—or dissatisfaction, it was hard to be sure—of seeing Wallace drop a piece of toast, clear his throat as if to speak, and then let the moment pass in silence. But there was something to be spoken, no doubt of that.

Walking back into the office that had been fitted out for him in the main lounge, Wallace sat quietly for a moment thinking about the breakfast conversation before unlocking the drawer of the mahogany desk and taking out his ledgers. Had Melanie meant anything by her mention of Clara? A

friend of Bunner's. He had never heard that, must ask Clara
(they had advanced to a first-name basis); he had always been
curious about Bunner's death. Something odd about it; he
wished he could discuss the matter with Melanie, but she
always withdrew from the topic—emotional about her brother.
The brevity of her mention of Clara indicated that she knew
no more. He was not such a fool as to give Melanie the
grounds for making outrageous demands in a divorce settlement. No gossip about this relationship would creep out, he
was sure. When it came time to talk money, only Melanie's
affairs would weigh in the balance.

Wallace was so stiff and unapproachable that no one had
told him how general was the knowledge of his misalliance.
It was the most exciting gossip to arise in Bourneham all
summer. He never discussed a business arrangement in front
of servants, fearing their loose tongues, but it did not occur
to him to hide his absorption in Clara from his valet. Melanie could have told him that servants are more interested
in the mere possibility of a love affair than in financial take-
overs. He would not have believed her.

This was no time to think about women, however. He
had to consider how to combat what had begun as a whispering campaign but, he realized from Melanie's description
of her interchange with Morgen, might soon erupt into the
press. A way of silencing the *Journal* about the Heron factory fire had to be found. There must be some city ordinance
Morgen was breaking. Certainly, Wallace put enough money
into campaign "war" chests to expect special treatment.
"Legal funds" was the heading in his ledgers. The invest-
ment had never failed him. Years ago he had been amused
to read a statement by one of the railroad tycoons: "If you
have to pay money to have the right thing done, it is only
just and fair to do it." That no longer seemed amusing to
him. Which recipient of Edmont money could be called upon
now? They were all afraid of the press. Lily-livered, terrified of yellow journalism.

The firm of private detectives Wallace relied on must

be contacted by Jessop and set to discovering just how the fire had started. There was always a chance that one of the other major property owners had hired an arsonist in order to throw suspicion on Wallace and make trouble for him. It would also be necessary to take greater precautions against fires. Improved fireproofing and additional fire escapes must be installed, and this should be done with the greatest discretion so that the actions would not appear to have been motivated by remorse for the Heron factory fire, thus accepting blame where none was due. For all his planning, he still felt apprehensive as to what new information Jessop would have for him. The trip seemed unconscionably long.

Melanie, too, was finding the trip tedious in her impatience to be in New York, to be with Denis, and at the same time she was wondering what Harry would be doing that day. For just a second she wished she had made love with him one last time. All the while, as an undercurrent, was her worry about what was happening in Bourneham. Rosamunde had seemed a bit feverish when kissed good-night. Then, too, the preparations for the ball were going on without her. She had an image of the camel standing by the side of the road in the midst of the farmland, waiting for her, searching the landscape with its huge wistful eyes.

She sighed and called Beryl to the stateroom to give her a massage and facial mask. It was the first time Melanie had traveled without Dena, who was still in the house awaiting Mrs. Woodruff's call to Villa del Destino.

After assisting Melanie to change into the cotton dressing gown used during beauty treatments, Beryl applied the clay facial mask, let it harden, and then after a few minutes removed it, first with warm, then with frigid water. This was followed by a facial massage with cucumber milk. Beryl had good hands. She made a better essence for the cucumber milk than Dena, having the patience to force the cucumbers through the sieve and cloth an extra dozen times before adding the alcohol, castile soap, oil of sweet almonds, and tincture of benzoin. Melanie told her to apply little makeup that day, merely a faintly tinted face powder, scented with dried rose petals from her garden, and a touch of almond oil on her eyebrows. Her hair was smoothed back into a chignon, rather than being piled in an elaborate pompadour atop her head.

Beryl placidly put out the rather odd combination of clothing Melanie had selected to wear upon arrival in New York. The lingerie was hand-sewn, the heavy peach satin petticoat had sixteen rows of lace made in Belgium and tiny diamond chips nestled in the tucks; the sheer silk chemise barely covered the nipples; lace trim and flaring ruffles decorated the drawers, and the thin silk stockings were exactly matched in color to the drawers and petticoat. The dress Melanie had decided to wear atop this elegance was simple, a plum-colored linen with a creamy lace Bertha, a high whalebone-stiffened collar showing a small row of jet beading, and modified leg-of-mutton sleeves with long lace cuffs. It was her wish to be as inconspicuous as possible. She was going to see her senile mother, hardly an occasion for ostentation. Thus the plainly cut dress. But Melanie was never inconspicuous; no simple dress or hairstyle could extinguish her.

As the *Falcon* approached New York Harbor, Melanie and Beryl came out on deck. Wallace was already present, looking at his watch. There was something uneasy, edgy about Melanie, he thought. Was something beyond the visit to her mother planned for today? But when he looked her over more carefully, he observed that she appeared just a trifle less willowy than usual. She must really be going to her mother's to have relaxed her lacing. He sent his valet to advise the captain of the *Falcon* to wait here for Melanie, take her back to Bourneham this evening, and then return to New York on Friday for Wallace.

The pier was crowded with workmen unloading the commercial vessels and footmen carrying boxes and trunks to and from the yachts. A short distance away were the rows of coaches and drivers, among them the carriage with the

Edmont crest and Cough, the coachman. Most drivers had been there for some hours, as they could not take the risk of arriving later than their masters.

Jessop was pacing up and down, nervously scanning the arrivals, watching for Wallace. Melanie was dismissed with no more than a glance: Jessop's eyes were only for Wallace; they lit up with a sort of passion when he saw his employer. There was an exchange between the two men and then they walked towards the carriages hurriedly, Wallace resting his hand on Melanie's arm absentmindedly.

"I will ride with Jessop. It is faster that way. Cough will take you to your mother's and then back down to the pier. I do not think you should go to the house today. Go directly to the *Falcon*."

"Yes, I told Junior I would only be gone a day. And of course I must complete preparations for the ball," she said pleasantly.

"Ah, yes, the ball."

"And what of you?"

"I will remain in the city tonight."

"Is there something I could do to help you?" she asked. He appeared so worried that though she was eager, indeed desperate to be away, she could not leave him in such a state.

He stared at her. "No," he said. "Nothing." He would shut her out always.

There was no way she could change that. She had failed in her attempt to enter his business life long ago when he had cared for her most. Loved her? Who could say that? He had been taken with her; that much was obvious. The memory of how sweetly he had smiled at her could make her heart ache even now. And she had accepted him gladly. Now she was going to Denis, Wallace to bury himself, busy himself in his office. He was so worried, harried. But when he sought solace, it would be with Clara. Everything was changing. And still she could ache for him, lined, tired, eyes bloodshot from the lost hours of sleep.

She watched him drive off and then climbed slowly into the carriage. As it pulled away from the pier, bumping over the broken pavement, she was again filled with the sense of anxiety, unease that had arisen during the Woodruffs' ball. She could not overlook the threat to Wallace posed by the rumors concerning the fire. Say it was not her business. And yet it was. Put it out of her mind; she was going to Denis. She could not. Whatever had been between them in the beginning had been dissipated, altered, lost during the years. Still, they had spent so much time together; it was a bond.

Foreboding, a vague fear that she was making a mistake cast a shadow on the day, over the anticipation. She knew Wallace to be a hard man in business affairs, and a divorce settlement was unquestionably business. While she told herself that her marriage had been a business and social arrangement, she unaccountably was filled with regret. Why could it not have been Wallace to satisfy her emotional life? It could have happened; she had been so eager for her marriage to fill her need for love, had been so determined to forget Denis—and for years. But there was never a chance of that, she thought, even before her infidelities. They hurt Wallace's pride, no more than that. His emotions were centered on his buildings, land, on his ledgers.

This meeting in New York was unwise. However good the excuse for being here, if Denis were seen in her company, people would talk. And talk had a way of coming to the attention of Armand Wolfe. With Wallace threatening divorce, a second scandalous report, right on the heels of that damaging account of her relationship with Harry, could be ruinous. But this was the only opportunity she could find to see Denis alone, to prepare him, subtly of course, for a marriage between them once Iris were safely away with Harry. That was what she wanted, what she had always wanted.

CHAPTER 19

Confessions

W hat should I do?" Mrs. Carle
replied to Melanie's urging that she resume the needlepoint
she had prided herself upon or read the gossip columns that
had so amused and fascinated her. "I wait for you to come.
I am interested in nothing else. I have nothing to do that
matters."

Her mother's frame for needlepoint had been pushed
into a corner; only Miss Robertson's knitting basket, the
needle sticking up out of the wool, was in evidence on the
highly polished end table. Melanie averted her eyes.

The drawing room, like her mother, was subtly altered.
Her mother's prized fans were nowhere to be seen. The collection was unique. There were fans with spokes of intricately carved ivory, others with mother-of-pearl set in onyx,
with tortoiseshell or bamboo. Set between these spokes were
panels of sheer silk covered with hand-painted landscapes,
or with feathers from brilliantly colored jungle birds, or lace
of the most unbelievable delicacy. Later Melanie would idly

open a cabinet in another room and come upon these treasures, put away by Miss Robertson to protect them from her mother's fluttering hands.

Melanie waited for a suitable moment to mention Denis, but one seemed no better than another and when at last she abruptly said he was to come this afternoon, Miss Robertson did not even change expression. The question remained, unanswered forever now, of how much she had known about Denis.

Mrs. Carle brightened when Denis came in, urged him to stay and wait for Bunner and Mr. Carle to return from the bank. She was quite gay, and then in the midst of her chatter, she paused, thought, and spoke again. "Why, Bunner is dead," she said in almost her old voice, then putting her hand lightly over her mouth, she murmured. "But we don't tell about it. Too awful. Died like a dog. Who said that? I don't remember. But I do remember Mr. Carle and I sat in this very room in the evenings in the autumn after his death and all that long winter. We did not entertain at all. Mr. Carle and I used to cry, yes, even he cried that winter. It was so cold. Nothing could warm us, and we would say, 'Why did it have to be Bunner? Pity it was the boy.'"

Knowing her mother senile made the words no less hurtful. Waiting for visits, and it was true her mother had nothing else to wait for, she nonetheless drove Melanie away. It was as if an evil spirit had taken possession of her in old age to darken it.

"I don't pay any attention when she starts in with that chatter. Half the time she doesn't know what she says." The governess again, offering comfort to her charge. What had Miss Robertson not done for her? *Make entry difficult enough and he will believe you.* The bond between child and governess was one of the strongest of a lifetime.

"Come, it is time for your nap, Mrs. Carle." Miss Robertson spoke firmly. "And I would like to lie down a bit myself." There was nothing of suggestiveness in her manner.

After they had left, Melanie walked to the door of the

drawing room and looked out. No one was in sight or earshot. Most of the servants had been dismissed and much of the house closed off. *Where can we go to be alone?* Anywhere now. The doors to rooms she had crossed with Denis so many years ago were shut. No need to hurry now. No one would come, calling her name.

Even with Denis beside her, she could not shake off the impact of the words her mother had just spoken. They took her back to everything she had spent years trying not to remember. The energy she had expended trying not to remember. Give a ball. Take a lover. Play with Rosamunde and talk with Junior. See Eleanora Duse play *La Dame aux Camelias*, Booth play *Hamlet*, Helena Modjeska sing, or Jumbo the elephant cavort at the Greatest Show on Earth. Purchase another painting by Greuze, Delacroix, or Millet. Order a $10,000 ball gown in Paris to wear just once. Read *Middlemarch* or *Vanity Fair*; read of other women's dreams of equality and suffrage. Play tennis, bridge; go swimming, ice skating. Who had more ideas than she to banish despair? Just listing them could occupy an hour. But ugliness was always there underneath: the distance in her marriage, bridged only occasionally by passion, then the frightening quarrels; the pleasure in her children dimmed by the fear of losing them to divorce; the hostility of the women; the tedium of the dinners, and always further back, Bunner's hideous death, the terrible words that had followed. Spoken once more.

The Edmont house farther north on Fifth Avenue was empty but for the small group of servants left to take care of Wallace's needs during the week. Wallace was in his office and certain not to come home before nightfall. He had told her not to go to the house today, giving orders as was his way; there could be no other reason. She was in charge of the servants; none would dare to speak to Wallace of her visit if she ordered silence. Still there was the possibility that someone would see her with Denis as they rode uptown. In the mood she was in, she did not care.

She rang for Beryl, who had been waiting downstairs in the servants' parlor enjoying the leftovers from lunch, then turned to Denis: "I don't wish to stay here. Let's go home."

As they drove up Fifth Avenue, Melanie sought to turn the conversation, wishing to make Denis recognize that being together was more important than restoring Carnaugh and the estates. If she could achieve this before he returned to Bourneham and learned that Iris was Harry's, not his, he would be prepared to act as she wished. It was best, she had learned long since, to raise weighty matters before love, while a man was at the peak of desire. Afterwards, sated, he was less receptive, less inclined to find ways of surmounting obstacles. That cooler mood lasted for a short time only, but a short time was all there was.

Denis agreed it would be his greatest joy for them to be together, not just for a few secret meetings but openly, permanently. Yet somehow he turned the tone of the exchange between them from serious intent to the sweet words of a lover not to be taken seriously. She could recognize the difference; he knew she could. For all her effort, nothing substantive had been said by the time they arrived. She would have to return to the topic later, no matter what his mood.

Melanie had not announced her visit in advance, but the servants were too well trained to display any emotion at her appearance with Denis. They were in full uniform, although Wallace never came home before evening. The house seemed stifling to Melanie as they entered, accustomed as she had become to the sea breeze, the airy rooms in Bourneham. Richard Morris Hunt who had designed the New York house had planned it for winter use, setting it at such an angle as to cause each room, except those allotted to the servants, to be warmed by the sun all day. The architect had expected anyone wealthy enough to be his client to go away for the summer and had failed to take into account the male propensity for work.

Melanie led Denis up the marble staircase and down one long corridor, flanked on each side with cabinets containing her collection of Italian majolica. As they came to the end, she turned to the right and led him all the way down another even longer corridor to a guest room at the very back of the house. Beryl, she knew, would follow and quietly place herself so as to be within call when needed to bring towels and cool drinks, to help with bathing and dressing. This was Melanie's favorite room, because it was secluded, removed from the rest of the house. Not a sound from the busy avenue in front of the house reached one here. To enter this room was to step into a magic box remote from all the world. The room was smaller than the others in the vast house and for that reason singularly well suited for love. When she closed the ruby damask curtains, the room was filled with a roseate glow. Warm, sensual. The ruby velvet bedspread covered a four-poster that occupied most of the floor space. The bed stood on a white rug of lamb's wool, so soft, so fluffy, one felt buoyant each time a step was taken. Everything was as it should be. They were together. Illicit lovers for so long, they knew they should not lose the moment. But for once, a sort of melancholy came over them, whether because of the thoughts aroused by her mother's words or the knowledge that he had come to marry Iris.

"I would like to have a child."

Denis's words filled her with dismay. All she had risked for this afternoon and his thoughts were not of her.

"That was not true in the past. I think I would not have been much better a parent to my son had he lived than my parents were to me. All the years of pregnancies and miscarriages and stillbirths, what I wanted so desperately was an heir. It was not really a person, but an heir who would become the seventeenth Marquess of Warburne, fourteenth Earl of Lowndes, eighteenth Baron Beaufort, someone to carry on the name, the tradition, the marquisate. But when Adelaide was expecting this last time and the doctors were saying that despite her age the pregnancy was advancing successfully, I began to think of the child as more than an heir, rather as someone close to me to care about. I would have made up to him for being without brothers or sisters, not let him be lonely as I was. In that sense, it will be easier for my future children."

Denis spoke without thinking of the effect of his words, did not see himself as callous. A marriage with Melanie was impossible as he well knew, and as in her heart she must know, too. He would marry Iris and she would bear his children. Those were facts. No need to gloss over the truth. But when he observed Melanie's recoil, he remembered that she had lost a brother and how cruelly her mother had spoken.

Abashed, he changed the subject, and asked gently, "Tell me what happened to Bunner."

"Why do you ask? He is long dead—in a hunting accident."

"It did not sound that way from your mother's words."

"My mother is senile."

"Can't you ever speak honestly to me? A quarter of a century of love and you offer me insincerities."

A quarter of a century of love and you offer me Iris in your bed, carrying the product of your lovemaking in her scrawny little body. Harry; suddenly she wished he were with her, never speaking the hurtful word, always kind. Now Denis was making a virtue of honesty. Speak honestly. All these years. And he returned to preface their lovemaking by telling her—honestly—about the pleasure he took in his prospective fatherhood. He came back to tell her, honestly, he would marry Iris Woodruff, a little girl. Oh, she knew how much he liked little girls, how easily he could make them like him. Still, she would win. The last trick in the game would be hers, and nothing else would matter. She would not be honest enough now or ever to tell Denis that she had pressed Harry into marrying Iris and ruining his plans.

"What do you care about Bunner? You never knew him." Thinking him insincere she spoke sharply. But then he touched her face. "You care; therefore, I care." There it was again, the unaccustomed softness that had never failed to melt her, despite her doubts. And she thought, after all, it

235

would be possible to tell Denis. What had happened had been so long ago that the horror should have faded. It was the secrecy, the lying, that had kept it alive for so long.

At first she chose her words carefully; the details were too disgusting to tell (only she had not been disgusted then, but wrung, tortured by the torture Bunny was enduring). Soon, however, Denis's manner of listening reassured her and she found herself able to speak of the horror of it, to describe it just as it had been. The terrible sounds of illness, the rapidly wasting body, the blue lips, *le mort de chien*.

Later she had objected to the lying, the insistence on an apocryphal hunting accident, but her mother said she was too young to realize how such an illness stained a reputation. "Many members of society would not allow a son to marry into a family with such a history, and I was coming into marriageable age. They were lying for me really, my mother said, though she never used the word. It was, I suppose, the way they thought of me: marriageable, to make a good marriage. My mother pointed out, as if this were a credit to them, that despite their tragedy, they still thought of ways to protect my future."

"Why didn't you tell me? I would not have thought less of the Carle family."

She might have replied that her mother was thinking only of husbands, not occasional lovers who are more easily satisfied about pedigree. It was the kind of sharp remark she was known for. But she would not be sharp with him, not after telling the truth about Bunny, not while she was feeling a relief greater than she would have imagined at having been able to speak openly at last.

"I think I could have comforted you—then when the pain was fresh."

"Comfort me now." She was thinking of all she wanted Denis to do with their lives, but he was taking her words in the more literal sense and began to stroke her hair. And the image of the miserable boy lying in his filth, smiling, with the strength pouring out of him, vanished.

Though Denis's hands caressed her, he appeared preoccupied. Seeing her questioning look, he said, "Your sad memories remind me of mine. What horrors we have hidden behind our carefully composed faces, Melanie. Our histories are so different, yet each carries a betrayal of love."

Melanie was startled. "Adelaide?" she asked.

"I speak of my mother." He had never before mentioned his mother. Men spoke too much or too little of their mothers.

"It is as if I never had a mother," he went on. "She was not a good mother, nor a good wife, nor a good marchioness, nor a good woman." But he felt a pang, as in his mind's eye, he saw her running, running in her velvet knickerbockers. Lady Aurora. Trying to run to where love would be. "She gave little love and I doubt that she found it. She left a note. It was for my father, but I took the words to include me as well. 'Any kind of love is better than no love.' 'Any kind.' How those words belittled me, haunted me."

As Melanie listened to him, it occurred to her that he had suffered. She had been so involved in her own suffering that she had never credited his. He had seemed a person with everything he wanted.

This was the first time in all these years, thought Melanie, that they had spoken to one another of matters that affected them so deeply. The very infrequency of seeing Denis had precluded this kind of revelation. Each meeting was an occasion to release sexual passion, little else. Only now, this feeling had broken out, perhaps due to her realization that their lives were changing and his instinctive response to her confession.

There had been some gossip about the mother, Melanie vaguely recalled as he was speaking. A love affair probably. Her mother and aunt had whispered about some old scandal just before Denis and Adelaide paid their first visit. Later, in a drawer of her mother's writing desk, Melanie had found the obituary cut out of the *London Times*. Something about the phrasing was odd, ambiguous, quite unrevealing.

Oh, where is Lady Aurora? Denis smiled wryly, recalling the only time he had visited her in Bath.

"Carnaugh," his mother had said, a wealth of expression in the word. "A mistake from the beginning, but oh, how long it took me to escape. And of course I never did. I think I have carried that vast aching emptiness and loneliness within me and it has not mattered where I have gone or with whom I have shared my life." She spoke so rapidly that he found it hard to follow. "They made me marry him, you know, my parents. There was someone else . . . I had thought . . . They would not listen, did not care. All they could see was the linkage between the two great families. I fit into neither of them, ever. Your father was no different young— stiff, priggish, self-important. Marital relations . . . he made them distasteful to me, repulsive." Young then, Denis had been embarrassed by such talk, he told Melanie.

"Yes, a mistake from the beginning. And now there is the viscount, Charles . . . I hear people call him an adventurer. He likes expensive things. But he has suited me. He is the only man with whom I have been able to tolerate, even in a limited way to enjoy, the sexual act."

"Mother!" Denis looked down at the table, refusing to meet her eye. She did not seem to notice, and spoke in so unself-conscious a way that his shock left him. Only she could make an unnatural confession appear the most natural thing of all.

"Except for him, I have only been happy with women. I think my body was not made to accommodate the male, so big, so rough, so heavy. Lying pillowed on Trude's soft breasts, I felt comforted. A woman can be gentle, loving. But still I found isolation where I thought love would flower.

"I owe a lot to the viscount, you see, Denis. But that is turning ugly, too. He is unfaithful—I don't mind that; I believe fidelity a most overrated virtue—but he goes to women of so low a class. I begin to study his body for the pox. It cannot go on. And what then? What then?"

At the table after dinner that evening with the viscount

238

sitting by her side, his mother had again recalled her life at Carnaugh. "There was no happiness to be found in that great stone pile and with that great stone image, Sir Stephen George David Tuncliffe, fifteenth Marquess of Warburne, twelfth Earl of Lowndes, sixteenth Baron Beaufort. Names, names, but where was the man inside?"

"I thought her disloyal," Denis told Melanie, though in truth that was how he saw his father. "But to speak so, and with the viscount sitting there, smug, self-satisfied."

One of his mother's thin hands turned the rings on the fingers of the other around and around nervously. He had never seen the rings she was wearing. The ruby ring with the sapphires held the viscount's ascot. And the blue-white diamond, remembered from his childhood, so large it had covered her fourth finger to the joint, was gone. He could not help but wonder whether tomorrow he would see it adorning the viscount's cigarette case. The viscount, following Denis's glance, was smiling; Denis thought he could not bear that smile of hidden knowledge.

At his expression, even his mother, always so quick and vivacious, turned quiet. Perhaps feeling himself an intruder in this scene—there was no reason to assume him completely lacking in sensitivity—the viscount excused himself.

All these years later, sitting beside Melanie, Denis remembered how it had felt, sitting with his mother at the table, unhappy, but unwilling to leave her. She had not rung for a servant to clear; the cut glass coupettes from dessert were still in front of them. Her face, almost unlined, looked little older than when he had been a child. He could imagine her in the jaunty school cap. Why did it not occur to her that the proper course would be to resume her duties as marchioness? She could be a mother, soon a grandmother. If only it could happen, even now, it would mitigate the circumstances of her going.

"What are you thinking, Denis?"

"You could come home."

She shook her head; the red-gold hair, only a little faded,

shone in the candlelight. "I can never go back, Denis, even if your father were to allow it, which he never would, you know." She paused, and then said passionately: "Ah, I wish I could wipe out the past."

"And then, Melanie, as if I had been struck, I thought of the note and her betrayal. I thought of all the things I had been trying not to remember since I decided to come."

"I know," he had said to his mother coldly, "including me."

"You?" She raised her thin, arched eyebrows, a darker red than her hair. He had at last penetrated her self-absorption.

"Can you have forgotten the note you left?"

"The note? The note was not for you, Denis. I wrote it for your father, the most coldhearted of men. I doubt that it affected Stephen much. I had not imagined even he would show the letter to you. Not that he was incapable of such cruelty."

"My father did not show me the letter. Nor is it his callousness that is at issue. But yours. So few words to say so much. Any kind of love is better than no love. No love. An all-inclusive term."

"I never thought that you might read the letter."

How could he have failed to pick up the thick cream-colored paper lying on his father's desk once he had recognized his mother's scrawl? "I should not have read it. But the words, the thoughts were there, Mother. And even if not intended directly for me, they did refer to me. Nothing changes that."

"No, no." She touched his hand with her slim fingers. "I was so angry with your father, wanted to find something to say that would hurt him and I could think of nothing worse than that the love of a woman outweighed everything he was. Stephen was proud of his virility, as if that were something to be proud of.

"You. Why, you Denis were the only person who held me to Carnaugh for so long. Do you think 'meine Trude' was the first? I had money of my own, nerve. I could have left at any time, except for you. I tried to explain it to you in my letters."

He had never read her letters, had not been able to look at any page that bore her scrawl. "If I could have taken you with me, Denis, I would have. But there was too much for you to lose. Even though I have never taken position or titles seriously, I knew that you, even as a boy, had caught that fever from your father. You would never have forgiven me for taking that away from you. And I never believed I would lose you so completely. I was naïve, Denis. I thought you would come to me on holiday. Why, I would have told Trude to absent herself during your visits. But you never answered my letters, so I knew you sided with your father against me. Bad Lady Aurora. Let us forget all about her." She seized his hand so tightly that the settings of her rings cut into his fingers.

"It wasn't that way," he said. "I thought you did not care."

"I cared," she cried. "Believe me, I cared."

"I wanted to believe her, Melanie. But even while she spoke, I knew that I had been right. I thought of how she had spoken of her time at Carnaugh that very evening. Not one pleasant thought, one memory. Loneliness. Misery. That was how she saw it. And all that time I was there, Melanie. She could have said, except for me—before I challenged her, not after. She had not thought about me at all. The note was, of course, as she said, intended for my father and in her self-absorption, she had quite forgotten she had a child. Later, I know she did remember, to the extent of writing to me, seeking to justify herself no doubt."

And even then, that night while she was saying how much she cared, the phrase ran through his head . . . disgusting, too disgusting to go through all that again. Those were words, too. A mistake from the beginning. How long it took me to escape. Oh, where is Lady Aurora?

"Believe me, Denis." Her green eyes were so bright with

tears, her lips were trembling slightly. It was quite as if she cared, he had thought, while still holding back a part of himself. Yet for all his resentment and disbelief, he found himself pressing her hand in return. Her hand was smooth, delicate, with no substance of flesh. Her lightness suddenly touched him. Oh, where is Lady Aurora?

All at once, he had a sense of peace. Love hovered in the air between them. He did not understand how it could be. What he was saying now to Melanie he had known to be true then. But was it altogether true? Even then, he had not been too young to know that Aurora might have meant all the things she said.

They had sat in silence, afraid that if they spoke, the tenuous link being forged would break. And he had remembered how it had felt to be happy with her, watching her hiding, one finger to her lips, in the old nursery, or running across the grass.

Finally, picking up his thoughts as if he had spoken them, she said, her voice lighter than before, almost girlish. "Do you remember my suit with the little waistcoat, and the velvet knickerbockers, Denis? Your father's tailor refused to make them; he was afraid of Stephen. So I had to go to Mrs. Pohl, the dressmaker, and she was so shocked when I told her what I wanted. Do you remember how I used to run around the lawns at Carnaugh?

"Oh, I ran and ran, faster and faster. I did that as a girl, too, around and around and around my parents' estate, only hobbled then in petticoats and long heavy skirts. Ran and ran faster and faster. This . . . this person . . . I cared for then . . . before your father . . . used to laugh at me, 'Do you think that if you run you get there faster?' Of course I did think so. But 'there' turned out to be nowhere."

She spoke these words gaily, laughing at herself like that "person" of old.

Afterwards she had urged him to go out, see Bath at night, directed him to a nearby public house. He had gone there and stood by the bar, drinking ale, wondering if they could make a new start.

When he had returned to the house, he found a scene of confusion. The lamps were lit in every room, the doors stood open and the servants were running this way and that, not knowing what to do. Oh, where is Lady Aurora? The viscount was nowhere to be seen. And so it had been Denis who at last followed the maid to his mother's room, flung open the door, and saw her lying naked on her bed, the blood running down the pink satin sheets to the cherubs in low-relief on the sides of the bedstead. Her hands, bloodied from the slashed wrists, covered her genitals, and the breasts and hips were so small that it might have been a boy lying there.

He found the note later. "I was wrong." Was this all she had to say? Did she mean that any kind of love is not better than no love? Or that she had failed to recognize his love had been there? He picked up the paper, and saw that she had started another page. "I should have kept on running with you. I know now . . ." and the scrawl had ended. Self-absorbed, she had not seen that there is cruelty in suicide. It was many years before he could pity her.

As he finished speaking, it seemed to Melanie that what he had confessed to her of his past that afternoon was an act of love of a kind more unusual in their experience than any sexual coming together. Custom in their world had always demanded control, dignity, a calm appearance, the ability to put a good face on disaster—the hunting accident, the am-biguously phrased obituary. They sat side by side, each still half lost in the tragedies that had haunted them for so long. The brilliance of the afternoon sunlight glowed through the draperies. Their afternoon was passing. There was this closeness, but it did not satisfy; they must be closer yet. Me-lanie wanted to arouse him from his absorption in what had happened on a long-ago night in a town house in a crescent in Bath. She stood up, half closed her eyes and bent ever so slightly forward from the waist. The movement was just enough to draw a man's eyes to her breasts. Even in the high-necked linen dress, he could hardly fail to become aware of the fullness of her breasts. The movement had never failed her. Knowing its effect excited her, too, caused her nipples to rise, hard, resilient, clearly evident through the fabric of the bodice. Wallace once accused her of practicing that movement before a mirror. She had laughed at him, saying this was the most natural and unstudied of gestures, but of course his accusation had been true. How else had she been able to calculate just how far forward to bend?

She had her ways did Melanie, thought Denis, rising to his feet, as excitement began to replace regret. Practiced, too practiced, and he remembered all the men who had possessed her. He had been first; that should be enough for anyone. It would have surprised him to discover that Wallace thought the same. Responding to her gesture, Denis threw off the dull, grieving mood. He took off his clothes and tossed them onto the white fluffy rug at their feet. Then he turned to her and began to undress her, carelessly crumpling the dress, the seductive lingerie she had so thoughtfully selected.

Melanie glanced down at her naked body, trying to see it as he was seeing it. Massage, emollients, exercise, care with her diet kept her figure firm, her flesh smooth. The expression on Denis's face was admiring; there was the heavy look of lust that invariably aroused her. Helped by cosmetics, she still looked young. But there were some signs of age. Harry never seemed to notice, but then Harry was not a man to look for imperfections.

Denis put his arms around her, feeling her body straining against his. Making love to her seemed an act quite different from the joyless couplings with Adelaide. Sometimes he could believe that his feelings were packed in ice; only with Melanie was there a great melting, did he come to life.

She waited for him to pull her upward sharply. It was the familiar signal for her to wrap her legs around his waist, re-create their initial encounter. It was his habit the first time they made love after an absence. Sometimes thinking about it caused an orgasmic shudder to go through her. She sensed a hesitation in him now. Love standing up. He was still strong enough to lift her, his hands on her buttocks, she light enough to be held so. But she sensed the hesitation. Would it be kindness to suggest that they shift to the easier classic position? It had never been her style to lead in lovemaking. There were many moments in her life when she resented the need to yield to a man, but not in the sexual act. The contrast between her regal appearance and imperious manner and her soft acquiescence in bed affected her lovers greatly, she realized. Each man thought it was due to him alone.

Denis picked her up, and it was fine, as it had always been. The moment, the movements took her back. Herself, fifteen, aching, aching. The rapture behind the door and then Adelaide and her mother in the drawing room. Despairing, jealous, filled with a terrible confused joy, she had nonetheless felt hope. And then—nothing had worked out as she had thought it would. Reality had intruded almost at once in Adelaide's swelling waistline and possessive manner, in the pregnancy and its finish in the bathtub alone, never more alone.

Their love affair was not over yet; she would not let it be, though she could not help but imagine Denis lifting Iris; why she was like a little bird. He would, he would pick up that fragile body. Iris to be mistress of Carnaugh? It must not happen, she thought, arching her back to look at Denis. Oh, to see him so—as when imprisoned in her corset long ago, she could not catch her breath. She had expected that much before this the moment would have come when she would see Denis as only a man like other men, no different; no better, handsomer, or more desirable. It had happened in every other love affair. The scales as it were would fall from her eyes and she would wonder that she had ever found the man sexually desirable. But not Denis, never Denis. Not even now. She could see him with a harsh clarity—observe the pad of flesh over the abdomen, the hair dark at the pubic region, but graying elsewhere. The signs of age made no difference; how desirable he still appeared. The phallus rose large and hard, the body was well muscled, the buttocks and legs firm.

He moved his hips forward and back, bringing her almost to the point of fulfillment. So many thoughts rushed through her head out of control. The camel waiting by the roadside, Harry plunging naked into the water at the cove laughing that the cold made his genitals shrink, Evangeline touching her arm meaningfully at the Woodruffs' ball, Clara offering her breasts to Bunny, Wallace at his ledgers, and Denis, always Denis embracing a pregnant Adelaide. The intrusion of events, places, times, names distracted her, drawing her away from fulfillment. She would have to drive away these images, fix her mind on the hard swollen phallus within her, on her muscles tightening and relaxing around it, and yield to the vertigo induced by his touch, by his lips, tongue, fingers, and male organ. She dug her long-nailed fingers into the flesh of his arms and shoulders, bit at his mouth. Passion, but anger, too, at his being so strong, capable of bringing such ecstasy and yet having failed her at every step of the way—from those first moments behind the door, failing her yet. Feckless, feckless. They called Harry feckless but this was the true fecklessness to throw away everything they could have had, throw it away with both his hands. His perspiration dripped onto her hair, into her ears. *My Denis is always so hot.*

Denis, holding her, was wondering if he would last in so awkward a position. Making love standing up had been easy at twenty-four, not so now. Feeling her hands moving down his back to the cleft between his buttocks, he nonetheless found uneasy thoughts breaking into his concentration just when it was most important for him to concentrate. He tried to close out the names impinging on his consciousness—Joseph Woodruff, the rumor had reached him, had been her lover. Surely that was an error. Not Joseph, so coarse, unattractive—and now this Harry Van Burgh of the gossip columns, unarguably Melanie's lover. And young, so young. No doubt he could maintain the act of love for any length of time in any position. Youth was the formidable rival. It almost did not matter who was the possessor. He moved at last to the bed. Easier so. Pressing his weight on her as he knew she liked it. If he could have been different, weak, ready to ignore his responsibilities, allow the estate to fall to ruin as his parents had been so willing to do he would have had Melanie.

Melanie, Melody. He stood again, lifting her, and groaned as her vaginal muscles tightened, loosened, then tightened again. He put her down, gasping, and they looked at each other, perspiring, flushed, the semen running down her legs and onto the white rug. The fluffiness turned into damp clumps, yellowing. Even in the dimly lit room, he could see the traces of makeup on her body, the color running down her legs with the perspiration and semen. But still, still so lovely. They lay down again, side by side, breathing in the smells of sex, spent, intimate, half asleep, yet keenly aware.

She pulled up the sheet to rub her damp face. Streaks of black, pink, and cream—the tints Beryl had applied so lightly, so subtly as to look natural—were visible on the lace-trimmed edging. Denis saw the streaks and smiled. But his smile was kind.

Without her speaking of the future, Melanie thought it was all being arranged for her while she lay here in his arms. She waited for him to speak at last of permanence, a sharing of their lives that went beyond being lovers, and then she observed that his eyes were hooded; he had withdrawn from her. She remembered that only Harry never held himself away from her. Climax did not bring sleep or emotional withdrawal; he would be with her, go on looking into her eyes, speaking the gentle words of a lover. That was illusion, too, however: Harry had been with her on time borrowed from what they both knew to be his real life, the life in which he would be Iris's husband just as Denis had come to her through the years on time borrowed from his real life with Adelaide.

Denis knew what she wanted, what she thought she had achieved by bringing him to this level of confiding, of confidence. But it changed nothing. After washing off the perspiration, the traces of Melanie's perfume and cosmetics, he would pick up his clothing from the floor, brush off the fluff from the silly little rug, and dress himself as neatly as possible. Cousin Malcolm and Woodruff would by now have completed negotiations on the marriage settlement. He would sign whatever agreements there were to be signed, make the promises, woo and wed the heiress. Or wed and woo the heiress. It made no difference which came first.

Everything will change if you marry Iris, Melanie had said. A threat, just a threat. She had said before that she would break with him and had never done so; she would not do so now. Willful and spoiled as she was, she must understand what a man's life meant. He must rebuild Carnaugh, restore the farms, buy back the Rembrandt. He must have a son who would in his time become Marquess of Warburne in the direct line, the title passed from father to son, from father to son and for seventeen generations.

CHAPTER 20

Horror on
the Lawn

Wallace. That was her first thought. His unexpected arrival alone would explain so improper a behavior: Beryl had rushed into the bedroom without having been summoned. In her entire life Melanie had never known a maid to do that.

Beryl was utterly distraught, stammering that they must dress, no time to bathe or even wash. She made an ineffectual gesture to wipe off Melanie's legs, bent down and with shaking hands picked up the garments from the floor, brushing off the fluffy wool.

"Mr. Edmont?"

Beryl did not respond to the question. "Listen."

It was than that Melanie realized she had been vaguely aware of sounds for some time. So deep in love, in talk, tight against each other in the secluded room, the windows closed and draped, the noise must have been loud indeed to reach them there.

Listening now, and with the door open, she could just

make out a buzzing, humming sound. How long had Beryl stood outside not daring to come in until her fear of what was going on outside overcame her?

Going to the window, Melanie saw nothing out of the ordinary, but these rooms faced onto the back of the house. "What is it, Beryl?"

"I have not seen anything myself, Mrs. Edmont. I could not leave you. But Bardon ran down the corridor to tell me he was going for the police and that I must warn you. People, men are on the lawn, shouting . . . threatening . . . A mob."

On the lawn. How could they have gotten in? A high wrought iron fence ringed the property. The gatekeeper was armed.

"Bardon thinks the gatekeeper must be dead," continued Beryl trembling. "He says the mob just tossed the man aside, threw him bodily across the road, and then broke the gate off its hinges."

She remembered then that the summer gatekeeper was one of the oldest servants, kept on out of the responsibility one had for longtime retainers, and assigned what had been considered the easiest of jobs. Still caught in the passions of the afternoon, Melanie felt dazed, unable to take in what had happened.

"Where is the gun room?" Denis appeared calm, unconcerned, the aristocrat, good British officer, rising to a situation. "How many men do we have?" His hands were steady as he drew on his underdrawers, pulled on his shirt, then his trousers, fastened his cravat, put on his waistcoat, his suit coat.

The gun room? Under other circumstances, Melanie would have laughed. Denis thought himself in an English castle. The gatekeeper had been given one pistol; there was another in the house, but she had never thought to find out where it was kept. As for men, well, Bardon was gone, so that left Cough, the coachman, and two footmen, both of them elderly. The butler and the more capable manservants were in Bourneham. Still, thinking of them, graceful in their brocaded livery with hair powdered for a ball, it was hard to imagine them holding a mob at bay. Could there really be a mob? Surely Beryl was exaggerating. Servants easily gave way to panic.

"I will go to see," declared Denis, not allowing himself to appear fazed by the news she gave him.

"Don't leave me here alone."

"Well, hurry then."

Even without the corset, it was hard for her to dress, and Beryl, terrified, was clumsy. Melanie decided not to waste time on undergarments, just stockings and garters, then the dress. But there were so many fasteners to close. Like all her dresses, this one had rows and rows of tiny buttons to ensure the proper tight fit. She would never be finished. Surely half the buttons were still undone when, following Denis, she ran back up the long corridor, took the turn, again up another long corridor, running towards the noise, which came at them in waves. It was an angry roar leveling off to a hum, a buzz.

As they reached the top of the great staircase, the crowd's roar became intelligible: "Edmont." Again and then again. The thought came to her that Wallace might be here after all, arriving after Bardon left and remaining downstairs to deal with whatever was happening.

"Wait. Let me go first," she gasped, out of breath. But Denis ran ahead, careless. It was not he who was at risk, she thought, forgetting that the greater risk was from the mob and that he was protecting her. Grasping at the banister to keep from slipping on the highly polished marble stairs, she rushed after him, still trying to keep him from entering the drawing room in front of her. Wallace was not there. The room was so dark with the heavy velvet draperies drawn tightly across the bay windows overlooking the front lawn that for a moment she failed to recognize the young man roughly dressed in shirt and trousers brandishing a pistol. Melanie recoiled, certain that a tough from the mob outside

251

had broken in and then she realized it was Bardon. She had never seen him save in uniform. Her heart sank. "Beryl said you were going for the police, Bardon." She had to raise her voice to be heard above the angry roar invading the room despite the closed windows and heavy curtains.

"I tried, madam, I had to change out of my livery. And by the time I had done so, the madmen were all around the house. They would have killed me as they killed old Musgrove at the gate. They would have torn me to pieces."

"Where are the other servants, Bardon?"

"They have gone down to the cellar and have barricaded themselves in the storeroom. Then I remembered Mr. Edmont's pistol. I was not sure what to do. Mr. Edmont will be angry with me for going into his dresser drawer. He has strictly forbidden it."

His fear of Wallace seemed almost as great as his fear of the crowd. *No one looks at my ledgers.* He was right to worry about his future in the house. It did not occur to her that there might be no future for any of them. Still more excited than afraid, she tried to reassure him. "You did the right thing, Bardon." And it was as she spoke those words that the enormity of the situation struck her, and she understood the danger they were in and the absurdity of his action. What good would one pistol do against a howling mob? And the cry of "Edmont" was getting louder.

Perhaps they should go to the cellar and wait there for rescue. It was bound to come. A police patrol checked Fifth Avenue at regular intervals, knowing the great wealth concentrated in the mansions there. It was the safest part of the city. (And yet, here was a mob on the lawn.) Who would come first—the police or Wallace?

Denis took the gun from Bardon as a matter of course. He was frowning. "From the sound of it, they appear to be standing still, not moving towards the house," he said. "Perhaps they are waiting for Edmont to appear."

Melanie thought of old Musgrove thrown across the road and shuddered.

252

Denis started towards the window. "No. No!" she cried out, caution reasserting itself even in the midst of her fear. Denis must not be seen here. She ran to the window, edged herself in front of him, and pulled the draperies and the lighter Austrian lace curtains aside just enough to allow a view of the scene outside. The crowd was made up entirely of men. There were fewer of them than she had thought from the outcry, but the atmosphere was one of menace. She looked from one man to the next. Surely that was the man with the knife. She would know his thin reddish hair, those misshapen hands anywhere. But of course, it was as she had realized before. All the poor looked alike, ragged shirts hanging out of trousers held up with twine. Any one of them might have been the man with the knife, the squatter with blackened hands, tattered filthy clothing, broken shoes. Dirt. Ugliness. Deformity. Emaciated or with unhealthy fat.

She opened the window a crack. An odor blew in to her on the afternoon breeze, rank, of bodies not merely unwashed now, but hardly ever washed at all, smelling of perspiration and the outhouse.

A man in the crowd caught sight of her with Denis a shadowy figure behind her and a cry went up. "Edmont." Hands were raised and balls of dirt and pebbles from the walk were thrown towards the house. She started in terror. This rabble could storm the house, assault, rape, murder. Melanie trembled and perspiration poured down her body; her close-fitting dress was damp under the arms, down the sides, stuck to her back. The thought of one of those men putting his dirty hands on her body, naked beneath the ill-fastened dress, made her feel sick with repulsion. She remembered how the tramp had looked at her breasts. A man like any other man when it came to this. She had never been helpless, never even conceived of being helpless, at the mercy of another. She remembered the day when she had been menaced by the man with the knife. Her fear had been tempered by the knowledge that Harry would protect her. And there had been only one attacker, not a mob of many.

Pure terror was a new emotion to her. Always, a ring of people surrounded her, keeping her from anyone who would harm her.

Wallace, too, was always protected. There were men in his office. Clerks they were called though no one would have given them anything to figure or to write: large, well muscled, powerful, their heavy shoulders and chests bulging in ill-fitting suit coats. Such men, bodyguards, if one dispensed with euphemism, were to be seen in many of the downtown offices. A necessary part of doing business in the increasing violence and criminality of New York.

She had always disliked seeing any of these men, had rather scorned Wallace for employing such guards. She understood the need for them now. Property owners, even the best of them, aroused hatred.

Looking over her shoulder, Denis muttered, "They think Edmont is in the house. They wait for someone else to come or for something to happen. I know what mobs are from my service in India."

"Perhaps it would be best to go down to the cellar."

Denis flinched. Could she possibly imagine that he, the last of sixteen generations of Marquesses of Warburne, would hide, craven, in a cellar? He was astounded, no enraged, at Edmont. How was it possible for a man to keep no guns in the house save this single pistol? In England, everyone he knew kept guns and the boys were taught to have good aim, shoot at a target, to hunt. In this country, apparently, men relied on others—police, bodyguards—to protect them, their property, their wives, children, and servants.

"I think that would be the wisest move for you and the maid, Melanie. But I must stay here. Mobs can be handled; I have done it before. Each man is a coward, after all, seeking strength in numbers. A show of firmness is often all that is needed. I will wait for the right moment to face them down. I have the pistol and Bardon behind me."

It was not so simple as that, thought Melanie. If Denis were to be seen here with her, she would be ruined. Even as this thought crossed her mind, she knew how inappropriate, trivial, was fear for her reputation. As at the moment when she plunged the knitting needle into her shrinking body she was face-to-face with the most elemental forces of life. Denis must not leave the house—not because it would create scandal and reduce a divorce settlement—but because he might be killed: Denis, his body trampled beneath the broken shoes of the ruffians unless she made him see reason. The men were shaking their fists at the house.

"No, Denis. You mustn't go."

It occurred to him that she was concerned whether someone would see him, link his absence from the Woodruff marital negotiations with his presence here. How like a woman, he thought.

"Surely you can see that appearances are not important now." But then as she clutched his arm, pulling him back from the door, he realized from her trembling how deep was her fear.

"Appearances? Surely you can see that you could be killed. And for what? The police will come. Fifth Avenue is patrolled. I cannot imagine where they are."

Denis could imagine. A hot afternoon. A stop for a cold glass of beer. Nothing ever happened on Fifth Avenue, nothing would. But he responded to the terror he read on her face. The dirty hands, she was thinking, foul breath, disgust.

Perhaps she was right. Sooner or later the police were bound to come. He could dare to wait for a little longer. Melanie was afraid, he thought, feeling tender towards her. (Had Adelaide flinched? He shuddered at the memory.) His upbringing had been such as to make him refuse to admit to a fear of death for himself.

"Go downstairs, Melanie. I won't leave this room unless it becomes absolutely necessary."

She shook her head, ordered Beryl to go, approached the window again. The scene held a terrible fascination for her; despite her fear she must see it played out. Denis came

255

up behind her and put his hand on her shoulder, comforting, to steady her.

She looked out and observed a man standing facing the house just below the window. Her first thought was that he had broken from the crowd to menace them. She opened the window a little wider and bent forward. The man was so close that she could have reached down her hand and touched him. He was holding something. A weapon? From this vantage point she could see what it was and could hardly believe in the incongruity. The man was holding a pencil and notebook and was busily writing. All at once she recognized him. It was Elmer Morgen, clothing shabby, shirt open at the neck, shoes dusty. In this guise, he might have passed for one of the mob. Looking up at the window and meeting her staring eyes he smiled. Oh, what a smile of triumph. I have you now. He held up the notebook in his dirty hands so that she could see what he had written. And it was not writing at all, but a drawing in thick black pencil lines so bold that its subject matter was clear: Melanie stood at the window looking at the mob outside, and behind her, a hand on her shoulder, one long finger touching her breast, a shadowy male figure.

Morgen's presence at the scene was understandable—a journalist following a mob to its destination in search of news. He did not appear afraid of the mob, had walked through their midst to come close to the house. Perhaps they welcomed him as someone to tell their story. Discovering her here in the company of a man must have been from his viewpoint pure good luck, enhancing the value of the report he meant to write.

Why the hideous frivolity of the drawing? The suggestiveness? The way he had made certain that she saw it? What was its relevance to this scene of menace and his presence here? There was nothing to indicate that he meant to come to her aid. Could the man be so evil that only his news story mattered to him? Observing her as if memorizing her appearance, Morgen made her aware of her own disordered state, her hair loose, her face gleaming with perspiration. He smiled then, waved as if to say he would return, and walked back into the crowd.

And then she smelled something, an odor strong enough to overcome the smells emanating from the crowd. It was a familiar homely sort of smell, and with shock she recognized it. Kerosene. She could feel Denis start. Melanie's heart began to pound, her mouth was dry. The house was to be burned down. They would have to escape, but escaping meant plunging into the hostile mob, which might not be escape at all.

The servants, she thought. "We must call the servants up out of the cellar, Denis, and get out of the house while we still can."

Denis shook his head. "Not so fast. They are moving away from the house. What is it that they are doing?"

The smell of kerosene grew stronger. Denis touched her and she realized a change had taken place. The clamor had stopped altogether, and the men dropped their arms and turned their backs to the house. Melanie's sense of dread increased. This was not the silence of peace restored, a crowd about to disperse. It was rather the stillness that precedes disaster.

"What are they doing out there?" muttered Denis. "What does this mean?"

The men had formed a huge circle on the lawn and in the center was someone or something she could not make out.

A sharp intake of breath, a gasp. It was as if all the men breathed as one, gasped as one. Then silence, and in that silence a sound was heard, not very loud, terrifying in its ordinariness, the sound of a match being struck. The smell of kerosene again, this time aflame. Had the moment come? She seized Denis's arm, uncertain of what to do.

Denis shook his head again. "Can't you tell? They are no longer interested in the house, Melanie, or in us." The smell of burning oil grew stronger. He gave a groan. "Oh,

257

my God! Don't look." He moved his body in front of hers, made as if to put his hand over her eyes, but she pulled away and looked out. A thin tongue of flame was leaping, rising above the heads of the crowd that blocked her view. The men were not facing the house; all their attention was focused on that fire. What was there that so fascinated them? What could Denis see or guess that made him look so sick? What lay in the center of that circle of men standing on the grass, on the beds of calla lilies, in the rose garden? There was a terrible smell, acrid, pungent, nauseating. A plume of blackened smoke rose from the fire. The fumes of boiling oil, grease mingled with another stronger odor, as of meat searing, cooking, crackling, roasting, burning. What were they cooking out there on the lawn that they stood watching so silently?

The appalling idea came to her that one of the dogs had been captured and was being cooked in a ceremony of revenge. Perhaps it was Wallace's favorite, Gorgon, the Great Dane. Yes, rich men were hated in these times. But listening keenly for sounds of yelping, barking, she heard nothing but the crackling of the flames. So the dog must have been killed before being put to the fire. That at least was a mercy. She turned looking to Denis for support, and at the expression of horror on his face, she leaned out of the window.

Just then the figures in the crowd shifted enough to give her a view of the fire on the lawn. It was burning furiously now, flames leaping in a brilliance that was almost blinding. In the midst of the flames, for just a second she caught sight of what it was that was burning, saw the body about to be consumed. The image was quite clear and though it lasted for less than a second she was never able afterwards to forget it. A person was kneeling there, a man. And while she stared, unable to close her eyes to the horror taking place on the lawn, the flaming figure fell forward onto the ground. She heard a gasp, a howl, and could not discern whether it came from the men in the crowd or from her.

She clung to the window frame shuddering. What she

had seen was mad, senseless. There could be no possible reason for such brutality, for burning a fellow human being. And why had the victim not screamed or struggled? He had not been killed first and then put to the fire as she had imagined Wallace's Great Dane to have been. She had seen the figure kneeling. Vicious beyond belief. To bring a man, alive, and burn him amidst the grass and flowers on a pleasant summer's afternoon.

One man then called out, "Murderer! Murderer!" And others took it up. Over and over the cry went up. The ground seemed to shake with it. But they were the murderers, thought Melanie. There could be no one else to blame. They turned and shook their fists at the house, and she drew back, frightened again, conscious of her vulnerability. Perhaps their appetites, whetted by one death, would require others.

All at once, she sensed that Denis, so close that she could feel each motion, had relaxed. " I think the worst of the danger is over."

Over? How was that possible when they were shouting murderer?

"I sense the change in mood," said Denis. "There is a moment when any violence is possible. And then it passes. The threat is less now."

Now she could tell that the voices were not so loud nor, despite the epithet, so threatening. It was as if the horror of the burning had served as catharsis, relieving them of the tension.

Suddenly weary, she left her position at the window and sank into one of the small armchairs. The contrast between the hideous scene on the lawn and the beautifully designed room, false doors on one wall balancing the real doors opposite to achieve the perfect symmetry decreed at Versailles, was jarring. For the first time she recognized that she and other rich people who lived in such splendor had separated themselves, had no connection with an outside world filled with suffering. And in that moment, she had a glimmering of what it was the mob had sought to achieve with its violence and Morgen sought to achieve with his newspaper.

The crowd had fallen silent when, with what she perceived as perfect irony, the sound of horses' hooves, whistles, shouted orders, clattering wheels, hoses being unrolled heralded the arrival of firemen and mounted police.

She rushed back to the window. Outside all was chaos. The men making up the mob were beginning to run even before the firemen finished unrolling the long hoses. Then came the torrent of water turned first upon the bonfire and then on the mob. It was not such a big fire, really. A moment or two and nothing was left but the charred grass with bits of what looked like rubble yet had to be ash and bone. The crowd dispersed in disorder, cursing and crying as the stream of water struck, knocking down those directly in its path. The police seized any men who could not move off the grounds rapidly enough. Three minutes, five minutes. The lawn would soon be empty of all save uniformed men and horses.

Turning to Denis in a sudden surge of warmth at the danger they had faced together, she saw him frowning. "The police and firemen will be here in a few moments; they would be at the door already if they believed you were present. I must be out of here before they come."

He was thinking quickly, she realized, and where only a short time earlier she had found fault with him for ignoring the risk to her, now she felt let down. This time it was he who was concerned for her reputation. Or was he only concerned about absenting himself from the Woodruff wedding negotiations for too long? He was right to leave; if he did not, she would regret it for the rest of her life. If he left quickly enough, no one would ever learn he had been there. The small group of servants knew better than to speak. Wallace did not deal with servants. They were her responsibility. But if Denis were called upon by the police to give testimony as a witness, sign a statement, everyone would know of his presence and assume that what had happened had happened. She might as well forget a divorce settlement then.

Denis was looking about, considering the possible exits. Despite the confusion outside, he could not hope to get out on the Fifth Avenue side.

"I think you could still slip out to the side street, Denis. The police will not be concerned with that exit, as the fence on the left side of the house appears to have no opening. But there is a small gate. You can see it only if you know where to look—exactly opposite the Japanese maple tree. I will give you the key."

He nodded.

"And where will you go then?"

"I will rejoin my future in-law who is no doubt translating my worth into dollars and put the balance of the day to good use." From the tone of his voice, she could see that he meant to be humorous, but the remark struck her unpleasantly. There was too much of truth here. He was displaying a nasty side, she thought. Certainly he could not have remained. But a word of farewell spoken with fondness would have comforted her. She was already suffering the reaction from the terror she had experienced. Harry would never have spoken in such a manner, however great the strain, she thought bitterly—Harry, whom she had sent off to elope with Iris. She would never see him again to talk as in the past, to be cheered by his attentiveness, his kindness. *Put the balance of the day to good use.* Nervous sarcasm. Even Denis was not immune to nervousness. The remark stuck in the craw nonetheless. Let him go to Woodruff, make his arrangement, and learn in time that it was all in vain.

But as she watched him go out of the drawing room, her resentment faded. He had shown courage, prepared, despite the lack of a cadre of men with arms from a gun room, to face the attackers alone. Unknown to the crowd, in shirt and trousers, he might have been able to make his way out. He had not abandoned her. If the rabble outside had begun to storm the house, he would have protected her. She felt better with these thoughts. Hating Denis would render all her plotting worthless; she would have given up Harry too soon and for nothing.

CHAPTER 21

Can He
Be Silenced?

The great knocker was lifted and fell. Melanie waited and then realized she was alone. For the first time in her life, she went to the door herself—it was so heavy she could hardly open it—and let in the police.

Upon learning from her where the servants were hiding, a policeman went to call them out. Though Melanie reassured the servants that there was nothing blameworthy in their action, they appeared hangdog. Beryl kept wiping away tears.

Melanie turned her attention to the police, who were courteously asking for her testimony. There was surprisingly little for her to tell them. How had the mob gotten here? Who was their leader? What their intent? She was asking more questions than she answered.

"The man who was burned. Who was he?" Nobody knew. Just a man.

Musgrove. She all at once remembered the luckless old

man, given the easiest job as summer gatekeeper. Now she learned he was not dead. An arm and both legs had been broken when he was thrown across the street. He had lain quietly, suppressing his moans, fearing that the men would come to finish him off if they heard him. The fire engine had all but ridden over him. One of the horses had broken stride at the scent of blood and Musgrove was found. He was now being carried to the hospital.

"The mob had no interest in him once they had breached the gate," remarked the police sergeant coolly.

At last after assuring her that men were being stationed on the grounds, the police left the house. Melanie could not remember when she had been so exhausted. It would be a relief to be alone for a while, to take a bath in softened, scented water, to have Beryl shampoo her hair and spray it with perfume, to be massaged and put into fresh clothing. Somehow it seemed impossible to take ordinary actions, resume her customary life after the overwhelming experience of the afternoon. Now sitting quietly in her living room, she felt the full impact. The image of what had happened on the lawn was all at once so clear it might have been taking place right then. She closed her eyes and saw the man with the kerosene poured over his body, then the flames licking at his feet, his legs, moving upward to his genitals, upward to the heart, the head, until the entire body was a flaming torch.

She went to the front door, barely aware of Beryl rushing forward to open it, and walked out between the columns onto the steps. There was still a smell of smoke, of burned meat, all the more repellent for her knowledge of what that meat had been. The odor filled her nostrils, her throat. The breeze had subsided. The air was heavy, humid in the late afternoon. It seemed that she would never be free of the memory; the image of the kneeling flaming body would be there behind her eyes, visible each time she closed them. She did not think that she could ever sit beneath the trees on the lawn again. It was sullied forever by the terrible scene played out there. Even the house appeared loathsome to her.

It was not only the horror, the memory that was intolerable, but the realization that they, the Edmonts, were not inviolate, that a mob could so easily force the gate and enter the grounds. Had they wished to invade the house rather than to stand outside watching the immolation, how could Denis have stopped them? She trembled at the thought of how narrowly she had escaped. There had been time for her to have been seized, raped, murdered before the horses had run through the streets drawing fire engines behind them, before the police had arrived. The man with the knife had been a portent.

She wished that Wallace would come. Though in her confusion she had not thought to instruct the police to inform him, she was sure that they had. It was Wallace's boast that every city agency and department reported to him, that he knew every major happening in the city almost as soon as the chief of police. He would come himself, she knew, to view the damage, determine his next course of action. For once she wanted him to be there to take charge, would not resent it, wanted to be taken care of. But then she realized what Wallace's arrival would require of her. She would have to be properly dressed and made up, have to pull herself together and give him an explanation he could accept for her presence here away from her mother's house. A pair of slippers wanted for the ball, a change of mind as to the jewels to be worn, the desire for an hour's peace after a heart-wrenching visit. She must be convincing, leave him no reason to doubt.

The smells were so foul; some nauseating odor different from that of the fire assaulted her. What could it be coming from? She walked down the steps, and there on the ground observed the little balls of dirt that had been thrown at the house. Bending closer, she knew with stomach-turning certainty that these balls were not of dirt, but of excrement. She retched and retreated up the steps.

With a sense that someone was watching her (she did not count the police), she turned and observed a man standing motionless under the trees. Knowing the police would not have allowed any unauthorized person to remain on the grounds, she looked again and saw the notebook in the man's hands. Of course, the journalist, the one person the police would not turn away. The chief of police was said to be afraid of Morgen, afraid of becoming a target. His men had instructions to cooperate.

Morgen's face was so blackened by the fire it was hardly surprising she had not recognized him at first. His clothing was disordered, dirty; there were holes in his trousers and jacket. He was smiling at her, his teeth white against his darkened skin. How did he dare to smile? It made her conscious that she looked as if she had come from bed.

Aware of her eyes on him, Morgen turned and walked over to the charred patch on the lawn and kicked at it. A fragment flew through the air. Bone perhaps, or ash.

Shuddering, horrified by his callousness, she turned away. And at that moment she recognized the danger she was in. Denis's presence here was known—and not just to servants who could be silenced—but to one of the most malevolent men in New York. He had made the drawing, the damning drawing. She could deny it, but no one would listen or believe. The afternoon with Denis had been a mistake. She remembered her foreboding. Everything they had done had been wrong. She remembered Morgen's triumphant smile. Yes, she had made a mistake in allowing Denis to disappear. It would have been better to have had his presence revealed openly and an excuse, however flimsy and unconvincing, offered. She would have to meet with Morgen; failing to do so would be another mistake. Perhaps she could persuade him to remain silent. He was a man, after all; she had always been able to manage men. Talk with him, and find his point of weakness. To allow such a person to enter her home by the front entrance was repellent to her, but she would be at a disadvantage talking to him on the steps.

Going inside, she ordered Bardon, by now uniformed

and at his post, to tell Morgen she wished to see him. Bardon was too well trained or too numbed by the events of the afternoon to exhibit any sign of surprise. He was to bring Morgen to the library; she decided it was more bearable to see the man there than in her drawing room.

Melanie indicated a place for Morgen to sit. His soiled clothing and filthy hands would leave marks on the cream-colored damask upholstery, but the servants would clean them off. There was something furtive about the way he kept looking up at her and then away. For the first time it occurred to her to wonder why he had remained on the grounds after the mob had left. Surely he had enough material for his newspaper article. She would have expected him to rush to the *Journal* office to see it into print. For the first time also, it struck her that he had been singularly unafraid of the ruffians in the crowd.

"I admired your appearance of ease when I saw you earlier, Mr. Morgen," she began. "You showed no fear of those rough men. I admired your courage."

"Thank you for the compliment, Mrs. Edmont. But the truth is I had nothing to fear. They think of me as one of them. I can fool rich people about my origins, but never people like them. I was one of those scorned immigrants, crowded into tenements of the sort owned by your husband. My father was a porter; I used to help him with the heaviest loads. It is easy to slip back: I put on shabby clothes, use a cruder form of speech, and I feel at home again, comfortable."

"And do you return to that life merely to feel comfortable?"

His smile was without humor. "Have you and your friends never wondered how I know so much about life in the slums, about the dregs of society, as you would call them, degraded, often drunken? I walk through the worst neighborhoods, take a room, a part of a room, that is, in one of the meanest of the old-law tenements, find employment hauling loads as my father did, looking no different from anyone else,

266

speaking no differently. It is because I am one of them that I know so much. I speak for them, write for them out of understanding, out of knowledge. When I write of their privations, I write for myself as a boy, for my parents, for my brothers, for the girl I once loved more than I have ever loved anyone since, dead, all dead. Typhoid, cholera. Dead."

The passion in his voice moved her. Despite the self-serving quality of his words, she saw justice in them and was close to admiring him.

"Perhaps you understand me a little better now."

In the silence that followed she looked at him again, observed his threadbare clothing, his broken shoes, dirty hands. And all at once she understood.

"You planned it." Her voice sounded hoarse.

He took her meaning at once. "No, no, I did not. The plan was made; I heard of it only this morning. There was no way of stopping it. I went along with the men. Their thinking was sound, even showed cunning."

How had a crowd of indigent men gotten so far uptown without being stopped by the police? Disreputable persons were not allowed in the better neighborhoods. But the police patrols for once were absent, and the men, coming a few at a time over a period of hours, bore forged letters declaring them to be repairmen, sweeps, and laborers for the unpleasant tasks of cleaning the chimneys and the water pipes. Such work was commonly done in the summertime.

"You could have stopped them. All you needed to do was go to the police."

"And have these poor beggars thrown in jail? They have a grievance, Mrs. Edmont, a real grievance. They wished to make a gesture, reveal the depth of their rage and helplessness. No harm was to be done."

"But why select Mr. Edmont? Surely, he is the best of the property owners."

Morgen shrugged. "Mr. Edmont is a symbol; they could hardly find a better one."

"What if they had turned violent, Mr. Morgen? What

would you have done then? Written it all down in your notebook . . . that they had burned down the house? Killed the servants?" She hesitated. "Attacked me?"

"I never expected to find you, Mrs. Edmont. I had assumed that you would be in Bourneham planning table decorations or using a facial mask or getting a massage, whatever it is you ladies do before a ball. It was a shock to find you here. But you would not have been harmed, nor would I have allowed your . . . friend or Edmont, had he arrived, to be injured. Of course, I know that crowds can turn violent. I had arranged for one of the young chaps on the newspaper to follow them on horseback and remain close by. If I gave him a signal, he would have made a run for the police."

Even if she were to believe him about this, and she was not sure she did, Morgen had known that poor wretch would be burned to death. She suspected him. Without the human in flames, the demonstration would not have made so good a story for his newspaper. Too good a story for him to have stopped it. The slight warmth she had felt for him vanished.

"Who was the man? The one who died? Surely if you know so much, you must know that."

He shook his head. "Nobody. Just a man. Slum scum— I should jot that down, a good phrase for my article. That is what your husband thinks, though he is far too polished, more polished than I, to say so. Who was the dead man? No one of importance, or conversely everyone of importance. Every man."

"But why was he burned?"

Morgen shifted ground. "I take it that Mr. Edmont isn't here. The leaders of this demonstration seemed to think he would be."

When she did not respond, he continued. "Tricked by the wily Jessop no doubt to send them away from Edmont's office, with possibly catastrophic results for you. But, I can assume, neither Edmont nor Jessop knew anything of your plan for the afternoon."

She remembered then that Wallace had urged her not

to come to the house. Had he foreknowledge of what was to take place? But if he had, surely he would have stopped it. For all Morgen's claims, the house might have been put to the torch.

"You have not answered my question, Mr. Morgen. Why did the mob put this man in the fire?"

"The mob, as you call these people, did not put the man in the fire." And then because Melanie appeared baffled, he continued: "They were horrified, too, though they agreed with the logic of his plan. He immolated himself by drenching his clothing with kerosene and setting it ablaze."

She stared at him in horror, unwilling to accept the meaning of his words.

"Yes. Self-immolation." Now the burning seemed more terrible to her than if it had resulted from mob violence. She wondered if the man had suffered, remembered having been told by a Catholic friend that martyrs burned at the stake worked themselves into such a state of ecstasy that they felt no pain. But that belief was held by the onlookers who, not feeling the flames, imagined ecstasy in the eyes rolled upward, the call to God.

"His wife and little girls died in the Heron factory fire. They were workers on the sewing machines."

"The man's grief must have driven him mad."

"That is one way of looking at it," remarked Morgen coolly. "Another is that he was quite sane. He had nothing to live for and wanted to make his death stand for something."

"For what?"

"A protest against conditions in the slums, against tenements and sweatshops owned by people who think the poor are of a different breed, deserving only filth, hunger, illness." He was lecturing again, addressing her as he would the readers of his newspaper. "Here on this lawn this one man expressed the suffering for which all rich people are culpable. And because I was here, the world will hear his protest."

"Because you were here," she repeated, recalling that

he had admitted having known, had come to see, relishing the spectacle, relishing the sensational reports he would then be able to write in his newspaper. "Why didn't you stop him?"

"Stop him? It was his life; surely a man has the right to do as he will with it." But he was not so cool as all that; the corner of his mouth was twitching, almost a tic.

"Mr. Edmont had nothing to do with the fire at the Heron factory, Mr. Morgen." It was the tic that gave her courage. "The poor wretch killed himself on this lawn in error."

"That would be a tragedy indeed," remarked Morgen. "If we could only reconstitute the bone and ashes and dispatch him to the proper place to burn himself again!" He paused. "Of course you are right in the particular. My sources are infallible. I know who owns that tenement and more than that, I know who set the fire and why. But it does not matter. Mr. Edmont is a symbol, I told you that, far better than Richard Quigley, who still lives in a modest town house on Lafayette Street and has, if I may say so, a retiring, uninteresting wife.

"If I know your husband at all," Morgen went on, "he will modernize those buildings he owns, have more fire escapes built, more windows cut through to the outside. And everyone will call it blood money."

"You will reinforce the belief in his responsibility by what you write, Mr. Morgen. Do you think that is fair?"

"I will not write falsehood, Mrs. Edmont. The reader can draw what conclusions he will. And if they are unfair . . . well, I hardly consider that relevant. The fact is that the effect of this burning will be greater if people are allowed to think Edmont is involved. He is a leader. Other property owners will follow his example and improve the conditions of their buildings. And things will be better, for a little while at least. That is why I write, Mrs. Edmont."

As he went on talking, her sense of distaste increased and it occurred to her that Morgen did nothing by chance. He had remained on the grounds after the mob left for a

270

reason. And she had let him in for a reason as well. The drawing. The damning drawing and all that it implied, all that he would imply about it in the accompanying news report.

Melanie raised her head and looked straight at Morgen. There was that in his manner now that showed him aware that her person was redolent of sexual activity. He had seen the shadowy figure behind her in the window, could not help but imagine her in bed with a lover. While putting forth a mass of verbiage, repeating his newspaper stories about the tenements, the vile exploiters, all the time he was thinking, she knew, could read it on his face, how it would be to start unbuttoning her dress, from its whalebone collar all the way down below her waist. No doubt he was wondering what she might be wearing underneath. Perhaps he even guessed she was completely naked under her dress. Her nipples showed against the tight linen bodice. There was the tic again.

She had not responded to his suggestive comments about her presence here and the person with her, but now she decided to move towards her goal directly, note his response and proceed from there. "When you were here before, you created a drawing, Mr. Morgen, and made certain I would see it," she said softly. "I would not like it to appear in the press. So unflattering in this plain dress."

Morgen did not answer directly; instead he began to talk again, nervously, foolishly. "When I left Bourneham, all society could talk of nothing but your forthcoming ball. Should you not be there, Mrs. Edmont, making certain sufficient ortolans and filets de boeuf are in your vast pantries, that orchids match the velvet hangings? I have even heard the rumor that you intend riding a camel. As a journalist, I have learned never to take anything for granted, so I have been to see the camel myself. It will be quite a performance—you and the camel. Two magnificent creatures!"

She stiffened at his unbelievable gall, impertinence, but he was oblivious of how improperly he had spoken. "I would like to see you together."

With difficulty Melanie held back the curt reply that would put him in his place. He held the power.

The tic was stronger now. And then she knew. It was clear to her why he had remained skulking about the grounds when he should have been rushing to his newspaper office. He had been unwilling to leave until he had played out his hand, had gotten the full advantage of his trump card.

He wanted to be invited to her ball. His mouth had a loose, wet look as if marked by passion. And passion it was. Though of a different type than the sexual, it could be quite as strong. He wanted the invitation with a desperate hunger—not as an opportunity to sneer—but as the pinnacle of a life, a proof of how far he had come from the dark crowded rooms in the tenement of his boyhood. How great must ambition have been to have lifted him out of the slums, made him, if not a gentleman, at least someone with whom gentlemen would speak. But not in their homes, not with their wives present. With his wife present if he had a wife. A Woodruff invitation had probably seemed as much as he could aspire to.

To attend the Edmont Ball, and in Bourneham where, though social events might be held for several hundred people, the conviction remained that they were intimate, inner-circle, in contrast with the large-scale balls in New York. Without that invitation, he would be no better than the townspeople peering through the fence at the camel, craning to get a glimpse of Melanie Edmont's legs as she climbed to her seat on the kneeling beast.

Like the rich man who discovers to his benefit and yet dismay that the politician believed beyond reproach could be corrupted, she felt a moment's regret that this man who had made his career as a reformer could, like any other social climber, so easily be bought.

Should she buy him with this invitation? Wallace would be furious; Genevieve, an ally she desperately needed, shocked and disapproving. Genevieve had cut off the Woodruffs for having Morgen at the table. But she could see that nothing else would serve. He had one last goal to achieve; single-mindedness had made him what he was. She would have to invite him to the ball.

A reason to give Wallace and Genevieve must be found. But, of course; Joseph Woodruff had shown her the way. Woodruff had deflected Morgen's pen from him to Edmont by so simple a device as an invitation to a ball. There were other rich men in New York for Morgen to attack. She would make Wallace and Genevieve see that this was the only way of drawing Morgen's poison.

Yes. She would head off scandal, and if all went well, she would yet be following Charles I and Henry VIII across the drawbridge and into Carnaugh Castle.

"Do you have a wife, Mr. Morgen?" she asked.

He smiled. The very question was an answer. Then his face clouded. Oh, he had a wife, she could see, a wife he was ashamed of now, taken from his early beginnings, perhaps from a squalid tenement, a wife to be concealed in his new way of life.

His wife was ill, he replied, did not attend social functions but always urged him to go. Melanie expressed her sympathy.

"My ball is held for my friends. I do not invite journalists, Mr. Morgen," she remarked in a light tone, noticing how his face fell.

"Is there something you would fear to have the public learn?" His voice was not so light as hers.

"I would not have the world at large know the details of the costume I plan to wear. That is privileged information for my own circle of friends." She was repeating the word.

"Could we not be friends, Mrs. Edmont?" he asked, uncertain of whether an invitation was or was not in the offing.

"My standards for friendship are very high." She gave the merest glance at the notebook sticking out of his suit coat pocket.

"I think I can meet them." Pulling out the notebook, he

tore out the page with the drawing on it and crumpled it in his hand.

She flushed at the vulgarity, the crudeness of his reaction.

He picked up her response and smiled. "Not to the manner born, you are thinking," he remarked. "And you are right. I have yet to learn subtlety. On the other hand, I am direct. And so I can be trusted."

She had learned long ago that those who spoke of their honesty were most often dishonest, those who said they were trustworthy most often failed in their trust. There was something sly about the man. Blackmail she understood. Pay Armand Wolfe and the nasty rumor was suppressed; no one would ever hear it again. But a man like this, he might yet betray her. She could still open the *Journal* and see the suggestive drawing. Morgen had torn it up, but drawings can be made again.

Concealing her distrust, she offered the prize: "Then I will expect you on Saturday, Mr. Morgen."

Well, she thought, he had played his trump card and she had played hers. Melanie rang for a footman to show him out. She had done all she could to salvage the situation; perhaps it would be sufficient, perhaps not.

Walking back to the drawing room and sinking into a chair, she felt too weary to move. Never had she held an interview where she had been at such a disadvantage physically, smelling of smoke, perspiration, sex.

CHAPTER 22

Wallace, Frantic, Rushes Home

Wallace, who had been calm when he learned that a mob had gathered outside his house, was beside himself at the subsequent report that Melanie had been seen at a window. As he set off on a frantic drive from his office, he was imagining all that might be happening to her at the mercy of those ruffians. Why was she there when he had told her to stay away? Oh, her headstrong ways would destroy her.

The police met his carriage as it turned up Fifth Avenue and assured him that the mob was dispersed, the house entered, and Melanie found safe. His anger increased that she had not returned to the *Falcon* but had gone home upon leaving her mother. It was so like Melanie. She would decide that she had to have the flower-patterned rose silk stockings or the lace-trimmed hankerchief. However trivial, if she wanted it, she had to have it. Home she would go, no matter how clearly she had been warned to stay away. The worst part of it was that he knew his warning had not been clear, unequivocal, but had been presented as a suggestion, and when had Melanie ever listened to a suggestion unless she chose to?

Of course, when he left Melanie at the pier, he had not really believed the mob would turn up at his house. He had not realized his home address was known to the rabble of the slums. There was not enough information then for him to say more, only rumors that Jessop had brought him, of bad feelings in the slums, threats against him. He had thought the rabble would go to his office if they went anywhere at all. That had happened before. A man could not own property in the slums and not have hotheads occasionally make their appearance at his place of business, howling invective and threats. They were easy enough to deal with. He had his boys—to himself he did not need to use the euphemism *clerks*. No, he had not been unduly concerned at the first report, but had merely thought it exigent to get to his office and start a counteroffensive against the flood of rumors. As a matter of fact, and the realization made Wallace uncomfortable, it had been Jessop who suggested that Melanie be told to keep away from Edmont property, Jessop who had shown in many subtle ways that he disliked Melanie. He saw her as profligate, spendthrift, qualities that were anathema to him, devoted as he was to conserving the Edmont wealth.

Within an hour of Wallace's arrival at his office, a deputation, well, what a name to give a group of ragged hoodlums, had indeed come there, declaring in their broken English to the clerk in the front room that it was known the *Falcon* had docked and insisting that they see Mr. Edmont. Scum. He would not meet with them. Jessop went to confront them, the boys at his side. The group was shaken by the sight of so much strength and fell back. Apparently intimidated, the rabble had dispersed.

Who would have thought a throng of poor and uneducated tenement dwellers would have the nerve to make their way up Fifth Avenue and convene at his house? Not foreseeing that danger, he had not sent a message to Melanie at her mother's house reinforcing his previous warning and ordering her to stay away—well, who could order Melanie to do anything?—but at least he could have apprised her of what was in the wind. Knowing her as he did, he should have insisted that a few of the boys be dispatched to accompany her from her mother's house to the pier. What a stroke of luck the mob must have thought it to have so valuable a witness in the house.

Warned that his grounds had been invaded, Wallace was prepared for devastation, desecration, but still, he was stunned to see the gate hanging open, its great hinges broken. The horses slowed out of long habit, as they made the turn around the driveway, circling the lawn. Its velvety surface was broken now, trampled, with bits of turf uprooted, bare earth revealed. Ruby-colored roses and calla lilies lay on the ground, their petals crushed, stained with mud.

Wallace shuddered as he made out a patch of sodden ground in the middle of the destroyed lawn. Blackness where the grass and earth had been scorched. It was as if his property had been attacked by an infestation of vermin, as if locusts had swarmed over the garden. Unclean. What did a rabble, a confluence of gross, crude men, understand of property? Or care about it?

He climbed down from the carriage, straight, tall, fashionable in his fawn-colored suit and flat-brimmed straw hat. Though the steps and the front door were spattered with foul-smelling mud, the house itself appeared untouched, peaceful. Looking up, he observed that the draperies had not been drawn across the windowpanes, which were, he thankfully observed, intact, and he could just make out through the lacy inner curtains the shape of Melanie's dark head. She must be sitting, as she so often did, in the emerald velvet armchair by the bay windows where the light was best. She was all right; it was as he had been told. He began to feel a little foolish at the wildness of his fears, hesitant to go in to face her. There was no predicting Melanie's reaction. She might turn on him, blame him for the failure of the police to come in time. On this occasion, he had to admit, for he prided himself on his sense of fairness, she had a reasonable basis for the accusation. The dilatory response by the police was his doing. He had thought himself to be behaving so rationally. His aim had been to show that an Edmont did not resolve a crisis in the godless manner of a Woodruff. During the strike against his foundries, Woodruff had issued instructions to fire on the strikers. Three men had been killed and dozens wounded. He had broken the strike, but a continuing series of depredations on his properties followed; Woodruff was one of the most hated men in the country.

And it had all been foreseeable. Wallace viewed business, he liked to say, as a chess match, considering each move and its countermoves, weighing all the possible modes of action until the one winning move was selected.

Send the police with orders to quell the riot using any means they wished? Fire on the mob? Leaders and followers would be hit indiscriminately; women might have accompanied their men. The countermove by the immigrants would logically be the destruction of the tenement property in which they lived to the detriment of the Edmont fortunes.

Fortunately—or so he had thought then—he had overheard the message Jessop had been about to send to the police, and had been able to countermand it and order that forebearance be shown. It had been at Wallace's insistence that the fire department had been called too, rather a brilliant stroke as there was then no hint that a fire might be set. Always prudent, Wallace had studied accounts of mob violence. He had learned that the most unruly mob can be controlled with streams of water as effectively as with bullets. Wallace had, therefore, ordered that police stand back outside the fence ringing the property for the few extra minutes required for the firemen to arrive with hoses and equipment.

It had seemed the height of wisdom and foresight . . . until he learned Melanie was in the house, and by then it was too late to demand immediate and harsh police intervention.

After having rushed home like a madman, Wallace stood uncertainly at the front steps, then turned and looked again at the appallingly altered grounds. The blackened, sodden, naked earth in the center of the torn-up lawn fascinated him, drew him. He walked towards it as if mesmerized. Always fastidious, he recoiled as the toe of his highly polished shoe, brown this season, touched the wet ground where death had taken place. Who had died? For what? For what? He was confounded, staring at the ashes where the horror, the burning had occurred. Surely, those lighter bits to the side of the puddle were bone not fully consumed, all that remained of the misguided creature who had destroyed himself here. On Edmont land. In full view of the house. The mob must have believed he would be present. Had Melanie not been there, no one would have witnessed the act. Wallace did not think of counting the servants. The man must have been mad. There was no other explanation. And yet how he must have suffered. Burning was a hard death, an agonizing, a slow death. What had the wretch thought in those moments after the match was lit and before the flames leaped up to consume him?

The mud had splashed a brown stain on his fawn-colored trousers. He wished he had not put on this particular suit today. Light colors were not his style; this suit, made at his tailor's urging, had never been worn before. Yet when leaving Bourneham he had instructed his valet to pack it. Somehow he had liked the idea of looking as if he were coming to New York for a social event rather than to deal with a business disaster. It had not been a good idea.

Turning away from the scene of tragedy, Wallace noticed a man walking around the driveway going towards the gate. As he stared in astonishment at the continuing incursion onto his property, the man turned the curve and Wallace got a look at his face. Why, it was Morgen, that filthy-minded muckraker, slinking about. Where could the man have been coming from? There had been no sign of him when Wallace entered the grounds. Morgen must have come from the house. Wallace was enraged at the gall of the man. No doubt he had been questioning the servants, seeking a scandalous story, and who knew what foolishness they could speak? He wondered then how the newspaperman would have learned so quickly about the riot. It did not seem likely that mere chance had brought him to the house.

"Mr. Edmont, I was hoping you would arrive before I left and save me the trip to your office," Morgen said in a flat voice that struck Wallace as insolent. At the same time the man seemed inordinately nervous. What could he have been concocting here? "I'm sure you would like to make a statement for the *Journal*."

Wallace knew better than to exchange words with a journalist. Anything one said could be twisted by a clever, unscrupulous writer. "Good day." Wallace spoke curtly, omitting the man's name though there was no reason to assume Morgen well-bred enough to recognize the snub. But why was he so nervous, furtive? Morgen shrugged and left the grounds.

Wallace sighed. He must not let himself be distracted by Morgen, but must consider the connotations of the demonstration, what it told of the potential for future mob violence, what response would be best for him to make. He must take action, prove once and for all that no one should dare to unlawfully enter and profane his property, but this must not be done carelessly or at random. He would have to order Jessop to send detectives into the slums to determine who had been behind the riot.

Bad as the prospects were, thinking about business relaxed him, helped him to put out of his mind his sense of unease that had Melanie been injured, he would have been to a large extent responsible, guilty himself.

Feeling apprehensive, he mounted the steps to the house. The door did not open at his approach. The servants were indeed in disarray not to have been watching for him. He picked up the heavy brass knocker, modeled after the bust of the emperor Marcus Aurelius, and it struck against the oaken door with a pleasing, rich tone.

As soon as he came into the house and saw Melanie, the disparate facts fit into one clear, whole pattern. It was Melanie who had brought Morgen to the house. That fact was obvious now. He was not sure why he knew it. Certainly, the desire to obtain a good newspaper story would have been enough to bring the man here. Yet Wallace was certain that was not the explanation, or not the only explanation. Wallace's steps were muffled by the thick pile of the rug and Melanie appeared so absorbed in her thoughts as not to be immediately aware of his presence. She was sitting in the small velvet armchair, staring down at the floor. He had never seen her in such an attitude of weariness. But for Morgen, he would have sympathized with her. Shoulders slumped, her arms hung slack at her sides. And then she looked up and he saw her hair straggling over her forehead and her neck. Her face was shiny and flushed, reddened a bit in patches as if from abrasion. He knew whose whiskers had abraded her soft skin. Her face was a trifle swollen. He knew that face, that look. Who would have thought it would hurt so much? Was the pain he felt that the man was Morgen?

He had been driven almost mad for worry over her. And she had come here not for the rose stockings or lacy handkerchief, but to betray him. What difference did it make whether it were this one or that—Harry Van Burgh or even, it had been rumored, Woodruff (though he found that too improbable to be believed) or Morgen? But it did make a difference. Dirtying. A man who earned his living sneering, casting aspersions on the wealthy and powerful. For Melanie to have been with him was to join in his sneering against her husband.

Having come to see Morgen, she had ended by becoming the object of the demonstration and had given it force and meaning, enabling Morgen to reveal everything that had happened, to accuse by innuendo where he dared not use direction. Melanie would not be spared. Gallantry, chivalry. One might as well expect it from one of the men making up that ragtag crowd outside.

This man, ill-born, ill-bred, of no particular grace or attractiveness had been, surely no more than two hours earlier to judge by the disarray of her hair, of her clothes, with his Melanie. And he had been frantic with worry.

Suddenly aware of his scrutiny, she straightened her back and held her head higher, these immediate responses the result of years of discipline. "I am pleased to see you have come through this experience safely, Melanie," he said, coldly, correctly.

"No more pleased than I. It seemed to me the police would never come."

He flushed. Guilty. But then he observed her nipples outlined in the fabric of her dress. She had come so precipitously from lovemaking, he thought, as not to pause for chemise, corseting, all the rest. Beneath the dark high-necked dress, her body was naked. He wondered whether the mob seeing her at the window had noted her state.

Hundreds, no thousands of his dollars were squandered each year on the satin corsets, the sheer silk chemises, the antique lace trim, the ruffled drawers, the taffeta petticoats, all handmade in Paris, cream-colored, rose, black, emerald green—and she came downstairs naked to face a mob. Underneath the severe dress he knew her skin to be soft, white, firm, demanding to be touched, yielding to the touch, his touch, Morgen's touch.

I asked you first, Wallace. He shuddered at the memory. The bloodied sheets. Her tears. And then the weight of years. The scenes she made. The money she tossed about— orchidaceous, profligate—Jessop was right, without a thought to the effort with which it had been earned. The men she had taken to her. But her body in the moonlight of those long-ago nights. *I asked you first, Wallace.*

Looking up at him, Melanie observed how troubled was his face. His eyes were glistening, as if brightened by tears.

He had worried about her, feared an injury to her. It should not matter. But somehow it did.

"What is it?"

She was surprised by his next words, spoken so softly that at first she was not sure of having made them out correctly. "Remember that summer, Melanie, that first summer in Bourneham?" That first summer. She remembered running across the lawn behind the Edmont mansion she was to remake into Île de Joie. A girl, newly married, aware of her body in the moonlight. Seduced by her own sensuality. She could almost feel the springy grass beneath her bare feet, the night breeze blowing up from the ocean against her breasts, her abdomen. That heat in the groin. Wallace. He had refused to come to her then. His parents might look out, might see. She had, oh, yes, that night on the lawn, aching in the moonlight, she had wanted Wallace enough to have been ready to give up her dream of Denis for him. There had been other nights. *Take off your nightshirt. I want to look at you in the light.* Never a chance. Never a chance. And here he stood in his fawn-colored suit, his eyes bright with unshed tears as if it were still possible for them to pick up again that old hope, that old promise, but at the same time he was ready, she knew it, to put her aside.

Her own body, her clothing repelled her. She longed to be clean, perfumed, wanted to use the commode. But somehow she lacked the will to act. The very air seemed to weigh her down.

Glancing up at Wallace, she observed his soft mood had passed and he appeared grim.

"So you came back here despite my urging you not to." He was ready for a quarrel. She could recognize the signs; he needed one to relieve his feelings. It did not seem to her that he had urged her. All she could recall his saying was that the *Falcon* would be waiting for her. In fact, she thought with a flash of anger, it had been disgraceful for him not to have warned her categorically had he known the demonstration was to take place. And certainly he must have known.

"I did not understand you, Wallace; you did not make me understand that you anticipated trouble. It is said that you have representatives"—the word used was *spies*, but she was speaking carefully, seeking not to exacerbate—"in every part of the city, know everything that happens."

"It is clearly time to change my representatives," he responded coldly, and she remembered a similar exchange with Morgen. "They gave me all the information, excepting the most important—which only reached me later—that you were in the house. As for that journalist, nobody mentioned him at all."

He realized belatedly that Melanie's excuse about coming to visit her mother was . . . well, fishy was the only way to describe it. Why had he not wanted to investigate further, considered what could possibly have induced her to leave Bourneham two days before a ball? Had he allowed himself to think about it, he would have had to know it could only be a lover. He might have had her followed, but he had long since given up such practices. What more evidence of her infidelities could he possibly require? (And still today, determined as he was to marry Clara, he felt despair at recalling the details of adultery that detectives had been all too eager to give as indication of how thoroughly they were doing their job.)

"It is a catastrophe that you were here," said Wallace harshly. "Do you think this . . . scum of a journalist will conceal that fact? For you? Are you vain enough to think he would do that when it will improve his story, add spice, that bit of gossip, scandal that every one of the foolish readers of his vulgar newspaper cannot do without? It will reflect upon me. In every way. I told you not to come here. They should have had an empty house to face. That would have blunted the edge of the riot. Not to have had my wife . . . my wife . . . as a spectator."

Wallace had raised his voice, something he never did, stung by anger that her presence in the house would be taken as an indication that the maddened slum rabble had won out over him.

Melanie was startled by his lack of control. In their arguments traditionally it was she who became overwrought, he who remained irritatingly calm and low-voiced. In a long marriage like this patterns were not readily broken. She studied him more carefully. Absorbed in her own concerns, she had forgotten the importance of being alert to him. It struck her belatedly that Wallace was dressed in a fashion unusual for him. A fawn-colored suit; Wallace never wore light colors, and it was more tightly fitted than the others in his wardrobe. Why had no one stopped the members of the mob making their way up Fifth Avenue? There were always police patrols. Where had they been today? Wallace had urged her to stay away from the house, being careful not to make his request appear sufficiently significant for her to ask questions. He had ordered the captain of the *Falcon* to wait for her, indicating that he expected her to return to Bourneham without delay. Why had it taken so long for the police to come? A pattern formed. He had not taken the threats of a ragtag mob from the tenements seriously. No mob had ever gone to a man's house before. Wallace had told the police to stay away, wanting to be sure there were no witnesses to what he planned to do. It was Clara for whom he wore the pretty suit, the bright blue silk tie with the red polka dots. Clara whom he had planned to meet in the house later today. Fat, plain Clara who would replace her. The unpleasantness of the idea was quite startling.

"Was my presence in the house undesirable because you anticipated the arrival of that crowd of rude men? Or was it undesirable for another reason?" (He might have arrived with Clara in time to surprise her with Denis.)

Wallace stared at her blankly. "What do you mean?" It seemed to her his voice was weak.

She hesitated, fearing she was adding another to the mistakes of the afternoon. But what did she have to lose by seizing the offensive? "Do you imagine I have not heard the gossip? It is everywhere. You have abandoned your customary discretion."

Wallace was so taken aback as to be unable to think of

a reply. She could not possibly know about Clara Ribley. She was lying; of course she was lying. The idea that there was gossip about him. It was not possible. Indiscreet? No one could have been more discreet, not that there was anything to be discreet about. The fact that he planned to ask Clara Ribley to marry him someday when he was free could not be known by anyone else.

At the same time an odd story that had been going the rounds at the club this week came to mind. It had not been told to him directly, but was ubiquitous and he had picked up snatches here and there. The story had it that Melanie had publicly embraced Clara at the Woodruffs' ball. He had dismissed the story as absurd, but now there was an explanation to fit the fact (that is if it really were a fact, and he could not quite believe that): Melanie had embraced Clara in the belief that Wallace was engaged in a surreptitious affair that would force him to make a generous divorce settlement for her.

"Well?" asked Melanie giving a nasty, suggestive smile.

Flushing, he was stung to reply: "Nothing I have done could be viewed as an indiscretion. Here. Anywhere. That is not how I act."

He realized the fatuity of the rejoinder as soon as it was spoken, and she pounced on the weakness. "Should I ask Clara Ribley then?"

"I do not know what gossips have told you about Mrs. Ribley," Wallace replied stiffly, "but there is nothing detrimental to either of us that could have truthfully been reported. We are friends. The idea that I would suggest an assignation to her, the idea that she would consent were I, were anyone, to do so is ludicrous. Mrs. Ribley is the most virtuous of women. It is absurd to insinuate that she would ever behave improperly."

Put it here, Bunny, right there, that's it. That's the way. It feels so good.

Now that the first shock had passed, Wallace was appalled, as if Clara were being sullied by the dirty thoughts in Melanie's mind. She could accuse him, accuse Clara when it was she who was false. It was Melanie, not he, not Clara who made assignations, who was flushed and hot, it was Melanie who panted, strained in a lover's arms.

"Why didn't the mounted police come earlier, Wallace? Why didn't police patrols stop the mob from forming? They must have had orders."

Wallace hesitated, as he took in the full import of her words. He had kept the police from responding to the mob as rapidly as they might have. But someone else must have given the order to the foot patrols to stay away. Might it have been Morgen? He was ruthless, single-minded, determined to bring down the rich.

"You summoned that journalist, the dregs of his profession, to the house."

Melanie was startled by his change of topic. What had that to do with the police, with Clara Ribley? "I did not bring him here, Wallace. He came because of the mob to get a story. He was with them, knew about them, had an informant."

"A good journalist's word, Melanie. I have never known you to use that word before. You are developing a new vocabulary." All at once she felt frightened by his sarcasm, the venom in his tone. "The fact is that he was leaving the house when I arrived. You allowed him to be admitted."

In her effort to conceal Denis's presence, she had forgotten that Morgen's presence posed as great, if not a greater, danger. It had not occurred to her that Wallace would link her and Morgen as lovers.

"Only to try to talk to him. Seeing him here I was afraid of what he would say in his newspaper story," and at the expression on Wallace's face, added hurriedly, "about you, I mean. I was afraid he would write that you were to blame for the fire and so for the man who burned up."

"You let him in." His voice was softer now, hers more shrill. The pattern of their quarrels was forming once again.

"That was later. The police were on the grounds. I could

not keep him out. The police who were on guard passed him through. A journalist can go anywhere. There he stood, with his notebook. It served as a pass, an invitation."

"Yes, an invitation; I believe that."

Her nervousness increased until it seemed to fill her lungs, her throat. "It is not as you think." She swallowed though her mouth was dry. "He was determined to get a newspaper story, vicious, ugly, heavy with innuendo about you, about the Heron factory fire."

"He confided in you the kind of story he means to write?"

She felt so hot; perspiration broke out again, running down her sides, but her hands were cold. "Of course not, but it was obvious. He was skulking about the grounds earlier. I saw him when I came to the window."

"And he saw you."

That had been the worst of her mistakes, she realized now. But she had been unable to remain waiting in the background as was proper.

Recalling how Morgen had looked, his smile of triumph, Melanie felt quite ill with apprehension. What did she know of a man like that? He might have been playing with her, pretending social ambition. The report with all its implications might yet be published. She had been so afraid of Wallace finding out about Denis. But the suspicion of a relationship with a man like Morgen whom he despised as beneath him was much, much worse. And she still had to reveal the invitation to the ball. She did not dare to keep Morgen out. Then there was the drawing, which could so easily be reproduced. She did not trust Morgen to withhold it. Perhaps she must tell Wallace about the picture now, explain it away, draw its sting so to speak.

"I was only trying to reason with him, Wallace."

She heard the gardeners outside begin their work of repairing the grounds. Death had been so close. A strong wind could have blown the fire to the house; the men could have broken in. So close. And now they sat arguing about who had made love with whom.

Wallace was watching her, waiting, his expression grim.

"He," she thought it better not to say Morgen's name to Wallace, "made a drawing showing me here at the window. I didn't want it to appear in the newspaper. So later when the police let him through and he came to the door, I thought to reason with him."

"Ah, yes, a drawing."

Wallace spoke as if he had seen that suggestive drawing with the shadow of a man behind her, unrecognizable, but unmistakably illicit, improper.

"Well, how did you go about reasoning with him as you put it? How did you induce him to suppress the drawing, alter the tenor of his news report so as to protect my interests?" As he spoke, he was looking at her, allowing her to observe how his eyes rested on her disordered dress, on her breasts. The rudeness of it astounded her. For a man to look so at a woman was lacking in respect. Perhaps, thought Melanie, with a touch of humor for all the danger she was in, he was comparing her to that pillar of virtue, Clara.

"I spoke with him. That was all. There was nothing improper about it."

"Well, what could you possibly have said that would outweigh the importance to him of a sensational news report?"

"I told him . . . I invited him to my ball."

"Your ball? Your ball? Surely you are joking with me. He is a serious man. As am I. And your story. Nothing improper. Why your appearance gives you the lie. I have seen that look. And not on the receiving line at a ball. In the bedroom, Melanie." He had never spoken to her so crudely, charging her openly, to such an extent. In the worst of their quarrels he had not directly accused her. Before he had always at least given the appearance of accepting her explanations. It was as if in the tensions of the afternoon, all pretenses were being abandoned. Ironic she thought that it was Morgen who had not been her lover who would do the ultimate damage to her reputation.

"Look at yourself. There in the mirror over the mantel."
He was shouting now. This time the servants would have a
different kind of quarrel to report.

She did not need to glance at the mirror to know her
hair was straggling, her face flushed and shiny, her dress
wrinkled, stained, and damp, clinging to her body making
her nakedness evident. Her guilt was apparent. That Wallace wrongly attributed the source for her guilt hardly less-
ened it. Barely hoping to convince him of her innocence,
she rushed on, hastily revising the events of the afternoon
to make them appear harmless. The reason for her return
home had been her decision to wear the ruby at the ball, the
ruby he had given her long before. It was in the safe at home.
Exhausted by the trip on the *Falcon*—she was unaccustomed to rising so early—she had lain down to rest, thinking
to wait for the afternoon's heat to abate before starting on
the long carriage journey back to the pier. Beryl had rushed
in a frenzy of panic to call her and had given her the news
of the mob outside. In the need for hurry, she had thrown
on her dress, not bothering with undergarments and corset.
Her voice remained firm, despite his obvious disbelief.

She stood up and walked over to the huge bay window
and looked out at the ruined lawn, flooded, blackened, trampled. Ashes, bone, nothingness. And in that instant it seemed
that belief, disbelief, argument were of no importance compared to the magnitude of the event that had taken place.

"A man died here this afternoon by his own hand. And
for whatever mistaken reason, still, he is dead."

She thought that if Wallace said it did not matter, that
one person out of the teeming populations of the slum was
not important, that the inhabitants were ignorant, worthless,
she would never be able to speak with him again. But he
nodded. "Yes." And after a moment: "What a tragedy. I was
thinking how he must have suffered. And for what?"

He walked over to the divan, sat down and began to
drum his fingers on the small end table. Wallace took pride
in having trained himself to avoid all nervous gestures. He

had told her once that he could read a man's true state of mind by looking at the movements of his hands and fingers no matter how impassive the face. It was an irony of fate, he thought. The police had held back on his orders. If they had gone in, the man who immolated himself might have been stopped in time. But many other lives would in all probability have been lost in the confrontation between an angry rabble and armed police. The odd thing was that he would have received less blame for that than this. He had thought himself superior to Woodruff in demanding moderation, but Woodruff was not the only businessman to call in armed men to disperse a mob. In time the outcry against such action died down. There would be another strike, another employer making use of force. But he, Edmont, would be unique, unforgettable. So dramatic, appalling was the episode that he would never live this down. The burning man, the act of self-immolation on his property would be associated with his name for the rest of his life, he feared. He had outsmarted himself. No. He would not think like that. It was beneath him. The way a Woodruff would think. A Jessop. He was a churchgoing man, upright, honorable. He had known the right thing to do and had done it. Lives had been saved by his action. But how sick he felt.

Wallace wished he could tell Melanie the whole story. She would understand, was more clever than Jessop, more imaginative. There were times when he had actually wished it were possible to bring her into the business. She was so clear-headed. Of course, she would never be able to give up the social life that meant so much to her. Plans for a ball, a dinner would occupy her for weeks on end. He had seen her arranging and rearranging the place cards for hours at a time.

She was standing by the window. Lack of cosmetics, of careful hairdressing did not alter the strong appeal that she possessed. In the midst of his worry, his despair at what had happened, his knowing her to have betrayed him with the most reprehensible of men, he was moved by her presence.

If anything, the carelessness enhanced her sexuality. Again, he was aware of the strange quality of her skin, unlike that of any other, making one desperate to touch her with one's hand, one's body. He had believed that one day he would be free of his desire for her. Instead, Clara forgotten for the moment, he wanted Melanie even now, in sight of the evidence of the scene of death and violence outside, he wanted her, could not imagine that the time might ever come when he would not.

Putting out his hand he touched her shoulder, took her arm, pulling it ever so slightly. She bent towards him as was her way in such moments, pliant, yielding. And as she did, he became aware of a faint odor. It was the aroma her body gave off after they made love, the perfume she placed at her throat, between her breasts, between her thighs, mingled with the smells of perspiration, of sexual secretions. Unmistakable. Morgen. He recoiled from her, dropped his hand. Morgen. Clara would help him to put Melanie behind him. Clara's eyes were clear and blue. No secrets lay behind them. A blameless life, free of the desperate sexual hunger that dominated Melanie, that dominated him when he was in her presence.

She recognized the change in mood, sighed, and went to sit down again. "What is your plan now, Wallace?" The misadventures of the day had become definitive. The mistakes she had made could not be unmade. Though she had never felt closer to Denis, nothing had been settled. She had thought to force the issue so skillfully that it would not appear forced. But the arrival of the mob had changed all that. Disaster. The burning man an omen of disaster. Of everything lost. Wallace. Harry. Yes, that too might prove to be a mistake in the end.

"Shall we return to Bourneham together?" she asked hesitantly.

He did not answer right away, weighing whether it would be wiser for him to remain in New York while setting his plan of action in motion, or whether he would merely be prey to the hordes of journalists who would be hot on Morgen's heels.

"I don't think you should stay here, Wallace. There may still be some danger to you."

He smiled, but without any humor or lightness, just a turning up of the corners of his mouth. "So you worry about me? Or perhaps you think I will not get to your ball to see your triumphant entry on camelback."

"I don't think that is funny, Wallace."

"You have often complained that I have no sense of humor. And perhaps I do not. No one but my mother and Jessop have ever laughed at my witticisms and Jessop is paid handsomely. But despite your opinion, I do see humor in many situations. I sit in my office sometimes thinking about them and smiling to myself. Spending five thousand dollars for the pride of a ten-minute appearance on camelback. Selecting the very afternoon a mob comes to riot to invite your journalist lover to our home. Humor. Yes, I can see humor in both these wildly contrasting situations. But I see no humor in what lies between us, Melanie. No humor at all."

CHAPTER 23

The Dogs of Villa del Destino

E merald Beach was shrouded in fog. Standing on the sand in the dawn, Harry had the sense—and it was pleasant to him—that nothing was there, an empty world, so no need to do anything. He looked up to where he knew Villa del Destino stood on the high ground and could make out no trace, not even the dimmest outlines of that great building.

Melanie had insisted that true to its name Villa del Destino held his destiny. Until yesterday she had appeared to be forgetting, or at least ignoring, the fact that he was to marry Iris. And then all at once she had become determined that he should do so. She had changed after she had seen the Englishman. Iris's Englishman. Melanie's Englishman.

As he stood there, the fog dissipated and sunlight brightened the beach and he began to think about Iris. Sweet little Iris. His heart melted at the thought of Iris waiting for him, counting on him, and wanting him even if Melanie did so no longer. Iris was his future and it was the future he wanted to have, to hold her light body against his, to protect her. The Woodruffs' yacht must already be gone from its berth, en route to New York. A wasted trip. For once Harry was wresting control over events from Woodruff. Iris was so helpless, depending on him, loving him. At last he had the opportunity to prove himself a man of action.

Harry left the beach and walked up the avenue to Villa del Destino, feeling strong, confident. Approaching the huge gate, he hailed the gatekeeper, old Bill, as he was known. Harry had often exchanged a few words with him. The man was a bit simple, but had enough wit to keep visitors straight. Old Bill stared at Harry, shook his head, and made no move to open the gate. Harry could not believe what was happening, and kept saying, like a simpleton himself, he thought later, "But it is Mr. Van Burgh, Bill. You know me."

Old Bill leaned forward and said in his hoarse voice, "She says not you, especially not you. It would be worth my job, Mr. Van Burgh."

Harry was startled, but not dismayed; he was rather uplifted by this evidence of Nellie's opposition. In his present mood the idea of foiling her was pleasant. There are many ways to enter a building and he circled the villa, looking for a place where he could climb over the wall. At last he observed a tree at a little distance. Harry was strong and having selected this as the best way in, got a running start up the trunk, grasped a branch, set it swinging and at the height of the swing leaped onto the top of the wall.

He prepared to make the jump down into the grounds, and in that moment heard barking and growling, the sound of heavy bodies throwing themselves at the wall. There was a moment of pure terror as he teetered on the narrow ledge almost certain to fall directly in the midst of the pack of dogs. Then he recovered himself, looked about and desperately reached back for the branch, now so far from his outstretched arms that his suit jacket tore at the shoulders as in a final lunge, he managed to catch the branch and hold tight. For a second before swinging away from the fence he looked over and saw the dogs jumping up frantic to get at him. Mrs. Woodruff must have ordered them released. Vicious Dobermans. He had seen the kennels where they were chained when visitors were present. It was common knowledge that the dogs were there to protect Joseph Woodruff from the many who hated him for his ruthlessness. But this time they were set loose to protect Iris.

On another occasion he might have thought it amusing to have someone find him, Harry, so formidable that a pack of howling Dobermans had to be unleashed to keep him at bay. He climbed slowly down the tree. Safe on the ground outside the wall again, Harry leaned against the tree, shaking from the effort, panting. Perspiration ran down his sides. His hands were bruised, bleeding, burned by the bark. That Nellie, that anyone he knew, should deliberately put him in danger was the most shocking realization he had ever known. Why, Nellie liked him. She could not have believed he would be hurt, must have thought that the mere growling of the Dobermans would scare him off.

The Dobermans were still barking and sniffing at the wall, excited by his presence. It was fortunate he was in good shape; another man might not have been able to stop himself in mid-leap; another man might be dead.

Now that it was over, he felt set up by his brush with danger; it would make a good story to tell Melanie.

What was he to do, though? How could he leave Iris like this? He recalled the reproachful look she had given him in the conservatory the previous afternoon. Surely Iris did not know why the dogs were loose. She thought he did not love her. Harry could imagine how her heart must ache. No, he must wait until a servant came out and offer a bribe for taking a note of reassurance to Iris. Her mother was not keeping her a prisoner; they would meet at Melanie's ball the day after tomorrow if he could not make his way inside the villa before then.

Harry's customary optimism reasserted itself. Nellie had won this initial engagement, but she had not hurt him and there would be other engagements that he would win.

More vividly than ever before, he imagined Iris in his bed. It would be for him to teach her physical love. Every man's desire. And all at once, with a sinking of the heart, he thought that perhaps she would not like it. Certainly if the married men at the club were to be believed, most women did not. Docile at best. Performing a duty. Since becoming Melanie's lover, he had come to think that women, even properly brought-up women, had as much sexual desire as men. But clearly from what he heard, that was the exception.

Suddenly Harry had the image of Melanie's passionate body straining in his arms. In the Englishman's arms now. That had been inevitable. Were it not he, it would be someone else. Harry's friends had urged him to enjoy the affair while it lasted; no one could hold her. He remembered how dazzling Melanie had been when he first became aware of her, how dazzling she was now. He had never believed he would possess her even for this short a time.

Harry tried to shake off these uncomfortable thoughts and make an effort to picture Iris's face. Then he remembered his mother in—what had been her favorite jewels?—emeralds. Gone now, along with all the magnificent furnishings inherited from past generations. His marriage was to make it possible to restore them all.

What if he eloped with Iris? Considering the excessive determination to keep him from her, one might assume that the Woodruffs would cut them off. But logic did not always hold sway. The Woodruffs adored Iris. But what if they did not yield? For the first time Harry allowed himself to consider whether it would be possible to manage without that fortune. Obviously he had often heard the homily that wealth does not buy happiness, yet the very people who said it spent all their time and energies trying to gain possession of money. Happiness? He remembered what Evangeline had said to him: no marriage is happy. Not Melanie's. And certainly Edmont gave her everything money could buy (and was she happy with him who gave her nothing?).

What of his own parents? He had not missed the expression on Evie's face at the time he mentioned them. When he thought of his parents together, the image was of his mother leaning towards his father as they walked. It was a movement somewhat like the one Iris made with him. But now that he was thinking about it, a memory came back that he had never before stopped to consider. It happened years ago. He had come into the drawing room where his parents were talking and was about to greet them when he saw that his mother's face, usually so pale and creamy, was flushed and she was breathing hard. She tore off her emerald bracelets and threw them, yes, quite literally threw them at his father. "Give them to her!" She had been almost screaming. "Give them to her!" Until this moment he had not realized what she had meant. She had seen him then and regained control so rapidly that he could hardly believe the episode had taken place. Smiling coolly, she had picked up the bracelets and held out her wrist for his father to fasten the clasps. But that was the only time. And maybe there was another explanation. All his other memories of them were happy. Bending. Sweetly. Like Iris.

Well, he could certainly earn more than he did. He had been acknowledged an excellent economics student at Harvard; a professor had predicted a career in finance. Often at the bank he could see opportunities that should be taken. But no one listened to him. Handsome Harry, they called him. It was said kindly. They were good fellows and they all liked him, he knew that, but no one took him seriously. Perhaps if a man were not taken seriously, it was his own fault. He would make himself heard in business as he should have done all along.

No one entered or left the villa all that morning. Harry walked back and forth, barely aware of the hours passing, of his growing exhaustion. What had he done all summer? What was he doing here? He had let the months pass as if dreaming them away, knowing he would awaken with Iris. That had been the assumption all along. He thought about Iris; it was as if he never had time really to think of her. It seemed to others, he knew, that he had been unbelievably lax in not making certain of her when it would have been so easy, when the Woodruffs had favored his suit. Why had he not done so? She was so pretty with her classic features and blond curls, her waist so tiny it was hard to believe that narrow frame could contain all the flesh and blood and organs of a real woman. His loving her had never been questioned; certainly he had told her he did. There had seemed no way not to when she looked at him with those adoring blue eyes. But now he knew that when he had stood on the beach in the early morning thinking about Iris, it had been the fact that she loved him that had moved him. His own feelings had been no more than accepting of that love, that dependency. Harry had never thought much about his own love for her, had taken for granted that he had to love her because there was so much need for him to do so. Yes, he knew why he had failed to act. There were so many reasons to marry Iris. He knew them all and all were good. And against them the one bad reason. Her summer toy. She had wanted him to come here to guarantee her the Englishman. He saw that clearly. Still, he would not marry Iris.

He should have been in despair. But as he walked away from Villa del Destino, his step quickened and the heaviness in his chest lightened and he realized that what he was feeling was relief. He had let everybody down—Iris, his mother, Evangeline. And yet he felt giddy with relief.

CHAPTER 24

Who Will Marry
Evangeline Now?

He dreaded facing her. In fact, it seemed to him that the worst part of the failed engagement was coming home, empty-handed as it were. Harry was hoping against hope that she would be out or would not have heard so that he could again postpone the unpleasant interview until some time when he would feel fresher. But he was aware it was a vain hope. His mother went out infrequently in the afternoon and as for not hearing, he had never been able to determine just how she obtained information, but she was invariably the first to know anything that happened. When his father had died at the club of a heart attack, the friends who came to bring her the news found her already in black.

Of course she knew. The very house proclaimed her knowledge. The draperies were open, clear evidence that she had given up protecting the colors of the upholstery and rugs. She would have to sell Rose Cottage now. The new owners would replace the shabby furnishings.

The sense of guilt that curiously had been absent when he left Villa del Destino had come upon him during the hours he stayed away from home. What made it worse was the realization that the relief he had felt upon walking away from Iris was with him still. He was not going to marry Iris after all; he was free. Then sick at heart, he thought, free for what? For whom? For Melanie? In the throes of a new or renewed love affair with the Englishman, she had urged the elopement. And were it not the Englishman—the dark knowledge came to him again—it would be some-one else. For had not Melanie in the beginning expressed the opinion that what intensified their pleasure in the ro-mance was its transitory nature? They had both known it. Yet when it had come to the actual moment of separat-ing himself from her he had not been able to bring him-self to be the one to force the actual ending. For once the optimism he had so often been warned against deserted him and he could not think that he would be Melanie's lover again or be able to make up for his decision to his mother and Evangeline. Who will marry Evangeline now?

As soon as he saw his mother, he realized that he had underrated her. It was her ability to respond rapidly to each emergency that had enabled them to continue following the only style of life she considered possible for people of their background. Forced to yield on one front, she would move to another where she could stand firm. In her way, she was as formidable as Nellie Woodruff.

Frail, appearing paler than usual in the brightened room, her voice was firm. "I have a plan for Evangeline, Harry. I hope you will help us with it." Not a question about what had taken place. Not a comment. Iris had been put aside. Harry felt like a heavy-footed dancer trying to keep up with a faster, more agile partner. Evangeline was to have been the chief beneficiary of his marriage to Iris. His mother had convinced him of that.

"Now that everybody is going to Europe, I do think that

301

Evangeline should go there, too," she said. Her words were bland, but there was something mischievous in her look.

"Genevieve Edmont has introduced us to a friend of the contessa's."

It took Harry a moment to remember that the contessa was Jocelyn, Wallace Edmont's sister, with whom he had played as a child.

Another potential suitor. The matter was becoming clearer. Harry wondered who it could be. Until now his mother had been able to do no better than Hiram Genever. A favorable Woodruff alliance had been viewed as the only way to broaden the choice. Now with the situation worsened, he tried to imagine someone even less attractive than Mr. Genever. And from his mother's earlier remark, he supposed he was to talk the man into accepting a deaf girl and Evangeline into accepting the man, however old, ugly, and encumbered with children. There was no way he could possibly refuse to do anything that was asked of him. It was quite likely, though, that his mother in desperation was seeing a suitor in a person who was merely being courteous. Harry foresaw a thoroughly embarrassing scene.

"He is staying with Genevieve Edmont."

It became evident to Harry immediately why his mother was so interested. A guest at Genevieve Edmont's house was per se desirable. Harry thought he could guess why he had not been apprised of the appearance on the scene of the new candidate. His mother had not wanted to relax the pressure on him to marry Iris. But then he realized that if the suitor had been in the offing, a position for a retreat prepared, his mother would not have been so frantic in urging him to marry, nor Evangeline so insistent on spinsterhood. Harry was sensitive to moods; he did not think he could have been so mistaken. Something had happened in just this one day. The man had appeared, and with Genevieve's help, his mother had approached him. It made Harry uncomfortable. He knew his mother capable of almost any action that would provide Evangeline with a husband. What had she devised out of her desperation?

"Who is this friend of Jocelyn's?"

"You have met him, Harry, at Genevieve Edmont's At Home and then again at the Woodruffs' ball. Signor Martelli."

Harry remembered now. The Italian; it had been difficult to converse with him in view of his halting English. Aware of Melanie nearby, Harry had been distracted and had not given the introduction its proper weight. He had believed himself to be Evangeline's only hope, and for all that he wished her well, felt somehow that he had been taken in.

What had the Italian looked like? Forty or so. Harry forced the recollection, cadaver thin, with a lined face, leathery skin and dark hair with a streak of white.

"Evangeline and I have seen more of him than you have, Harry. We dined together, just the four of us, at Genevieve's last night, and he came here to lunch today. I had rather hoped you would be here."

He had stayed at the club until late the previous evening, had come home only when he was sure she would be in bed. At that time he had been planning the elopement with Iris and had not wanted to see his mother until everything was settled.

"Signor Martelli is returning to Italy next week, so there really is not much time. I have told him you will be calling on him within the next day or two."

Harry was stunned by this speech and its implication of a serious suit. What could his mother be thinking? The man was an Italian, and that was all very well for Jocelyn Edmont who could hear and had not only her mother, but the powerful Wallace Edmont and the Edmont fortune behind her. It would be quite different for Evangeline, unable to hear and impoverished. He felt a sense of responsibility for her. Until today, making a good marriage had been all that was required of him as a brother. But now that he had ruled out the marriage to Iris, he owed Evie more than this.

"Just a minute, Mother. I cannot believe that something so important has been settled in just a few hours."

"We are certainly not going to act precipitously, Harry," his mother replied unperturbed. "Signor Martelli has invited us to visit him in Italy and while I do not think that is proper, Genevieve has suggested that we stay with Jocelyn and the count while arrangements are being made."

It sounded fairly precipitous to Harry, this visit at which arrangements were to be made.

Even while they spoke, Harry could hardly believe that things had gone so far—unless it were that his mother was building on the foundation of a daydream.

"I will not allow it, unless I am convinced that Evie wants it. And I doubt very much that she does." Harry had never spoken so strongly to his mother, to anyone in his life. But his feeling that he alone was there to defend Evangeline aroused him. "Why, only yesterday she was claiming vehemently that she didn't want to marry at all. Now you tell me something has developed between this man and Evangeline? Since yesterday? I must say that sounds most improbable."

"Not at all, Harry. Have you no spirit of romance?"

Harry was taken aback. Everyone knew he was the romantic in the family.

"It is really a sweet story, Harry. Until yesterday we had no idea that he was interested. It was such a grim day you know. You had gone to Iris, but so reluctantly, so slowly. You know how it is, Harry; suddenly there is a moment when you stop hoping. You'll laugh at me, Harry, but I told Evangeline that she could get a hearing device. I had the wild idea that somehow it would bring us luck. Superstition. I laughed at myself. But it worked."

Genevieve Edmont had sent a footman with a message inviting them to a quiet family supper. Her houseguest, it appeared, had revealed an interest in Evangeline, had asked whether it were true that she was engaged to Mr. Genever. He had seen them together at social events. Despite the language difficulty, Genevieve quickly ascertained that Signor Martelli had indeed been admiring Evangeline, that he had been longing to meet her, considered her his feminine ideal of beauty. Knowing how short a time her houseguest was to remain in this country, within minutes Genevieve set things moving.

"The strangest thing, Harry, is that Evie had been taken with him, too, but you know how she is, she never mentioned it. Any other girl would have made an excuse to be with him or asked her mother to arrange a meeting but she did nothing. We had to do it all, Harry, Genevieve and I. But isn't it romantic?" For the first time Harry almost believed her. She was in the best of spirits, preparing to capture her quarry, with Genevieve as ally. "At the luncheon table today, Harry, you should have seen the way the two of them were looking at one another with melting eyes."

Looking. The language barrier made it possible for Signor Martelli to remain ignorant of Evangeline's handicap. Harry wondered whether the man had been told, or if the impression that she merely did not know the language had been allowed to stand. His mother, totally honest in all other ways, was capable of such duplicity when it came to making a marriage for her daughter. Nor would any of the other women in their set have censured her for it. Wait until the man was won before revealing unpleasant truths. If the arrangement fell through then, well, at least one need not reproach oneself for having failed to do one's best.

Of course, Evangeline was lovely and Harry had been quite sincere in saying that any man would be lucky to get her, but even a man in love might balk at such deception. Nothing good could come of it. Sooner or later Martelli would have to find out and trouble surely follow. Harry began to dread the interview.

"What is his family background?"

"He is from one of the best families in Milan and you know that Milan society is viewed as the best in Italy." Jocelyn's count was Milanese. "The Martelli family is close to the count's. I believe a cousin or aunt married into the count's family. They have known one another for generations."

"Has he never married—an Italian, a man of that age?"

"His wife died several years ago. She was barren."

"Mother, do you expect Evie to be able to read lips in Italian?"

"She says she will learn," replied Louise.

By now Harry was convinced the Italian knew nothing of the handicap. Surely, however, he did know about the Van Burgh family's financial position. While women might conceal a physical drawback, to deceive about money was beyond the pale. Harry could believe that Signor Martelli was looking at Evangeline with melting eyes, but marriage to a penniless girl was quite another matter and he still feared his mother was building a flirtation into a serious proposal.

"So you think Signor Martelli wants to marry Evangeline." He spoke in a wondering way as it would be the height of discourtesy to express this as a question.

"He is lonely," said Louise.

"With all of Milan society—the best in Italy—to amuse him?"

"Well, he does not live in Milan itself. His estate is located some miles away . . . in beautiful country, I understand."

Harry saw it now. Farmland perhaps. Acres. Isolated. Lonely. His face must have shown what he was thinking because Louise added hastily, "I am sure he would go to Milan more frequently if he were married, Harry. There is some money, not a tremendous amount, but enough."

The late afternoon sunlight streaming in through the windows made the room so bright that Harry found it unfamiliar. He had forgotten that the divan, gray in the customary dim light, was covered in satin of a robin's-egg blue. Evangeline came in then. The light that accentuated Louise's fragility and pallor revealed Evangeline's high color. There was a vividness about her that Harry had never noticed before. It was because of him, Harry thought, that Evangeline might spend her life with an uncommunicating husband on an isolated estate miles away from anyone she had ever known. He began to doubt his decision; perhaps he must go

306

back and win Iris, face the fact that free choice was only for the wealthy.

After Louise had left the room, he turned to Evangeline. "I know how Mother is when she gets an idea in her head. But you don't have to do this, Evie. I can take care of Mother and put a stop to the whole thing. You're so pretty; there'll be other men."

"I've always wanted to see Italy," replied Evangeline coolly. "I was too small when Papa took you and by the time I grew up, we didn't have the money."

"You don't need to pretend with me."

"Harry, has it never occurred to you that I might be tired of having people sorry for me? Poor Evangeline with her handicap. A burden. Harry's burden."

"Don't say that. I don't feel that way."

She smiled meaningfully and he colored, feeling guilty that he was not marrying Iris.

"This man, Signor Martelli—Enrico is his first name, though I have not yet called him by it—Enrico, he sees me. To most people I am invisible, but he sees me. He leads an isolated life. Few women will put up with it. But I have been isolated by my deafness for much of my life. I will be no lonelier there than here, less perhaps, because there, it is natural, caused by the condition of life; here it is unnatural, unique to me."

"That's unfair, Evie. You have us."

"I know, but you go out every night, and I can't blame you; this house is so gloomy. That leaves Mamma and me— somehow we don't get on. I know what a disappointment I am to her. But it is hurtful to know that. I hold it against her. There's no helping that."

"But Evie, yesterday you were speaking out against marriage."

She smiled; her dimples showed. "Yesterday I thought marriage for me meant someone like Mr. Genever. I had seen Signor Martelli at the At Home, then at the ball and there was something about him. I noticed him looking at me, Harry, the way men look at other women." Andrew Arnold had looked at her that way once. No one since. "But what made me bitter was the realization that any other girl could have arranged to talk with him, charm him. But not I. Harry, I was discouraged. And then, after you left yesterday, the strangest thing happened. Mamma said I could get a hearing device. She has always been so set against it, has insisted on pretending that I could hear if only I would try. I knew in that moment that she had given up hope for me. It was a relief, but a source of despair at the same time. And then, less than an hour later, there was Mrs. Edmont's footman with the dinner invitation. Mamma thought she would have to insist, that I would refuse to go; I usually do, you know. But then I thought that maybe he would be there and I said I would go."

It was true; his mother had not been making it up. Had he no spirit of romance?

"But Evie it's so fast. You hardly know him."

"The Edmonts know him and Jocelyn's count. There are no dark secrets about him."

Harry was still troubled. For all his mother's gushing about romance, for all Evangeline's unaccustomed smiles, there was still something of danger in the situation. "Aren't you afraid, Evie, going to a foreign country like that with a man who is almost a stranger?"

He knew she would not lie to him; she never refused to face harsh truths. "Just a little, Harry. If anything should go wrong, I'll be alone far from home with no one to turn to."

"I'll come if you need me, Evie, anytime. You can count on me."

Now that he thought of it, there was a way to give her some protection: he could arrange a marriage settlement that would provide her with control of a certain sum of money, allow her passage home. And afterwards he would visit her regularly (somehow he would raise the money to pay his way) and make certain that she was well taken care of, show Martelli and his family that she was not alone and defenseless.

Evangeline looked at him a little doubtfully and then she smiled. "I think you really do mean that, Harry.

"If you want to view this marriage logically, aside from the attraction between us"—she paused, hardly able to believe she was actually saying such a thing—"Signor Martelli is the best of the lot. He is not young, but not so old he requires nursing, not so old he could not make me a mother. And as for his looks, he is thin, and I prefer thin people to fat." It had been a satisfaction to her to see Andrew Arnold take on flesh.

"Does he . . . know?" Harry raised the question that he had not dared to ask his mother.

Evangeline gave a wry smile. "Mamma wanted to conceal it—until we had captured him. She was quite severe with me, arguing what a mistake that would be. And Genevieve Edmont—can you believe it?—agreed with her. But I told him the truth today after lunch, with Mamma seated in the corner, signaling me not to do it. I had to use signs, move my hands around to show what I meant. He did not know the words in English and I know no Italian. He didn't seem to mind it really once he got over his surprise. After a few moments, when I thought he might just get up and leave, he said, oh, Harry, he said . . . he knows that much English . . . he likes my smile." My pretty. Not quite the same. Never the same. Rejoice at his paunch, but still she ached at the memory.

"But Evie, surely you will need to say more than that to one another."

"I will learn Italian—to read and write anyway." She feared she could not speak a language she had never heard. "Perhaps I can learn to read lips in Italian. If not, we will converse by writing."

"Evie," he said, speaking hesitantly out of his sense of guilt. "I think perhaps you are putting a good face on this to make me feel I have not let you down."

"It is Mamma who puts a good face on things, not I."

"What if I had married Iris, Evie? What if I were still to do so?"

"For me? Oh, Harry, you touch me, but I never believed that you would marry Iris."

"I believed it."

"With half your mind and less than half your heart. I was never fooled. Melanie Edmont is too old; she has been with who knows how many men before you." Again he flinched at her uncompromising accuracy. "But she spoiled Iris for you."

Had she not spoiled all other women for him? Evangeline was smiling. Harry could see why Signor Martelli liked her smile. And then she put her arms around him and said, "Oh, Harry, I'm glad you are not to marry Iris. For me as well as for you. This way I'm going to escape from Bourneham and New York and all the people who have always pitied me, the people to whom I have always been invisible. I couldn't have done that with an American husband. For the rest of my life, I would have known people were thinking how lucky I was to have had you buy a husband for me. No one can say that now or doubt that . . ." After a long silence, she added, "That a man desires me."

The light was dimming now, at the beginning of one of the long twilights that were so beautiful in Bourneham. Harry, deep in thought, climbed the stairs more slowly than was his custom, avoiding the places where the carpet was most worn. He had an invitation to dinner, as he invariably did, but tonight he would not go. It had been unforgivable carelessness to give such short shrift to business for so long. He could go back to New York later this evening on the van der Cleeves' yacht. When Jon van der Cleeve invited him the previous day, Harry had refused. To rush to and from New York for the second time that week had not seemed worthwhile. Better to finish out the week in Bourneham and get back to the bank refreshed on Monday. But now he felt an unfamiliar compulsion to be at his desk. The weariness of setting out on the return trip to Bourneham before dawn on Saturday appealed to him in his present mood, hardly able to believe he had been so feckless in the past. He would see

Melanie at her ball that night, tell her what had happened and what he thought should be done about it. Harry had always wanted an easy life. For the first time it occurred to him that this was not necessarily the best, or even the happiest life.

CHAPTER 25

Hours of Anxiety at Île de Joie

Fire and fear. All the way back to Bourneham on the *Falcon* the fresh sea breeze could not dissipate the memory of the smell of charred flesh; it seemed to Melanie that it hung in the air, impossible to breathe at all without breathing it in. The scene of horror replayed in her mind overwhelmed everything else she had experienced that day. Her mother hostile in senility, Elmer Morgen and his plots. Denis. Yes, even Denis. The memory of their bodies wet in one another's arms was trivialized by what she had witnessed, what had happened.

The poor. A volcano smoldering; Morgen had used those words the night of the Woodruffs' ball, having already set in motion the series of events leading to the catastrophe on the lawn, the fiery conclusion of a life. The wretch burning in front of the lilies, the rose bushes in bloom. Fire. How had Morgen described it? Young girls, children really, hair aflame, skirts and petticoats blazing, jumping from the tenement building, the tongues of fire leaping behind them. Great billows of smoke. Everything reduced to ashes. And on the street, the men weeping, the sparks catching the hairs of their eyebrows, their mustaches.

At first, upon learning of the Heron factory fire, she had not quite taken it in. The fire was terrible, but there was no connection with her. It was a disaster, the kind journalists sought to discover, remote from her life. But since that miserable human being set himself ablaze on the lawn, her lawn, believing himself wronged by the Edmonts, she felt a connection. It made no sense; the man was in error. Yet she could not escape the feeling that somehow he was their victim.

Morgen declared he wrote to arouse the public to vote against evildoers, to throw out of office those who defrauded, profited from the misery of the poor. Female suffrage had become his cause, not out of any abstract interest in justice, but because he thought that women would be less involved with profit, more with people, and would correct social wrongs. But what was a social wrong? Melanie had been brought up in the belief that any man could rise from poverty by his own efforts. Her father had expressed that view frequently, as did Wallace. Never Joseph—he had been convinced he was unique. Perhaps he was. Because if a man were to kill himself so horribly, endure such excruciating pain, then perhaps the belief that anyone could rise to wealth and power was false. Morgen would surely say so; she did not want to think Morgen right about anything.

Morgen. She could not trust him. Fear again. Later today she might pick up the newspaper and read the despicable article. There was no way to be certain that the desire to achieve social prestige by attending her ball meant enough to make him abandon so sensational a news report.

And what had taken place in Bourneham during the day she had been away? She wondered if at the very moment when the man set fire to himself on her lawn, Harry had been arranging to elope with Iris. Perhaps at this very moment they were escaping from Bourneham, from Nellie

313

Woodruff, on the way to find a minister to marry them. Or could that have occurred already and at this very moment Harry was making Iris his? Melanie could imagine them in the small secluded country inn Harry had spoken of—romantic. They were together, surrounded by the rosy brown dimness a room takes on in the afternoon with the doors closed and the curtains drawn, the air still and heavy with perfume, perspiration, semen. How many times in just such a dimness, on just such an afternoon, had she been with Harry, closed the door and closed out the world?

The *Falcon* was cutting through the water, rushing her back to Bourneham. It was necessary for her to be there to make the final preparations for her ball . . . her ball that Harry would not attend. There was nothing to look forward to in Bourneham. Not since the days of the terrible boredom that had driven her to Woodruff's bed had she been without something to look forward to. The moon was full, but its brightness seemed muted by her mood of despair. All summer she had felt a glow, Harry's glow. She had given him up—no, he had never been hers to give up; she had merely speeded him on the way he had been going all along.

Exhausted by the events of the day, Melanie was nonetheless too disturbed to rest. Undressed for the night, she found it impossible to remain in her stateroom, but dressed again and went on deck followed by a confused and tired Beryl. In the darkness she could just make out the figure of Wallace standing by the rail, erect, staring out over the water. Before boarding the *Falcon* he had taken off the fawn-colored suit and was sober as usual in dark coat and trousers. Coming closer, she observed his somber expression; he had not smiled since he walked into the house in New York and saw her sitting there, limp, exhausted, ill-kempt, ill-dressed, damp with perspiration. Lost in his thoughts, he did not appear aware of her presence. Melanie wondered what plan he was evolving to mitigate the effect of the disaster. Another man might be ruined by it. But Wallace would not be the loser; he never was.

She recalled how often he quoted his grandfather, whom he had respected above all other men: "Put yourself in a position where you cannot lose. However poor the alternatives, there is always a choice that favors you more. Win on the grand scale or on a lesser scale. But win you must."

When, as a bride, she had first been proffered these remarks as proof of the old man's acumen, she thought them fatuous. But over the years she had found that the maxim always worked for the Edmonts. Wallace's grandfather had fought city condemnation of a row of tenements, but when the order passed the council nonetheless, it turned out he had already found a buyer for the building materials that would be left by the wreckers and had contractors ready to begin constructing new housing that would provide him with rentals high enough to cover the costs. He had opposed a projected highway to cut through valuable farmland, but in time collected a sum for the rights that was sufficient to support an even more profitable business venture. Now Wallace was raising objections to plans for a subterranean transportation system, insisting publicly that it would cause sidewalks to buckle, buildings to fall, and property values to plummet. But Melanie had overheard Wallace discussing with Jessop the purchase of property in the districts to be served by the transportation.

There had seemed no way for an Edmont to lose. Even she. The first indication she was not so protected had come with the threat of divorce. Even there, with the death of Adelaide, the discovery of Clara, it had appeared she might yet benefit. Now it seemed to her what had happened that afternoon was pointing inexorably towards failure. Wallace's finding her at home in New York counterbalanced the advantage she had possessed in knowing about Clara.

What was Wallace thinking as he stared into the dark water? She could imagine the ugly divorce suit now, herself presented as the guilty party. Wallace believed she had been with Morgen. There was snobbery even in cuckoldry. Melanie now saw the drawing, which she still feared Morgen

315

would publish, in a different light. The shadowy figure in the background could be any man, Morgen as much as Denis. To Wallace it would appear that Morgen was bragging about his liaison with Melanie, proclaiming it to all New York.

An unsavory, ungenerous divorce would destroy any chance she might have of convincing Denis, who was refractory even now. In that moment she realized that Harry's elopement with Iris guaranteed her nothing. She had believed that everything depended on it, that what Harry did would bring Denis to her. Now it appeared that just as much depended on what Morgen did. Even if Denis lost Iris, he could nonetheless be lost to her in the ensuing scandal. The death on the lawn and its aftermath affected everything. Anxiety seized her.

It was still dark when they arrived in Bourneham at last. She could hardly believe that not quite twenty-four hours had passed since she started out for New York. The events of that day would haunt her for the rest of her life, might even change its course.

As the carriage started around the sweeping driveway to Île de Joie, she closed her eyes for a moment, not wanting to see the expanse of lawn, resodded each spring, watered, and tended. The lawn in New York would be replaced. By tomorrow it would be emerald green like this one, velvety, perfect.

Side by side, but not touching, Wallace and Melanie mounted the steps to the house. Once inside he handed the night footman his hat, gloves, and cane, and without glancing back, walked heavily, head down, up the great staircase to his study. He would always choose work over rest, thought Melanie. She, too, could not rest until she found out that Rosamunde's fever meant no more than a cold. Then she was suddenly so weary she had to take Beryl's arm to help her to her room. No message from Harry was waiting for her, though she had thought he would contrive to let her know. Could he have failed with Iris after all?

Wallace at his desk was making a great effort to busy

himself preparing a directive to reduce unrest and hostility in the slums, but with that woman in the house it was hard to concentrate on anything else. Never before in his life had he feared the delivery of the newspaper from New York, knowing that any attacks on him were calumny—and would be recognized as such by all who knew him. But now he could guess what Morgen would say about the self-immolation on the lawn and also how he would imply a relationship with Melanie—and it would be recognized as truth by all who knew her.

As soon as it was light he would go to breakfast with his mother, tell her his decision to divorce Melanie and after a suitable time lapse marry Clara Ribley. Despite her opposition to divorce, he expected the unconditional support his mother had never failed to give him.

After a few hours of restless sleep, Melanie was awakened by the sound of Wallace's footsteps going down the stairs, and then the heavy front door closing behind him. At that moment Beryl, who had been hovering outside the room, waiting for the first sound of Melanie's stirring, tiptoed in with a note. Denis, thought Melanie. Predictable. Resolved to retain her as his lover, he would woo her, counter the effect of having left her after the tragedy of the previous day, his intransigence in refusing to give up Iris. She knew his pattern so well. But the handwriting, a large clumsy scrawl, was not Denis's; the note was from Joseph Woodruff asking her to meet him immediately or she would regret it. Regret was spelled with two t's. Threatening: each man had his pattern of behavior; that was Joseph's. Iris's disappearance had no doubt been discovered by this time; the insistence that Melanie meet him must have to do with the elopement. Should she dress quickly and go to him? There was nothing Melanie could do about the elopement now, but she recognized the menace and did not dare to refuse him.

Joseph was waiting for her in the arboretum where they had been used to meet in that long-ago time (unbearable to think of now) when he had been her lover. The trees had been transplanted from a New Hampshire forest on Joseph's orders and at his expense. The Woodruffs had been new in Bourneham then and seeking to buy their way into society. The trees were taller now, the shrubbery thicker.

Joseph looked her up and down crudely, indicating how well he had known her, how very well. She felt disgusted by that look and by the realization that it was justified. "You don't show your age, Melanie. Watching you walk into the grove here, it seemed like no time had passed and you and me were still together."

Small flatteries were not his style; they made her more nervous. She did not respond in kind, did not change expression. He smiled at this, came closer, put his hand on her arm, letting his fingers brush against her breast. Melanie recoiled, and at the same time remembered the mixture of repulsion and desire he had once aroused in her. She shuddered at the ugliness of her memories; he had been her biggest mistake. What did he want of her? It was essential to be on her guard.

"I remember how much you like to have . . . fun," Joseph remarked coolly, dropping his hand. "And why shouldn't you have something on the side? I hear Edmont is doing the same thing."

How could she have put herself in a position where he might speak to her like this? The blood was rushing to her face and she hoped the powder kept it from being obvious to him. "Why did you ask me to meet you today, Mr. Woodruff? If your intention is to insult me, kindly select a day when I am not so occupied preparing for my ball."

"My intention," he stumbled over his repetition of the word, "is to tell you something, Melanie: you're not going to make a fool of me. I'm warning you. Have fun if you want to. But it stops right there. Make that clear to Warburne. And tell Handsome Harry that if he tries to run away with Iris, he'll be sorry. You make sure he understands that. I can make him sorry, Melanie."

She gasped, remembering his violence to her when she

had tried to break away. What would he do to Harry? Melanie shuddered; her hands were icy. She had put Harry at risk by brushing aside his doubts, urging him to act. Odd that Harry had seen the danger from Woodruff when she had not, had thought only Nellie wanted the marriage, that Joseph preferred Harry to an English nobleman. He scorned foreigners; she had heard him speak of them in disparaging terms often enough. How could Harry have been so right and she so wrong? And she had reassured him about Woodruff, claiming her intimate knowledge of the man when this very intimacy should have told her how Joseph would react to being foiled. From Joseph's words it seemed he did not know Iris was gone—perhaps the elopement had not yet taken place. In that case, she could still warn Harry and stop the elopement. Denis's marriage to Iris would proceed without obstacle, but she could not let anything happen to Harry.

"Have you told your daughter about all this?"

Joseph gave a short harsh laugh and continued; it had never been possible to deflect him. "I know where you was yesterday afternoon and who was with you. You and Warburne must have thought me an idiot to let him walk off like that with important business going on. Of course I had him followed. I was sure you'd be cozy in Bourneham having a fond farewell with your pretty boy. So I had to figure out why you wasn't. And you know, Melanie, it wasn't at all hard to do."

His expression was cold, frightening. "There's Edmont with his woman and you with Warburne. Very neat. And Van Burgh—he fits in very neatly, too. Except for one thing," Joseph continued. "I won't let Warburne off the hook. And you know something? He don't want me to. This marriage is as important to him as it is to me. He may have lost his head over you this week—he ain't the first man to do that—but did he ever tell you he'd break off with Iris for you? I'll bet he didn't. Take it as a fling and go back to that good-looking Harry. Now there's someone who's crazy enough about you to give up Iris for you. And you'd better see that

319

he does. You don't want him to get hurt, do you, Melanie? And he will if he gets in my way.

"You take my word for it, Melanie, this marriage to Warburne is going to happen. My daughter will do like I say. I ain't talked to her since getting back from New York; she's been sleeping in her room the whole time. But Iris will go through with it, I promise you."

Upon returning home, shaken by the encounter, Melanie immediately sent Beryl to Harry with a note (she would not entrust it to a footman), telling him to postpone all action until he had seen her.

Beryl returned soon thereafter. "Mr. Van Burgh was not at home."

Did his absence mean the elopement had taken place? In that case, she would have to face Joseph, use what influence she still had with him to mollify him, mitigate the consequences. Remembering how his fingers had brushed against her breast, she knew what Joseph was thinking; she was to be the consolation prize. Or perhaps the prize itself. Indeed it was quite plausible that his whole idea had been to make her his lover again. Now that she had given him the place in society he had lusted for enough to release her, he wanted her back, and was using Harry as his tool. Yes, she knew what he was thinking: he had found her weakness. That was the way he dealt with others in business, in his personal life. Find the weakness and exploit it. But whatever his underlying motive, his threat against Harry was real. Somehow she must disarm him. What had he said to her in those long-ago days of intimacy that he would not like to have used against him now, particularly when she had Morgen's ear? Had he not once boasted to her, after they had made love, of having years earlier arranged a fire in a railroad train to keep a rival's shipment from reaching its destination in time? She would exploit something like that if she had to.

What an ugly scene it would be, but she had lived through ugly scenes before. All that mattered was that it should succeed. And perhaps the elopement need not be stopped altogether but postponed.

320

She would not make a decision until she was able to determine how great the danger from Joseph truly was. Her plan would also depend on whether Morgen published the drawing, bringing down on her head a scandal no one, certainly not Denis, would excuse. In that event, there would be no point in advising elopement. Unless, of course, Harry wanted Iris that desperately and somehow Melanie seldom accepted this logical reason for his precipitous marriage plans.

In the meantime no matter how heavy a strain she was under, she realized that the preparations for the ball had to be completed. Wallace would be returning home from wherever he had gone so early and be suspicious if she were not deeply involved in the activities of a household in the throes of frantic preparation for the next day's ball. Gardeners were straining as they dragged pots of small trees and shrubs from the greenhouses and placed them on either side of the walk from driveway to house. A windbreak was constructed before each major ball, as on the hottest nights of summer, a breeze would blow up from the ocean, delightfully cooling the mansions lining the shore, but disturbing the women's hair, which had been artfully combed, each wave and curl arranged to reveal a cluster of jewels. No other hostess offered such consideration to her guests. It was often mentioned in Melanie's favor when her failings were under discussion.

With relief, Melanie felt the household close in around her. During her absence, the cleaning of the chandeliers had been completed. The scaffolding erected by the workmen so they could reach the two-stories-high ceiling had been taken down. Each hanging crystal drop, polished by hand, caught the morning sunlight. The marble walls were glowing, the pile of the rugs brushed high. When she came downstairs the groundskeeper was waiting to show her the plans he had made for the entry of the camel—the ramp leading onto the terrace and into the ballroom, the unfinished pine boards placed over the floor. Coming into the ballroom, Melanie observed workmen emptying wheelbarrows and raking the burden of sand over the boards and under the tables where three hundred people were to dine the next night. An oasis had been created at the far end of the room where the orchestra usually sat; the date palms had been shipped from the botanical gardens at Kew in England.

A small balcony for the orchestra was being constructed on the wall closest to the music room where the dancing was to take place, the ballroom floor being under sand. The rugs had already been lifted from the music room floor and the wood polished to so high a sheen that the dancers looking down would see themselves, ghostly figures as in a dark mirror.

The great ballroom would be at its most spectacular that night. The maids and footmen were mounting hundreds upon hundreds of candles in sconces, in high silver candelabra. The soft quality of candlelight would make the beautiful even more beautiful, would soften and conceal the lines, bags, and jowls of those ravaged by time and good living.

The thousands of tiny flames would be reflected in the mirrors and in the panes of the French doors facing the back lawn. In the course of the evening the doors would be opened from time to time to let in the cool night air and the flames would dance and flicker. After the doors were closed again, footmen with long tapers would circle the room, moving slowly and with great dignity as they rekindled those candles that had blown out.

A willow tree had been planted outside the doors and the breeze would blow its leafy branches against the panes. The sound of that gentle tapping and rustling added a touch of mystery.

Watching the workers put the candles in place, imagining them lit, Melanie again had a sudden spasm of nausea. The flame of the candles was not so different from that of a bonfire. Well, she would not spend her life avoiding fire to the extent of recoiling from glowing candles as well as knitting needles. What was called for now was the creation of the most brilliant ball of the Bourneham season, a ball to be remembered for years.

The camel trainer and his boy had orders to lead the camel up Ocean Drive to Île de Joie in the predawn hours tomorrow and have it tethered on the lawn between the house and the ocean before any of the neighbors were up and out of doors. A small shed had been constructed to shelter the beast. Melanie had arranged to have a tent put up as well for her to use to change back into her ball gown after the camel ride. The townspeople were sure to crowd against the fence, peering through any openings to catch a glimpse of her. They were the same individuals who at other times paid a dollar apiece to stand, faces pressed against the windows of the Emerald Beach clubhouse, to ogle the dancers at the Friday night balls.

The plans were made: as soon as she entered the ballroom on camelback, the Worth gown would be carried downstairs and placed in the tent on sheets spread on the grass, alongside the corset, stockings and petticoat, a small table holding a glass lamp and the creams and tinted powers to retouch the makeup so carefully applied earlier. Beryl was given charge of the box of jewels.

The camel's big hooves would kick up huge divots of earth and grass as it made its way across the back lawn. Squares of turf had been made ready so that the entire lawn could be re-created rapidly. But as the gardeners must attend church services on Sunday, Melanie feared the unsightly appearance of the lawn for the balance of the weekend would annoy Wallace, who already took a dim view of the camel ride.

Returning to her sitting room, she began a final check of the seating plan. A place must be found for Morgen. If he came to the ball and were well treated, his continuing silence became likelier, yet there was the danger that he would be chilled by her very proper guests. Then she had the perfect solution: Evangeline Van Burgh. Morgen would be flattered at being placed next to a member of New York society's most inner circle, and so determined a man would not be put off by her deafness. Wishing to make the most of the connection, he could be expected to take the trouble that conversation with her required. If Evangeline did not react, her aloofness could be attributed to her handicap, but Melanie thought it likely that she would respond to him, considering how few people tried to talk with her. The arrangement would suit them both.

As for the Woodruff party, she could not reveal prior knowledge, and so had placed Denis next to Iris, Harry at another table. In all probability, she thought, having still no word from Harry, neither he nor Iris would attend. She dreaded the thought of facing Joseph; for all her bravado, she was not fully confident of her ability to divert him with threats of exposure.

She paced nervously. What if Wallace in pique did not attend the ball? Everyone knew he was in Bourneham. There would be no possible excuse for his absence, but the real one. For once Melanie could see no possible way to save herself if her worst fears proved true. Today she found it hard to dismiss the thought that Wallace would seek to have the children taken away from her. For all the myriad details awaiting her attention, the need to see them was suddenly strong. It struck her, as it sometimes would in the midst of her preparations for a ball, that what she was doing was unimportant compared to her life as a mother. She made as much time for her children as she could, more than any of her friends did, but still it never seemed enough.

She sent Beryl to call Junior to her and inform Rosamunde's nurse of her wish. The children lifted her spirits. Rosamunde, ignoring her cold and merry as always, shouted and jumped up and down with joy, and Junior ran up to touch Melanie's hand, knocking over a vase as he did so, eager to show her a botanical drawing he had made for her during her absence.

Then Miss Abbott, the dressmaker, holding the Worth gown reverentially, was at the door. Melanie did not allow her figure to vary by so much as half an inch, but even a fraction of that necessitated a few stitches to maintain a flawless fit.

The gown was of a deep red silk satin covered with an overall pattern of velvet flowers in the same hue. The neckline was cut so low that when Melanie was tightly laced, one would think her breasts would be revealed in their entirety when she moved; however the gown was so ingeniously fashioned as to stay in place whatever she did. Careful seaming below the breasts curved inward to the sharply accentuated waist. It had taken many fittings to achieve the perfection Melanie and Mr. Worth demanded, to have the fabric over the rib cage and around the waist lie without the smallest fold. This faultless smoothness was achieved by the ruby satin corset, created in the Worth workrooms; no front grippers, ribbon, or bit of lace marred the line. Lacings in the back and small elastic insets on the side held in the waist. The sleeves to the gown were no more than narrow bands of satin, one edged with gilded lace, the other with a ruby ostrich plume. The skirt was drawn up in the back, with a fullness hinting at the bustles of the seventies and trailing gracefully on the floor. In front, the fall of the satin overskirt was arrested at the knee in a cascade of feathers and cut back to reveal a panel of eighteenth-century point d'Angleterre lace, cream in color and glowing over a burgundy petticoat.

As Melanie studied her reflection in the triple mirror, Mrs. Abbott and Beryl circled her, placing a tiny chalk mark at each place where a stitch should be taken. In the total concentration required for the fitting, the anxiety receded briefly.

Now she had to change her clothing and go out for the final practice to the road beside the farmland outside Bourneham, the road where the camel was waiting for her. Surveying the scene on camelback, at each turn in the road, she found herself looking for the horseman. Denis. *I have often imagined you riding, Melanie.* And then that decision, disastrous now in retrospect, to meet him in New York. He might not come to her again. The thought of what had happened, the waste, the loss, was so painful that again she almost slipped down over the camel's curving neck. Abdel and Ali ran to her prepared to catch the reins, but she waved them away. She lifted her head, in control again. So would she ride up the ramp into the ballroom. Proud, triumphant, outdoing all others by the extravagance of her action.

Returning from the camel ride, she was seized again by her fears for Harry. The suspense was not to be borne. And there was nothing she could do about it, had to wait, hoping someone would send a note or telephone. Most of the people she knew in Bourneham had the new device; not the Van Burghs, of course.

While Melanie was brooding over the possibilities, all seeming dark, Dena came to the open doorway of the dressing room, timidly knocking against the frame. She had changed her mind, she said, wanted to remain with Mrs. Edmont. Nellie had changed her mind for her, Melanie thought, but in her present mood, the girl's miserable face touched her. Girl. Why, Dena had grown old. Her face was quite lined, there was gray in her hair. The past they had shared. Blood. Filling the bathtub, making a trail on the floor over the rugs, then on the bedclothes. Dena had mopped up the blood, cleaned the bathtub, washed Melanie's body, and remained silent for years. A confidante to be relied upon. Until Nellie appeared. A spoiler like her husband. Those letters from Denis. Dena had kept them hidden for months while Nellie moved inexorably forward, forward again, then consolidating her gains. Dena, Denis. She remembered the girl she had been, how titillating the similarity between the names.

Somehow she could not bring herself to reject the appeal, send Dena away to nothing. "Beryl is my personal maid now, but Mrs. Karling will find you other duties in the house."

After Dena left, Melanie was too agitated to busy herself with any task. The newspaper from New York was due. And still she would have to wait, as it had to be brought to Wallace first. Even so, she went out to the landing to look down and see if the paper had been delivered. At that moment Wallace was coming out of his study, the newspaper in his hand. He stopped short on seeing her. Melanie tried to read his expression but found it inscrutable. He cleared his throat and after a pause asked how the preparations for the ball were going. She was too startled to respond. Wallace had never before inquired as to such matters, viewing them as her province. The idea crossed her mind that Morgen had printed the destructive news report, Wallace had read it and was asking the unaccustomed question to torment her, to keep her waiting longer. While she had never before hesitated to ask for what she wanted of him, she could not bring herself to request the newspaper.

"The preparations are proceeding according to plan." In the effort to control her voice, it came out strained and weak. Unable to stop herself: "I see the newspaper from New York has been delivered."

"Yes," he replied absently, "I thought you might want to read it." But he did not offer her the newspaper. "I have been to see my mother." She looked up at him, disquieted, but he said nothing more and only stared at her with an intensity that alarmed her.

Wallace thought he could never tell Melanie what had passed between him and his mother that day. He had initially been astounded by the vehemence of her reaction and subsequently by the direction of her argument. It was not the divorce itself that she was objecting to, he realized with shock. Instead, for the first time in his remembrance, his mother had actually differed with him, criticized him, told him he was in error. And what he was in error about was Melanie. He had been prepared for her to urge restraint, to tell him that although Melanie had indeed behaved abominably, still divorce was not a proper course for an Edmont. He had in fact prepared a response. But his mother refused to agree that Melanie had behaved abominably. If anything, she appeared to think it was he who was behaving wrongly.

"Clara Ribley?" she had asked. "You would leave Melanie Edmont for a Clara Ribley? I cannot believe it, Junior."

"Don't you hear the gossip about Melanie, Mother? Everyone in Bourneham talks of her."

"Of course there is gossip. What would you expect? You married a beautiful woman and then express surprise that others find her beautiful. She does you credit; she does the Edmont family credit. And she has borne you an heir. Gossip. What does that matter? A woman of beauty and spirit will always be talked about. That is the way with our society. We Edmonts take it in stride. We ignore it. They will not gossip about a Clara Ribley.

"As a woman, I think I know Melanie. And I view her as a daughter, Junior. You make a mistake to allow the denigrating words of envious people to affect you."

When he explained that Melanie had been found in the most compromising situations, she remarked blandly that men always sought to put beautiful women in compromising situations because they thought it reflected well on them.

The tenor of the argument stunned Wallace; he had come to count on his mother's unquestioning approval of his actions to the point where he even thought she would accept the otherwise unacceptable course of divorce.

A Clara Ribley. A Clara.

It was more than gossip. Melanie had been having an affair with the journalist. Why, she had actually invited that cur to her ball, insisted that it was necessary to keep him from vilifying them in his infamous newspaper. Maybe so. But perhaps, and it certainly was the likelier of the alternatives, she wanted him to see her in her greatest beauty in the ball gown. It had certainly cost enough. Not that he was unable to afford the price, but it was absurd to spend money so wantonly. *Wanton*, that was the word for her. Not only the journalist, but young Harry Van Burgh—Handsome Harry, they called him at the club—who had been too careless or improvident to silence Wolfe. And all the men before these two. His mother was too innocent to recognize what was going on. But then, seeing that her eyes were unnaturally bright, he thought that perhaps she was aware of the romances, but did not consider them important. His father, there was no use denying it, had been an overt philanderer and she had maintained the fiction of a solid, even happy marriage. Maybe it had not been fictitious, despite his father's having died in that woman's bed in New Orleans. Melanie had told him that his mother complained she was lonesome since that death. His mother confided in Melanie; it always surprised him.

"You know, Junior, there are people who are so attractive to the opposite sex. They cannot help the effect they have on others." His mother's voice was softer; perhaps there were tears in it as if she too had been remembering his father, remembering that she had for years been the not-wholly-deceived wife of a dashing man. "A woman like that. You cannot make too much of each little flirtation."

"But think of my position. Do you know what people say of me?" Cuckold. He had come as close as he possibly could to the crux of it.

"As far as I can see, everyone envies you, Junior. Every man, certainly. And every woman envies Melanie for being your wife." His mother spoke with utter conviction. He shook his head. Genevieve put her hand on his arm gently. "No one will gossip about a Clara Ribley," she repeated. "If that is your criterion of what a woman should be, then you would be making the proper choice." He would not have believed his mother capable of such sarcasm. "The men will not be flocking about, seeking to slip her notes, and bribing her maid. Not at all. Why should they?" Wallace was surprised that his mother knew of such stratagems, but then he realized anew that she knew everything that went on.

He wanted to tell her that he loved Clara, but the words would not come. Clara was his refuge, offering a safe harbor after the stormy seas of life with Melanie. But a Clara Ribley.

His mother's defense came to his mind as he stood on the landing staring at Melanie, haggard despite the careful makeup. She was afraid, he realized; and all at once he saw how it must appear to her, recognized what an unsavory divorce could do to her.

"Did you have a good visit with your mother?"

"Yes, yes, of course."

Thrusting the newspaper at her so swiftly that she had to grab to keep it from dropping, he walked back into his study, closed the door, opened it again, looked at her as if to speak, and then closed it.

The newspaper rustled in her shaking hands as she went back into her dressing room and sat down. Wallace had not really seemed hostile, yet his manner had been so strange it was impossible to guess whether Morgen had written the article she so dreaded.

She scanned the front page apprehensively; the Heron factory fire was still prominently featured beneath large headlines. Having wrung all the human interest out of the tragedy, the articles now were devoted to interviews with city officials deploring the lack of fireproofing and vowing more stringent legislation. The name of the owner of the tenement was given. No reference, real or implied, to Wallace Edmont was made. Nor had Morgen written about the related fire, the fire on the Edmont lawn, nor of the body blazing amidst the flower beds and the velvety grass.

At first Melanie felt relief, and then she realized that this could represent no more than a reprieve. Morgen might be playing with her and planning how best to use the frightful drawing revealing the two figures at the window, male and female, risen from bed, rushed from their lovemaking to witness the angry crowd, the man aflame.

CHAPTER 26

Three Men at Melanie's Ball

The unthinkable was happening: the van der Cleeves had arrived with their guest, Clara Ribley. Wallace had planned this, taking cruel advantage of the custom of bringing houseguests to social events without forewarning, on the assumption that Bourneham was too informal for the rigid protocol demanded for a New York City entertainment.

Melanie despised him for the small-mindedness that caused him to set the stage for a scandal at her ball, instead of having it out with her in private. Wallace was revenging himself on her—for the affair he believed she was carrying on with Morgen, for the summer toy appellation in the *Bugle*, for the years of conjugal strife, for the extravagant gesture with the camel, for her orchidaceous style. This was how he was paying her back. And she would have to get through the evening, ride the camel, the object of all eyes. And surely all eyes were on her now to see her reaction. Everyone knew about Clara. She had never felt so compro-

331

mised as she smiled and welcomed the van der Cleeves and their guest.

But surely it was not good sense for Wallace to bring Clara here when there was still some doubt as to what Morgen meant to do. Until he had evidence—or what would be construed as evidence—of a relationship between them Wallace should not be so confident that her affairs would be viewed as more reprehensible than his with Clara, flaunted now. The action was out of character, but then she thought that however deep his involvement with Clara, he still had not liked to think of his wife with Morgen, and jealousy made people behave foolishly.

Barely able to conceal his feelings, Wallace was horrified by Clara's action, having been certain she would find a pretext for staying away, as he had avoided the Woodruffs' ball upon learning she was to attend. As a houseguest of the van der Cleeves, there was precedent for her presence. It was tradition to come, but Wallace would have wished her to stay away.

Another woman might have been reluctant to appear to poor advantage, dimmed by Melanie's good looks and extravagant style, but Clara had no such fears. Always plain, she had when young found in libertinism the way to attract boys of good family, and in middle age had found that solidity of form and character could count for more with some men than beauty. In fact, it was her very stoutness that appealed to Wallace. His muscles tensed as Melanie turned her bright, false smile on Clara; yet he had nothing to be nervous about. Melanie was the one who invariably (and deservedly) was the object of scandal, not Clara, not he. His relationship with Mrs. Ribley was perfectly correct; at any moment, anyone, his mother, anyone, could have entered a room where they were tête-à-tête. However, Melanie was unpredictable, capable of anything she thought would serve her purpose. If she snubbed Clara, or made one of her nasty cutting remarks in a carrying voice, it would fuel a scandal, convince everyone that he was indeed in the midst of a love affair. She would not even have to speak. All Melanie needed to do was to look over at him in a suggestive manner and everyone would know. It seemed to him that the entire roomful of guests was aware that this meeting was portentous, was waiting for something to happen. Melanie made a mockery of virtue, he thought, growing angrier.

Seeing the two women standing next to one another, he was struck by how much older Clara looked than Melanie, though there could not have been more than a very few years between them. He liked that. A woman gained dignity by admitting her age. It was ridiculous the amount of time—and money—Melanie spent in efforts to maintain her youthful appearance. (But how young she looked tonight, glowing in the red gown, slender waisted, her breasts high and firm.)

Tensed for an excessively unpleasant scene, he felt almost let down when Melanie greeted Clara affably, revealing no emotion. She turned to someone else. The moment had passed.

Melanie, too, was relieved that the meeting with Clara had gone so smoothly. She knew how easy it would have been for Clara to have by some glance indicated her special role in Wallace's life, in this way embarrassing Melanie as wife, denigrating, making her look pathetic standing there in all her splendor, particularly because of her splendor, because of the satin Worth gown with the ostrich plumes, because of the forty-six-carat ruby on a golden chain around her neck.

The air of calm Melanie exhibited was such as to make Clara wonder if the situation with Wallace were as settled as she had believed. Surely it was impossible for Melanie's ignorance, displayed at the Woodruffs' ball, to have lasted through this week.

As Melanie with Genevieve beside her swept through the great hall to greet the other guests, Wallace followed his own path, a little to the left, a little behind. The separation was so slight as to be unnoticeable to any but those most aware of social nuances. Genevieve gave not the smallest sign she knew of trouble brewing—except for the fact that she had been the first arrival, in striking contrast to her customary practice of appearing just before the dinner was to be served. Knowing precisely what his mother's promptness expressed, Wallace felt depressed.

Melanie forced herself to create an aura of warmth, welcome, confidence, looking each guest in the face while desperate to glance over her shoulder to see whether Harry had come, whether Harry were safe. She felt she could not endure her fear for him any longer. At the same time she was watching apprehensively for Morgen. Were he not to appear, she could take it as a sign that the compromising drawing was yet to be published.

Finally the announcement of his name allowed her to turn and see Morgen enter the room. Wallace gave a stiff, cursory greeting barely this side of discourtesy. Melanie for her part had to guard against being too effusive. Were she not still so worried about Harry, she would have been quite limp with relief.

At last a ripple of conversation, a sense of excitement sweeping through the room signaled the arrival of a party of unusual interest. Nellie and Joseph Woodruff were making their entrance and in an instant she would know whether Harry was there, whether the elopement had taken place. Iris slowly followed her parents into the great hall; Denis was beside her. Harry was nowhere in evidence. For a moment Melanie had the wild fear that they had eloped, been followed and caught by Joseph and violence of some sort done to Harry. But if that were so, Iris must surely appear distraught, frantic, and her face was merely sad, calm. Harry had not come to her after all.

Nellie Woodruff had outdone herself; the other guests appeared positively modest. Every inch of her considerable bosom and of her arms, as big around as an average woman's thighs, was covered with a dazzling display of sparkling diamonds, emeralds, star sapphires, golden balls, and baroque pearls. She was glowing with pleasure at being there, welcomed by Melanie and Wallace, triumphant, with her daughter and her prize, Denis. But Joseph did not seem happy, despite having gotten his way. Had Melanie's guess been accurate, that he had not wanted to win? Would he have preferred to have her pleading, begging him for Harry's safety? Observing this reaction, Melanie thought that in the end if she handled it skillfully, Joseph might yet accept an elopement and let Harry have Iris. What if that were to happen? Why, Denis might not be lost to her.

Iris was barely whispering her greeting. She was dressed in taste as perfect as her mother's was vulgar, in silk chiffon of the palest peach with a simple necklace of pearls around her long, slender neck. Her waist, circled by a dark blue velvet ribbon, had been laced to a circumference of a hairsbreadth less than sixteen inches. This was the body too frail for any man, thought Melanie, that was to receive her Denis. How old he looked next to Iris's fresh flowerlike beauty, her name so aptly chosen. For a moment Melanie could see how Denis must appear to Iris, an aging gentleman, with lined leathery skin and gray in his beard. Iris had no memory of Denis young, infinitely desirable to any woman. That body of the past only Melanie perceived in the older body of the present.

As they moved forward, Melanie noticed how his hip just barely brushed against Iris's. Seeing Denis beside Iris, standing a little apart from the rest of the Woodruff group, obviously coupled, should have been intolerable. Melanie waited for the familiar stomach-turning wrench at seeing her lover with his next sexual companion. But it did not come. Curiously she felt almost indifferent. It was as if Denis's capacity for making her suffer had at last been worn out. For an instant she found it possible to imagine her life without Denis in it. Desire would return, she knew; she was merely exhausted by the excess of emotion she had experienced, by the realization only beginning to sink in that her plans had failed. Tomorrow, she thought, tomorrow, she would see him again as he was, had been, in the music room, aroused in

335

his tight trousers. And it was not necessarily true that her plan had failed. Postponed perhaps, no more than that. As she had told Harry, he could elope with Iris until the day of the wedding. Oddly, this thought brought her little comfort.

Nellie was flushed and, despite the breezes from the artfully placed windows cooling the room, overheated. Perspiration stains were already evident under her arms and on the back of her fuchsia silk taffeta gown. "I am planning to hold a party myself as soon as we are all back in New York," Nellie told Melanie in a whisper clearly heard through half the enormous, high-ceilinged room. "The very first Saturday."

It did not seem the moment, nor did Melanie consider it her responsibility, to inform Nellie that she was about to commit a major gaffe. Genevieve, by virtue of her position, always held the first social event of each season; until she had done so, no one, however prominent, would even think of scheduling a party. The custom was unspoken; everybody knew of it. Were someone else to hold a ball, no one would attend.

As they spoke, exchanging pleasantries, Denis skillfully slipped a note into Melanie's gloved hand. She did not need to read it to know what it would say; there had been so many such notes over the years, often passed at a social gathering, passed right under Adelaide's nose. Now it was Iris's. No change, the status quo was to continue. Only she was weary. Not even angry or, tonight at any rate, disappointed. But weary. And frightened. Denis had not come to her aid when they were young; he would not do so now.

She was frightened, despite the fact that her appearance displayed confidence and vitality. Anxiety was becoming constant. The whole unpalatable business of divorce hung over her. Wallace, across the room, was so carefully not looking at Clara Ribley that Melanie could sense the effort. If Denis did go through with the marriage to Iris, what would become of her? She crumpled the note and, as a footman passed with a tray, dropped it into a half-empty glass of champagne.

"When is the wedding to be?" she asked Denis coldly, the slightest biting edge to her tone.

Nellie overheard and interrupted. Her tutor had improved her speech, but had not dared to comment on her manners. "You have guessed our little secret, then?" she said. Her voice was a trifle sharp as well; Melanie must have learned about the marriage plans from Harry, and Nellie was still a little uncomfortable about him. She wondered how he had described her role in the loss of Iris. There was no way of guessing from the charming way Melanie was pressing her arm, telling her how lovely she looked. To be sure, Melanie might very well be pleased with Nellie, delighted at the way things were turning out. Were she Melanie, she would be in no hurry to have Harry married.

"How could I not have guessed?" replied Melanie. "Iris's blissful expression simply gives it away."

How could she have said that? It was her weakness. Seeking to improve matters, she went on: "And where is the wedding to be, Nellie? Your magnificent house in New York might have been designed for such an event."

Nellie was eager to present her greatest coup. "Castle Carnaugh is even better suited for so important a wedding, Melanie dear. Lord Warburne insists that the wedding be held on his estate."

Denis's insistence was clever, thought Melanie with cynical understanding. Glancing at his impassive face she thought of the sums the Woodruffs would surely allot to repairing the castle and its grounds for the so-important wedding—a few hundred thousand dollars by the most conservative thinking that would otherwise have gone to decorating the Woodruff mansion. A veritable army of craftsmen and workmen would be dispatched to Carnaugh. Guests would no longer force themselves shivering into tubs carried to the bedrooms each evening. Nellie would have bathrooms installed and additional sources of heating. Never suspecting his motives, Nellie was thrilled by the prospect of inviting (or failing to invite) to Carnaugh those in New York society who had sneered at her.

Of course, Melanie was wrong to assume naïveté. Nellie knew exactly what Denis was doing. It was not so long since she had been forced to plot to extend limited funds in ways no more subtle than this. Knowing his subterfuge only made Nellie admire the marquess the more.

The work on Carnaugh would hold up the wedding for several months that could be used to advantage by Harry. Where was Harry? What had gone wrong? Once she knew a problem, she could solve it, but she felt curiously lacking in ingenuity tonight. What had seemed so easy a few days ago seemed difficult now.

Aware of Denis's eyes on her, speculating as to whom she was awaiting, she colored. When Nellie walked away, taking Iris to speak to the van der Cleeves, he remarked softly: "You returned to Bourneham without further incident, I trust."

"And you I see in triumph."

"In triumph?" He frowned.

"Perhaps the triumph is as much due to your cousin's skill as your . . . charm." She was taking a perverse pleasure in being unpleasant. "I believe it is he who so skillfully handled the arrangements—surely to your satisfaction."

"Malcolm is always skillful. As for my satisfaction, the word has many meanings not all of which apply." He had dropped his voice, though his manner still would indicate to any onlooker that he was making the most casual small talk. "I fulfill my responsibilities as I must. You have always understood me."

"I think I have not," she replied. "But I understand you well enough now."

Malcolm was observing the exchange. His eyes were cold; there seemed to be no light within. A good negotiator for Denis, he was the only cousin who, being childless, had no interest in the succession. He disliked Melanie, made no bones about revealing it. Attractive in an ugly way, as was characteristic of Denis's family, he had seldom if ever faced sexual rejection and had shown a nasty streak when, on a visit to England long ago, she denied him. She had wondered if he were aware of her relationship with Denis; there was that about him, a touch of meanness, caddishness, that made her believe he probably had surmised and been moved by suspicion to try to win her.

"Why not me?" he had said when she refused his aggressive approach. "You take on practically everyone else. It's common knowledge." Were he not so unquestionably an aristocrat, he could never have spoken so. Were he not so unquestionably odious, he could never have selected so cutting, so cruel a remark. And in retrospect she understood that the insulting, insufferable words had been deliberately chosen, with the intention of reversing their roles, making her the one to be rejected, degraded, not he.

He walked over then to join them. "I am sorry to have missed seeing you the other day when we were all in New York on our various . . . businesses." Malcolm affected the upper-class mumble that made one uncertain of understanding him. His tone was suggestive, as if he knew the reason for his cousin's absence during the afternoon, though considering Denis's reserve, it was unlikely he could do more than guess.

"Ah, yes. I came with Mr. Edmont on the *Falcon* to visit my mother. Perhaps you remember her?"

"I can't say that I do."

Ignoring the superciliousness of his manner, the rudeness of his response, she continued: "I am so pleased your visit has coincided with my ball."

"It is indeed pleasant to be here to see the engaged couple. I believe my cousin is satisfied, as any man would be with a bride so young and lovely."

Satisfied; again the word with many meanings. Malcolm was smiling at having found, he thought, the way to wound her. Neither Iris's youth nor her loveliness is my rival, only her promise of great wealth.

The encounter with Malcolm revived Melanie by its very unpleasantness; she felt buoyed by nervous energy, ready for anything. She looked about and observed that the appearance of the strangely assorted Woodruff party had aroused speculation and gossip. And when Harry Van Burgh accompanied by his mother and Evangeline entered the great hall and approached Melanie, conversation stopped, as each person waited to hear, not quite knowing what there would be to hear, but sensing the significance.

Harry was unharmed. She could not allow her relief and joy to show on her face. In the circumstance, Melanie dared not ask him what had happened, could not even meet his eyes, could barely make the most trivial small talk. Anything of a serious nature must wait until they contrived to be alone. That would be possible when she left to change for the camel ride; she was certain Harry would be watching for the chance. Wallace was studying her; Harry's arrival had diverted his attention from Clara, thought Melanie.

Something was different about Harry, though. If it had not been Harry, she would have said he was careworn. Though as impeccably dressed as always—the tailor discounted the price knowing that wealthier men would seek him out thinking to look like Harry—there were signs of distraction. His shoes were not shined to the highest possible gloss, nor was there a boutonniere in his buttonhole.

Melanie's smile was so agreeable, so impersonal, that Harry could not tell whether she was angry with him, disappointed that he had failed to elope with Iris and leave the Englishman free for her. The knowledge of her preference for the other man was painful. Was Harry never to be her lover again? Edmont was standing just a little apart from Melanie and Harry thought how unhappy he looked when he could have been joyously proclaiming to the world that Melanie was his wife. Certainly Harry in his place would have done so. Edmont's greeting was predictably cold.

What an intolerable evening this was. Now he would have to face Iris. With a spasm of guilt he observed how sad, how reproachful, was her expression. She was not yet experienced in hiding her emotions. He had led her to expect more of him and he had not been lying; until yesterday he

340

had not known he could not marry her. Evangeline had said it truly: Melanie had spoiled Iris for him.

And there were the Woodruffs dressed in their formal clothes and smiling just like everyone else, as if they had not set the killer dogs on him. Still, at the moment, Harry felt relief that the Woodruffs were protecting Iris to such a degree that he could not manage to see her alone. What might he tell her that would not make her more unhappy? Better for her to believe her parents had forced him away than to recognize that he did not love her.

At the same time Harry was miserably aware of the man at Iris's side. Warburne. Melanie's lover. He could hardly bear to look at the man, the object of her passion. How old the Englishman looked, though surely that was not how Melanie saw him, Harry thought with despair, sick with jealousy. Even so, he did not need to surrender so easily. Nothing could be worse than the way he was feeling now. He could at least see Melanie and tell her of his decision not to elope with Iris—not soon, not ever, tell her of the reason for his decision. And then? Well, from her reaction he would know what to do, what to say.

Looking about for Evangeline, he was stunned to see Melanie introducing Elmer Morgen to her. One would not have expected to find Morgen in this house and Harry wondered at Melanie. How unpleasant it was to stand there, Harry thought, to smile and watch that crude journalist daring to offer attention to Evangeline. To be present in an Edmont home conversing with a Van Burgh must surely have been beyond the man's wildest dreams a short time before. Melanie was unconventional in some ways, he knew, but she did not flout tradition without very good reason. She wanted something from Morgen, wanted something suppressed more likely. Morgen would not take a cash bribe as Armand Wolfe would do, but an invitation to the greatest ball of the Bourneham season, an introduction to a Van Burgh: Harry thought as Melanie did; he knew the value.

About to go over to lead Evangeline away, he observed

341

how she was glowing at Morgen's attention, glowing and glancing under her eyelashes at Signor Martelli who was watching the scene. She was flirting, thought Harry, like any other young woman, using one man's interest to arouse the other. How had she learned to flirt?

Observing Evangeline smiling at Morgen, Melanie was struck by how much she resembled Harry. Why, she was pretty. Melanie had never thought of Evangeline's looks somehow, and never counted her among the beauties. No one did really; she was excluded from such consideration by her handicap. Yet who among the women present had eyelashes so long and lips so perfectly formed? And her waist— even Iris's was hardly smaller. What is more, this evening Evangeline appeared less retiring, less modest than usual, had abandoned her custom of filling in the neckline of her evening dress with tulle or chiffon and had allowed the low-cut gown to reveal the cleavage between her breasts, surprisingly full for one so slender. Her color was high, whether (even Melanie could not tell) due to excitement or to rouge.

Louise certainly had made recourse to cosmetics. They were applied with too little skill to leave anyone in doubt. It did not matter. Nothing could detract from her dignity. Alone among the women she appeared in a gown worn at other balls not only this season but for four or five seasons past. Her manner in greeting Melanie was so charming that only a dropping of her lids to veil her eyes as she spoke indicated her coldness.

The Italian, Signor Martelli, who was Genevieve's houseguest, was hovering nearby and the warmth in Louise's manner as she turned to greet him was quite startling in contrast. Melanie supposed Louise was making a point; she could not imagine the two were friends. How cadaverous the man looked; still upon arriving he had kissed her hand with true European courtesy and he did appear quite taken with Evangeline, vying with Morgen for her attention. Maybe there was a match to be made, only Louise would never see it. Perhaps a word to Harry.

Melanie glanced at him moving through the great hall at ease, taking a glass of champagne for his mother, another for himself, selecting the crabmeat mousse canapé for Evangeline, urging the caviar on Louise. He gave every appearance of someone enjoying himself. But of course with a man as trained in proper social behavior as Harry, one could never tell what he was thinking.

Groves, the butler, quietly informed Melanie that all the guests were present and the time had come to lead them into the ballroom. There were gasps as the desert transformation was seen, the date palm oasis, the sand brushed under the tables and covering the floor area usually reserved for dancing. The doors to the adjoining music room stood open and guests moved freely from one room to the other.

Bourneham's up-and-coming businessmen sought out Wallace, wishing to take advantage of the occasion to obtain his opinion on matters of business, hoping perhaps to catch him off guard and learn something to their advantage. Wallace for his part was finding it hard to concentrate on the discussion of land rights, legislation affecting property, and political maneuverings that usually engrossed him. Even the speculation as to whether a subway would be dug under the city making the buildings unsound and destroying property values (or so he said and others thought) failed to entice him. The feeling that he was not in full control was so unfamiliar that he was unnerved. His life had always gone according to his plan. Each step had logically followed the one before. Perhaps he had overlooked the shaky condition of her father's bank when, dazzled by Melanie's beauty, he had impulsively asked for her hand. Even then, he was not long into the engagement before his customary prudence had caused him to call for the balance sheet. He had calculated what it would cost him to keep the bank afloat and the figure had been well within his means. One could not call that a careless, profligate decision. In fact, no one could say he had made a careless, profligate decision in any aspect of his personal or business life. This was the way he had been prepared by his grandfather, who had indicated that it was Wallace's duty to make up for his father's lapses, for the astonishing, incomprehensible disinterest in the business that kept them all. When necessary, Wallace had taken risks, but always with the full knowledge of each possible outcome and how it would be managed. Flood, earthquake, fire, yes fire; even those factors had been weighed for the effect they might have. Now with all his care, all his planning, he had lost control.

Blame for the Heron factory fire in which he took no part had made him and his family the target of troublemakers. He would have to increase the number of bodyguards by introducing them as extra footmen into each of his houses. That matter of the self-immolation on his lawn would haunt him for years.

Glancing across the music room, he observed Elmer Morgen standing close to that deaf girl, Van Burgh's sister. The man was smiling, looking as benign as his sinister features would allow. Melanie's lover, Wallace thought, unable to keep from grimacing at the image that called forth. When Melanie told him she had asked Morgen here to protect him, Wallace, he had viewed that as a ridiculous defense, not worth serious consideration. But tonight he found himself considering it. Calmer now than on that terrible day before yesterday in New York, he could see that the fact of the man's being her lover would hardly be sufficient to explain the invitation. It was sure to be talked about; Morgen was after all no Harry Van Burgh to be invited everywhere as a matter of course. Perhaps Melanie knew what she was doing. For all her failings, she had a great deal of sense about such things. He had to give her that; it would not have occurred to many women to bring Morgen here and to introduce him to the one member of a good family who would not rebuff the upstart.

Good sense or no, the man was her lover and the only way for Wallace to take charge of his personal life again was to put her out of it. Clara stood at the opposite end of the ballroom. How womanly and modest she appeared in deep blue crepe silk, a bertha collar of white lace covering her buxom figure to the waist. It was, he thought approvingly, the simplest and most tasteful gown in the room. But Wallace could not help noticing that except for Josephine van der Cleeve, Clara was being snubbed by the women. It surprised him; dignified, matronly, of good if not the best family, she was just the type of woman who was most sought after by other women. He knew that Melanie's flamboyance, attractiveness to men, refusal to look or act her age aroused envy and suspicion.

Despite Melanie's assertion, Wallace failed to recognize that gossip had already linked his name with Clara. Thus her appearance at Melanie's ball—for a ball was credited to the hostess not the host, as were all social occasions—was a major error. The suspicion was raised that Clara had timed her visit to the van der Cleeves to coincide with the ball, to force an invitation on the basis of social custom, creating by her presence an incident that might cause Melanie to make a scene, Wallace to declare his intention to divorce.

Instead, it was as if at her presence, a wave passed over the room, carrying with it a change of mood. In the space of a moment, attitudes were altered. The women had been whispering about the divorce for the last couple of weeks, enjoying the gossip, taking a kind of pleasure in the thought of Melanie's misfortune. But not one of them had really believed it. They had taken it as a threat Wallace was making to force Melanie to behave in a more conservative manner. Now, seeing the situation at first hand, the meanness of Wallace in bringing his new woman into the house, to flaunt her in front of Melanie, they were disgusted. Divorce ceased to be a topic for titillating gossip.

Melanie was one of them, a wife and mother, what is more a wife of long standing. If she could be put aside, replaced on a husband's whim, could any wife be secure? It now seemed outrageous that Wallace should think to justify himself on the grounds of her behavior. Melanie was no longer the shameless one from whom no man was safe, but rather a woman whose beauty demanded the kind of admiration she received. This adulation should have made her even more treasured by the husband who possessed her. The relationship with Harry that but minutes earlier had been considered depraved was now transformed into a perfectly natural—almost, one might say, innocent—friendship between an older woman and a younger man. "Summer toy" ceased to be applied as an epithet, but as the charmingly descriptive term for a harmless flirtation. Those who had criticized the forthcoming camel ride as excessively showy now spoke of the gallantry of making so great a demand of oneself at a time of such strain.

Melanie, sensitive to every nuance, was aware of what was happening—and was appalled. Disapproval, envy, jealousy were abandoned, as the wives rallied around Melanie. It was Wallace now who faced their disapproval.

Clara should have known that this would happen; she was a member of that very group, thought as they did, but she had been swayed by her desire to alter the anomalous position of widow to that of Mrs. Wallace Montague Edmont V, a desire so great that she had convinced herself she was in love with Wallace, though they had spent only a few hours alone together and she had been somewhat bored by his correctness. Unwisely, she had indeed believed that her appearance at the ball would create the definitive scene, either on the spot, or more likely, for she was not so foolish, between husband and wife in private later.

Catching sight of his mother, Wallace realized that she was observing him observing Clara and he became so disturbed that he had to take out his handkerchief and wipe his forehead. He knew that never breaking the flow of her conversation or appearing to gaze anywhere but directly at the person with whom she was speaking, his mother followed everything that went on in every corner of a room, could afterwards comment on the direction of each covert glance, the theme of each conversation, the unusual in groupings or pairings.

No one was more adept than Genevieve; without any overt movement or speech, she could make clear her approval or disapproval of a person, group, or behavior. She was disapproving of him now. He could not get over it. Seeing her, being near her, had always calmed him. Aware that he was watching, Genevieve left the group she was with to go to Melanie's side. Small, plump, she was no less regal than that other small, plump figure, Queen Victoria. Suddenly Wallace felt trapped in his own house. Once again, he took out his handkerchief and wiped his forehead. Before he spoke with his mother, he had been so certain of his course. And surely there were no possible grounds for becoming uncertain. Clichés were true: detectives had long since proved to him that where there was so much smoke, there had to be fire. Wallace had thought that everyone, anyone would agree that he was wronged, that he had been far too patient with his faithless wife. He had believed in—counted on in a sense—the gossip, the viciousness of the rumors about Melanie, the hostility to her of the other women, and expected to be treated with the greatest sympathy. His mother set an example for all New York society, no, go further, for all American society. There was no question about it; he was shaken.

A sudden buzz of conversation broke into his musing. One of the guests, Peter de Witte, had slipped out to reconnoiter and had seen the camel on the back lawn, with its exotic keepers, gazing with melancholy eyes at the ocean. A crowd of townspeople, he was reporting with excitement, had gathered outside. Some had gone around to the beach, hoping to climb up onto the lawn from there, but that approach had been foreseen and forestalled by a wall topped with sharp-edged stones. Everyone turned then, Wallace, too, towards Melanie dominating the room with her presence, radiant in the brilliant deep red satin gown. Between her partially revealed breasts, Wallace observed the forty-six-carat ruby he had bought her at Christie's in London so long ago. It had seemed the least he could offer her. And how she had smiled.

He had come to her and she was lying in bed, warm in the cold room, her perfumed hair spread out upon the pillowcase, the rose satin sheet pulled all the way up to her face. And just as he approached the bed, she had pulled down the sheet and there, glowing in the soft dim light, he saw it. The golden chain around her neck, the ruby between her breasts. Her skin as if lit from within. Nothing else. She had seen that he was shocked; he was still young then, not yet accustomed to her ways. And the excitement he had felt, she had seen that on him, too. How she had smiled. *My Wally, my prince.* It made his heart ache.

The orchestra on the balcony struck up just then, but no one moved. A sense of anticipation was evident. Seeing Wallace standing immobile across the room, Melanie was unable to force a smile to her lips and held up her fan to conceal her fear. He was not moving, she thought, did not mean to start the dancing with her, was as good as announcing the break now in front of society, in Clara's presence. All that was required was for him to select another partner. It did not have to be Clara; it only needed to be anyone but his wife. Watching him more intently than usual, it struck her that Wallace had never looked so well. Homely and awkward as a young man, in middle age he had taken on a quality of distinction. The sober air that in a young man had put people off was now compatible with his years, his dignity. He had gotten heavy, as who among the older men she knew had not, but with his height and broad frame and a tailor at least the equal of Harry's, he carried it well. Perhaps he was looking his best tonight because of Clara. Melanie knew what a new love affair could do for the appearance. He was not coming towards her.

Painfully aware of glances being exchanged, she could tell that everyone was thinking as she did. The women's looks were kindly. It was not to be borne. That she should be pitied, supported by the very women who had always envied her, been hostile to her . . . the knowledge was galling to her. Genevieve moved closer. That support, for all the love behind it, was bittersweet to receive now.

348

Wallace, not in the mood for dancing, sighed, knowing that no one else would go onto the floor until he did. About to cross the room, he became uncomfortably aware of Clara's attention, met her eyes. There was something about her look that made him realize she thought he would start the dancing with her. He was startled. Surely she could not have thought him so ill-bred as to have made an overt, incorrect gesture. For that matter, he did not see how he could dance with her at all that night. Again he wished she had not come.

Wallace began to walk across the floor. Coming up to Melanie for the dance he thought how her skin would be hot to the touch. And as always when close to her, he wanted to feel that heat. He recalled how over the years, after he had become aware of her infidelities, he had waited, longed for her to age, lose her sexual attractiveness, lose her beauty, grow old as other women do. Then he would be free of her. He had said that to her once when angry, had been satisfied to observe the shock, more than that, the naked fear on her face. But it was not true; Melanie would never be like other women. She appeared to possess unending youth, had borne a child at forty. Her infidelities would never end; in old age, she would still be tormenting him. The only way to be free of her was to leave her. It was too much to bear to have these personal worries just when he had so much to contend with in business.

Melanie's head was high, her back straight, and she greeted him with her customary bold and winning smile as she preceded him to the music room. But when he put his arm about her for the dance, he felt her tremble. No, it was more than that, a shaking, waves of shudders were passing over her body. He tightened his arm around her instinctively. Guessing how she must have interpreted his hesitation—he knew custom as well as she, had been preoccupied, thoughtless—for the first time in their lives together, he pitied her. Remembering Clara's look, he knew that Melanie had thought he would open the dancing with another. What kind of a man did she think him to be, capable of so graceless, so harsh an act? But then with a sinking heart, he realized that he had become just that kind of man, a man who planned to divorce his wife. She deserved it; she was an amoral woman. Only he wished she were not trembling so.

Wallace was looking at her moodily. He had opened the dancing with her simply to avoid flouting convention in the presence of his mother. Oh, she knew him so well. The action had no meaning aside from that. Melanie thought of how he had spoken to her after the Woodruffs' ball. A ruthless man. He would put her aside, ruin her reputation, leave her in the discredited position of a divorced woman. She wondered at the unhappy face presented by this man, the wealthiest in New York, this man with two women to choose between. He looked away over her shoulder, at Clara no doubt. Wallace would rest on Clara's ample bosom . . . where Bunny had once lain. No moment ever stood clean and whole; each carried with it the memory, the perfume or the stench, of previous moments.

They were dancing well together, effortlessly, flawlessly; childhood dancing classes produced a skill that lasted for life. But Wallace could sense a stiffness about her and she would not meet his eyes. "Look at me," he said softly, then thinking she would read too much into his words, added, "Everyone is watching us," and when she looked him full in the face, he saw her eyes were brimming with tears. Her head was high and she was smiling, but there were the tears. He could not think what to say to her in the face of those tears. "I see you are wearing the ruby . . . It makes me remember." Looking at the ruby he also had to look at her breasts, half revealed in the low-cut dress. "Sometimes," he went on, "I wish I could forget all of the things I remember."

"All of them? There are good memories, too, or don't you think so?"

"Those are the memories I would most like to forget."

She stumbled in the dance—Melanie, who never missed a beat; she had taken his meaning. But was that what he meant? Forget all that connected him to her? For years he had been telling himself that was what he wanted, it had begun to seem real when Clara had entered his life. But forget? The bloodied sheets, her cries of ecstasy. *My Wally, my prince.* A high-spirited girl, wanting to take part in his business. How serious she had been. It had been laughable, ridiculous, but so appealing coming from her. She had been reading his ledgers; he could not have that, had raised his voice to her. But at the same time it had touched him. Everyone had warned him she was too vain to bear children, yet with what difficulty, what repeated pain and effort, she had given him an heir. His mother had remarked on it.

Melanie had recovered her footing, was gliding gracefully on the highly polished floor. The tears were gone, but her eyes avoided his.

"It's time for me to prepare for the camel ride." Her voice was trembling very slightly.

"Wait . . ."

She looked up, startled. What if he were to say now that none of the past bitterness between them mattered, gossip, his suspicions, Clara? They both felt these words trembling on his lips, hanging in the air, unspoken. Perhaps it was true that this marriage had lasted so long that the unhappiness, incompatibility, infidelities could be swallowed up in it.

Wallace drew back, uncertain whether he were not once again being swayed by her physical presence. He must think about this again, in solitude, tranquillity, when she was not there, her skin glowing, her perfume arousing. At that moment, Morgen passed them on the dance floor, Evangeline in his arms.

Without another word they completed the dance, and at the final notes, Melanie smiled in courtesy, left him and walked rapidly across the dance floor and out of the room. Wallace watched her go; as her skirt brushed against the doorway, a ruby-colored ostrich plume fell to the floor. There was a growing excitement among the guests. All at once, despite his scoffing and disapproval of her extravagance, he

351

was as eager as any of them to see her dramatic reappearance on camelback. Then as he looked idly around the room, he observed Harry Van Burgh detach himself from his friends, place a partly eaten canapé and half-full glass of champagne on a footman's tray, and go towards the doorway, stopping on the threshold to pick up the feather. So there it was. Wallace's spirits sank. Always someone to follow Melanie out of a room. Going to stand beside Clara defiantly, he wondered that his mother could continue to praise Melanie.

CHAPTER 27

The Night of the Camel

He was not without a heart after all, had been briefly affected by his memories of their past. It meant nothing. No significant words. Probably by now Wallace had gone to stand beside Clara, self-satisfied at having opened the dancing with Melanie. That duty done, he could spend the rest of the evening, the rest of his life, with Clara.

And what of the rest of her life? Denis had come with Iris. Melanie recalled how she had told herself once before it did not mean he would leave with Iris. But strangely, the mood of indifference that had seized her when she saw Denis standing with the Woodruffs was still upon her, though she knew it dangerous to be affected by a passing mood.

Waiting for Harry in the little room next to the conservatory where the flowers were arranged for the house, she was painfully aware that she would have to use this opportunity to move him to the action that would win her Denis. She wanted that; at least she had wanted it, and knew she would

353

want it again. The tables had been washed, but the scent of flowers remained, heavy. She felt hot, feverish; it was an effort to focus her thoughts on what had to be done. Harry would tell her what had happened, and together they would remake the plan. But the thought of planning wearied her, she who thrived on plans and planning. All she felt like doing was to see Harry in their old way, reality forgotten. Perhaps that had been their mistake all along, to have allowed themselves when together to forget Iris, forget Wallace, Denis, all the other people who made up their lives. It had been a mistake before the *Bugle* had plunged them into reality by stiffening Wallace's resolve to divorce, convincing Nellie of the rightness of her actions. A false, lying scandal sheet, right just this once to such effect.

Harry came in without knocking. It was hot in the room, humid, as hot as it had been in the Woodruffs' conservatory, but this time he was unaware of discomfort.

Though agitated, Melanie was filled with a sense of well-being at seeing him. "I was so afraid for you, Harry."

Afraid? Could she already have heard about his narrow escape from the jaws of the Dobermans? His pleasure in her fear for him was dimmed by the realization of what it really meant: she recognized that he had been in real danger and so did not blame him, was not angry with him for having failed in the elopement. Knowing Melanie's determination, he thought she might suggest a way for him to circumvent the Woodruffs and gain Iris still.

"You were right about Woodruff, Harry. He forced me to meet him and then threatened you, said I must stop you from eloping.

"I was frantic with worry, particularly when I learned you were not at home. Why didn't you get word to me, Harry?"

"I wanted to tell you in person, Melanie." He had come here to reveal to her his change of mind.

Melanie supposed he wanted her to assure him that all was not lost and of course she could. Now she should tell him she had realized what Woodruff was really up to, that

354

she thought she could handle him and Harry could win Iris in the end. But she felt reluctant to say all this.

Harry put his arms around her and felt how hot her body was beneath the heavy satin and boning; heat always lay beneath her skin as if a fire burned there.

"What happened? What happened?" she whispered, but she was kissing him, too, running her hand across his shoulders, down his back in the way she had. Her kisses, her touch, and in a moment, he thought, he would forget how eagerly she had sent him to Iris, that she would send him to Iris yet. Holding her like this, he wondered that he could ever have believed he could give her up.

Thinking again that she must tell Harry the truth about Joseph, the pain that, oddly, she had not felt upon seeing Denis with Iris struck her now. These were the arms, this the body that would belong to Iris—if Melanie had her way. Never had she felt so confused, thinking about Denis and Carnaugh's crenelated towers, remembering that unforeseen leaning towards Wallace and being at the same time so aware of Harry. She pulled away. "There isn't much time, Harry. I must prepare for the camel ride."

But there was time. No one was more adept than she at changing clothing rapidly. A string trio was to entertain the guests while they waited for her reappearance on camelback. Melanie could hear the musicians tuning up.

With a sense of being looked at, she glanced through the window and was startled to find herself gazing into the large, sad, round eyes of the camel, wistful beneath its scraggy eyelashes. The men must have been walking the beast around the back lawn. Restless. The camel, too.

"Harry, what happened?"

He thought of old Bill the gatekeeper, the Dobermans unleashed to hold him at bay. And then he remembered that Melanie had sent him to the villa. "It was the strangest day, Melanie. I couldn't believe it when it was happening. I can't quite believe it now. I awakened early feeling somehow listless, dreamy. I went down to Emerald Beach; the sun should have been rising by then, but the fog was still so heavy that the sky was quite gray. I could hear the ocean, but not see it. I stood there on the beach and I thought about Iris and your insistence that we elope."

Was there something acerbic in his manner? "I never insisted, Harry. The decision to marry Iris was yours from the start."

"In the beginning, yes, it was mine and of course my mother's. Not yours; you never liked me to talk about it. And then all at once my marriage to Iris became of overriding importance to you. I realized that what I had sensed when you returned from your camel ride was true. I had not known of your connection with the Englishman before. It is said that no woman ever gets over her first lover however he has treated her. Why should it be different for you?"

"You know, Melanie, Mrs. Woodruff is no doubt convinced she is doing what is best for her daughter by finding her so illustrious a fiancé. Only Iris does not see the marquess with her mother's eyes clouded with the desire for a noble connection—or with yours, Melanie, clouded with memories of passion."

The way he was speaking was uncharacteristic, had a bitter undertone, though he spoke quite calmly. Jealousy, she thought, familiar to all lovers. She could not tell what he was thinking. Was the game played out? She should urge him to try again, but felt curiously indecisive. So much had changed for her over the past days, over the past hour, that it was hard for her to recall what she had been so determined to achieve. Denis, tonight, greeting her with the same look of complicity as in so many years gone by. Too many years. And it had been the hope of Denis that had caused her to drive Harry into the elopement.

Harry was looking at her oddly; something was expected of her, but she was not sure what. "Were you very disappointed? You can still win Iris, Harry. I think I can manage to bring Woodruff around."

"Oh, I've no doubt you can manage Woodruff or any man, but no, I was not disappointed. In fact, Melanie, I was

356

relieved. At first I could not understand why that should be. Now I do."

His conversation had always been made up of pleasantries, charming commentaries on each situation. Now he spoke seriously, driven. And listening to him, caught up in his intensity, Melanie lost awareness of the ball going on outside this little room, the camel on the back lawn.

"All this summer, Melanie, I have been lost in this feeling I have had for you. So lost that I let myself forget how serious a situation my mother is in. I have been like a boy taking a vacation from school, careless of the coming fall semester. When I thought of her plight at all, I justified myself by saying it was the last lighthearted summer of my life before settling down to be a steady husband and sound businessman. The last summer when I could be your lover. Even so, it came as a rude shock to have you send me to Iris as if I were a package, inanimate, the toy Armand Wolfe described me as being."

The *Bugle* again. "I do not view it that way, Harry. I thought I was helping you do what you most wanted. It was always my understanding that you saw yourself as my summer lover. You love Iris; that has been taken as fact by everyone. And she is without question madly in love with you."

"Perhaps I would rather be your summer lover than Iris's great love."

"The summer is ending."

"I was not speaking literally. You know what I have been thinking, Melanie? I have been thinking how nice it would be to be married to the person one desires passionately."

If she did not know how lovers talk and how little meaning can be ascribed to their words, she would have thought this a proposal.

"When I was very young, Harry, my father explained to me that marriage is a business arrangement with a very few additional factors to be taken into account. He was very serious. You would not seek an association with a person who

357

was disreputable, dishonest, foolish, wasteful, or impoverished. Instead, you accept a business relationship only with
someone of stature, honesty, intelligence, means, and prudence—all the best criteria for a husband, too."

"You have had one marriage like that."

"Perhaps. But you have not yet had yours."

"The rumors that you and Mr. Edmont will divorce are
ubiquitous. What do you think of your so-proper marriage
now?" Harry was aggressive now. Attacking. She could hardly
believe it.

"Whatever happens"—there was no point in denying the
divorce rumors to Harry—"it was the only kind of marriage
possible for someone like me, like you, too, Harry."

"I am unconvinced. And I am also unconvinced that you
love the Englishman. I know you so well, Melanie. You cannot bear to fail. That old affair went badly; you want to make
it come out right in the end. Only we have all gone far beyond that, so far that I can never marry Iris."

He was suffering a reaction from the debacle at the
Woodruffs'. That would pass. "If you do not make it up with
Iris, you will marry another rich girl. Your mother is proba-
bly already making the selection."

She did not take him seriously. Marry one rich girl or
another. Harry who had always lived for the moment saw
the future she was presenting to him: Iris or Eleanor de Witte
or Jenny Olney at his side, in his bed where Melanie had
lain in his arms, happy, no, more than that, in ecstasy. With
Melanie that word did not seem excessive.

"My mother is a formidable woman, Melanie. She has
found a husband for Evangeline—that Italian friend of Jocelyn Edmont's who is staying with your mother-in-law. He is
here tonight. And to my surprise, Evie seems more pleased
than not."

Melanie remembered Signor Martelli hovering about the
Van Burghs; it had not occurred to her that he was already
a suitor. Louise was indeed formidable. Harry was relieved
of one of his burdens, she thought idly.

"I have not applied myself to my work as well as I should have, Melanie. There are opportunities in the bank and I plan to make the most of them from now on.

"I am quite ready to let the proper, profitable marriage pass for something better. For you, Melanie. You would not be so rich, but wouldn't you be happier with me than you have ever been with Mr. Edmont?"

It was a proposal after all. A fantastical idea, not to be taken in earnest, to be dismissed. Yet for just a second she had a daydream of what it would be like to be with Harry (even in a daydream she could not use the word *married*), to see his smile brighten the dimness of the room, to put out her hand in bed at any time, three o'clock in the morning, and feel his body (so little did she think of marriage in connection with Harry that she did not consider the separate bedrooms).

How charming Harry was being; no one she had ever known could play at being lovers better. And he was looking so solemn that perhaps he actually believed what he was saying—for the moment. It was not as easy to send him away as she had thought it would be. *How can I resist you?* And all the times after that, the golden glow that had filled the room each time he made love to her. If she were not so clear-eyed, she might have gone on playing that game with him, forgetting that he had been following the convention of the time, the last fling before the wedding. A common enough occurrence. She had better put a stop to his talk right now before the situation became embarrassing to them both.

Deliberately she spoke the one sentence that she knew would put his words in proper perspective. "Don't forget the difference in our ages, Harry." That should do it; she had never before referred to how old she was.

"No chance of my forgetting that," Harry replied. "My mother reminds me of your age daily. She finds it of more significance than I do."

He found it of less significance because he did not understand it. "I still look young, Harry. What will you say,

359

what will you think, feel, when I do not?" The very thought of all that would in time be needed to look young—the facial masks, massages, exercises, diets, intricately constructed corseting, cosmetics, hair tints—exhausted her.

"Your beauty does not mean as much to me as your spirit, the excitement you carry with you, your enthusiasm. These will last. You think too much about your looks, Melanie. Your age is not important to me." Melanie's age and experience were in fact among the attractions she held for him. He remembered how he had admired her when he was a boy, had imagined becoming her lover without ever daring to dream it could become true.

He took her hand, stroked the palm, and she smiled and shook her head. How charming Harry was being, she thought again, touched. In the silence she could hear the music. She had almost forgotten that everyone was waiting for her. "I must go."

"Of course. The camel awaits." And as she turned away, he added, "As do I."

She left the room shaken, forcing herself to think of nothing now but the camel ride. To avoid walking through the ballroom, she went down the long passageway leading to the back stairs. She had planned to take this unaccustomed route later so that the guests would not see her in costume before she made her spectacular appearance mounted on camelback.

Someone was standing there in the back hallway. The light was so dim that all she could make out was a figure in evening dress, a dark head, a strong build. Why it was Wallace, she thought. Her life would be easier if Wallace stayed with her. But would it be better?

She recalled how he had given her the newspaper, how tightly he had held her in the dance. He was not so certain of his course. She could still sway his senses. When he looked at the ruby between her breasts, he had been remembering what he wanted to forget and could not; the years they had spent together, the moments when affection and desire had linked them. But he had drawn back, remembering also, as she did now, the quarrels and affairs and anger. A pattern repeated so often that they could not break it. And again she thought that her life would be easier with Wallace, but would it be better?

Then the man lifted his head and she saw it was not Wallace after all but Denis, Denis whom she had given up on, who had passed her a note she had not even read, knowing what it would say. *Any kind of love is better than no love.* Those were the words he had grown up on. It was hardly surprising that he had taken so little of love for himself, allowed her so little.

He came forward and put his hand on her bare arm, confident. For the first time in a quarter of a century of loving and waiting her body did not respond; there was a hint of the weariness she had felt earlier that evening.

"How did you find me?"

Even as she spoke she knew he had tipped a footman, bribed a maid. The servants were agog about her using their staircase. It still smelled of lemon oil, so carefully had it been cleaned.

Denis was wearing impeccably tailored evening clothes, but the heat of his body had already caused his shirt to wilt. *My Denis is always so hot.* "I had to see you, Melanie; you looked at me so strangely upstairs, almost coldly. It is not easy for me either, to stand beside Iris." (Not easy, but his hip had brushed against hers so naturally.) "Surely you know I could not endure my life without you in it."

He sensed there was a crisis. The series of events that had been set in motion by a few words in the *Bugle* were reaching a climax.

"And how do you see my life while I am making yours endurable? I think the divorce will go through after all. I will be free, while you again fasten fetters around yourself."

Now that he had seen Clara and recognized the significance of her presence, Denis no longer questioned the divorce.

"I thought I had made you understand my reasons."

"I understand them. Perhaps you find the idea that I will be alone attractive to you."

"Come now. You will never be alone. You will marry again." She saw the future he envisioned: a new set of partners to be deceived; that was the only difference. "I have an idea. Why not marry my cousin Malcolm?"

Denis had at last succeeded in shocking her. She was not sure whether she was expected to laugh at the audacity and outrageousness of his suggestion or pretend to take it seriously.

"Why Malcolm?"

"His lands are contiguous to mine."

"Ah, that would seem to be the prerequisite for two most happy marriages."

"I know it sounds insane; it seemed so to me when the idea first came to me. But think more carefully, Melanie. You will have to marry someone, and were it Malcolm we would be so close. And he has money. You will have need of that."

He appeared to be half-serious at least. Perhaps the idea would not seem so absurd to someone in his situation. A night when a camel entered a ballroom was a night when anything at all might happen, the most bizarre ideas seemed logical. But Malcolm. She could imagine his supercilious face on the pillow beside her.

"You have become thoughtful of me."

"I have reproached myself all these years for failing to protect you. My only comfort is to look at what you have been able to do with your life nonetheless—Wallace Montague Edmont V, whomever you would wish as his successor now."

"And you think it should be Malcolm."

"He is eminently suitable."

He had reminded her that he had failed her in the first crisis, even though, as he pointed out, she had recouped by means of her marriage. But she had been rescued by Wallace, not him, and now all these years later she was to be rescued by Malcolm. It was laughable really.

362

All at once she faced the fact that she would never be mistress of Carnaugh. Perhaps she had known it without taking it in at the moment she saw Denis brush his hip against Iris's.

"Oh, I know you have never particularly liked my cousin; he is not the most likable of chaps. But a sensible marriage makes strange bedfellows." He gave the witticism without a change of expression.

"You would not mind the knowledge that I was lying with him in his bed, the actions we would be performing, the image that would call to mind?"

"I would have gone mad long since if I allowed myself such imagery."

He had more self-control than Melanie who had tortured herself over the thought of his body lying atop Adelaide's, his mouth on hers, hard within her. Now he would lie in Iris's body. Yet this newer image was less painful than the earlier ones. Scar tissue forms over the wound one thought would never heal.

"What I suggest is the way the world works, the way one can wrest a little happiness for oneself while not failing to meet one's obligations. Let us be honest with one another, Melanie. Love is for love affairs, not marriage. The basis for marriage is not now and never has been love."

His statement was only slightly different from those her father had made and she had just finished repeating to Harry. The code Denis described was her code. She had married by it, stayed in her marriage through bad years, conducted her affair with Denis, with her other lovers, on just that premise. It no longer satisfied her.

"If you really cannot abide Malcolm, why another Englishman can be found," remarked Denis smiling, seeking to lighten the mood. "I can think of a widower with lands to the north and I do believe there's a bachelor with an estate to the west of Carnaugh."

His humor was more obvious now, but there was something of seriousness at its core. "I do not think I can muster up the necessary cynicism," she said.

"Ah, cynicism is a word. Love is a better one."

She knew what he meant by *love*—the letters with his compliments, the long absences. Now he would have Iris conceive and bear the heir, while Melanie was there nearby, fulfilling her obligations to her new husband, doing her marital duty. As he did his. But waiting. Always waiting. She knew what Denis meant by *love*. And she would not accept that any longer.

The meeting on the road during the camel ride when she had devised the plan that was to rob him of Iris and assure him to herself had seemed to her to be the culmination of a lifetime of desire, of longing. Yet perhaps even as she had talked, plotted, tried to convince him, the relationship had been slipping into history.

She waited for the sense of loss. What would she do with her life without Denis to look forward to? But like the stab of anticipated jealousy when he had touched Iris, it did not come.

"All these years," she said, "I have wanted to see us together at Carnaugh. Only that would wipe out the memory that has haunted me, the memory of how we began. I have never found it easy to see myself as victim. And now I can never change that image."

"A victim? You? Surely not. You have never been afraid to take risks. I have been haunted, too, Melanie, Melody, for having let you down. But you were never a victim. Not even then. Had you known what would come of it, would you have refused your chance at joy?"

That afternoon in the music room, not knowing what he was to do, but knowing that he must do it, that she could not bear it if he did not. All she had feared was that he should stop. Had she foreseen the pain, the blood, the risk, yes, the knitting needle, the letters with his compliments, the long silences, the absences, she would not have drawn back. A victim? Surely not.

"You wept for me once."

"Melody, Melody." And after a long pause: "I will not need to weep for you again."

364

Another woman faced with divorce would be lost, helpless, thought Denis. Not Melanie. She would marry again of course. Advantageously. "If you and Edmont break, I cannot doubt that you will find . . ." he hesitated, ". . . your way."

With a smile of farewell, she turned and started to climb the stairs, erect, not touching the banister. Her future looked as bleak and hazardous as ever in the past and she was no longer young. What was to become of her? *You will find your way.* Harry's astonishing proposal came to mind, the proposal she had not taken seriously, should not take seriously. Young, too young. *You will grow old and lose your looks and I will be free of you.* The harsh words followed her up the stairs. Too young. Too young. You will grow old. You will grow old and lose your looks. Louder and louder, the voice followed her up the stairs.

Hurrying now to her dressing room, she reached the threshold, looked in and saw him lying on the chaise longue, waiting for her as he had done so often that summer, his head golden in the lamplight. At the sight of him, she realized whose voice had followed her up the stairs. Not Harry's voice. It was not Harry who had spoken those hateful words, but Wallace. He was the one with whom her future looked dark: he was the one who would put her aside. She could make him give up Clara now when she appeared young, still aroused desire in him. But what when she did not? Another Clara? *Your age is not important to me.* It was not Wallace who had spoken those words. Not Wallace. But Harry.

Put yourself in a position where you cannot lose. Perhaps for all her mistakes, she had succeeded in doing just that. The choice would yet be hers. *Win on the grand scale or on a lesser scale.* She would be a winner still.

Dena and Beryl rushed to the doorway, wanting to put her into the Bedouin costume; she waved them away and walked into the room, to Harry. He was looking out of the window and did not hear her light step.

"Harry." Sure that he could hear the emotion in her voice, she expected his eyes to light up as they always did when she appeared. Harry rose politely; there was no brightness on his face.

"I saw you, Melanie; I followed you, thinking to come up to your dressing room and talk with you before you changed. You see, I thought I had won you. And then I saw the Englishman waiting for you, clearly an arranged meeting. He reached out his hand and touched you as if you belonged to him. I couldn't stand to watch, so I went back to the ballroom, but I couldn't stand to be with people either, so I came up here.

"You left me and went straight to him, Melanie." He sat down on the chaise again, oblivious to the fact that she was still standing.

"Harry, let me explain."

"You've explained it already; somehow I didn't believe you. My mother will find another rich girl for the proper marriage you urge upon me so sensibly. And how will you remember me, Melanie? In that belittling way I was described in the *Bugle*? No, I think not. That would be unkind and you have never been unkind. Your summer love. That's how you will think of me."

"No, as so much more than that." But he was hardly listening. Melanie did not know what to say to Harry; she had never seen him like this before, could not change the tenor of the exchange between them.

She came closer to him then and he reached out and encircled her with his arms. His face against her thighs, she could feel the fever in his skin and the warmth of his breath. He lifted the ruby petticoat, the skirt, and pressed his lips against the bare flesh above her silk stocking. And for all the years of learning how to inhale in her tight corset, she could not catch her breath, but swayed fainting. She put her hands behind his neck, pressing him against her more tightly, feeling the silkiness of his hair, but Harry drew away. His eyes so golden brown were still sad and he said with a slightly bitter half-smile: "You'd like me to make love to you now, wouldn't you, Melanie? You see, I know you so well. You'd keep your guests waiting still longer for that. Making love would seem to you to be fitting for the occasion, the last touch needed for the night you'll ride a camel."

"Yes. I would like you to make love to me. Now. On the night I am to ride the camel. But not because it fits the occasion."

"As a farewell gesture then? For the end of summer?"

"No, Harry, because you did win me."

He stood up, drew in his breath audibly, still serious, only half convinced, uncertain of how she meant him to take the words she was saying. "What have I won you for, Melanie? To go on being your lover? I want more, more than I've had, more than any of the many men who have loved you has ever had of you."

"I want more of you, too." Harry as a husband. That had been the one possibility she had refused to consider. No one thought it strange that Denis, older than she, was replacing a middle-aged wife with a young girl. Denis and Iris were viewed as an unexceptional couple by everyone (except Iris herself). But people reacted differently when the woman was the elder. They would remark cattily about her age, his youth. Why should she care what others thought if she were in the marriage Harry had described, the marriage to someone passionately desired? Certainly Harry would not be swayed by opinion.

She had told Wallace that this would be remembered as the summer when Mrs. Wallace Montague Edmont V rode a camel into the great ballroom at Île de Joie. Next summer, perhaps, would be known as the summer when Melanie Edmont and her young lover were married. And afterwards? Well, who could tell? As a couple, they would not face the ostracism of an earlier era. Society was changing; it was not so restrictive as in the days when Genevieve had refused to meet the Woodruffs. Louise. How she would weep! Yet what could she do but accept them in the end?

She must not allow these ideas to cloud her clarity of vision. Marriage to Harry was a risk. Still, Denis had spoken

367

truly; she had never refused a chance at joy. Many of the experiences that had given her life its savor had carried a risk. Passion carried a risk. A few minutes, no more, standing up behind a door—and had she realized where it would lead her, she would have done it nonetheless. Would she do less now for Harry?

She had always been sure that what she felt for Harry was the pleasure of mutual attraction, not love; love was Denis. But perhaps she had not known how to define love. Must it be made out of darkness, misery, loneliness, broken only rarely by flashes of rapture? Love might be lightness and sweetness; passion might be born of happiness.

Golden Harry. What kind of a husband would he make? She had believed only a Woodruff would be able to afford him, had seen him as a temporary delight, not as someone to go through the winter with, to go through life with.

If she went to Harry, there would be no camels or date palms in the ballroom, no Arctic snow, no favors of crystal and gold. But if one were to share life with someone desired and desiring, would not that be worth the price?

As Melanie told Harry she loved him, she thought how often before she had given promises of love when in his embrace. Only then. Pillow talk, and she always made clear that it need bear no relationship with the truth. Telling him now was telling him for the first time. Harry had spoken of love at other times, but she had dismissed his words: no one could play at being lovers better than Harry, she had thought. Had he stopped playing without her noticing?

"And the Englishman?"

"Habit, Harry. Habit. A habit so long-lasting, so ingrained, that I was not aware until tonight that it was no more than that."

He wanted to believe her, but felt a doubt. Looking at her, radiant in her ball gown, he thought of all the powerful, rich men who had desired her, would desire her. Even as he put his arms around her and felt how quickly she was breathing, how her heart was racing, there was the doubt.

His friends had said he would never hold her, and how could he—patronizingly called Handsome Harry, penniless, young, without her experience of life—how could he hold her?

All at once he knew how much he had to offer; he alone recognized her dream. What other man in their circle understood that a woman might desire a life that included but went beyond shining in the ballrooms and bedrooms of New York and Bourneham? Not Edmont certainly, nor any of the prominent businessmen who sought her out for her beauty. What other man would encourage, take pride in her achievements?

"Melanie." He gripped her shoulders so tightly that a tiny brightly colored plume came off in his hands. He reached out and gently, so gently stroked the feather across her lips, softer than a kiss. "When we are married, we will be lovers, Melanie, but more than lovers: we will be partners. I believe you have always wanted that more than the conventional marriage you spoke so convincingly about. I have come to think you married Edmont because you wanted to share his business life as well as his home. He never let you do that, Melanie; no other man will. But I will do anything I can to help you achieve your dream."

Ah, what could Harry do after all? Still, Melanie was deeply touched by his understanding of her dream. And then she thought, what if—it was a wild idea—but what if she were to bring Harry into Carle & Company? He was bright, able, newly aware of how much more he could achieve in his work. A replacement for her cousin was needed, and if Wallace were her husband no more, the directors would have to come to her. They would view a visit to her as a formality, to obtain her signature on a document giving someone else the right to run her business. But no one could force her to sign.

Melanie did not delude herself that it would be possible to serve as bank president herself. She had passed beyond such naïveté. The directors, the bank's customers, would never accept a woman. But Harry could fill that position. He had a great name, social connections, youth, some experience at another banking house. There would be objections, of course, but she thought Harry would be able to deal with them. A failing bank. Not many men would be eager to take on the bank's presidency at a time when Edmont support would be removed. Accepting the position would be seen as tantamount to agreeing to preside over a bankruptcy, a wake. Only Melanie did not think Carle & Company needed to fail. With Harry's help, she could make it succeed. For the first time she was seeing Harry as more than the charming companion of her summer.

No one looks at my ledgers. There was the dream again, never quite abandoned in all the years of reading *The Wall Street Journal, Bankers' Magazine,* and *Commercial and Financial Chronicle.* Reading in secret for fear of Wallace's sneering. She had encouraged Joseph to speak to her of business rather than love, had learned how many were the opportunities for profit if one were but bold, if one were but able, if someone would but listen. Harry would listen.

"How could you know and understand when nobody else ever did? Nobody else, Harry. My father laughed at my ambitions. Once I believed Wallace would support them, but that turned out to be false. Oh, there were men who talked business with me, but they would have been horrified by the idea of my sharing that life with them openly as a partner. No. Nobody else—in all my life."

She bent towards him then in the way she had and he came still closer to her. His hands went to the fastenings of her gown, the tiniest of buttons and hooks and eyes, covered with narrow piping, concealed with intricate seaming. He smiled at her, baffled, and she sent him out to call Dena and Beryl still hovering in the adjoining bedroom.

The maids' practiced fingers found and opened the fastenings that gave the dress its flawless fit. They eased Melanie's arms out of the gilded lace, the ostrich-plumed sleeves, let the heavy red silk satin gown fall forward, lifted one of her legs, then the other so that she could step out of the skirt without touching the fall of point d'Angleterre lace, the cascade of ostrich feathers. The ruby satin corset she would not wear for riding a camel was unlaced and removed, as were the chemise and the creamy silk stockings. Harry, watching from the bedroom, sighed as she emerged from the gown. In another moment the maids had left the room and Harry returned.

He came to her, still fully dressed, and put his arms around her. The wool of his suit was rough against her bare body, the buttons pressed into her flesh. She was vaguely aware of the sound of the townspeople outside the fence, the music rising from the ballroom—and quick, quick. As in another time, quick, quick someone will come. Then they were skin to skin, her breasts tight against his chest, and he drew her down onto the chaise longue, his long legs between hers. The cleanness of his body, firm, strong, straining against her, yearning towards her. They had captured every possible moment for being together all summer, but this was the first time they had made love as more than lovers. He kissed her throat.

The greatest joy she had ever known, would ever know: had she truly believed that had happened years ago in the music room with Denis?

Later after Harry had dressed and left the room, she called Dena and Beryl, who silently helped her into the Bedouin costume, touched up the smudged cosmetics on her face. He was too young. Much too young. But how young she looked in the mirror; her eyes, lined in kohl, were shining, brilliant.

The great burnoose was in place, the hood settled firmly above her forehead, and she was ready for the camel ride. Head high, Melanie walked down the hallways, down the stairs, and out the back door. Stepping onto the thick velvety grass, she walked around the house until she could look through the French doors to the ballroom glowing in the candlelight. The guests were unwrapping their golden favors with expressions of pleasure, shuffling the golden sand beneath the thin soles of their dancing slippers. From where she stood she could not make out the faces, the couplings.

The orchestra began to play an Arabic chant; two footmen came forward, and all activity ceased.

Melanie turned and ran across the lawn out of sight as the footmen opened the French doors and set lanterns in rows along the terrace to light her entry.

There was an outcry. The townspeople were massed against the fence peering through the openings. Ignoring the onlookers, Melanie walked in the darkness to where she knew the camel would be. She moved swiftly, feeling the damp warm air against her face.

Down by the wall dividing lawn from ocean, the trainer Abdel and his boy were waiting, holding the camel on a long rope. They had been standing there for hours, but showed no hint of weariness. The camel knelt, dutiful, tamed. The men helped her to mount, holding her a fraction of a second too long.

The camel lurched upwards then to a standing position. This was the bad time when she feared she would become ill, dizzy, or faint. Then it passed. She was high above the scene, able to see the townspeople crowded outside the fence, the white surf breaking against the shore, the brilliantly lit house with its French doors standing open for her. This was her moment. Whatever was to come. This was the summer Melanie Carle Edmont rode a camel into the great ballroom at Île de Joie.

And joy came over her, triumph; her future appeared as golden as this moment and her doubts faded in its splendor.

The guests were already beginning to applaud. The camel tore up earth and grass as it clumped heavily across the lawn. Seated on top of the hump, Melanie felt light, heady, in control. Riding towards the ramp, she saw the men and women in the ballroom rise to their feet the better to see her approach. A figure was standing in the shadow cast by the huge beechwood tree. There was no movement or sound as she rode by, but she knew without any doubt.

Harry, you glow in the dark.